ABOUT THE AUTHOR

Elaine Ramsay grew up in Ruislip Middlesex. She attended Newnham Primary School (of celebrity Fearne Cotton fame) and Pinner County Grammar School (which gave the world such notables as Elton John and Simon Le Bon). Ruislip Woods are where she spent many hours walking her dogs, and Park Woods in particular provides the backdrop to the woodland setting of 'The Pit'. Ruislip Woods border the grounds of St Vincent's Hospital and prompted the original idea for the story. She now lives with her husband Gavin and two cocker spaniels in Market Harborough Leicestershire, and has expanded the backdrop of the book to include the rolling East Midlands countryside with the nearby Nature Reserves, Rutland Water and Pitsford Water.

Elaine attended Thomas Huxley Teacher Training College in Acton, where she qualified as a primary school teacher in English and Drama. She gained a BA with the Open University in English and Social Studies. When her family were young she worked in hairdressing and social services and later in the Civil Service. Now retired she is an avid member of the U3A (University of the Third Age) and belongs to two play reading groups and a creative writing group. She is a member of The Leicestershire and Rutland Wild Life Trust, The Woodland Trust and The Leicestershire Wild Life Hospital.

For years Park Woods has been a haven of protection to the many creatures living there, but the peace and tranquillity has generated an attitude of indolence and complacency, leaving the animals vulnerable to danger. Now something sinister lurks deep in a pit nearby and every day its toxic poisons spread further, contaminating everything around it. The poisons invade a colony of rats, polluting their minds as well as their bodies.

When Cory, a popular and dutiful hedgehog, discovers the poisoned stream, together with disfigured, dead and dying rats, he is compelled to initiate an investigation. The young hog is full of self-doubt about his ability to lead, but his determination, sensitivity and charisma succeed in mobilizing a number of apathetic, belligerent, meek, and traumatised animals and birds. Cory's 'army' eventually march out to face overwhelming odds.

This is the story of an ordinary, unassuming little guy, pitted against something hostile and destructive. But it is not just a battle between good and evil, because these two characteristics are found on both sides: it is about personal battles to confront doubts and uncertainties. It is a race against time, and the final confrontation can only be won by overcoming individual weaknesses, using ingenuity, showing courage, learning to look out for friends and, for some, making the ultimate sacrifice.

*The story of The Pit revolves around nature and the environment –
themes that have always been close to my heart, and I hold nostalgic
memories of similar themed books like, 'Watership Down' by Richard
Adams, William Horwood's 'The Duncton Wood' series and the
wonderful 'Wind in the Willows' by Kenneth Grahame. My long-
term interest in the preservation of our woodlands and wildlife
inspired me to eventually open the laptop and begin to write. A
donation from the proceeds of the sale of this book will go to the
'Leicestershire Wildlife Hospital Trust.'*

Elaine Ramsay

www.elaineramsay.co.uk

"An engaging and exciting plot. The environmental theme is an appealing one with descriptions of nature that are both well observed and effective. The animal characters are colourful and strongly realised and the narrative cleverly uses their antics to comment implicitly on human behaviour."

Brian Keaney (award winning, popular author, and Royal Literary Fund Fellow at Goldsmiths College, University of London 2011/2012).

The Pit

Elaine Ramsay

Matador
9 Priory Business Park
Kibworth Beauchamp
Leicestershire LE8 0RX, UK
Tel: (+44) 116 279 2299
Fax: (+44) 116 279 2277
Email: books@troubador.co.uk
Web: www.troubador.co.uk/matador

ISBN 978 1780884 172

British Library Cataloguing in Publication Data.
A catalogue record for this book is available from the British Library.

Typeset in 12pt Garamond Pro by Troubador Publishing Ltd, Leicester, UK

Matador is an imprint of Troubador Publishing Ltd

MIX
Paper from
responsible sources
FSC
www.fsc.org   FSC® C013056

Printed and bound in the UK by TJ International, Padstow, Cornwall

For Amy and Sarah

"It is in truth not for glory, nor riches, nor honours that we fight, but for freedom alone, which no honest creature gives up except with its life."

(Adapted from the Declaration of Arbroath, Scotland's right to Independence & Freedom)

"Those who are brave are free."

Lucius Annaeus Seneca.

CONTENTS

LARGER SIZED ILLUSTRATIONS

CHAPTER 1

STORM CLOUDS GATHERING

The truck reversed slowly under the canopy of trees and came to rest at the edge of the pit. The motor died and the lights went out; silence except for the ticking of the engine as it cooled. A door opened and clicked quietly shut. A man approached the lip of the pit and peered down into the darkness; he could just make out the shadowy shapes of drum containers, plastic bags, rotting boxes and wet sacking. The acrid smell of chemicals, rot and decay hit his nostrils and sent him into a fit of coughing. *What a stink! The pit was almost full – it would be his last trip.* He unbolted the back doors of the truck and dropped the tailgate down with a thud. An owl screeched and something soft brushed the top of his head – *a bat? – the finger of God?* With a shudder he glanced around furtively then leapt up inside the truck and rapidly began unloading its contents down the ramp and into the pit. *Christ, he was jumping at shadows; this would definitely be the last trip, there were too many risks.* A sharp gust of wind set the leaves rustling and dark clouds scudded across the moonless sky. There was a rumble of thunder and his sense of unease grew: *storm brewing.*

Working quickly, he lifted the tailgate and rammed the bolts home. He climbed into the cab, his nervousness making him fumble with the ignition switch before the engine kicked into life, sending his lucky bunch of dried heather jiggling and batting against the windscreen. Dipping the headlights, he moved the truck slowly out towards the narrow rutted path. A flash of lightning lit the sky and for a brief moment the woodland was bathed in a ghostly blue light that exposed the writing on the vehicle: **T.X.I. & CO – MEDICAL WASTE DISPOSAL.** The first heavy drops of rain began to fall.

CHAPTER 2

THE SWIFT

The bird was coming out of Africa. Swift by name, swift by nature, she had covered almost two thousand miles never stopping; feeding off insects as she flew. She soared high, balanced on warm, friendly air currents. Her journey had taken her across part of the hot Saharan desert  and then on up the coast of Spain, through France and finally over the cold grey waters of the North Atlantic Ocean. Her little heart beat wildly; she was weary, but she was coming home. Sixteen years, thirty-two journeys; wintering in the warm Sub-Saharan continent and returning each spring to the same nest in the place she called home. Home, where she had raised so many chicks, seen them grow and gather strength for the long journey back to Africa in the autumn. But the journey this year had been different. She had been impatient to return, with a longing that had prompted her early start before any of her family and friends: she was alone. There had been no mating and now, for the first time there would be no chicks. Well so be it; she was getting old. It was best to leave those things to the younger ones.

For some hours she had been tailing a storm but now the wily quarry had turned in its tracks to confront her. Buffeted unmitigatingly by air currents that had grown mean and spiteful, she needed all her skill and strength to remain on course. The heavy rain was becoming torrential; it beat down on her relentlessly and the weight of her sodden feathers dragged her lower. Gasping for breath, she searched for a place to cling to, somewhere to shelter. An ear splitting crash of thunder coupled with a great fork of lightning spun her around. Momentarily stunned, deafened and blinded, the swift plummeted towards the ground.

CHAPTER 3

CORY, SCUMBLE AND SPIKE

The morning after the storm Park Woods stood resplendent; fresh and shining under the early watery sun. Grasses and ferns beaten down by the heavy rain were already recovering as the warmth of the spring day began to dry everything out. The carpet of bluebells, safe under the protection of mature oak and birch trees, breathed their sweet scent into the air. Even the last of the daffodils remained upstanding, on parade in defiance of the elements. Water droplets on the webs spun between branches of the hornbeam glistened like precious jewels. The rain had washed away the last vestiges of winter and the woods rejoiced in the prospect of new birth.

On the edge of the coppiced woodland, backing onto the common, a family of hedgehogs had made their home. The last members of two litters remained with their mother, Patience: Cory, born in the previous June, and the twins, Spike and Scumble, born in September. Patience looked upon the twins as her two little miracles. Not many September litters survived the winter – there was too little time to fatten up for the hibernation period. However the twins had survived, even Scumble the runt of the litter.

Although physically small and weak, he showed a determination and courage far beyond his size. Spike, though bigger than his brother was still relatively small for his age, but what he lacked in stature he made up for in attitude. Spike was not one to let others have the last word. Patience was proud of these three sons as only a mother could be; even more so because all her other children had now fled the nest and made new lives for themselves. Of course she was not blind to their faults; the twins exasperated her with their mixture of arrogance and vulnerability and there were few days that ended without her having lost her temper at one point or another. She often wondered what irony had caused her to be named Patience. Some joke played by the Great Pan himself she supposed. Pan: considered by some to be nothing more than an overgrown sprite with an impish sense of humour, whilst others accused him darkly of destructive and evil maliciousness; either way Patience conceded, Pan was trouble. If it wasn't for her eldest son Cory, Patience would have been tempted into turning them all out of the nest and sending them on their way. She dreamed of a summer free of youngsters – a time for herself, a time to reflect. After many years of being at everyone's beck and call, what luxury to have time just for herself. But she would miss Cory; sensible, intelligent and reliable, she could thank Pan at least for Cory.

Cory, Spike and Scumble were spending the day in search of food. This was proving to be a relatively simple task as the rain had brought a variety of worms, bugs and insects within easy reach. Their dedication to feeding was born not only out of the need to build up strength after weeks of hibernation, but from an innate unsurpassed enjoyment of just filling their bellies. They had breakfasted in the shade of the woods, foraging amongst the bracken and brambles; washing each delicious mouthful down with water from the rain pools caught between the roots of the oak trees. Now it was almost lunch time and they had made their way out onto the common in the hope of catching any early grasshoppers. The common was mainly frequented by rabbits but also accommodated any number of smaller rodents, who mainly kept themselves to themselves out of a sense of preservation. There was no shortage of predators in the form of stoat, weasel, fox and occasionally badger, to keep any little body at the end of the food chain on his or her toes. There was also a quantity of bird life endeavouring to raise their young and maintain their species against all odds. Nature could be cruel but also full of wonder; always new life growing regenerating the old.

Cory felt good, he felt satisfied; all was well with the world. He lifted his snout to the warm breeze and scented life. It made him restless and he thought, not for the first time since he had awakened, that now was the time to leave. He wanted to explore, to find his own life, discover a new exciting world: he wanted adventure. Spike and Scumble were bickering as usual, or rather Spike was. Cory moved out of earshot and tried to shake off his irritation. He refused to let Spike spoil this beautiful day. Sometimes he wished Scumble would stand up for himself more. The more he allowed Spike to dominate, the more domineering

Spike became. It wasn't that Scumble was afraid of Spike, indeed he seemed to adore him and agreed with most of what he said and did out of love for him. But Cory was beginning to think it was a misplaced love and one that was not doing Spike any good, making him selfish and insensitive. He looked around in time to see a group of young hedgehogs come out of the woods.

***

Spike was angry with Scumble but if someone had asked him to explain precisely why, he would not have been able to. The main reason he supposed, was because he was always expected to look after his weaker brother, always expected to be responsible and he felt trapped. He noticed the group of hedgehogs approaching and his heart sunk. How he wished he could make friends with them, or even just some of them; but he was rejected because of Scumble. Scumble was different and was looked upon as a bit weird. Scumble had fits – he called them dreams, but they were fits where he lost consciousness and called out strange things. He frightened the other youngsters who took to bullying him, and Spike was trapped into having to protect him. At times Spike was sorely tempted into joining the others against his twin, but he was afraid of what Cory might do. Also there was something that Spike felt ashamed of that he kept in a small dark and secret place next to his heart. The previous autumn he and Scumble had been looking for a comfortable, safe place to bed down for the winter sleep. He had discovered a particularly quiet, dark den covered in leaves, sticks and tree branches. It was cosy and warm – the ideal place. Spike felt proud. But instead of praise from Scumble, he got a load of nonsense about how it didn't feel right – how Scumble felt an impending sense of danger; although he was unable to specify what danger. Spike was tired and in no mood to humour a brother who was frightened of his own shadow. He'd told Scumble to bugger off and find his own place, before curling up and very quickly falling into a deep sleep. He was woken some time later by a distraught Scumble who was shaking him in an effort to get him up. The air was thick with smoke that filled his lungs and stifled him. His eyes stung and smarted and he could not see which way to go. The heat was fearful and all that Spike could do was quiver with terror. If it had not been for Scumble shouting encouragement and pushing him in the right direction he would not have found his way out. He knew he would not have survived; he knew that Scumble had saved his life. What made it even harder to bear was that Scumble had taken the worst of the heat and many of his back spines had been burned. They remained charred and blackened even now, a constant reminder to Spike of his brother's bravery and his own stupidity. It was worse than this however, because Spike had afterwards related a very different story. Rather than admit his lack of knowledge about bonfires and his subsequent inability to act sensibly, he had lied. Glibly and with eloquence, he laid the blame on Scumble's slowness and clumsiness, even letting it be known that it had all been Scumble's idea in the first place. What surprised him was Scumble's mute acceptance of the lie and his willingness to take the blame. Even now, months later, no creature knew the truth; but instead of feeling gratitude towards his twin, Spike despised him for what he saw as weakness.

The group of young hedgehogs were standing a little way off but their sniggering and snorting could be heard quite plainly. They were bored and wanted to brighten up their day by having a bit of fun at Scumble's expense, but they were wary of Cory and did not venture too near.

'Hello Scumble,' shouted a big, well grown hog at the front of the group. 'Had any dreams lately?'

'Come on Dumb-bell – tell us your dreams,' called another hog.

'Yeah tell us yer nightmares; 'e's a bleedin' nightmare 'imself,' a voice from the back cried out amidst raucous laughter.

Cory reared up and confronted the group. 'That's enough of that Bugle, or I'll be round to your mother first thing. Go on, off with you. I can see you Trefoil, hiding at the back. You should all be ashamed of yourselves.' Cory moved towards them slowly and deliberately, carefully looking at all their faces. After some hesitation they backed away; Cory's authority was still respected. However, as they made their way back towards the trees, scraps of a song they were chanting wafted back to the three brothers:

'Bumble – Scumble – 'e's a Dumb-bell
'bout as sharp as sugar plum crumble!
Who's a fright?
Who's a sight?

Who's the hog got set alight?
Tried to run, but burned 'is BUM!
Shame, shame 'e's ter blame;
The hog's no 'ero — brains are zero!'

Spike stood with his head down, intently studying the residue of a half eaten worm; for once he could find nothing to say.

Cory took charge as usual. 'Come on you two,' he growled softly, 'don't mind them; useless morons! Let's do some exploring.'

Scumble sighed and shrugged. 'Think I'll just go by myself for a bit. Don't worry about me Cory, I'm OK.' He gave a crooked little grin, 'Need some thinking time.' He wandered off across the common in the direction of the spinney. Cory was undecided what to do. If Scumble found more trouble, Cory would be in hot water. But he couldn't be his brother's keeper forever. Scumble needed the chance to learn for himself.

Spike had already started walking away. 'Let him be Cory,' he shouted.

With reluctance, Cory turned his back on Scumble and followed Spike. Spike plodded on towards the top of Park Woods where the trees were thickest, away from the family home. There was no sense of purpose of where he was going, only that he wanted to leave the common as quickly as possible. He could hear Cory following behind but the truth was he couldn't care. He found no comfort in Cory's company. *Cory the blessed; the talented! How he hated him!*

Cory called to him, 'Let's go down to the stream, it'll be cool and shady there and we may be lucky and find some of those big slugs.'

Spike did not answer but once he reached the trees veered off to the left towards the stream. Park Woods had originally been used by Man for hunting, and the game had been contained and protected by massive earth mounds. These were now covered with a tangle of ancient hornbeam and a mixture of almost impenetrable plants. In places the mounds had been dug out, mainly by rabbits and badgers, but mostly these burrows were now old and deserted. There was a forlorn air of loneliness and decay. The stream started somewhere further north on the other side of Whylder Wood, more commonly referred to as the Dark Wood by the locals. By the time it flowed down through Park Woods, it had become a fairly substantial water way. It meandered along the edge of the common until it merged with the River Rushlep and continued its journey to where – the hedgehogs never knew.

Over night the stream had been fed by the heavy rain and Cory could hear the noise of rushing water as they approached. The ground underfoot became soggy and slightly unpleasant but nevertheless, cooling to their paws. There was a dank, malodorous smell of wet mud and damp vegetation. Cory laid a friendly paw on Spike's shoulder. 'Don't worry about Scumble; there's more to him than you think.'

Spike shook him off angrily. 'What do you know about it?' he muttered bitterly. 'How would you like to be tied to a twin who's a lame brain?' He moved away from Cory and shook tears of frustration from his eyes. 'Anyway, it's alright for you – everyone likes you; they look up to you; they listen to what you have to say.'

Cory chuckled. 'I'm not sure that's true: *you* don't listen for a start!' Before Spike could reply, a movement in the stream caused Cory to lean forward and peer more closely. 'Great Pan in the pasture, what's that?'

The dead body of a rat, caught in the current, was lodged against the reeds. It was in a sorry state; patches of fur were missing and what remained had turned a dirty white in colour. Its pallid wrinkled skin was blistered and scarred; but more horrifying was the sight of its face frozen in a death mask of fear and its little paws clenched tightly into fists of pain. As Cory and Spike moved involuntarily nearer, an eddy released the rat, spinning it slowly around in front of them before carrying it further downstream, where it eventually disappeared from view.

CHAPTER 4

THE PIT

The swift lay half conscious; trapped between wet sacking and decomposing cardboard boxes. Her fall had been cushioned by the thick foliage which now formed a sheltering canopy above her. The pain came in dizzying waves and she knew that her wing was broken; if she did not get help soon she would die. To her left were the ruins of an old house: crumbling brickwork, rusted pipes and rotting window frames. Only part of the house remained standing, some of it had fallen into a deep pit caused by subsidence. The pit was full of rubbish which gave off a deeply unpleasant pungent smell; it caught in her throat and made her eyes smart. A noise to the right made her turn just in time to see the head of a rat emerge from a crate near the top of the pit. In its mouth it held what looked like silver paper. The rat saw the bird immediately and froze. It stared and she stared back, unblinking.

Baldlice the rat was weary; weary to the point of exhaustion. For five years he had been the undisputed pack leader, securing his place in the hierarchy largely by his size and strength; but he was not a stupid rat. He was clever and cunning and had an innate sense of self-preservation. Lately however, he had frequently been called upon to defend his position of leadership. Younger, stronger, more ambitious rats were challenging his authority and his body carried numerous wounds and scars as a result. A particularly nasty scar running diagonally across his face had almost blinded him and he no longer had full sight in his left eye. On top of all this he was fast becoming crippled by constant arthritic pain. It would not be long before he was bested in a fight and either exiled or killed.

The discovery of the pit and its contents had been a revelation. Those rats brave enough to descend into its depths could be rewarded by finding miraculous cures and antidotes for all manner of ills. The powders and potions were indeed a panacea from the great Pan himself. Pain was eliminated and the mind pleasantly numbed. Sometimes the panacea evoked weird and wonderful dreams; vividly colourful and hypnotic. Sometimes if you were unlucky, the dreams took on a threatening, nightmarish quality; dark and terrible. His regular forays had taught him to distinguish between the various powders and through trial and error he was now able to keep his pain in check as well as maintaining a transient feeling of well being. Initially there had been a number of terrifying accidents when rats who had delved too deep were burned by hot corrosive liquids. Others had died agonising deaths after ingesting the many poisonous substances spilling out of bags and boxes. The place had come to be known locally as "Pan's Pit of Pleasure and Pain" and most rats now kept their distance. Only a few hardy souls such as Baldlice were willing to take their chances, in the optimistic hope that pleasure would ultimately win over pain.

Baldlice narrowed his eyes and scrutinised the wounded bird. She was trapped and vulnerable and he assessed how he might take advantage of the situation. How might this add credence to his diminishing power? A dead carcass might feed a small portion of the colony for a couple of days perhaps, but what if she was kept alive? The stare from her unblinking eyes was becoming absorbing – hypnotic and he was drawn towards her. Tail held high he made his way across the chasm of uncertainty; balancing on the topmost crates and yellow plastic bags.

With supreme effort the swift calmed her beating heart until it was only a faint and distant throb. Trance-like, she felt the warm winds of Africa wash over her, ruffling her feathers. She smelled the desert's heat and the odour of ripe fruits, flowers and the dark continent's spicy perfumes. The throb of her heartbeat slowly began to match the throb of the heart of Africa, and she saw the dancing figures rhythmically rocking and swaying to the beat of the drums under the thin black columns of palm trees. The rat was directly in front of her now: she marked his old, grey scarred face.

With deference he laid his gift before her. 'For you, my queen,' he murmured, 'it will take away your pain.' He looked long into her bright black eyes and she took his mind.

CHAPTER 5

THE SPINNEY

Scumble entered the spinney at the farthest end of the common. He was glad that neither of his brothers had followed him. He wanted to be alone. It was upsetting that he seemed to be a figure of fun to other young hedgehogs; but Scumble was not one to dwell on the negatives of life. It would be nice to find a friend but if that didn't happen then so be it. He was what he was and could not change it. Scumble quite enjoyed his own company and took much delight in observing what went on around him. The flora and fauna of Park Woods; its changing nature through the months and seasons, was a never ending joy to him. He had grown knowledgeable about all sorts of plants, especially those with medicinal properties and was fast becoming adept at advising which plant best suited which illness. Scumble also enjoyed observing the antics and behaviour of other inhabitants of the woods. It was not that he wished to be drawn closely into the lives of other animals, or to be judgemental about what they did or said; but he liked to evaluate cause and effect. He was interested to see the outcomes arising from certain behaviour and

often successfully predicted what those outcomes would be.

By and large Scumble was a stoic, self-contained, contented little hedgehog, except for one thing. Every so often and with no warning he would lose consciousness and enter a dark world with disturbing dreams. Usually the visions were accompanied by strange voices saying things that he strove to remember and interpret when he regained consciousness. He referred to these periods as "dreams" but from an onlooker's point of view he appeared to be having a fit. Sometimes when he "awoke" he found that his tongue was bleeding or that he had damaged himself by threshing around on the floor. What was most worrying was the fact that, whilst in a fit he was incapable of rolling into a ball and was subsequently left unprotected.

His thoughts were interrupted by the sound of muffled sobbing nearby. Scumble had not planned on company and would have preferred to ignore the intrusion, but for a sense of unease. 'Hello,' he called, 'are you alright there?'

'Go away,' came a muted reply.

Scumble sighed. 'I don't want to go away,' he muttered. 'I came here for some peace and quiet; let's make a pact not to bother each other.' He closed his eyes and let the warm sunshine play over his body. The plan was to hide in the spinney until tea time and hope that by the time he returned home both Cory and Spike would have forgotten the embarrassing incident that afternoon. He thought that if he tried hard enough he would forget it too. Some minutes elapsed before he was aware that the sobbing had started again and, being a kindly soul, he went over to investigate. A bedraggled female kestrel crouched pathetically in the long grass, her little body shaking with the effort to contain her sorrow. She turned her head to glance back at him and a tear rolled resolutely down her already very wet beak. It dropped onto Scumble's nose and was followed in quick succession by others. 'Hey,' he said gently, 'I didn't ask for a face wash! Come on now, things can't be that bad.'

As there was no reply he settled himself down comfortably beside the bird and took stock of the situation. Apart from the sobbing and the chattering of a squirrel overhead, everywhere was peaceful. He noticed two men with guns approaching across the common, but they were making for the other side of the spinney and he judged there was no call for alarm. A family of crows had also spotted the men and the birds rose like a huge black cloud, hanging in the sky for some seconds, before circling once and flying away in a cacophony of noise. The disturbance interrupted the kestrel's self preoccupation and with one or two hiccups she ceased to sob. Scumble had been scratching around for food and took advantage of her silence to push a few choice worms and a half chewed beetle in front of her.

'Not much of a feast, I'm sure,' he smiled ruefully at her, 'but as my mother always says, "it's the thought behind it that counts."' The kestrel thanked him and pounced on the meagre meal as if she had not fed for days. It galvanised Scumble into fresh attempts at hunting, until he had successfully compiled a veritable banquet and they both tucked in with gusto.

'My name's Echo,' said the kestrel, between mouthfuls of food. 'Who are you and what's happened to your back?' She eyed Scumble's blackened hindquarters with sympathy.

'I'm Scumble,' he replied and for the first time in his life he began to talk openly about himself. Echo was a good listener and Scumble was amazed at what he was prepared to reveal about his life, his thoughts and his feelings. He told her of his dreams where he heard strange voices; how it was difficult to always remember or interpret what they said, but that sometimes it helped him to make predictions about the future. Sometimes in his dreams he was flying and sometimes he would find himself falling – plunging frighteningly down into blackness. Worst of all was the feeling of despair and of struggling against being held down, trapped by something sinister and unknown. He told her about the incident with Spike in the bonfire and how he had been burned; how he had always felt himself to be the runt of the litter, weaker and less effective than his brothers and how other hedgehogs called him "Dumb-bell Scumble" because he always seemed to be doing something wrong in their eyes. In true Scumble fashion, the little hedgehog related all this in a matter of fact way; he did not whine or whinge about his lot but accepted it pragmatically and even, at times, with humour. He certainly did not ever point the finger of blame and Echo felt a growing regard and respect that made her feel ashamed of her own self-centred, emotional behaviour.

'I don't think your brother Spike seems very nice,' she whispered. 'I can't help but say it.'

'Ah but then you haven't met him and you can't understand. He is always in Cory's shadow and feels he has much to prove. He has a great deal of pride and he cares very much about what others think of him.'

'And I think that you are *not* influenced so much by other's opinions,' said Echo, 'you do not have an over-inflated sense of pride. I will think of you as "Humble" not "Dum-bell" you are so modest and have such a generous spirit, I'm glad that I met you today.'

'I am glad that I met you too, Echo,' Scumble replied. 'I feel peaceful now. You have helped me straighten some things out in my mind. No creature has ever encouraged me to talk so much and to listen so well. I hope that we will always be friends.'

Echo sighed. 'I think that when you get to know me better, you will learn to like me less,' she murmured.

This sparked Scumble's curiosity and he turned to her in surprise. 'Won't you tell me why you were crying?' he asked. Echo opened her beak and then looked up, startled at a loud commotion in the tree above them. The noise arose from an altercation between a squirrel and a crow. The crow, apparently having just arrived, was being loudly accused of encroaching on the squirrel's space and food

store. The squirrel, in his rage and determination to give emphasis to his accusations, had foolhardily thrust his face periously near to the crow's sharp beak. The bird stood his ground with his chest feathers puffed out and a steely glint in his eye.

'Move on free-timer,' growled the squirrel. 'No freeloaders welcome here.' He glanced quickly at a spot near the roots of the tree where it could be assumed his cache of nuts and seeds was buried.

The crow drew himself up to his full height. 'I hope you're not threatening me,' he said silkily, 'because I don't take kindly to threats, no way, no sir!'

'Button yer beak bird brain!' spat the squirrel. 'I've met your sort before; sneaking around riding on the backs of the workers. How many times have I sweated my nuts off to fill a larder, only to have you freakin' fobs filch it from under my nose!'

The crow sniffed. 'I was under the impression that you lot were liberals.' He smiled sarcastically. 'I *was* of the opinion that you believe in equal rights for all; you know share and share alike and all that.' He became aware of Scumble and Echo staring up at them and he began to rapidly preen his feathers. 'I'm sure I don't know what I've done to offend you,' he said huffily. 'I don't want your precious nuts.'

The squirrel had also become aware of their audience and changed tack a little. 'Well excuse me! I'm just saying!' he repeated lamely. Their attention was drawn to a man stepping out from under cover of the spinney and walking purposefully away across the common, his arms swinging freely. They watched him disappear into the distance.

'Well that's that then,' said the crow, 'I'm off home.'

He made ready to launch himself off the branch but was held in check by Scumble's cry of 'STOP!'

The crow teetered dangerously on his precarious perch, desperately trying to regain his balance. 'What the...?' he spluttered.

Just then a dark cloud in the sky revealed itself to be the returning crows, who swept noisily back into the spinney. They were instantly greeted by loud reports of gunshot and the onlookers witnessed a number of hits: little black bodies fell like stones out of the sky to be followed more slowly by a cascade of drifting feathers.

The crow screamed in anguish. 'That's my family; there go my friends,' he wept.

The squirrel looked stunned. 'Tough luck pal,' he murmered, 'y'know it stands to reason, if two men go in then two men must come out, innit?'

Scumble felt sorry for the crow. 'When the man leaves we'll all go over if you like,' he said. 'There maybe some wounded we can help.'

The crow looked down at the little hedgehog with surprise. 'Thanks, I'd like that.' After some thought he added, 'You know you probably saved my life – I owe you.'

After the man (who now carried two guns) had disappeared in the same direction as his collaborator in crime, the hedgehog, kestrel, squirrel and crow all made their way over to the scene of carnage. The man had taken away the dead but there were three wounded birds lying on the ground. Some returning crows were already attempting to help them, although it was clear they had little idea of what to do and were relieved to take orders from Scumble, who directed them to find various roots, leaves and nettles that could alleviate pain or stem the blood.

By the end of the afternoon progress had been made in saving the lives of two of the wounded, whilst the third less fortunate one had at least been given a decent burial. What was just as important was that progress had been made in cementing a friendship between the two animals and two birds. Before they parted, Sheard the squirrel committed himself to being available for any future similar engagements; whilst Scally the crow vowed he would always be indebted to Scumble and would come whenever he called.

CHAPTER 6

MAD MAGGIE MINCHIN'S &
THE ACOLYTE PRIESTS

Whylder Wood to the north east of Park Woods had been left un-coppiced for decades and was now mature high forest consisting mainly of oak, birch and hornbeam. Plant life on the ground was limited under the dense shade, but bramble, bracken and a variety of ivy, nettles and fungi struggled successfully for survival. Close to the stream where the soil was wetter, there were alder, willow and buckthorn and a good quantity of pond weed, speedwell and stitchwort. Sunlight had difficulty penetrating to the floor of the wood, making the whole place darker, colder and more forbidding than its cousin to the south. A few hardier animals, like Braxton the badger had chosen to make it their home and Freeman the fox, ever the opportunist, visited regularly. Man rarely visited and the advantage of Whylder Wood was that it offered more security and protection to the shy and the vulnerable. Nevertheless, its relative isolation and pervading mystery served to make it a place to fear and so it had come to be called the Dark Wood.

Almost two centuries ago an imposing house was built on the outskirts of the Wood, under the direction of

Alderman J.R. Minchin, a wealthy land-owner. How he had made his money no one could say, but he had certainly made a number of enemies. He lived in the house with his family and servants until expiring tragically one night, after tumbling top to bottom down the spectacular marble staircase. Various rumours abounded as to the cause of his fall but as nothing was ever proved, the incident passed quietly away into the annals of history. With his death came the gradual deterioration and death of the house. Other family members died in their turn or departed for cheaper, warmer climes. The servants were let go and both the house and its gardens fell into disrepair. The last surviving member of the family, Aunt Maggs, ended her days there caring for dozens of local feral cats, whilst valiantly fighting off regular visits from the bailiffs. Eccentric she was, but harmless enough and nothing sinister or untoward had ever been proved against her. Time, however, had been less than kind to her memory and the ruined remains of the building were now always referred to, with a frisson of fear, as "Mad Maggie Minchin's house".

Most of the building had collapsed through subsidence and what was left standing was crumbling and rotted. No windows or doors remained intact and the skeletal roof, minus most of its slates, welcomed in the elements to continue their insidious damage to the heart of the house. Ivy and bindweed clung like parasites to the brick and stonework; squeezing out the last vestiges of its life. Nettles and weeds grew in abundance in the gardens and had also gained a stranglehold in the hallway and most of the downstairs rooms. The suppurating chemicals that leaked from the pit into the surrounding earth gave sustenance to only the most hardy and poisonous of plants: a few ravaged oleander shrubs; deadly nightshade; lethal-looking malformed fungi and a proliferation of tangled thorn bushes. In sharp contrast there were swathes of bare, barren soil that promised only sterility and emptiness. Neglect and decay were everywhere.

Under the direction of Baldlice, the swift was moved to more comfortable quarters inside the house. The chemical fumes were less here and she was able to see and think more clearly. Two female rats, Myrtle and Luthian, were assigned to attend to her needs and in general the rats that came to inspect the new phenomenon went away satisfied that she was no immediate threat. Some of the covert glances, however, were at the very least suspicious; some were clearly malicious and she was under no illusion that should she lose her power to control Baldlice, it would be the end of her. Luckily so far she was maintaining a good hold over him. His mind had grown considerably weaker due to the effects of the many powders he was taking and she found it relatively simple to keep him hypnotised. Besides, he needed her as much as she needed him; they had read each others minds and knew their shared purpose. Their plan was to found a religious order that offered both structure and a higher sense of being; something to bring the colony together in community spirit and fellowship and to transcend the current daily mundane activities of fighting and bickering. The swift had some knowledge of African religious cults and what she lacked in fact she was confident she could make up for by imagination and invention. If the plan worked it would buy both her and Baldlice more time.

Her nest had been placed in what had once been a room to one side of a flight of steps leading down into the cellar. Much of the room had fallen into the cellar but what was left housed her comfortably enough and afforded a fairly unobstructed view of what went on below. Part of the roof covered her; but whilst it offered shelter it cut off her view of the sky. For a bird that had lived most of her life flying free on the wing, this was a devastating plight to be in. She felt bereft of all she had once loved or valued. Her whole being cried out to escape but the only way she felt this might be achieved was to concentrate all her effort on the plan. Already Baldlice had galvanised a party of rats into clearing the cellar of its detritus. It was to be the place of worship and its high walls and cavernous ceiling gave it the acoustics that would prove impressive. A block of marble, a relic of the once imposing staircase in the hall, lay on its side forming a high altar. As the swift looked down, Luthian was decorating it with dried ferns and flowers.

'Things are going well Iya Nla,' whispered Baldlice in the swift's ear. 'I have brought you the acolytes for priesthood duties. Many rats volunteered but I have chosen six of the strongest or most knowledgeable. Perhaps you would care to consider them.' The swift turned to face the six rats that had formed a semi-circle in front of her. She indicated to one at the end to step forward and as he did so she held him with her eyes.

'My name is Earle,' he said gravely. 'I am an elder and have earned that right by wisdom and diplomacy; the wisdom to change things for the better when I can and the diplomacy to leave well alone when I can't.' The swift nodded and he stepped back with a bow. She indicated to the next rat to step forward.

'I'm Gram, Your Highness.'

'She is the High Priestess, the Great Mother and you will refer to her as Iya Nla,' hissed Baldlice.

'Beg pardon, Iya Nla then,' said Gram with a shrug. 'I'm strong and not afraid to fight, especially if it's in a good cause,' he smirked and stepped back. The swift looked at him long and hard.

'Wimund's my name,' said the third; a rather sober female rat. 'I am flattered to be one of the chosen six; I welcome you to our home. Your idea is inspirational: I feel I am made for the priesthood, it is something I have been looking for all my life.' The swift held her with her eyes, before the rat stepped back into line.

'Atol,' said the next rat with a deferential bow. He was a good looking, well made rat with a pleasant expression. 'I am here to learn and I am a quick learner.' The swift held his gaze intently before he stepped back with a nod of his head. The next rat, thin and nervous, shuffled forward.

'I'm Ware,' he whispered hoarsely, looking down on the ground in front of him, 'and I offer my support to you.' He stepped back.

'What are your strengths?' asked the swift. The rat looked up briefly in time to meet the bird's eyes.

'I can be very loyal to those in whom I trust,' he answered quietly.

The last rat stepped forward. He was of small stature but solidly built. 'My name is Holt,' he declared, 'and I am here at the request of my father.' He turned to look at Baldlice. 'I am willing to perform the duties of a priest out of respect for him.' He stepped back and the swift sighed.

'That is not reason enough,' she said. 'It must be your own desire if you are to perform with credibility.'

'My desire is to please my father. I may come to believe in the doctrines of the creed when I have been tutored in them,' he responded.

'Very well,' said the swift, 'at least you are honest.' She turned to Baldlice who was looking uncomfortably at his son. 'Baldlice I will accept your choices, you will begin their indoctrination tonight. The place must be kept private, it will be best to mount guards outside. It is important that the acolytes begin to physically withdraw from other rats; they must maintain an air of mystery to command the necessary respect due to their role in the priesthood.'

'It will be done Iya Nla,' replied Baldlice and he ushered the six rats from the room.

Left alone, the swift reflected on what had just taken place. She was disturbed. Two of the rats had kept their innermost thoughts from her; she had been unable to read their minds. They had not completely bent to her will and therefore she was not ultimately in control. The pain from her broken wing was becoming almost unbearable and she was counting the minutes until Baldlice returned with her medication. She knew that like Baldlice, she was becoming dependent on the white powders to relieve her pain. Already it would seem, her hypnotic powers were diminishing and this could only get worse. Well there was nothing else she could do and she resolved to make the best of things; at least for the moment she had the majority of acolytes under her control. It was enough to buy her time – time perhaps for some miracle that would save her from a lonely, painful death in this strange forbidding place.

CHAPTER 7

CORY AND SUNNIFA

It was a hot afternoon in May and Cory sat motionless in the tall grass under a ring of oak trees, on a rise overlooking Bluebell Grove. It was his favourite spot: private enough for solitary thinking but not too isolated or lonely to be dangerous. Its elevation gave a good view of the surrounding woodland and there were a number of bolt holes for little animals amongst the tree roots, should any predator chance to come. Despite the warmth of the sun and the comfort of his seat however, Cory was not happy. He was worried about a number of strange, unpleasant things that had been happening recently, which were all unaccountable. Ever since the day he and Spike had seen the dead rat in the stream, things had gone from bad to worse. Three other rats had been sighted in much the same sorry state and another one, only yesterday, had been found dying on the outskirts of Whylder Wood. The hedgehog who had found him reported that the rat was in terrible pain and foaming at the mouth. His dying words were a warning to stay away from Mad Maggie Minchin's house. On top of that, last night had been disturbed by the howls of a fox that had gradually risen to unearthly screams. They were not the screams of a fox caught in a snare; mostly a fox in that predicament was struck dumb with the shock and pain. Besides why should Man bother to lay snares in Whylder Wood, it made no sense? Cory felt ashamed that he had listened to an animal in such agony without going to its aid. He tried to assuage his conscience by asking himself what possible help a lowly hog could be to a fox. Nevertheless, Cory considered his inaction to be cowardly. To cap it all, only this morning, Scumble had had another fit, ranting and raving, 'Cows on the common; Cows on the common!' Cory felt frustrated and, at the risk of being "Scumble-like", a sense of foreboding. He lifted his head and stared about him: he sensed a presence, a feeling of being watched. A rustling behind him made him spin round but he could see no creature. 'Who's there?' he called, but there was no reply. 'Who's there?' he called again. A soft wind rustled the leaves and momentarily set the grasses dancing and swaying. He thought he heard the faintest sound of tinkling pipe music, which was gone before he was certain. *I'm getting too doom laden and jumpy* he thought, *time to go home.*

Just then his attention was drawn to a movement on his right and a shaft of reflected sun-light made him blink. It came from something that sparkled and glistened on the ground. Remembering one of his mother's cryptic comments, "all that glitters is not gold", he approached cautiously and recognised an object belonging to Man. It was made of something solid but he was able to see into it and observed a wood mouse caught inside. The mouse was scrabbling frantically around without being able to find its way out. Cory had seen this sort of thing before:

small animals attracted by the smell of food were enticed inside, only to find that they were trapped and often stayed trapped until they died. Cory cursed the thoughtlessness of Man who endangered woodland life in this way. He could see how the mouse had got in; the anticipation of food had emboldened its endeavours to squeeze through a small hole. Unfortunately the little animal now lacked the impetus to squeeze back out, especially as it had grown plumper after its recent repast! Cory placed his nose near to the opening and whispered encouragement but it was no good; whilst the mouse continually approached the aperture, it would come no further than its whiskers.

'OK little feller,' said Cory, 'change of tactics: turn round.' To Cory's relief the mouse did as he was told and by a concentrated effort Cory was able to grab the prisoner by its tail and, with a whoosh and small squeak, it regained its freedom. With hysterical chattering of its appreciation and gratitude the little rodent disappeared through the grass, hopefully homeward bound.

'That was kindly done,' said a voice behind Cory, and on turning round he saw a female hedgehog watching him with bright twinkling eyes. 'Not many hogs would have bothered with such a small creature. Who are you?'

'I'm Cory,' he replied, with an uncharacteristic feeling of shyness. He was surprised to feel so awkward; it was unlike him. 'I haven't seen you around before, who are you?' he asked rather huskily.

'My name is Sunnifa,' she smiled. 'I have been living on the other side of Park Woods where I was born, but now I've come to live with my aunt, near the common.

Until of course I set up my own home,' she added with a sweet laugh, and for a moment Cory thought he heard the tinkling pipe music again. 'I have heard of you, Cory,' Sunnifa said. 'All good things and now I believe them; you seem so thoughtful and gentle. Do you have to go yet? It's nice here, we could sit and talk.'

Despite his feelings of awkwardness and embarrassment, Cory could think of nothing nicer than to sit in the sunshine with this lovely female. He sat down in the tall grass amongst the creeping wood sorrel and patted the ground for her to join him. Sunnifa came and sat closely beside him. 'When I first heard of you,' she continued, 'I imagined you would be independent by now, not still living with your mother. It seems strange because nobody thinks you are a mummy's boy.'

Cory could feel her studying his face, so with a great effort he turned and looked at her. 'Mostly I stay because my mother needs me,' he explained, 'it's not my first choice. She has had a difficult time with my twin brothers, Spike and Scumble; September babies you know, never big or strong.' He sighed, 'I had planned to leave the nest this spring, but apparently she is now expecting another litter and I'm beginning to feel trapped. Please don't get me wrong Sunnifa,' he added quickly, 'because I love my mother dearly.' Sunnifa shifted closer and he felt her paw resting on his. It was comforting but also arousing; Cory had never felt this way before, he was in uncharted territory and did not know how to proceed. Her scent was in his nostrils and he felt her warm breath on his cheek. There it was again, that music.

'C-c-can you hear that?' he asked hesitantly.

'What?' she replied with pup-like naivety, but there was a mischievous twinkle in her eye and she

grinned at him. 'It's only Pan practising on his pipes, nothing to be nervous about. Long ago, Pan fell in love with a nymph called Syrinx, but sadly she did not return his love.' Sunnifa's touch became a caress and she leaned closer. 'Pan became angry and jealous,' she whispered, 'and he turned Syrinx into one of the water reeds he fashioned into his pipes. But sadly, once done it could not be undone. That sound is the music of longing – the music of love.' She reached up and kissed him. Cory lunged at her in a half clumsy, half terrified way and found himself embracing the warm scented grass where she had been sitting. Sunnifa was already running through the grass giggling, her little rump swaying provocatively. Cory, entranced, followed at a fast pace and was just about to capture his prize when they both stopped in their tracks, aghast at what they saw.

Freeman the fox lay almost comatose amongst the roots of one of the oak trees. He was breathing hoarsely and his thin flanks rose and fell erratically. He regarded them through heavily lidded eyes that were cloudy with pain.

'Help me,' he croaked.

'How can we help?' asked Sunnifa. 'What's the matter with you?' Freeman's lips curled back to reveal a tongue and gums that were burned and blistered. One of his paws was in a similar state.

'Can you follow us?' said Cory. 'The stream's not too far, the cold water will do some good.'

'No way,' wheezed Freeman, 'wetted my mouth in the stream up near Mad Maggie's. The stream's gone bad... poisoned.'

'Have you been in pain all night?' asked Cory. 'We heard a fox crying out, I'm sorry no creature has tried to help you.'

The fox sniffed and a brief tear trickled from the corner of one eye. 'That was my mate, Wilda,' he whispered. 'She drank the water and burned her insides.' He shuddered, 'It was a terrible death. No creature deserves to die in that way. We'd been together for years, my lovely Wilda.' Cory was at a loss as to what to say next, but Sunnifa busied herself by examining the extent of Freeman's injuries.

'Erm, we've heard some other recent stories about Mad Maggie's place; all bad,' Cory said eventually. 'What were you doing there?'

Freeman glared up at him. 'Ever heard the saying "curiosity killed the hog"?'

'I thought it was the cat,' said Cory.

'Same difference,' muttered Freeman.

'Look,' Sunnifa interrupted, 'I've got an idea. Can you walk to the common do you think? It's just the other side of the rise.'

'I can, if you think it'll be worth the effort,' said Freeman.

'Yes I do,' replied Sunnifa and she proceeded to trot off in the direction she had indicated, but almost immediately stopped. 'Cory,' she called, 'we will need to bring the thing that the wood mouse was trapped in; it should be possible if we nose it along together.' Looking bemused Cory followed her and, limping slowly, Freeman tagged on at the back.

The cows were on the common! Cory could not believe his eyes, usually they did not arrive before the end of June: another successful Scumble premonition – or perhaps not. Perhaps his brother had already seen them the day before, in which case there was nothing magical about his dream at all. Under Sunnifa's directions, Freeman had settled himself as near to one of the cows as possible whilst still remaining under cover. The cow was lying down basking in the sunshine. Sunnifa went up to it and politely asked if she would mind them taking some of her milk. The cow replied that she had no objection as long as they knew what they were doing.

'Have you ever milked a cow Cory?' asked Sunnifa.

'Have you?' he replied incredulously. 'I've heard the stories but thought that's just what they were – stories.'

'No it's true, I've done it before, my mother showed me how. Move that jar thing over here.' Sunnifa crouched down and began to knead the cow's udders which were resting on the ground. A few drops of milk splashed into the jar. Cory watched intently to see how it was done and then joined in until the drops became a trickle and then a flow of frothy creamy milk. The cow mooed in appreciation and Sunnifa laughed delightedly. She suddenly directed a stream of milk at Cory; it hit him squarely on the snout and he tasted its delicious warmth and flavour. Heady with a culmination of emotions he had encountered already that day, Cory directed a stream of milk back at Sunnifa until her whole body was covered entirely with the sweet liquid. Only the blackness of her eyes showed and the pinkness of her tongue as she threw back her head and laughed with abandon.

'When you two have quite finished,' Freeman groaned, 'I would appreciate some help.'

With apologies and concerned looks, the hedgehogs carefully nudged the jar towards the fox until it was near enough for him to lap up what remained of the milk. It was not ideal; there had been some spillage, but it was better than nothing. He found the warmth and sweetness comforting, it gave him strength. Sunnifa went in search of medicinal healing plants, whilst Cory pushed the jar back underneath the cow and began to fill it again. The cow had obligingly moved nearer to them and so the whole process became easier. Sunnifa arrived back with a quantity of nettle leaves and some tiny early flowering cowslips; torn and shredded into small pieces and mixed with the warm milk it made a relatively effective poultice which, when held in Freeman's mouth, relieved much of his pain. Sunnifa also made a poultice for Freeman's paw, holding it in place by binding it with long grass.

'It won't hold if you walk on it,' she said, 'but if you stay here for the night it should be a lot better in the morning.'

Freeman shook his head. 'I can't stay out another night,' he mumbled through the mouth poultice. 'Wilda and I left a litter of cubs at home. I must get back to them. I'll stay until the sun goes down and then be on my way.' He smiled grimly, 'Who'd have thought I'd ever need the help of two little hogs. I shan't forget this and if I survive you can call on my help another time.'

'Of course you will survive,' retorted Sunnifa. 'I am a very skilled practitioner in the arts of healing.' She gently touched Freeman's face, 'Make sure you stay under cover whilst you are here, the man will be coming to collect the cows soon.'

'Well let's hope he doesn't notice one cow's yield is light,' said Cory. 'Goodbye Freeman and good luck, we may well call on your offer of help one day.'

The two hedgehogs made their way back home via Bluebell Grove but their mood had changed and there was no more teasing or flirting.

'I was very impressed with how you handled that situation,' Cory observed. 'Where did you get your knowledge of healing plants?'

'A little bit from my grandmother,' said Sunnifa, 'but I have always been interested and just picked it up really.'

'You know, my brother Scumble has the same skill and no creature taught *him*. I always thought it was a bit strange and mysterious.'

'Well there is more to the world than you or I know Cory. I am so glad we know each other now; we are friends, aren't we?' She stopped so that he would turn and look at her. There was a lump in his throat that made it difficult for him to speak but finally he was able to tell her that he regarded her as one of his best and closest friends. He remembered his earlier sense of foreboding and now he sensed it again.

'How long were you watching me this afternoon, before you first spoke?' he asked her in what he hoped was a nonchalant manner.

'Oh not long, I was going for a walk and came up on you just as you got hold of that little mouse's tail. Why, you don't think I was spying on you do you?'

'No Sunnifa,' Cory shook his head, 'but I did feel that some creature was.'

They said their goodbyes on the edge of the woods and promised to meet up the next day. Cory sincerely hoped that they would meet up. He was charmed by Sunnifa and part of him felt a fool at his clumsy attempt at lovemaking. He resolved to find out more on the subject so that next time he would know what to do properly. He prayed to Pan that there would be a next time and that Sunnifa would give him another chance. As Cory returned home, musing on the day's events, the eyes that had watched him throughout, blinked then continued to follow him. Spike was wending his way home too.

CHAPTER 8

THE CELLAR IN THE DARK

She was flying; gliding effortlessly on high, warm air currents. She banked and dived; swooping deliciously downwards and the rush of cold, clean air as she drove through it was exhilarating... liberating. The sky was a clear blue backcloth; a canvas to paint whatever wonderful patterns she chose to weave and she was powerful, she could paint a panorama. Her little heart beat joyously: she was going home.

Something broke her dream: *a noise, what was it? There was some rat in the cellar.* She peered down into the deepening shadows but could make nothing out. She could not see the sky but she knew that it must be night and a moonless night at that, for there was little light filtering through. The rat was standing before the altar with its back to her. Its shape was distorted and unfamiliar. Its head and shoulders were covered with something; she could not make out what. During recent weeks the altar had acquired some new embellishments and was now decorated with a number of Man-made artefacts, brought back from rubbish dumps by gangs of foraging rats.

There was a large, elongated container with the image of a formidable rat on it. It was decorated with bold red and black markings, some of which were weather stained and obscured, but the pattern that remained was pleasing to the rats:

RAT KILLER

The logo on it of a skull and two crossbones fittingly matched many of the articles found in Pan's Pit and thus the container had become deified as the "Spirit of the Pit".

Next to it was a knife with a pretty ivory-coloured handle that was pleasantly smooth and tactile to hold. The blade was chipped but still sharp enough to do damage, as the rat who found it could testify: it had sliced his paw deeply and the wound had now turned septic. The pit housed dozens of various sharp pointed objects and the knife was considered to be a good representation of them. It had become deified as the "Spirit of the Impaler".

There was also a magnificent gold and silver coloured object that magically reflected back the image of anything placed in front of it. Many a rat had stood before it in thrall at perceiving its own self staring back; this glittering object had become deified as the "Spirit of Self-Perception".

Of all the artefacts, the most powerful and commanding took centre stage and dominated everything else. It had taken two teams of twenty rats to transport it from Mad Maggie's garden, where it had been discovered buried under a mountain of tangled weeds and brambles. Although weathered and damaged it was still recognisable as a majestic beast, with a mane of hair, sharp pointed canine teeth and long curling talons. It was made of stone and very heavy and in all it had taken two days and nights to complete the journey. Under the direction of Baldlice the rats had dragged it into the cellar through a gap where part of the wall had collapsed, using ropes and twine taken from the pit. It was placed in front of the altar as it had proved impossible to lift onto the marble slab. One attempt had been made to lift it, but cruelly it had toppled sideways crushing a number of rats. Ironically, considering the tragic accident, the beast was named "Sacred Spirit of the Stone", by Iya Nla, as a representation of the life force of the rat.

Without attracting its attention, the swift – or Iya Nla as she was now deferentially referred to – continued to observe the rat before the altar. It worried her that she was unable to identify it. She watched it preening and posturing in front of the Spirit of Self-Perception. It ran its paws over the face of the Sacred Spirit of the Stone, stroking the nose and mane; then made a mocking bow before it in a parody of referential worship. Suddenly it leapt onto the marble slab and snatched up the knife. It stood for a while closely examining it, absorbed in its detail, then threw back its misshapen head and let out a high pitched squeal of laughter that chilled her blood. Before she had time to collect herself, call out and question the rat's right to be there; it had leapt down from the altar and disappeared into the shadows.

She felt fear: a sense of doom. The worsening smell and fumes in the cellar were obscuring her inner vision; her ability to think clearly. She was losing control and her plans to unify the rats might well be high-jacked by individual ambition for power; what she had just witnessed indicated that this was already happening. With her waning ability to read minds it was uncertain whether even Baldlice could be trusted any more. She must summon her strength and probe deeper; she resolved to call a meeting of the acolytes.

'WILL YOU ALL HUSH UP AND LISTEN!'

CHAPTER 9

THE MEETING IN BLUEBELL GROVE

Cory had called a meeting in Bluebell Grove. Dozens of woodland creatures were congregated in the late afternoon sunshine under the oaks, whilst the trees themselves housed a multitude of birds of various breeds and creeds. Some of the party were aware of the nature of the meeting and had come to offer their services. Others had arrived out of curiosity, whilst for many it was a social occasion for meeting and greeting and a chance to gossip. The noise was pandemonium. With the help of Spike, Cory had manoeuvred himself onto a large gnarled oak tree root, where he could be seen easily and with a few 'errs and ums' and clapping of paws, tried to bring the meeting to order. This proved no easy task until Sheard the squirrel swung himself onto a branch near Cory's head and bellowed:

'WILL YOU ALL HUSH UP AND LISTEN!' which immediately got everyone's attention.

'I have asked you here,' began Cory, 'and by the way, thank you for coming.' A small hedgehog giggled and was cuffed into silence by its mother. 'I have asked you here,' continued Cory, somewhat daunted, 'because of the terrible things that have been happening in Whylder Wood.

There have been lots of dead rats, both in the stream and in the wood itself, especially in the area around Mad Maggie Minchin's house.' He took a breath and went on, 'The deaths all appear to be related and the rats without exception have died in agony.' Cory paused and surveyed the sea of serious faces looking up at him.

An elderly rabbit with a worried expression spoke up. 'My name is Bede and I speak for all rabbits when I say that we also have suffered a plague of agonising deaths in the past. Gladly we have been free of the terrible illness for some years now, but perhaps it has decided to attack rats instead.'

'Thank you Bede, what you say is plausible but I don't think it is the answer. Some of you already know how Sunnifa and I met Freeman the fox and how his mouth was burnt from sipping water from the stream in Whylder Wood. You all must have heard those terrible screams from his mate who had drank long and deep from that same water. She died in the self-same agony as the rats. It's not an illness.'

'Sounds more like poison to me,' said Scally from his perch above Scumble and Echo. 'What about the stream that runs through Park Woods, has anyone tried drinking that recently?' This was met by a number of negative head shakes and the inevitable buzz of conversation.

A weasel raised its paw to say that he and his family had drunk from the stream the day before and to his knowledge none of them had suffered any adverse effects. 'Anyway I'm here to tell the tale,' he said smugly.

A voice from the back asked sarcastically whether indeed it was just a tale and was it perhaps only "weasel words" the company was hearing; which set everyone off again until Cory managed to calm them down.

During the noisy interruptions, Spike noticed a female hedgehog giving him the eye. He knew her name, Neldar but had never spoken to her. She was sitting with Sunnifa and Sunnifa's Aunt Mae. Ever since Spike had secretly watched Cory and Sunnifa together a few days ago he had not been able to get the thoughts of Sunnifa out of his head. Many times since the meeting had begun his eyes had been drawn to her; but she had eyes only for Cory. Neldar must have thought he was interested in her. He looked across again and Neldar smiled invitingly. Well that was a turn up for the books; at last Lady Luck was favouring him. He gave Neldar a wink and she dissolved into giggles. He turned his attention back to the meeting, feeling somehow a little bit more self-important.

One of the starlings was speaking. 'There's something very nasty about Mad Maggie's place; the air is difficult to breathe and it makes your eyes smart. We don't go there anymore.'

'No, nor do we,' chirped a hedge sparrow, 'we don't even fly near it, there's a horrible smell. A stoat volunteered the information that a group of rats he had seen recently in Whylder Wood had been acting very strangely; laughing hysterically at nothing in particular and talking gibberish. They had passed by right under his nose and none had spotted him.

'It was like they were away with the fairies,' he said.

'Excuse me,' said a small voice near to Scumble. On

looking down, Scumble saw a caterpillar balanced on its tail, stretched to its fullest height, trying to get itself noticed. It was a dark brown, almost black in colour with reddish bands along each side and a splash of white on its rear. Altogether its camouflage was amazing; it was practically invisible against the bark of the tree roots, the bare soil and leaf mould on the ground. Scumble gently picked it up and let it stand on his paw.

'Good grief,' squawked Scally, 'a talking bird dropping!'

'Well that's the general idea,' retorted the caterpillar, 'else we'd be easy pickings for the likes of you.'

Cory held up a paw to hush the chattering that was breaking out again. 'Did you wish to address the meeting?' he asked. 'If so it might be easier if you came here.' Without further ado Scally plucked the little grub off Scumble's paw and deposited it onto Cory's paw with great dexterity.

'I have news of the rats that you are talking about,' the caterpillar said breathlessly, after his unexpected flight. 'Important news,' he added, folding his top front legs across his chest. 'My name is Vincent.'

Some weasel laughed, Cory frowned and some creature else said, 'Shut up and give the little feller a chance.'

'What is your news?' asked Cory.

'The colony of rats living in Mad Maggie Minchin's place is going mad,' Vincent looked around dramatically for effect and then continued. 'They are living next to a big pit; they call it Pan's Pit, but it is full of Man things; not nice things. Things that smell, that sting the eyes and burn the throat when you breathe; liquids and powders that burn the flesh right off you if you touch them and things that scald your insides if you eat or drink them. Poisons in the pit are seeping into the earth and spreading wider. They are seeping into the stream.' Vincent stopped for breath.

Cory bent down gently and whispered, 'Where did you get this information?'

'From the ants,' Vincent replied.

'What!' Cory exclaimed before he could stop himself.

There was a general hubbub, where those near enough to have heard the caterpillar repeated his story to others further away. Spike took advantage of the interruption to look across at Neldar and she returned his gaze, before laughingly pointing a paw at Vincent and tapping her forehead to indicate the likelihood of his insanity.

Vincent drew himself up to his full height and looked Cory straight in the eye. 'We caterpillars have an affinity with ants,' he said slowly and clearly. 'We have always been able to communicate as long as we are near together. I hatched under a leaf in Mad Maggie's garden and from the start made close friends with the ants. In fact we are mutually good for each other,' he said with great pride. 'Many have already lost their lives to the seeping poisons and it is getting worse. They asked me to spread the word and warn all the woodlanders.'

'If your story is to be believed,' said Cory with caution, 'why do you say that the rats are going mad?'

'The ants say that many of the rats have started eating or sniffing some of the white powders and it makes them act weird,' Vincent explained. 'It's as if they've lost control of what they say and do. They become reckless. There have been some strange killings,' he added darkly.

'Sound like a lot of smack-heads,' said a large rat appearing from behind Cory's oak tree. Two other well-built rats followed. There were a few screams and scuffling, with adults protectively manoeuvring youngsters behind them. 'Let me introduce ourselves,' continued the lead rat in a calm voice, 'I am Aldin and these are my companions, Heaton and Clowes.' The two rats nodded to the assembly. 'We are from the south, downstream along the Rushlep River. Forgive us for not making ourselves known sooner but we did not want to frighten you.'

'Yeah, yeah, yeah,' said Sheard, 'fo shure, but how do we know you aren't spies from Whylder Wood?'

'You don't,' said Aldin, 'except to say that I am a rat that has travelled far and my two friends here have lived on the banks of the river all their lives. Apart from that you will just have to take our word for it.' He slowly surveyed the crowd with unblinking eyes.

Cory felt intimidated but, as the organiser of the meeting felt responsible for keeping things calm and good natured so, with a restraining paw towards Sheard, he turned to Aldin and said, 'What do you mean "smack-heads"?'

'Acid heads: addicted to drugs,' Aldin answered in a matter of fact way. 'The white powder makes them feel good so they take more of it. Soon they need to take even more to keep feeling good.'

'Sounds OK to me,' called out the weasel who had spoken earlier. 'Who wouldn't want to find something like that so you could feel good all the time, what's wrong with that?'

'I am a city rat,' said Aldin, 'and I've seen similar behaviour there. The more you take the white powder the more you need to take it. In the end you *have* to take it; not to feel good, but just to stop feeling ill. You will do anything to get it, even kill for it. And if you take it too much it will eventually kill you.'

'Yes,' Vincent spoke up, 'it's what the ants said: the rats who are taking the white powder don't care what they do...some of them are dressing up.' There was some nervous laughter at this but Vincent ploughed on. 'They are holding ceremonies in the cellar of the house, and seven of the rats wear ceremonial cloaks. The cloaks are made from dead rats; the skulls and innards have been removed, the rats have been skinned. The seven rats have great power and all the other rats have to do as they are told. Oh yes and there is a bird,' he finished rather lamely.

'What bird?' squawked Scally. 'How can a bird be in the cellar with all those rats?'

'I don't know,' Vincent answered defiantly, 'but I believe the ants, they have never lied to me before, why should they lie now?'

'Why indeed!' said Scally with sarcasm.

Sheard lent over the branch and spoke to Vincent. 'Don't take that ragging to heart little feller, you may look like a bird turd but man, I like your style.'

'Well,' said Cory, 'I am inclined to believe Vincent but whether he is right or not, I don't think we can afford to ignore what is happening. If the stream is being poisoned it's only a matter of time before it spreads and does a great deal of damage. We *must* investigate. I would welcome any ideas and any offers of help.'

Bede the rabbit stood up again and spoke. 'As you all can see I am the sole representative for rabbits here. We are a timid lot and that is not so surprising giving the amount of enemies we have.' He eyed the weasels and stoats suspiciously. 'Long ago we had a great leader; a rabbit who was courageous and inspired others to be brave also. It is said that he led a group of rabbits out of the jaws of death and because they believed in him they followed where he led. A long and arduous journey until finally, they arrived on the top of a mountain where they made their home and lived in peace and contentment for many years. So the story goes but we have not seen his like since Pan was a boy. I am afraid that no rabbit now will volunteer to tackle anything dangerous.'

'I understand,' said Cory, 'but perhaps you will be able to persuade them at the very least to keep their ears open and report anything that may be of relevance.' Bede nodded and said he would try.

Cory looked up into the trees and spoke to the birds. 'There are many of you,' he said. 'It would only take a few to explore Whylder Wood more closely. Surely one or two of you at least would be prepared to go to Mad Maggie's house and report back on what you find there?'

The hedge sparrow fluttered her wings in dismay and flew up onto a higher branch. 'I couldn't possibly,' she trilled. 'We've already explained how difficult it is to breathe in that place; we could be inhaling the poison as we fly. I can't afford to do anything dangerous like that, I have the responsibilities of motherhood to consider.' She puffed out her chest. 'I have an exceptionally large and beautiful chick to feed and it takes me all my time just to keep him from starvation's door. In fact I have been away from him far too long already.' She flew off the branch and without another word, disappeared in a matter of seconds.

'Dozy Dunnock's got a cuckoo in the nest,' Scally said. 'Serves her right!'

Cory looked at the kestrel. 'Echo,' he said, 'perhaps you could visit Mad Maggie's? You would be able to hover high enough above to keep clear of the fumes, but be able to stay in one spot long enough to notice what is going on.'

Scumble felt Echo shudder beside him.

'N-n-no I-I couldn't,' she answered in a very subdued voice. 'I-I'm sorry C-Cory. I have t-t-to do something else. I-I can't, I can't.'

'Fo' shame!' cried Sheard. 'First a doofus drama queen and now we've got a self- proclaimed diva.

'That's not fair, Sheard,' called Scumble, 'we shouldn't expect others to do what we are not prepared to do ourselves.'

'Nuff said,' Sheard replied. 'Cory, I volunteer to help in whatever way you think I can, but I'm afraid I can't hover!' He looked daggers across at Echo, who hung her head miserably.

'Thanks Sheard,' Cory looked at the kestrel in puzzlement. 'Don't worry about it, Echo,' he said kindly.

The three rats were now huddled together in close discussion. Other voices became raised and opinions more vehemently expressed as individuals pressed home arguments for and against further investigation or, what some termed, "risky interference". Spike tried to make eye contact with Neldar but she was gazing at Cory with seeming adoration. Both she and Sunnifa were giving a good impression of two fawning neophytes worshipping at the shrine. A bolt of jealousy shot through him and anger blazed within. *Typical – Cory wins again,* he thought.

A female stoat raised her paw to ask Cory why there were not more creatures from Whylder Wood at the meeting. Cory said diplomatically that he thought it was probably because they had not received news of the meeting in time. Privately he believed it was because they were too frightened. He explained that Freeman had sent word apologising for his absence as he was still suffering from his injuries and had the motherless cubs to care for. Freeman had given assurances that he would be available to help in any way at a later date. This was met by some sarcastic laughter and a few cynical comments which Cory ignored. He went on to say that there had been no word as yet from Braxton and that he was becoming anxious for the badger's safety. His set was not far from Mad Maggie's place.

Although Cory managed to maintain a calm and purposeful front he was beginning to feel quite desperate inside. He was rapidly coming to the conclusion that he made a poor leader – weak and inadequate; obviously not inspirational like Bede's historical hero. It was with some relief therefore when he heard a small party of crows offering to fly as close as they dared to Mad Maggie's and report back on what they could learn.

'Scumble was good to us once not long ago,' explained

one crow, 'and we owe you hedgehogs a favour.' This offer encouraged two hedgehogs, Bugle and Trefoil, to volunteer to visit Braxton. Cory recognised the two hogs as those he had spoken sharply to on the common when they were ragging Scumble and he was pleased they did not appear to be holding any grudge against him. Orva the female stoat said that she was prepared to show them the way and Cory accepted gratefully. He had already decided to seek advice from Drew the owl, whose reputation for having a grounding of common sense surpassed the more questionable one of being worldly wise. Both Scumble and Sheard said they would go with him and Scally offered his services as a guide.

The shadows under the trees were growing longer and the sun had sunk low in the sky as the meeting came to a close. Many had already left after promising to report back on any new piece of information. Sunnifa had volunteered to be the point of contact for the reports in the absence of Cory, and Neldar excitedly said she would help her. Cory was about to officially end the meeting when Aldin, Heaton and Clowes approached him.

Speaking in a low voice Aldin said, 'Look Cory, our path leads us through Whylder Wood; we've talked it over and are agreed that to reconnoitre Mad Maggie's won't be too much out of our way. We are not in any hurry and it's likely we could get away with being in the area without necessarily being suspected of spying. If you are agreed we would prefer that our destination is not made public; no point in enlightening the enemy and putting ourselves at a disadvantage.' Cory felt a sense of relief. It was still not clear whether these three rats could be entirely trusted but he liked their manner. He judged that they were honest and hoped to Pan that he was right.

'I'm grateful,' he said. 'I suggest you follow the stream as closely as possible and you will come to the place. If what we hear is correct the smell will draw you on anyway.'

Vincent spoke up. 'I think I should go with them,' he said. 'If I can get near enough to communicate with the ants then it might save us unnecessary danger.'

'And I should go as well,' cried Spike, before he knew what he was saying. He wanted so to impress Neldar and from the look on her face he considered he had done just that.

Aldin however did not appear to be impressed. 'We planned a covert operation,' he said with suppressed irritation, 'a swift and silent reconnoitre and we do not need extra baggage.'

Spike coloured with embarrassment and anger, 'I'm not baggage,' he hissed at Cory. It was a dilemma: Cory could see that the rats would be quicker, more agile without the encumbrance of a caterpillar and hedgehog. Nevertheless, he was loath to belittle his brother especially when he had volunteered for a mission that none of the other woodland folk were brave enough to tackle. For a number of reasons he wanted Spike onside, not against him.

'Look,' he said to Aldin, 'although it may well slow you down, I think the advantages outweigh the disadvantages. It would be useful to have a number of witnesses as to how Vincent communicates with the ants. We need to be certain that what he believes to be true, is really so. I also think that if Spike is with you, you have the option to continue on your own journey afterwards without the need to report back here. Spike can do that instead. What do you say?'

Aldin was not totally convinced by Cory's argument but he had a growing respect for the young hedgehog and therefore nodded his head. So it was agreed and all parties thought it best to begin without further delay, whilst there was still light enough to travel by. With a sinking heart, Spike saw Cory and Sunnifa take an affectionate leave of one another. In turn he said his own halting goodbyes to Neldar, who told him she thought him very brave. Thus with raised spirits he followed the three rats and Vincent out of the grove in the direction of the stream. The crows then made what was for them, a relatively subdued departure towards Whylder Wood.

Cory turned to Bugle, Trefoil and Orva the stoat and wished them a safe journey. 'Don't go doing anything foolhardy,' he warned. 'Just go straight to Braxton's and stay the night if he lets you. You can report back to Sunnifa tomorrow.'

'Will do, Captain,' Bugle said with a jokey salute.

'We'll be back before you've 'ad a chance to miss us sir,' Trefoil laughed.

Cory gave them both a grave look. 'It's not a picnic you're going on. Take it seriously, stick close to Orva, she knows the wood well.' He watched them climb the steep slope of an earth mound and disappear from view over the ridge.

'Well that leaves just us chickens,' said Sheard. 'Lead on Scally, let's get moving.'

The last party started off in the direction of the common leaving Scumble and Echo alone to say their goodbyes.

'I'm so sorry Scumble,' Echo said mournfully, 'sorry for being so useless!'

Scumble brushed a gentle paw across her cheek. 'I don't know what trouble you are in,' he answered quietly, 'but I understand that you feel you must face it on your own. Just remember that I am here for you if you need me.' He gave her a lopsided grin, 'Keep in touch,' he whispered.

Echo watched him chase after Cory and the others, his little burnt backside with its blackened prickles making him look somehow very lost and vulnerable. He was her friend and she had let him down. Echo watched with tears in her eyes.

CHAPTER 10

FALSENESS AND DUPLICITY

Baldlice had arranged for the meeting to be held where the swift's nest was located as she was too weak to be moved to a more private, secure room. To discourage prying eyes and ears, he had placed sentry guards around the perimeter and the guards had sworn an oath of allegiance to Iya Nla. The six acolyte priests plus Baldlice now sat in a semi circle around the bird. Seats had been fashioned out of bricks and flat stones.

The meeting had begun in the usual way, with each rat reporting briefly on what he or she had been doing in the last few days. The biggest piece of news, reported by Holt, was that the birth rate had gone down. Less than half the numbers of rats were now being born than had been the case in March. What was more worrying was that many of the rats being born were born dead, or were so weak that they lived only a few hours; at the most days. Incredibly there were a high proportion of rats being born grossly misshapen. Initially the deformed pups had been killed immediately by the mother rats, but Holt suspected many mothers were now hiding them and keeping them alive in secret. This might be a travesty of Nature and probably death to the long-term future of the colony, but understandable when a mother failed after many attempts to produce a healthy, normal pup: what was to be done?

Earle spoke with authority. 'Iya Nla, it would appear that the fumes and poisons from the pit are adversely affecting the female rats' ability to breed healthy offspring. I propose that all females of breeding age should be housed on the other side of the building, where the air is cleaner. In the meantime we must eradicate all rats found to be deformed in any way: they must not be allowed to breed.'

'With respect Earle,' said Holt, 'whilst I agree with your first proposal, I cannot countenance what is tantamount to the full scale slaughter of helpless rats, deformed or otherwise. We would risk an uprising of angry parents against any attempt we made and we do not have the strength in numbers to counter such rebellion. There would be anarchy.'

'Perhaps there is another way,' pondered Atol. 'It is clear that breeding females should be kept as far away from the pit as possible. However, is there really a need to exterminate young rats, simply because they may look a little different from what we are used to? Nature is forever evolving; do we have the right to interfere in that?' He stood up and bowed to the swift. 'Iya Nla, would it not be more profitable to allow the strongest of these deformed rats to live; to grow and develop under the jurisdiction of the priests. If they are tutored by us, who knows what positive benefits the colony may reap. We cannot say at this stage what intellectual abilities they will have and, for all we know, Nature may compensate their feeble bodies by giving them exceptional brains.' Atol turned and slowly surveyed the other rats before taking his seat again.

'Does any rat wish to add something before we put this to the vote?' the swift asked. 'Wimund, what is your view?'

Wimund inclined her head as if searching for inspiration. 'I think that under ideal circumstances it would be wiser to put these poor apologies for rats to death. I feel that in a healthy colony they can only weaken the structure. However, as we surely must all agree, this is not a healthy colony and as Holt has pointed out, our number is fast diminishing. Perhaps therefore, we should be circumspect and let the best of them live. I like Atol's idea that the priests should be responsible for their education and welfare. So to that end I propose that we create a nursery, separated from all other adult rats. I cannot see that the mothers would contest this if they were assured their offspring were being taken care of.'

'Thank you, Wimund,' the swift said. 'Now if no rat else has anything more to say?' She paused before continuing, 'Let us take a vote... Baldlice?' She looked quizzically at the old rat and he stepped to her side.

'Who favours killing *all* deformed rats?' he said solemnly. Earle and Gram raised their paws. 'Who favours killing only those with the most debilitating deformities?' Baldlice continued. Atol and Wimund raised their paws and after a furtive glance round, Ware raised his paw also. 'And finally,' said Baldlice, 'who favours setting up a nursery to be run by the priests?' There were raised paws from all but Earle and Gram.

The swift blinked and sighed. 'Very well,' she said. 'Wimund, I appoint you Head Priest of the nursery, come to me tomorrow with your plans for the day to day running of it.'

Wimund stared angrily at the bird. 'I am not a nursery maid,' she said indignantly. 'Just because I am female does not mean I want to spend the best part of my time with screeching juveniles!'

The swift smiled, 'Do not take offence, Wimund. Many creatures and birds, both male and female, jointly share the responsibilities of raising their young.' She swallowed and went on quietly but firmly, 'My mate and I brought up dozens of chicks over the years, our roles were always the same. I thought you would want the major role in the nursery considering it was your idea.'

Wimund appeared to be in a sulk, when Atol stood up and with a shrug said, 'It worries me none, I am happy to take the role of nursery Head Priest if that's acceptable to the rest of you?'

There were murmurs of assent and the swift said, 'Well that's settled then, report to me tomorrow, Atol. And now I would like to discuss another issue. Is there something you have not been telling me?' she directed her gaze at Earle.

Earle was startled and somewhat embarrassed, 'I think you might mean our ceremonial cloaks, Iya Nla?' he replied.

'Yes,' said the swift, 'the wearing of dead rat skins – how did that come about?' She looked at all of them in turn, 'Whose idea was that?'

'As to whose idea it was, I cannot say specifically,' said Earle, 'it seemed to present itself to each of us at the same time.'

Gram interrupted. 'Six rats were crushed when the Sacred Spirit of the Stone fell on them. I remember thinking afterwards — *six — that's more than coincidence; it's a sign from the gods!* I believe I may have mentioned it to the others,' he said smugly.

'I think not,' retorted Wimund. 'I distinctly recall that it was I who suggested it.' She glared at Ware who was nearest to her.

'I don't remember,' Ware answered vaguely.

Holt scratched his nose. 'I seem to remember that it was you Atol, wasn't it?'

'Possibly,' Atol answered with a smile, 'but I think Earle is correct when he says we all seemed to think of it together. I think it was you, Holt, who pointed out we were one skin short for Baldlice and I said I would endeavour to get one. It was fortuitous that the rat that had cut his paw on the Spirit of the Impaler, died that very night.'

'Not so fortuitous for him,' muttered Holt and Gram giggled. Baldlice scowled at him.

'Iya Nla,' said Atol, 'I hope that you are not displeased with us? You, yourself gave instructions to set ourselves apart from the colony. What better way to command respect and obedience than to appear grand and awe-inspiring.'

Baldlice cleared his throat. 'The argument *was* persuasive,' he explained, turning to the swift. 'When the accident first occurred I ordered four of the rats to be taken immediately to the burial grounds. The other two were initially only injured and therefore taken to the healing rooms. When I discovered later that both had subsequently died of their injuries, I accepted the idea that it was a sign from the gods. You cannot deny, Iya Nla, that the cloaks are very impressive and are being put to far better use than if left to rot in the ground.'

The swift eyed them all in turn and then said quietly, 'We established this place of worship as a device; a device, to bring the colony together in fellowship and union. It is a useful device but that is all. It is dangerous for us to believe in magical charms and signs from gods of whom we know nothing. I asked that you should set yourselves apart from other rats. I did not mean for you to set yourselves above them. Do not think yourselves more important than those who you teach. Remember all lives are sacred.'

She gestured to Baldlice to close the meeting and they took their leave of her. The swift sank down into the nest and closed her eyes, the meeting had exhausted her. Her power to read minds was continuing to wane and some things remained obscure to her, but she could sense falseness and duplicity. She considerd the two rats that were able to close their minds to her. Her feelings towards one were ambivalent; she had yet to make up her mind. The other filled her with dread. It seemed likely that one, or both, were using mind control over the other rats; in the same way that she was able to control Baldlice. Hence the vagueness about who had first suggested skinning the dead rats. What was more disturbing was the fact that all three injured rats had died so quickly before there had been time to bury the four dead ones. It was too much of a coincidence, especially as it had been reported by her two handmaidens, Myrtle and Luthian, that the rat with the cut paw was making a good recovery. No, the priests' story stank of lies and she had to conclude that murder had been committed three times over. The air was thick with the vapours of treacherous poisons that were corrupting the mind as well as the body. The swift felt nauseous and weak with pain. She waited patiently for Baldlice to bring her medication.

CHAPTER 11

ECHO'S STORY – PART 1

Echo watched Scumble until he disappeared through the trees and under the fence onto the common. The shadows were growing longer by the minute and she determined to start her journey before night fell. She planned to make for The Grange which she had been told was somewhere northeast of Whylder Wood. How long it would take her she had no way of knowing, although she assumed it must involve crossing the road and she was adamant she would not attempt that in the dark. Breathing deeply to counter the churning in her stomach, she rose into the air for about ten feet and set her course towards Whylder Wood.

To begin with she made good progress; there was enough light to see her way and she was becoming skilled at twisting and turning to negotiate the gaps between the trees. Once she reached the "Dark Wood" however, things became more hazardous. The trees were taller and grew closer together and the pathways were overgrown with brambles. The effort of keeping herself aloft at such a low level sapped her strength and she had rested in the undergrowth on three occasions before eventually reaching, what could only be minutes from the road.

From her shelter in a crevice between some tree roots she heard the whine of an engine approaching rapidly. The noise reached a crescendo, blocking out all other sounds, before gradually diminishing and finally fading away altogether as the motor continued on its journey. Echo shivered and fought down a feeling of nausea. She lacked the courage to cross the road and the only alternative was to spend the night here. The shelter was not ideal but she was too tired to search further, besides she had spent many recent nights alone on the ground and was getting used to it. Just then, a movement in front caught her eye and instinctively she summoned the last of her strength to fly forward and pounce on the unfortunate vole that had left it too late to reach the safety of its home that night. The meal was manna from Pan to Echo, who had been subsisting largely on insects and grubs for some time. This piece of good fortune gave her the motivation to search for better sleeping quarters and she was rewarded by finding an abandoned rabbit burrow close by. It was warm and dry and after a while she had relaxed enough to feel sleepy. With some trepidation she closed her eyes and almost immediately found herself re-living the nightmare that continued to stalk her both day and night...

***

When Echo woke up that morning she was filled with a sense of excited anticipation, for today would be *the* day – the day she would leave the nest for the first time.

Full of impatience she nudged her brother Marlin: 'C'mon Marlin, today's the day – the world is waiting for us out there.'

'Leave me alone,' he grumbled, 'what's the rush? You're always so pushy,' he turned his back on her and snuggled further down into the warmth.

The nest was high in the hollow of an oak tree on the edge of Park Woods. Echo and Marlin were the third brood to be born to a pair of kestrels who had returned here for three years running. On this particular morning the youngsters' mother was out hunting for their breakfast, whilst their father would shortly be returning from his visit to Great Bowden Water some miles away. Bowden Water was a favourite spot of both adult kestrels and they had promised to take their offspring as soon as they were strong enough to do the journey.

From her vantage point, Echo peered out over the woods; she could see as far as the spinney at the other end of the common. She could smell the fresh new growth of green vegetation and her keen eye caught the bright yellow shades of meadow buttercup and celandine as they lifted their faces to the morning sun. Along the hedgerow, the tall grasses were spotted with the dusky pink of early campion and just visible beneath the trees was a white carpet of wood anemones. The sky was a pale blue with scudding white clouds and the breeze was strong enough to set everything dancing and swaying as if to say, 'Welcome – won't you join us?' Echo could not restrain herself from giving Marlin another dig.

'Marlin, *do* c'mon, let's give Mother a surprise. Don't you want to test your wings? Don't you want to see how strong you are? I feel so strong I bet I could touch those clouds up there.' Tipping herself forward to inspect the clouds she toppled out of the nest, and with a shriek and excited giggle, landed clumsily onto a branch below. Looking up she saw Marlin's worried face peering down at her.

'Are you OK?' he asked. 'How are you going to get back?'

'Marlin!' said Echo with exasperation. 'Why do I need to get back? I have flown the nest and my future lies elsewhere.' She stared expectantly at her brother who finally, with a sigh of resignation, fluttered down to land at her side.

'Well we've done it now,' he gulped, 'I don't know what Mother will say, she told us to wait until she got back.'

Echo shrugged. 'Look if we keep practising we'll be proficient by the time she does come back. Think how proud she and Father will be.'

'Proficient?' Marlin mulled the word over, 'half the time I don't understand what you say, Echo,' he muttered.

'Never mind that, just follow me.' She rose into the air and with a screech of ecstasy flew straight to another tree thirty yards away. Landing heavily and swaying to keep her balance, she turned gingerly to face her brother. 'You can do it Marlin, I swear it's as easy as sucking on slippery shrew spleen. C'mon!'

After a great deal of encouragement on her part and a great deal of reticence on Marlin's, he eventually joined her. They rested in silence for a while, Echo hoping that the break would bolster her brother's courage, while Marlin scanned the skies hoping in vain to catch sight of their returning mother.

'Right!' said Echo impatiently. 'Let's go, on the count of three: one – two – three.' She lifted off and headed across the tree tops towards the common. With one last despairing look for his absent mother, Marlin sighed and followed her. Echo had always been bigger and stronger than him and she had always considered herself to be more daring, although Marlin preferred to think of it as more headstrong. Nevertheless, he had to admit that he was quite liking the feeling of freedom and the comforting way the breeze caressed his feathers. This could be fun. They rested again in a tree at the edge of the common before Echo led them in a straight flight to the spinney. A crowd of raucous crows and starlings were noisily competing for their first feed of the day, pecking at the moist earth in the shade of the trees. There were a number of disputes and altercations but all in all there proved to be plenty for every-bird and the two kestrels were pointedly ignored.

'Well,' observed Echo. 'It seems it's the luck of the early bird to get the worm, that's for sure.'

'Good luck for the bird,' agreed Marlin, 'bad luck for the poor ol' worm!'

Echo chuckled; she loved her brother very much, even if he was a bit of a scaredy chick. She scanned the ground and concluded that there was little chance of getting any breakfast here. 'We'll fly over that way,' she said, indicating the south part of the common. 'We'll have more luck of catching something if we're on our own.

'Echo no…no further,' Marlin protested, but she had already gone.

The rest of the day was spent perfecting their flying and hovering skills. Echo even managed to catch a field mouse to share; which only added to her already inflated feelings of self importance. Marlin's whinging and carping was beginning to get on her nerves but in truth she had to admit that she was feeling just a teensy bit guilty that they had not returned home earlier. As the day grew older the breeze had strengthened, and by the time they found themselves at Clacks Farm they were being buffeted by a strong wind. The sky had darkened ominously and black thunder clouds were gathering. Swooping down, Echo negotiated a few outbuildings before entering a large barn and crash landing onto a beam. Marlin followed ten seconds later.

'Welcome,' said a smooth, rather mournful voice and looking round the kestrels saw a large white owl gazing unblinkingly at them. He was bigger and weightier than both of them put together, but his heart shaped face seemed kindly.

'Hello,' Echo replied brightly. 'Sorry if we've disturbed you.'

'No matter,' replied the owl.

After a few minutes of silence, in which the two young birds began to feel rather uncomfortable, Echo ventured to say that they hoped the owl would allow them to rest for a while before they went home. The owl continued to gaze silently and benignly on them, so Echo was encouraged to recount the day's events, with Marlin chipping in at intervals.

'Well,' said the owl at last, 'it would seem you have had quite an adventure. It's probably safer to stay here for the night. There is a nasty storm brewing.'

'We *must* go home,' Marlin said firmly, 'Mother will be so worried.'

'Oh for Pan's sake!' cried Echo. 'You are such a drag, Marlin. If things were left to you we would do nothing – *know* nothing!'

'And what happens when things are left to you?' Marlin retorted, 'Danger and anxiety that's what!'

Echo spluttered. 'Exaggerating again Marlin, what's wrong with taking a little risk here and there? The trouble with you is, you lack courage.' She looked at the owl for support.

'Hmmmm,' he said. 'Maybe courage *is* being able to stand up and say your piece; but remember that sometimes it is also about being able to keep quiet and listen to someone else's point of view.' He smiled at the youngsters and added, 'Never let a little argument spoil a good friendship.'

Echo felt irritated. Surely it was better to be a bird of action: one had to be decisive to get things done. The owl's attitude annoyed her; she had expected him to give her credit, even praise, for what she had achieved that day. So for no other reason other than perverseness, she changed her mind about staying and told Marlin that after a short rest they would start their journey home. The owl pointed out that it had begun to rain, but on scrutinising Echo's exasperated expression decided that perhaps silence was the best policy. Marlin could hardly contain himself with the prospect of returning home and characteristically immediately forgave Echo her indiscretions of the day. By the time they were ready to leave the rain had become a downpour and the rumblings of thunder more distinct. Nevertheless, both kestrels were determined to go, despite the owl's efforts to persuade them otherwise. They said their goodbyes and flew out of the barn and up into the dark sky. The old owl sighed and muttered about the arrogance of youth. The trouble with the world was that fools were always so certain of themselves, whilst those who were wiser were always so full of doubts. He turned his back to the barn door and tucked his head comfortably under his wing.

Echo had not been in the air for more than a few minutes before she realised her mistake. It was obvious that they should have remained under shelter in the barn. The driving rain not only obscured her vision and deafened her, but the weight of it was painful on her body. She wrestled with her conscience and came to the conclusion that she could not bear to lose face. Instead she resolved to keep encouraging her weaker brother in the hope that a positive attitude would see them both through. Her thoughts were interrupted by a flash of lightning that eerily lit the trees around them and this was quickly followed by a loud clap of thunder. 'Keep going Marlin,' she called, 'follow me.'

Echo was becoming anxious, the scene that had been illuminated seemed totally alien to her. She did not recognise where they were and was uncertain of what direction to take.

'Where are we Echo?' Marlin panted, 'Where are we going?'

'Not long now,' she called back, trying to keep her voice light and cheerful.

The weight of the rain was keeping them low to the ground and Echo debated on whether to land and shelter under a hedgerow. It was not just the prospect of being lost that worried her, but the rising storm was becoming frightening in its intensity. She could feel Marlin right behind her rather than hear him, but she sensed his fear also. Whilst she was still debating, they came upon a large Man-made pathway; a road, she thought it was called. There was no recollection that they had passed over it earlier in the day, but she decided to follow it in the hope it would lead them somewhere familiar. 'We'll follow the road,' she called to Marlin. 'Keep together and keep low.' This last instruction was superfluous as they were both so wet by now that their feathers were almost waterlogged and it was as much as they could do to keep airborne.

Suddenly, without warning, a truck appeared round a bend in the road and raced straight towards them; its headlights blazing and its engine roaring. For a few confused seconds the kestrels were blinded and mesmerised with fear. As the truck bore down on them, Echo saw the driving rain bouncing off the windscreen like a waterfall; she glimpsed a man in the cab, hands tightly gripping the wheel, his face frozen into a grimace of terror. She veered to the left but was not quick enough and the truck caught her off balance; with a thud she glanced off the roof and was sent spinning onto the embankment. She heard Marlin's squeal of horror, 'Noooooooo!' as, with a screech of brakes, the truck skidded across to the other side of the road and overturned into a ditch. It lay there for a few awful seconds and in the silence a small bunch of heather fell out of the smashed windscreen onto the bonnet, before the engine finally exploded and engulfed the truck in flames. Echo dragged herself under a fence and into the long grass before losing consciousness.

When Echo came to, the storm was over and the truck was a burnt out skeleton. It lay with its bare bones exposed; stark yet vulnerable like some long dead monster stripped of its power. The grass and hedgerow surrounding it were burnt black and there was a sickly smell of oil and petrol. She gingerly stretched her wings and was relieved to find them undamaged, but her chest hurt her and she was finding it difficult to breathe. She lifted her head and called to Marlin, but all that came out was a croak. Painfully she made her way up the bank onto the road and in the grey light of dawn surveyed the disaster scene. Involuntarily she vomited up the partly digested field mouse so proudly caught the day before: so much for that! But where was her brother? Not daring any attempt to fly, Echo hopped around the area croaking Marlin's name, but there was no sign of him. Eventually, utterly exhausted, she hunkered down under a hedge and fell asleep.

It was midmorning when she awoke and after spending what seemed like hours searching and calling for Marlin, she resolved to find her way home in the hope that he was there. Her chest was still painful but she managed by dint of determination to fly low over the ground for short bursts until, with overwhelming relief, she found herself in familiar territory. It was not long before she reached the place where the old hollow oak should have been... but everything had changed. With a feeling of dread and a presentiment of doom she saw that the tree lay on its side, split wide open. Its once proud trunk and familiar branches burnt and blackened to a skeleton in mock imitation of the truck. Without doubt it was retribution visited upon her by Pan; her punishment for selfish, thoughtless behaviour. Echo groaned and if there had been any contents left in her stomach she would have brought them up. Where was Marlin? Where were her parents? No bird answered her calls which became increasingly despairing as time passed. Just when she felt it was time to find some shelter and was considering where to go, she glimpsed the still shape, partly hidden under a branch of the decimated oak. She approached slowly, her heart thumping; blood turning to ice for what she dreaded to find. The fears were well founded: her mother's body, with blackened charred feathers, lay cold and lifeless on the ground. Echo felt she had discovered the limitless cruelty of the vengeful Pan and her despair and remorse knew no bounds. It was all her fault; her wayward disobedience had caused the death of a man, the death of her beloved mother and probably the death of her brother as well. Pan had sent the wrath of the storm to punish her and she deserved it.

With a cry of desolation she lifted into the air; beating her wings relentlessly as she rose higher and higher. For a moment she hung suspended, then everything faded into silence; dizziness took hold, it was difficult to breathe and she dropped like a stone to the ground. Shocked and stunned, she lay gasping for breath before retching again and again on her cramped and empty stomach. It took some minutes before she plucked up the courage to try flying again and this time she resolutely stayed as low as she dared. Flying in short bursts she made her way back to the burnt out truck; she was desperate to discover what had happened to Marlin. Again and again she flew over the area, calling to him; her keen eyes searching for any sign of movement or, Pan forbid, his still, lifeless body. But there was no sign of him. Echo hardly dared to hope that he had escaped injury and might possibly be flying around searching for her. She gazed with expectation into the sky only to be disappointed. The alternative did not bear thinking about; she glanced at the truck surrounded by black and scorched vegetation and shuddered. With an effort she rose into the air once more and with a heavy heart retraced the route that she and Marlin had taken the day before. By the time she reached the spinney she knew that she could fly no more that day. She crash landed under the trees and crawled deep into the undergrowth.

***

As the cold light of day seeped into the rabbit burrow, Echo shivered and woke from her dream. For a minute she could not imagine where she was then memory came flooding back. The nightmare would never leave her. She lay quietly, shivering now and then, trying to collect her thoughts and go over her plans. She intended to make for Great Bowden Water in the hope of finding her father and perhaps – Pan willing – even Marlin. A number of woodland birds had given her directions; the general consensus being to break her journey at The Grange where she might obtain more specific directions from the swallows nesting there. One piece of unexpected good news came from a friendly fieldfare, who remembered seeing a kestrel hovering over Park Woods two days earlier. The kestrel had last been sighted making off in a north-easterly direction towards Great Bowden Water. Echo hardly dared to hope that this could have been Marlin; but she clung fiercely to the thought that at least one other member of her family had still been alive two days ago. As much as she loved Scumble and would have happily helped him and Cory under any other circumstances, it was impossible for her to attempt anything now except to concentrate on her own problems. Besides, what possible use would she be – a kestrel who couldn't fly? She sighed deeply at the thought that she might have lost the friendship of the little hedgehog: a bitter pill to swallow on top of everything else.   Feeling lost and forsaken, Echo summoned up her courage to face the next challenge, she would have to cross the road. It was still rather gloomy and she decided to wait until the sun had risen higher in the sky before making the attempt. She hoped that a road in daylight proved to be a safer prospect than one at night.

CHAPTER 12

INITIATION

The initiation of the acolyte priests was to take place that night when the moon was full. Iya Nla explained that this was because the potency of the moon's power was important in these types of ritual ceremonies. In more practical terms of course, it would be the only source of light in the darkened cellar. There was feverish activity all through the day to bring everything together in readiness for the great occasion. Baldlice was in his element; directing operations like a General. He was energised and high on a mixture of drugs. Nevertheless, the old rat had to admit to himself that these medications were no longer primarily to counter his painful arthritis and general feebleness of body. Their addictive use was more to bolster his growing uncertainty and lack of confidence. He realised that the more he took them, the more he came to rely on them; but this was his dilemma because he now believed he could not function without them.

Today, however, he felt at the height of his powers and appeared decisive and visionary. Driven by the drugs, Baldlice had achieved a momentous change in the ancient, crumbling cellar. Foraging parties of rats had returned with more artefacts for the altar; mostly bright, shiny objects. A swathe of red velvet cloth was draped across one wall and a ragged tear to one side had been cleverly disguised by an arrangement of tall grasses and ferns, deadly nightshade and some flowering ramsons. The pinnacle of his achievements however, dominated the lower end of the room and consisted of an assortment of metal pipes: rods, canisters, cartons and tins arranged around a large drum barrel that had been hauled out of the pit. The acolyte priest Ware had volunteered his services, proving to be a veritable musical genius and together with the old rat's ingenuity they had assembled a unique and workable band. Interested prospective players had been auditioned and those with the best rhythmic musical skill had been chosen. It was exciting times and, well before the allotted time of commencement, dozens of rats were already gathering outside the entrance waiting to go in.

The swift in her role as Iya Nla was moved closer to the cellar drop so that she could look down unimpeded over what was left of a crumbling parapet. Myrtle and Luthian stayed by her side. As the fullness of the moon's light began to light up the centre of the cellar, Baldlice gave instructions to let the congregation in. The musicians played an erratic, rather discordant background piece of music written and orchestrated by Ware; but what it lacked in melody it made up for in enthusiasm and rhythm. The dance floor accommodated roughly a hundred rats standing shoulder to shoulder and the maximum capacity was very quickly achieved. Whilst most of the centre was lit well enough to distinguish the identity of individual rats, nothing could be perceived clearly in the shadowy corners.

The rats were allowed some minutes of mounting curiosity and restlessness before the six acolytes made their entrance following in the wake of Baldlice. All seven wore the ceremonial cloaks of the skinned rats and a hush fell around the room. The cloaks made the priests appear bigger than they really were and the effect of wearing the skinned heads on top of their own heads with the snouts pulled low over their faces made them look misshapen and awesome. The disguise produced the desired effect that no individual priest was recognisable, except for the leader with his arthritic limp and scarred body. At a sign from Baldlice, the congregation fell to the floor in a mixture of fear and reverence and the music ceased. The six acolytes knelt before the altar, whilst Baldlice addressed the congregation and in ringing tones expounded the creed of the cult. The rats were to understand that the duties of the priests were primarily to heal the sick and afflicted. In order to do so they would conduct rituals to call on the help of the spirits; or to pacify the spirits if any rat transgressed against the well-being of the colony. Loyalty to the colony must come first; followed by loyalty to the spirits and lastly loyalty to the individual. The priests would give sole concentration to the worship of the spirits and as such, would not mate or be part of family life. They would remain separated from all other rats and practice their art until they grew proficient in all priestly things. Soon they would gain the wisdom to read and interpret dreams; make predictions and tell fortunes; they would learn how to cast spells to invoke protection; they would create love spells and death spells and finally they would learn the secret of the powders and potions to be found in the pit. The priests would become the protectors of the colony and also its advisors. Any rat wishing to consult with a particular priest could do so by arrangement with Baldlice.

The old rat indicated the four main spirits: the container with the logo of the skull and crossbones – Spirit of the Pit; the bone handled knife – Spirit of the Impaler; the gold and silver mirror – Spirit of Self-Perception; and the beast – Sacred Spirit of the Stone. These were the talismans that held spiritual powers; they were the spirits which the colony would worship. The Supreme Being who had created the universe was too far away for personal relationships and thus It had sanctified the worship of these lesser deities. Here, Baldlice beckoned to four rats that approached carrying a large, heavy vessel; as they placed it awkwardly onto the altar some liquid slopped out of it.

The swift leaned forward. 'Ah,' she said, 'this must be the mayflower and honey mead.' She looked to Luthian for confirmation.

Luthian nodded. 'Yes, Iya Nla,' she replied. 'It was made as you instructed and buried these last few weeks deep in the warmth of the earth. It has fermented well.'

They continued to watch as each priest made their vows to the four lesser deities and afterwards drank in turn from the vessel. Then the six priests rose to stand with Baldlice and the congregation were invited to file pass; to pay homage to the spirits and to receive a blessing from the priests. Some movement in the shadows behind the altar caught the swift's attention but it was a while before she could discern what was going on. More drinking vessels had been carried in and as each rat finished paying homage it drank its share of the potent wine. There appeared to be a never ending supply of the liquid; many rats were drinking greedily and excitedly running round to join the queue again.

'No!' cried the swift. 'Quickly Myrtle, go and fetch Baldlice and bring a sample of the wine here. I did not instruct that the congregation should be offered the drink. Luthian, what rat ordered the making of more wine?'

Luthian seemed confused. 'I do not know Great Mother, but I do not think it was Baldlice,' she said after some hesitation.

'No Iya Nla, I did not order it,' Baldlice appeared at her shoulder and stood looking down at the scene below.

The orchestra had begun to play and the deep throb of the drum was a fitting accompaniment to the party-like atmosphere unfolding in the cellar. Some rats had begun to dance, gyrating slowly to the music, whilst many others noisily surrounded the drinking vessels. There was a general air of relaxation and merriment and Baldlice smiled at the swift. 'Whatever rat ordered it had the right idea, don't you think? Try some yourself, and he offered her some wine. She drank and it was good, sweet and full flavoured, but strong and heady. She felt dizzy.

'Baldlice, go and make sure that the vessels are taken away. The rats have had enough; we will not be able to control them if they become too drunk.'

Baldlice bowed and left the room, but he appeared to do so reluctantly. The swift watched him remonstrate with the rats in charge of the wine and it seemed that they were loath to obey his orders. Baldlice became agitated and began to wave his arms around, but to no good effect. Whilst she looked on with sinking heart, she noticed a number of different groups of rats huddled together in the dark corners of the cellar. There was a furtiveness about them which clashed oddly with the cheerful festivities taking place on the moonlit dance floor.

'What are those rats doing in the shadows?' She turned to Luthian and Myrtle with a look of despair.

'They are dealing in the powders from the pit,' Myrtle replied. She saw the swift's look of horror and went on hesitatingly. 'Some rats that are brave enough to enter the pit collect the powders and barter with those who want them.'

'They trade,' Luthian said, 'things or…or favours are exchanged.' She looked down at the ground in embarrassment.

'It's a risky business,' Myrtle went on, 'many rats that enter the pit never return, or if they do they have been burnt or poisoned terribly and usually die quickly.'

'But they say that the pleasure of the powder outweighs the risk of the pain,' Luthian muttered. 'That is what they say, Iya Nla, but I do not know…I have not tried it.'

Myrtle gave Luthian a long, hard look but said nothing. By now the music had quickened a pace and the gyrations on the floor were becoming more extreme. Rats danced shoulder to shoulder with little room for much variety of steps, but this did not deter them from leaping up and down whilst simultaneously throwing back their heads and shrieking shrilly.

The swift scanned the cellar looking for the priests but it was a near impossible task. She noted one priest by the orchestra which might possibly be Ware but there was no certainty. She eventually caught sight of two other priests on the dance floor, cavorting drunkenly with a total lack of regard for their sanctified position, but again she could not identify them. She thought she spotted a fourth watching the dancers; it had its back towards her and was unrecognisable. Finally, after much searching, she saw a fifth priest standing in the shadows behind the altar; but of Baldlice and the sixth priest there was no sign. Suddenly there was a commotion by the gap in the cellar wall and a party of guard rats entered dragging two bound prisoners with them. The rats on the dance floor were pushed and jostled out of the way until a path was cleared all the way to the altar. The priest from the shadows leapt up onto the altar and the swift froze in horror at remembrance of when she had seen it do this before. The priest did not appear to say anything but almost immediately the orchestra ceased playing and the dancers came to a faltering standstill. All attention was now focussed on the new arrivals.

A large muscular rat, apparently the leader of the group, stood before the priest on the altar. 'Two spies, caught sneaking around outside,' he said. 'They wouldn't say what they were doing and put up a hell of a fight when we tried to apprehend them.' He held up a badly bitten paw to verify his story. Other guard rats also displayed their wounds. There were a few gasps from the congregation accompanied by drunken murmurings, whisperings and accusations. The larger of the prisoners, a female stoat, was thrust forward towards the priest: she was covered in deep bites and scratches.

'It would seem,' hissed the priest, 'that the spirits have sent us a gift to mark the occasion of our initiation; a fitting tribute to our hard work and deference. For no ceremony is complete without the sacrificial lamb.' It paused and bent down. 'Or should I say the sacrificial stoat,' it whispered. And before the swift realised what was about to happen, the priest picked up the Spirit of the Impaler and, holding the stoat down upon the altar, drew the deadly blade across her throat.

The priest then leapt from the altar and knelt before the Spirit of the Stone with arms held aloft, his paw still gripping the bloody knife, 'All hail to the Spirit of the Stone,' he cried. 'Accept our sacrifice, which we offer as a token of our esteem for your love and protection.' He stood and faced the congregation with arms raised. 'All praise to the Spirit of the Stone.'

And the congregation, in a state of shock and nervous excitation joined in. 'All praise to the Spirit of the Stone.'

Two more priests appeared by the altar but they seemed at a loss to know what to do. One could be seen directing some of the guard rats to remove the body of the stoat and take it outside. The other looked desperately around the cellar and then upwards towards the swift. The second prisoner, a hedgehog, stood before the altar held tightly by three remaining guard rats. It had been bound the length of its body with twine to prevent it from rolling into a protective ball; it had also sustained wounds to its face and paws.

'Raise me up,' the swift commanded to Myrtle and Luthian. 'Hold me up high.' They raised her until she was in full view of all below should they choose to look up.

The priest with the knife had yet to sate his bloodlust and continued to intone the ritualistic chant, encouraging the congregation to greater supplication, whilst it eyed up the prisoner. It nodded to the guards who swung the hedgehog onto the altar, where it lay belly up. In the moment that the priest raised the knife above the defenceless animal, the other priest, who had been seeking help from the swift, grabbed its arm and grappled for the knife.

Taken by surprise, the chant of the congregation stuttered and ceased, and in the silence that followed the swift screamed out: 'Stop this abomination! Iya Nla does not sanction this! The hedgehog must not be sacrificed!'

All eyes turned up towards her and witnessed the maimed and sick bird suspended like magic in the air, for in the darkness neither Myrtle nor Luthian could be seen. Surprised that she had commanded their attention with so little effort, the swift pressed home her advantage quickly. 'It is a sacred animal. The spirits venerate its special powers and it is a sacrilege to take its life. Take him to the healing rooms and see to his wounds. Bring him to me tomorrow so that I may judge his powers.' She glared down at the priests by the altar. 'He is worthy of our hospitality and must not be injured, mark well what I say.' She turned again to the congregation. 'We have done well tonight. Your contribution has ensured that the ceremony of initiation has been a success.' She lurched a bit to one side as Myrtle and Luthian struggled to keep her aloft. 'Depart now,' she added quickly. 'We bid you all a peaceful good night.' The bird disappeared rather abruptly from view as her two stalwart supporters collapsed in a heap on the floor.

'That was inspired, Iya Nla,' gasped Luthian. Myrtle quickly peeked down over the edge.

'They're going,' she breathed excitedly, 'they're actually going. Oh Great Mother, well done.'

The swift lay almost comatose in the nest, the events of the night had exhausted her, but it was not over yet. 'Myrtle,' she whispered. 'Quickly, go and inform Baldlice that I want to see all the priests immediately, there are to be no excuses – hurry.'

As Luthian fussed over her trying to make her more comfortable, the swift's mind was racing; her suspicions had been correct and she was faced with the prospect of rebellion. A renegade, possibly two, were intent on subverting her original plans to suit their own dark ambitions. *How best to handle this? What to do, what to do?* In the precious time remaining before the priests arrived, she searched her memory for an idea... a way to save the hedgehog. Down in the now almost deserted cellar, a shaft of moonlight momentarily lit the marble topped altar where a pool of viscous blood mixed with wine and white powder dripped steadily onto the floor.

CHAPTER 13

ON THE WAY TO CLACKS FARM

Scally, Sheard, Scumble and Cory had made good progress as they journeyed towards Clacks Farm. Scally led the way, hopping from branch to branch or flying ahead for short excursions to spy out the lay of the land. Sheard was next; chattering constantly and listening to nobody. He was followed by Scumble with Cory bringing up the rear. Cory had deliberately chosen his position at the back because he wanted time to think. He was full of doubts about whether his decisions had been the right ones and he was uncomfortable that his decision to head for the farm may have been perceived by others as the safe and cowardly one. He was doing a lot of soul searching lately about his ability to be a leader, especially now that he had seen the composed way in which Aldin was able to take charge. The rat had a natural authority about him that Cory found enviable. For some reason that he could not fathom, the woodlanders had always looked to Cory for guidance and his young heart felt weighed down with the responsibility. By sending out groups to glean different information he had hoped to spread the risk of any direct confrontation with, what sounded like, an irrational and dangerous adversary. But now he regretted sending Spike to the Dark Wood and was uneasy about the outcome. The three rats were quick and agile, older and more experienced in the world than the little hedgehog; if the group met with any threatening opposition, violence even; he feared that Spike would be the one to suffer.

To be fair, Cory's decision to seek out the wise owl Drew at Clacks Farm arose from a genuine need for advice and guidance and was not influenced by the fact that it was the safer option. Not consciously influenced anyway he thought, but he was left with a niggling doubt that he *was* a coward. Cory had never had the opportunity to get to know his father; male hedgehogs were not expected to stay around and help care for their offspring, this was the natural order of things and as far as he knew it had never been questioned before. Nevertheless, Cory questioned the merit of this when it left so many young male hedgehogs without a true role model, or the chance to acquire basic knowledge just by talking with some hog older and more experienced. His thoughts were interrupted by Scally squawking, 'Road ahead!'

Sheard stopped abruptly with arm raised. 'Yo!' he cried, whilst Cory and Scumble piled into the back of him. 'Look,' said the squirrel, 'we have to cross this road my friends but there will be no problem if you do what I tell you, so listen up.'

'Understood Sheard, over and out,' said Cory. Scumble giggled.

'Don't be a doofus man!' cried Sheard in exasperation. 'Ignore my instructions at your peril my spiky friends. You hogs have a ghastly track record for becoming instant bird fodder, so let's keep it real.' He turned his gaze intently on Scumble, who immediately adopted a serious expression. 'Rule one: look both ways and listen hard. Rule two: be quick and don't dither. Rule three: keep moving and DON'T roll into a ball – simple really. And if none of that works then it's tough patooties. Now follow me.'

He led the way up the embankment, pushing through the long grass and cow parsley and stopped behind a clump of dead white nettle. Scally was already on the other side of the road perched in a hawthorn tree keeping look-out. Sheard peered across and gave a start of surprise. 'What the...' he muttered, squinting through the gathering gloom, 'What in the name of Pan is that?' A little way further up the road was what looked like the burnt out carcass of some huge animal.

'Looks like a burnt out truck,' called Scally. 'It's harmless.'

Sheard shrugged. 'No worries; gave me a start though – weird man.' He shivered slightly. 'Right, let's get going.'

A curious noise behind him made him turn. Scumble was lying on his back, thrashing from side to side whilst Cory was frantically trying to restrain him.

'He's having one of his turns,' explained Cory breathlessly. 'Not much we can do I'm afraid, except try and stop him hurting himself. He'll come out of it eventually,' he added when he noted Sheard's stricken expression. 'Most often happens when there's a moon, but not always.'

Scumble had started a low moan which was increasing in volume by the minute.

'Falling!' he cried. 'Down... Deep Down... Dark! Noooo....Echoes in the dark!' he opened his eyes for a moment and grabbed Cory by the throat: 'Help! Help me! Be warned... it's dark... it's wet!' Cory couldn't breathe; he was being strangled. He struggled to release himself and with a great deal of effort managed finally to prise Scumble's paws away. Scumble closed his eyes and became quieter, he moaned softly. 'F...a...l...l...i...n...g!' he repeated. 'Echo, Echoes in the dark. Watch your step!' Gradually his agitation subsided and he became peaceful.

'Well stone the crows! Never seen anything like that before,' said Sheard. Scally, who had flown back across the road to join them, gave a squeal of indignation. 'You watch your language tree rat!' he glared at the squirrel.

'All right you two keep it down,' Cory said quickly before the argument could escalate. 'He's coming round. Now don't make too much of this; my brother gets very embarrassed if he knows his blackouts have been witnessed.' He looked beseechingly at his two friends, who nodded in sober assent.

Scumble stirred and opened his eyes. 'What happened?' he whispered to Cory.

'Just a little blackout,' Cory replied, 'nothing to worry about. You mentioned darkness and falling. You've had that dream before haven't you? Do you feel strong enough to go on? We've still got to cross the road.'

Scumble got to his feet. 'Yes I'm OK,' he said. 'A bit dizzy but that will pass. I...I'm sorry for being a burden.'

'No burden,' Sheard answered emphatically. 'Now let's get moving and mind what I said.'

With a final glance towards the skeleton truck etched blackly against an ominously darkening sky, Scumble shivered and took a deep breath. Scally returned to the other side of the road and the two hedgehogs followed Sheard hesitantly onto the wide expanse of tarmac. The squirrel kept up an encouraging monologue in the hope of inspiring a more confident approach and things went fine for a while until suddenly Scally screeched. 'Car coming, car coming, get off the road!' The sound of a motor could be heard in the distance, the drone getting louder by the second.

'Advance!' shouted Sheard. Cory, running instinctively, fixed his eyes on a lone pink campion flower that was just visible on the roadside verge ahead. He had almost reached his goal when he heard Sheard screaming behind him: 'This way Scumble! Move it! THIS WAY! NO! NO! NO!' As Cory watched, powerless to help, he saw Scumble dither one way then the other, his eyes glazed in panic and confusion. He had reached the middle of the road when he appeared to give up the struggle and rolled into a ball. The car was almost upon them, its motor roaring, when Sheard raced back and gave the little hedgehog an almighty kick, which sent him rolling down the camber of the road; gathering momentum as he went. For a few seconds he could be seen teetering on the edge of a storm drain at the side of the road before disappearing from view.

The car passed by and the noise of its engine began to diminish. Cory was in a state of shock and hardly dared to look; he expected to see the remains of Sheard squashed flat on the tarmac. As it was he saw who he now regarded as his hero, hopping on one leg and clutching his foot.

'Hedgehogs from hell!' the squirrel screamed. 'Freakin' prickles! Probably maimed for life!' He limped over to the storm drain and peered inside. Cory and Scally joined him. With a feeling of relief they saw Scumble safely caught in the sump just below the grating; he was half immersed in stagnant water, but apart from that none the worse for his adventure.

'Sorry to cause you so many problems; thanks for saving my life Sheard and er – sorry about your foot.'

'Mmm, no probs,' Sheard muttered. He lay down on his side and put an arm through the grating; stretching to the limit until he was jammed right up against the iron works. But he was no where near reaching Scumble, even though the little hedgehog stood upright on the tips of his toes.

Cory pushed forward. 'Move over, let me try,' he said gruffly, because he was becoming worried. However were they to rescue Scumble? He seemed so near and yet so far. Cory snuffled around but could find no way of opening the heavy grating. He peered inside then lay on top of one of the steel bars and put his arm down. It was impossible to reach Scumble. He breathed in deeply and leaned over as far as he dared.

'You're not going to do it that way,' Scally said and then gasped as Cory overbalanced and disappeared inside.

'Shit!' Sheard exclaimed and looking inside the drain he saw both hedgehogs looking up at him sheepishly. 'This is becoming farcical,' he said.

'Yes,' said Cory, 'sorry.' The water they were standing in was cold and very uncomfortable. 'Look,' Cory said to Scumble, 'try climbing on my back; you might be able to reach Sheard's paw.' Just then a large pebble fell from above and landed at Cory's feet. He looked up in surprise to see another one on its way down and Scally's face peering through the grating. 'Oi!' yelled Cory. 'What do you think you're doing?'

Sheard's face appeared. 'Stand back,' he yelled excitedly. 'If we can drop enough stones down you can use them to raise the level.'

'Yes,' said Scally, dropping a biggish stone. 'Never mind about stoning the crows, we're stoning the hedgehogs!' He omitted a shrill screech that might have been laughter.

Cory and Scumble took refuge at the sides of the sump and as more stones fell, arranged them as best they could to form a platform. The platform looked a bit precarious to Cory, but if nothing else he was grateful that the stones had actually displaced the water and he and Scumble were now out of the wet. Trying to asses the situation with an authority that he did not really feel, he climbed gingerly onto the stones and lowered his spines flat.

'Climb on my back,' he said to Scumble. 'Let's see if this mad brained scheme works.'

So with much huffing, puffing, pushing and pulling; together with enthusiastic encouragement from above, Scumble finally found himself perched on top of Cory. Balanced haphazardly and holding his breath, he reached for Sheard's extended paw and found to his delight that he could now grasp it securely. The squirrel clenched his muscles, gritted his teeth and hauled the little hedgehog up and through the grating to safety. The mingled shouts of 'Hooray,' were drowned by Cory's cry of alarm as the stones

beneath him began to dislodge and with legs and arms spinning he was precipitated backwards and downwards towards the bottom of the drain.

He was falling, falling into darkness and his cry of despair echoed eerily around him. With quick presence of mind he curled into a ball seconds before he landed with a thump amidst a shower of stones. He rolled a little way and came to rest with a mixture of relief and frustration. He would be a laughing stock. He imagined the taunts: 'Follow our illustrious leader – but only if you fancy a roller coaster ride in the Park Woods drainage system!' He looked up and could just distinguish faint light coming through the grating with the shadows of three little heads looking down at him.

'I'm OK!' he yelled. 'No bones broken!' *Thank Pan for small mercies,* he thought grimly. He felt he should take the

initiative quickly to recoup any wavering belief left in his authority. 'You go on with Plan A to Clacks Farm,' he called. 'I'll improvise with Plan B,' he muttered sarcastically to himself; but his muttering sent echoes bouncing off the walls up to his listening friends.

'What's Plan B man?' shouted Sheard.

'To find the ruddy way out!' Cory grunted.

A loud squawk came echoing back. 'Think I know where the drain comes out,' called the bird. 'I'll keep an eye out for you; you'll have a few miles to walk before you get there.'

Cory sighed, he'd better get started, they had wasted enough time already. He heard Scumble's plaintive plea to be careful and tried to set his brother's mind at rest with a jocular retort, before setting off into the dark unknown. As frightened as he was, and he had to admit that he *was* frightened, Cory was also a little excited. He had always longed for adventure and now it had happened upon him quite unexpectedly. He could not fail to remember Scumble's recent dream and pondered on its relevance to his current situation. Did his brother's ramblings refer to Cory's fall? At the time Cory had thought Scumble may have been talking about his friend Echo the kestrel; but now it seemed more complicated. Whatever the truth of the matter, it had to be acknowledged that Scumble had an extraordinary talent for predicting events. Cory also remembered the day he met Sunnifa and Scumble's prophesy of the cows on the common. His thoughts turned to Sunnifa. He felt a deep attraction for her but had not yet managed to convey it satisfactorily; when in her company he became tongue tied and was easily embarrassed. He felt sure that she liked him but he also felt that he may well look a chump in her eyes. He dreaded to think how she might react on learning how he had clumsily fallen into the drain. Nevertheless, he thought it best not to dwell too long on negative feelings. He gave a mental shrug, pointed his nose in a southerly direction and set off on his journey.

It was dark although, thankfully, not completely black, but as yet he could see no light at the end of the tunnel. Keeping close to the wall he concentrated on putting one paw in front of the other. Both the walls and floor of the drain were running with water and soon Cory felt wet and chilled to the bone. Worse than this however was the silence and the loneliness; he felt as if he was the only creature left alive in the world. There were moments when he had to stop and breathe deeply to suppress the rising feelings of fear and panic. At one point he could not stop himself from calling out in the hope that there might be help somewhere nearby. However his faltering cry only elicited a number of strange and fearful echoes that spiralled away down the length of the drainage pipes and then bounced back at him, sending his head spinning.

He did not know how long he had stumbled on his way and was just beginning to think that he could bear it no longer when he noticed a faint luminescence in the distance that became brighter as he approached. With racing heart and a prayer to Pan, he broke into a trot and found himself at the next drain inlet. But his excitement dissipated as quickly as it had come when he saw that the problem remained the same. The grating was way too high for him to reach; he was stuck as before without the means to climb the slippery vertical pipe. Even though he knew it was hopeless he continued to examine the smooth sides closely, praying that he might yet discover some unevenness in the joints of the pipes that would encourage him to attempt a climb. Dispirited and on the verge of giving in to his feelings of dejection, he heard a welcome squawk and there above him was Scally with his little black head pushed between the bars of the grating.

'You're a welcome sight,' Cory said, relief flooding through him. 'Can't say I enjoy being down here much… any ideas how I get out?'

'Obviously not here,' replied the crow. 'Don't worry though, there's bound to be a place somewhere. The road is downhill from here so there might not be such a drop at the next inlet. I'll keep looking,' he said cheerfully.

'You do that,' muttered Cory, 'and you might consider fetching Braxton and his family to dig me out if the worst comes to the worst!

'Oh I'm sure we won't need any badgers. Don't despair we'll laugh about this one day.' And with that Scally flew away.

Laugh, I'll give him bloody laugh! thought Cory. But there was nothing left to do except continue onwards, buoyed up with the thoughts of what he'd like to do to the crow if he ever got the chance.

He had been travelling for what seemed like hours and was beginning to notice an uncomfortable emptiness in his stomach, when he heard the sound of voices approaching nearer from around a bend in the drain. Immediately, with an instinctive act of self-preservation, Cory rolled into a tight ball and remained motionless in the shadows at the foot of the wall. The voices got louder until they sounded right above him. He felt something touch him and he was pushed a few inches along the ground.

'Ouch! Those spines are sharper than the needles in Pan's Pit.' The voice was harsh and rough.

'Yer own fault fer touchin' 'em,' growled another. 'Haven't yer ever seen a hog before?'

'Best left alone,' said a third. 'We've wasted too much time already and there'll be hell to pay when we get back, especially now we're one short.'

Cory heard footsteps pattering off and the voices became indistinct. He lay still for many minutes, his ears attuned to the silence of the tunnel, before cautiously uncurling. Normally he would have waited a good deal longer before exposing himself to danger but he was cold and hungry and his nerves were in shreds. He sped round the bend in the drain and continued to run as fast as his legs would carry him; intent on putting as much distance between him and those voices as he possibly could. Head down and breathless from his exertions he hit something soft that yielded with a sound like, 'Ooof!' Cory peered into the shadows and saw a small scrawny rat flat on its back with legs in the air. As the hedgehog quickly contemplated his next move, the rat bounced upright and squared up to him, jabbing at him with his two front paws.

'Keep your distance, back off!' it squeaked as it danced around on its hind legs. Cory's fear rapidly vanished and he strove to suppress his laughter at the little creature that, in spite of its efforts to appear aggressive, only came across as comical.

'I'm sorry,' said Cory. 'I had no intention of knocking you over it was very clumsy of me. I hope you're not hurt?' The little rat appeared somewhat nonplussed at the sincerity in Cory's voice and sheepishly lowered its paws. 'I'm lost in this drain pipe,' Cory continued. 'I fell through the grating hours ago and I have no idea how to get out. I think some of your friends just passed by me but I rolled into a ball; just to be on the safe side. I ran into you because I was panicking. I hope you forgive me?'

'I'm not hurt, sir. Those other rats are no friends of mine and you did well to protect yourself; they would have done you mischief if they could.'

Cory felt exhausted but he also began to relax in the rat's company so he crouched down with his back to the wall to rest. The rat sat down next to him and they remained for a while in comfortable silence.

'My name is Fag, sir. I was part of a scouting party sent out to forage and scavenge and collect information. I disliked the company I was in and absconded. If I am caught I will be punished,' he shivered, 'and I don't much fancy what form that punishment will take.'

'My name is Cory. I too am part of a scouting party and you might well say that I have also absconded; although not deliberately,' he chuckled. 'May I ask where exactly your party came from?'

'Our colony lives in Whylder Wood, some call it the Dark Wood. I believe that the place is known by local woodlanders as Mad Maggie Minchin's house. There have been great changes there in the last few months and not for the best I am sorry to say. There is a big pit close by which is full of rubbish that is dangerous. Some rats climb inside to collect white powders. It is said that if you sniff them or eat them they make you feel happy; they make you feel strong and you don't need to sleep so much. They also take away pain. The rats that collect the powders sell them to those who are willing to pay the right price.'

'And have you tried them?' Cory asked.

'No,' Fag replied with a shudder. 'Not me sir, I'm not prepared to pay the asking price; it would mean servitude and slavery to those in power. Once you have tried them the powders take a hold on you and it is difficult to become free. I have seen rats driven mad by their need for more and more of the powders. They will end up doing anything for them. They lose all self respect and they can only think about when they can get the next powder. Those in power have become mean and aggressive. There is much cruelty. I don't ever want to go back there.' The rat stared dejectedly into the darkness of the tunnel and Cory felt a wave of sympathy and compassion for the little fellow.

'We have heard something of this,' Cory said quietly. 'There have been reports of strange things going on in your colony. I have seen creatures that have been burnt and poisoned; not just in the Dark Wood but in Park Woods as well.'

'The poisons come from the pit,' said Fag, 'and they are fatal. That is why only a few rats venture to go inside to collect the powders. Sometimes a rat will climb in and no rat ever sees it again. Sometimes a rat will come out but it will be horribly burnt or poisoned and it will die a long and hideous death. This used to happen a lot at first until the rats learned the difference between the "happy" powders and the poisonous ones. Even now mistakes are made. We call the pit "Pan's Pit of Pleasure and Pain".

Cory dipped his nose into a stream of water that had begun trickling past. His throat felt parched and he lapped at the water; it tasted metallic but good, it quenched his thirst. 'We have also heard reports of a bird that has become part of your colony,' he said. 'How can that be, is there any truth in it?'

'It is most strange, sir,' replied Fag. 'I believe she is a swift; they usually spend most of their life in the air, but she has a broken wing and is now earthbound. Our leader, Baldlice, has taken it upon himself to protect her, but for what reason I cannot rightly say. We have been told to call her by the name "Iya Nla" or "Great Mother", which are titles given to the High Priestess of our religion. She and Baldlice have appointed six rats to be priests and their purpose will be to govern the colony. They will also learn the art of healing and of prophesy. For the last few weeks we have been working hard to complete the hall of worship for the Initiation Ceremony. Our party should have returned in time to witness the ceremony but I fear we have left it too late. Unless the returning rats can come up with an important piece of information that will excuse their lateness, they will be punished. I suspect they will use my absence as the reason that delayed them.'

Cory suddenly noticed that the trickling water had become more like a stream that was gaining momentum as he watched. He realised that he and Fag were now sitting waist deep in the flow which was decidedly cold and unpleasant.

'Need to go,' he muttered curtly and with one accord they both started down the tunnel as fast as they were able. The force of the water swept them forward and Cory knew that it would not be long before they were swept off their feet and would have to swim for it. With relief he saw a patch of light ahead and shouted encouragement to Fag. His relief was short lived however when he saw the grating high above them with no means to climb up to it.

'This is no good,' he said despondently, 'the grating is still too high.' He looked at Fag for help.

'Not to worry, sir,' said the little rat. 'A rat can climb up easily enough but it is too steep for a hedgehog; we must travel a little further.' He gazed rather vacantly into the blackness of the drain pipe.

'Will we ever find light again Fag?' Cory asked trying to muster his strength.

The rat smiled wistfully. 'Oh yes sir; there is always light at the end of every dark tunnel. Follow me sir, and I will show you a little piece of heaven.'

'Hurrumph,' Cory snorted; he could think of nothing more appropriate to say.

Together they forged the stream again and soon felt their feet lose grip on the slippery floor of the tunnel. They were swept along; paddling frantically whilst their bodies were swirled around and thrown painfully against the sides of the pipe. The water was rising and just when Cory felt that they would both be drowned – ensuring an ignominious death and a pathetic end to his adventure – he saw the welcome light and an exit grating straight ahead. Within seconds he was slammed against the ironworks and, looking down, saw the cascade of water plunging into the turbulent current of what could only be the River Rushlep. Part of the grating had been bent to one side and Fag was already squeezing through the gap.

'Come on sir,' he panted, 'there must have been a rain storm; river's running high and we have to cross to the other side. Better sooner than later.'

The River Rushlep was a good deal wider and deeper than the Park Woods stream that fed it. Now, filled to capacity with iron grey water flecked with white foam and roaring tumultuously along its course, it looked a dangerous and ominous adversary. Cory's paws froze on the grating and his throat went dry. A familiar squawk broke into his paroxysm of fear and Scally alighted on the grid next to him.

'Be careful,' was the crow's totally unnecessary warning. 'The current's strong enough to carry you down to the Welland Marshes and it'll be a devil of a job to get you back from there.'

'Yes well thanks for that, much obliged I'm sure.' Cory thought the bird had probably missed his note of sarcasm. However Scally's arrival and inane remark had gone a long way to reviving Cory's spirit and he began to inch his way through the grating until he was clutching the bars on the outside, huddled closely to Fag.

'We need to get to the other side as quickly as possible sir, try to swim in a straight line. Aim for that tree, its roots will be under the water; they will give you something to hang onto before I help you up the bank.' Fag's teeth were chattering with the cold; he was soaking wet and his tiny body looked frail and half starved. Cory didn't hold out much hope that the little animal would have the strength to haul him out of the river.

'Keep your mouths closed; don't swallow the water,' screeched Scally, 'it might be poisonous.'

That's all we need, thought Cory, as with eyes and mouth tightly shut he opened his paws and felt himself plummet down into the icy turbulence below. The shock made him open his eyes at once. Fag had landed a little ahead of him and was already striking out towards the opposite bank. Kicking his legs, in what Cory could only think was a laughable parody of Fag's excellent swimming action, the hedgehog attempted to follow. Scally's warning about the current had not been an idle one and he struggled against the force of the water that would have had him spinning out of control if he had put up less resistance. What made it worse was that whilst the current was pulling him to the left of where he wanted to go, the undertow was pulling him down. By the time Cory was halfway across only his nose and a few spines were visible above the swirling waters and his waterlogged body had taken on a vertical position. He paddled his aching legs furiously in order to maintain buoyancy but he was making little headway. Fag had reached the bank and Scally was hopping up and down screeching instructions which could not be heard above the noise of the river.

Cory was reminded of the attempt to cross the road earlier that day, or was it yesterday? It seemed incredible that so much had happened since. He remembered Scally screeching in the same way; Scumble panicking and Sheard running brilliantly to the rescue. The adventure might well have ended there and then with Scumble's death and perhaps Sheard's death also. But it hadn't and if he had anything to do with it then it wouldn't now. Cory fought down his panic and fixed his eyes on the tree that Fag had pointed out and with a determination dredged up from where, he did not know, he swam irresolutely towards it. Gasping from his exertions he opened his mouth and the cruel waters rushed in, choking him; he was drowning, there was a ringing in his ears and his eyes glazed over, but somewhere a spark of life kept his legs moving. Something propelled him from behind and he landed amongst the roots of a willow tree, where he gratefully grasped a sturdy prop to steady himself.

'Well done sir! Now if you would just allow me to push a bit more from behind...no disrespect sir; one more heave and up...you... go!'

Cory felt himself slithering up the grassy bank and there was his saviour: wet bedraggled Fag who now appeared in front of him with a little sinewy arm held out to haul him to safety.

'Not so bad was it sir?' said Fag as they lay together coughing, spluttering and gasping for air. Cory could feel his heart pumping so hard that he thought it would explode. It was hammering so loud that he was certain both Fag and Scally must hear it.

'I wouldn't have made it but for you,' Cory said softly, 'I am indebted to you, Fag.'

'Please don't mention it again, sir,' the rat replied, 'I value your company and am only too pleased to help.'

Cory looked at the tiny wet, brave creature and saw his loneliness and vulnerability. 'If there is anything I can do to help you just say the word,' he said.

'There *is* something, begging your pardon sir,' said Fag earnestly. 'Would you travel with me a short time more? I would like to show you heaven.'

CHAPTER 14

OF POLITICS, PANDORA AND PITS

The swift was sleeping, but it was a restless, wearying sleep punctuated by macabre dreams. The bird was filled with guilt at what her well meaning plans had unleashed. It would appear she had opened Pandora's Box of evil tricks and Pan no doubt was finding it all most amusing. She could see no way to retrieve the situation. Her weak and aching body kept her imprisoned in the nest and her once bright mind had become dulled with the noxious fumes of the pit. She lay for most of the time in a drug induced lethargy. But even in this semi-comatose state she fought to retain her own self; the essence of her and what she had once been. Images of happier past remembered days came and went intermittently. Sometimes she could feel the warmth and comfort of her mate beside her. She missed his steadfast companionship. They had learned to be good, capable parents over the years they were together. In their youth and inexperience they had made mistakes and perhaps some chicks had died needlessly, but last summer's brood had been the best of all. Five fit and healthy chicks full of confidence, with an eagerness to learn and explore the world. How proud they had been of this family and so certain that they would repeat it this summer when they returned to the same happy nest. She moaned softly and her eyes flickered open. She sensed rather than saw the shape of a rat pull sharply back into the shadows behind her.

'Is that you, Myrtle?... Luthian?' Her parched throat could barely utter the words. 'Baldlice, are you there?' There was no reply only the intake of breath; a hiss before the sound of something scuttling away into silence. She lay quietly, reliving yesterday's meeting following the Initiation Ceremony. No priest had owned up to the killing of the stoat and there had been no clue as to who it was; although there had been many accusations amongst the six rats; each it would seem intent on laying the blame on another. *So much for the general philanthropy of the priesthood*, she thought sourly. The cold blooded killing had shocked and terrified her. It had taken her completely unawares and she felt helpless to deal with it.

She peered down into the cellar and saw that the severed head of the stoat was now displayed amongst the deified spirits on the altar. The pelt had been fixed to the wall covering the torn red cloth; the decorative grasses and flowering ramsons had gone. She assessed her options and concluded that her priority must be to try and save the captured hedgehog's life. At that moment footsteps heralded the arrival of Baldlice and the hedgehog that was supported on both sides by two large guard rats.

'Iya Nla, I have brought the prisoner as you requested,' said Baldlice.

The swift nodded her head and indicated that the guard rats should go; which they finally did after a protracted argument with Baldlice. They exited muttering darkly about reporting this dismissal to the priest in charge.

'What priest in charge?' the swift said sharply to Baldlice. 'Which priest is setting themselves above the rest?'

'I cannot tell,' the old rat answered, 'I am no longer in their confidence.' He shrugged.

She breathed in deeply to suppress her feelings of anger and frustration at the old rat's apathy. 'You may leave us Baldlice; I will call you when I need you.'

'As you wish, Iya Nla,' he replied and left the room.

The swift surveyed the creature in front of her and the hedgehog returned her stare. He was still bound tightly along the length of his body to prevent him from curling into a ball; what spines remained free stood erect in fear. He was making a puffing noise to show his displeasure and uncertainty. The bird was pleasantly surprised that she could read his mind. He was young and his mind was not complex; she judged him to be simple, but steadfast and honest.

'What is your name and where do you come from?' she asked gently.

'Me name's Trefoil and where I come from's me own business,' the hedgehog replied boldly. 'Who are you to be questioning me and how in Pan's name did you get 'ere?'

The swift smiled at his spirit under such duress; she indicated her broken wing and answered softly. 'As you can see I am badly wounded and cannot fly. The rats have taken me into their colony and I am looked after well enough. I am called Iya Nla, it is a name given to the High Priestess in our religion. We have seven other priests who share the leadership of the colony; you and your – er – stoat friend arrived in the middle of the priests' Initiation Ceremony. It is very regrettable what happened; please believe me when I tell you how sorry I am and that I will do all in my power to keep you safe from harm. Tell me what brought you to this place and how you were captured?'

Trefoil blinked and looked around him; there appeared to be no immediate escape for him and the bird's soft, calm voice was soothing to his frayed nerves.

'I can't breathe properly with this binding wrapt round me,' he said emphatically, 'If yer want a long conversation yer'll 'ave to gerrit taken off.' He stared directly at the bird, 'I won't curl inter a ball; can't think that would do me any good in this situation.'

'I'm afraid you're right it wouldn't,' said the swift; 'we'll have it removed.' She called for Baldlice who arrived so quickly that it was apparent he had been only just out of sight, most probably attempting to listen to the conversation. On the swift's instructions he gnawed at the bindings until they came away and Trefoil could breathe easily again.

'Thank you Baldlice,' said the swift. 'Would you please tell Myrtle and Luthian I shall need their services in a little while?' She nodded at the rat to dismiss him and he went with an inscrutable expression on his old scarred face. 'Now,' she said turning hurriedly back to Trefoil, 'make yourself comfortable, we have no time to lose.'

Trefoil hunkered down beside the bird's nest but as he did so he caught sight of the cellar below with the dried head of the stoat in the middle of the altar. With a start he craned his head forward and tears misted his eyes.

"Er name was Orva,' he murmured; 'we 'ardly knew 'er but she led me an' me mate Bugle to where we wanted ter go.'

'And where was that?'

'We was tryin' ter find Braxton the badger. We thought 'e might be ill; what with all the poisons in the stream and maybe some of the plants in the Dark Wood. We were lookin' ter 'elp 'im.' Trefoil gazed accusingly at the swift; 'We meant no 'arm but we was overtaken by a rat patrol – 'bout a dozen or so of the bleeders; they didn't want to talk only ter fight. Well they got what they was lookin' for; Bugle an' me was proud ter fight alongside of Orva, she was unstoppable. Five of the bleeders got tossed up an' thrown inter the undergrowth; two of 'em landed in a briar patch an' stuck fast. But they was too many fer us an' Orva was worn down. I was taken captive; Bugle must've escaped... I 'ope to Pan 'e did 'cos that'll mean 'elp is on its way. Course 'e could be lyin' out there hurt or – or – dead.' A tear trickled down his snout and he laid his head sorrowfully on the floor between his two front paws.

'Now listen to me,' whispered the swift, 'and believe what I say. I cannot prevent your being sacrificed at the altar unless you can prove to these rats that you deserve to live. I have led them to believe that you have magical powers and that you are protected by your own god – the Moon Goddess Ishtar; Goddess of Justice and Healing and what is of more importance, Goddess of Reincarnation.' She paused when she saw Trefoil's look of incredulity.

'If I weren't so bleeding terrified I might just 'ave a right good laugh at that,' he said. 'Do I look and sound like some goddess's favourite hog? No rat's goin' ter believe it.'

The swift dismissed his remark impatiently. 'As it happens, if any of them are intelligent enough to make enquiries they would learn that Ishtar *is* the protector of all hedgehogs; myth or legend, it is not I who make this up, it is a story that has stood the test of time. However, you and I must embellish it; we must convince them that Ishtar would bring retribution to them should you be harmed. She is called the "all seeing eye of heaven" and her familiar is the sacred lion.' There could be heard a scuffling outside the room and the swift dropped her voice even lower, 'Just follow my lead and try to act the part...

'Is that you Baldlice?' she called. Baldlice entered with Myrtle and Luthian in tow; they all gazed at Trefoil who returned their stares imperiously. 'Baldlice, I wish for the hedgehog to remain here with me, he will be useful to us. With the help of the other priests I want you to construct a five pointed star within a circle on the floor: the hedgehog must be placed in the centre of it. You will instruct the Priests in a spell that I will teach you; an incantation that will confine the hedgehog within the pentacle and prevent him from escaping. For maximum potency, mind that the points of the star are of equal length and that the angles are symmetrical. I feel sure that you will be able to achieve this.' She looked at the rat long and hard. 'I have every faith in you.'

'I hear what you say,' Baldlice said sceptically; 'but I'm not sure I can convince the other priests to go along with this. Why should they believe he is worth keeping when it is becoming hard enough to find untainted food and water for us rats? They will question why we should bother housing a different species.'

'You must have faith in what I tell you,' the swift answered calmly. 'Have I been wrong so far? It is likely the hedgehog's prophecies will help the colony to solve its problems. But tell the doubting priests this: if after a week the creature has not been able to help us then I give the priests the right to decide what should be done with him.'

'Very well Iya Nla, I will convey your message and I will set guards outside the room until such time as we are convinced the magic of the eight pointed star will hold him.' Baldlice bowed and left the room.

The swift sighed for she had hoped secretly that Baldlice would forget about the guards and so afford Trefoil an immediate escape route, but this was not to be; the old campaigner was not as gaga as he looked. She set Myrtle and Luthian to work making sure that the hedgehog was fed and made comfortable, whilst she settled down into the nest; her mind racing on how to devise a plan to save him. She clung to the thought that in the story of Pandora and her box, not all the contents had been evil; hope had remained.

***

Baldlice hurried along what remained of the old hallway towards the nursery where he hoped to find at least some of the priests. His mind was in turmoil and he was filled with trepidation. Not only did he feel weakened and diminished by the frequency he was now impelled to take the medicinal drugs, he was acutely aware that the Iya Nla was also struggling to keep a grip on the situation. Things had not gone according to their original plans for a united and peaceful colony. Indeed the introduction of this religion and the priesthood had only served to divide the colony even more. Between them they had created a dangerous predicament where the enemy was obscure, unidentified and yet dangerously malevolent and vicious. Baldlice would have gladly returned to the situation as it had been before the swift arrived; at least then he had known who his enemies were. Now he did not know who to trust, perhaps not even Iya Nla herself. It was becoming increasingly difficult to read each others minds and doubts were creeping in on both sides as to their sincerity and truthfulness.

These troubled thoughts were interrupted as he saw a tall figure emerge from the nursery further up the hall. In the gloom he could barely make out who it was but he guessed it might be Earle. The priest glanced up at him, hesitated, then walked rapidly towards him; averting his head as he passed and disappearing in the direction of the cellar steps. He looked agitated and angry. Baldlice slowed his pace and glanced back. Earle appeared to be on a mission and the old rat was in two minds as to whether or not to follow him. Whilst he was considering he heard raised voices coming from the nursery, so without further thought he continued towards it, pushed on what remained of the door and entered the room.

The reception room was large and airy with a high ceiling, most of which was intact; two other doors on the opposite wall led to adjoining rooms from which arose a hubbub of sound. Wimund stood with her back to Baldlice; hands on hips with her tail raised threateningly high in the air. Atol faced her some yards away with his forepaws folded across his chest and a stubborn expression on his face. The two of them were obviously arguing but they quickly changed tack when Baldlice appeared.

'Welcome,' Atol said; 'it's not often we have the pleasure of your company here Baldlice, what can we do for you?'

Just then a rat came slowly out of one of the rooms. It could only have been a few weeks old but, although its head appeared to be of normal size, its body was enormous and an extra thick growth of bone on its neck and shoulders gave it a distorted humped back. It must have weighed a considerable amount as the legs, which were puny in contrast to the rest of its bulk, appeared useless in the purpose of either support or mobility. The creature moved by dragging itself over the ground on its belly and using its tail, which was thick as twisted rope, like a rudder to steer by. As it moved it made a soft mewling cry. Baldlice stared, struck dumb with horror whilst Atol said calmly, 'Ah, another unexpected visitor, do not be afraid, he is curious to see you, Baldlice. It shows a measure of intelligence that he is inquisitive, do you not think? But he must learn not to visit this room unless invited.' Atol raised his voice, 'Scabious, you have mislaid an important personage, please come and collect him, now.'

One of the large guard rats, who had helped Baldlice take the bound hedgehog to Iya Nla, appeared in the doorway. With a deferential glance towards Atol he strode in front of the deformed rat and, with a waving of paws and stamping of feet, managed to persuade it to turn around and return whence it had come. As Baldlice watched it lumber away he looked aghast at Atol and then Wimund.

'In all that's abhorrent, what in Pan's name are you keeping in those rooms?' he croaked.

'Don't overreact, Baldlice,' Wimund cut in; 'you were part of the democratic vote that agreed to keep some of the deformed babies; don't go all squeamish on us now.'

'It was agreed to keep the strongest,' Baldlice retorted, 'to let the best of them live. Are you telling me that – that monstrosity is one of the best?'

'Do not be so quick to condemn what you know nothing about,' Wimund replied, 'in its mother's eyes at least it is not a monstrosity. Should we not show some compassion to those less fortunate than ourselves? Come Baldlice, you are not the most handsome of rats yourself.' Wimund tilted her head cajolingly to one side but Baldlice saw a smirk flash fleetingly across her face.

'Do not fret, Baldlice,' Atol said. He came forward and laid a paw on the old rat's shoulder. 'Come, I will show you the nursery. Once you get used to the deformities you will see past them to the rat beneath.'

They entered the room in which the deformed rat had retreated and Baldlice stared around in mute dismay. Dozens of juvenile rat-like creatures lay on the floor or crawled around the room. The noise was incessant and the smell appalling. All were misshapen. Some blind, others with incomplete bodies, or with extra limbs and growths. He noticed one that had grown a second head which hung uselessly on its chest. Another youngster had grown so many teeth that it could not close its mouth. He wondered how it managed to eat.

'I cannot sanction this!' Baldlice cried. 'This is a travesty against Nature herself. You cannot think that Pan would accept what you have done!'

'I have to disagree,' said Atol. 'We have not caused this; we are only dealing with a situation that none of us asked for. Who provided the poisonous pit? We have to assume that Pan allowed the pit for a reason.' He held his arms wide, embracing the room. 'These young rats are as much the children of Pan as we are and who are we to harm them?'

Baldlice, his poor brain weary with the effects of the drugs could think of no rational argument to counter Atol's verbosity. 'I will have to report this to Iya Nla and she will put a stop to it,' he muttered.

Atol smiled and led him out of the room. 'Do not play games with me, old rat,' he said softly. 'We both know that Iya Nla's days are numbered. She has passed her usefulness and is only kept as a figurehead to pacify the colony. Now my friend, tell me what was the purpose of your visit?' Falteringly, Baldlice explained Iya Nla's wishes regarding the captured hedgehog. After Atol's opinions on the bird, Baldlice expected an emphatic denial to comply with her wishes but was surprised when Atol laughed and nodded.

'We will humour her in the little time she has left. I will help you. I have some understanding of diagrams and angles; together you and I will construct a magical pentacle that will please her. The results should be interesting, don't you think?'

As he turned to leave, Baldlice bumped into Luthian who had the grace to look embarrassed.

'I – I have come with a message for Atol,' she mumbled, staring down at the ground.

'Well make it snappy,' Baldlice answered irritably and left the room. He felt confused and anxious. He was aware that Atol had bested him in the argument but that did not mean the Head Priest of the nursery was right: once Baldlice would have spoken more eloquently, more authoritatively but that was beyond his powers now. Why, he had not even thought to question what was being held in the second back room. Nor the fundamental question of what the poor deformed rats were being fed. He was left with a sense of frustration and despair at his failing intellect. He would have liked to try and find Earle; perhaps he also was against what was going on in the nursery. He stared along the empty hallway, his confidence had been shattered and his body ached interminably. With a sigh he turned back the way he had come and went to report to Iya Nla.

***

When Earle came out of the Nursery and saw Baldlice approaching he was in two minds as to whether to confide in him. Earle had been shaken at what he had just witnessed and heard from Wimund and Atol, and he was incredulous at the stubbornness they both showed in refusing to listen to him. Earle had always prided himself on his ability to make concise informed judgements on any given situation. He considered himself to be a realist and did not hold with fanciful or emotional views on life. He was a forceful, opinionated rat and until now had always been able to persuade or coerce others to accept his arguments. What he saw as the nursery priests' intransigence filled him with impotent rage. Nevertheless, in regards to Baldlice it would be prudent to keep his own council for the time being he thought and decided instead to go and find a priest who he was certain shared his views. He went in search of Gram.

He descended the cellar steps and with purposeful strides crossed the floor by the altar. He noted that the stoat's head had been given pride of place alongside the Spirit of Self-Perception. He stopped for a moment and appraised himself in the mirror. Earle had taken to wearing his ceremonial cloak most of the time now; it gave him a grandeur that he felt he deserved. He rubbed his paw over what could be seen of his face, smoothing down the greying hair and stroking his long whiskers. He was ageing well he thought, eyes still bright and snout still black and wet. *Yes, quite distinguished; altogether quite an imposing figure. Nothing wrong with his brain either; still agile, quick to see the flaws in other's arguments. He could outwit them if he put his mind to it.* He smiled and his image smiled back at him.

Earle crossed the cellar and went outside through the gap in the wall. He passed the pit and made his way towards the stream where he could see Holt directing a number of rats in building a dam. They were attempting to stop the water flow by constructing a tightly knit mass of vegetation, tree branches and the crumbling rubble from the walls of the house.

Holt looked up and saw him. 'Hello Earle!' he shouted, 'How do you like our handiwork?'

'What's it all in aid of?' Earle replied, moving nearer.

'Water's poisoned,' Holt climbed up the bank breathing heavily. 'The damn's to stop the water travelling downstream to Park Woods. Temporary measure I know,' he said as he noticed the condescending look on Earle's face. 'Best I could think of at the time. Of course it's made the stream quite deep this side of the dam but once we've made the thing secure it will act as a bridge as well; haven't made too bad a job of it so far, though I say it myself.'

Earle felt his anger returning. 'Where's Gram?' he said, his voice sharp with impatience.

Holt surveyed the arrogant priest for a few seconds before replying. 'No idea, haven't seen him all day.' He turned to go.

'Wait!' cried Earle. 'I have just come from the nursery. Are you aware of what Atol and Wimund are doing there?'

'Not in any detail, haven't been there for a while – not my scene. Is anything wrong?'

'Wrong! It's all wrong,' Earle shouted. 'The colony is being destroyed before our very eyes and we play at building dams, making music; getting off our heads and cavorting on dance floors!' He spat contemptuously on the ground close to Holt's foot. 'Why in the name of Pan are we all still here surrounded by this stench and pollution? The sensible thing to do is move the colony to a healthier place.'

'And how do you suppose we might do that?' said Holt curtly. 'Even if the strong and able wanted to leave – which I doubt very much considering that many of them are now addicted to the white powders – it would be impossible to move the sick, disabled and the dying. Do you propose that we march out on them leaving them to their fate?'

'It is the only answer,' Earle's voice cracked like a whip. 'The alternative is that we all eventually become sick. The colony dies if we remain here.'

'Wimund and Atol believe that the longer we stay there is a chance we will become immune to the poisons. They are making a study of the deformed with that in mind.' Holt shrugged, 'And who knows, they might be right. It may be Pan's wish. Nature *is* very adaptable you know.'

'Utter tosh,' retorted Earle. 'It's more likely that those two have other, more self serving plans afoot.'

'Well if it sets your mind at rest I will go and see for myself; but remember Earle, there's nothing stopping you, or any rat who wants to leave.'

Earle narrowed his eyes and scrutinised Holt. 'Do as you will,' he said, 'I'm off to find Gram.'

The priest strode away towards the pit and Holt watched him go. Earle was in a dilemma: he knew that what Holt said made sense in that he could leave the colony anytime he wanted. So why didn't he? He had to admit that he enjoyed the privileges of being in the priesthood. He welcomed the authority and respect that it conferred on him. And there was no doubt that he had earned those privileges. Ever since he could remember he had believed that he was a cut above other rats; that he was destined for power and leadership. He was loath to throw it all away so easily. He skirted the rim of the pit, holding his nose as he peered down into it. He had walked halfway round it and was out of sight of the rats building the dam when he came across a heap of plastic bags and containers that had undoubtedly been removed from the pit. He stood on the edge and squinted through the rising vapours down into the hole. It was deep; he could not see the bottom. Why had the things been removed? As he pondered he heard a small sound behind him, but before he could turn round something struck him forcefully in the back, sending him tumbling headfirst down into the cavernous blackness.

CHAPTER 15

TWO VISITS

Scally, Sheard and Scumble's visit to Drew at Clacks Farm had not proved to be particularly helpful so far. Scumble worried that if Cory had been with them they might have got more out of the owl. But it was not to be; the owl had listened politely but had offered no specific advice and so they must make the best of what they were given. The most interesting news, for Scumble at least, was learning of Drew's encounter with Echo and her brother, Marlin. Putting the pieces of the jigsaw together it seemed that something terrible must have happened to the kestrels after leaving the barn and in particular to Marlin. Drew was disturbed that he had not been more persuasive in getting the two birds to remain safely undercover in the barn, but he recalled how determined Echo had been to have her own way.

'You know it is regrettable but true how many of you youngsters will throw yourselves at life; scornful of any suggestion that you might get hurt,' he mused. 'Is it any wonder that you often have to learn the hard way?'

'You're preaching to the converted,' said Scally, who was perched next to Drew high up in the eaves. 'The only

youngster here is that little hedgehog down there and he seems sensible beyond his years,' Scally indicated Scumble sitting on the floor next to Sheard. Drew leaned forward magisterially and surveyed the little figures, then blinked slowly and turned back to the crow. As he did so he released a pellet which fell with a splat in front of Sheard.

'Oh man, gross,' muttered the squirrel. The brownish black and white dropping reminded Scumble of Vincent the caterpillar and he wondered for a moment where the little fellow was and what he was doing.

'Well, well,' Drew broke into his thoughts. 'Lovely as it is to have met you all, perhaps we should call it a day. This is my rest period you know and I need my sleep.' He shifted on his perch and stared down at Scumble. 'Please give my regards to your brother Cory; I am sure between you – you will find a way to solve your problem.'

'With respect sir,' Scumble stood on his hind legs to give emphasis to his words, 'it's not just our problem, soon it will affect the whole…'

Before he could finish, Scally let out a high screech of warning. Instinctively Scumble wanted to roll into a ball but he was conscious of his friend next to him. Turning round they were confronted by one of the farm cats, a huge tabby with spiteful yellow eyes and a mane like a lion. As they turned it pounced, missing Sheard by inches. The squirrel scrabbled up a nearby roof support onto a low beam. Spitting and yowling, the cat made to follow whilst Sheard bared his teeth, claws at the ready; daring him to try. Scally, screaming abuse, dive bombed the furious creature and while it was distracted Scumble darted in from behind and clamped his sharp little teeth around the cat's hind leg. With a final yowl of pain the animal made its escape through the barn door leaving a relieved and jubilant trio.

'Yo!' cried Sheard, 'That'll be something to tell the grand-cubs, innit!' He grinned at Scally and Scumble; 'what a team fo shure!'

'Well,' said Drew softly, 'there's certainly more to you than meets the eye.'

Scumble, feeling he should try and capitalise on the owl's new found interest in them, stood on his hind legs again. 'Before we go sir and leave you to your rest, could you not give us some piece of advice? If the stream in Park Woods is already poisoned it won't be long before the land surrounding Clacks Farm becomes bad. The problem affects us all.'

Drew closed his eyes and the three friends waited patiently. At last the owl spoke. 'You have just proved most adequately that different species of animal and bird can unite in a common cause. That is an important lesson to have learned. Every individual has both strengths and weaknesses and each individual must learn to recognise what they are. We need to know ourselves; what each is capable of and what we *might* be capable of if we try hard enough. A united group must learn how to use the different strengths available to them to the best advantage – as you have just done.' Drew gazed at Scumble benevolently. 'Your brother Cory had the right idea in proposing an investigation of the rat colony. Any experienced campaigner will tell you that the more you know about an adversary; his strengths and weaknesses; the more likely you will be able to defeat him.' The owl paused here and regarded each member of the trio with serious scrutiny, 'But it is important to keep open minds about whether the rats are truly your enemy. There is good and bad in all species and from what you tell me, the spreading contamination does not appear to be the fault of the rats. Man, as is so often the case, appears to be the culprit here. If this pit that you speak of is full of Man's artefacts then only Man could have put them there. On the one hand I would say that you have a choice to leave well alone. If the poisons are as virulent as you say then it is likely the colony of rats will die without your intervention and Nature herself, in time, may well be able to heal the wounds of the earth. The alternative I think is to bring the state of affairs to the attention of Man and let them resolve the problem that they themselves have created.'

'Whoa!' Sheard cried, 'Hold hard my friend. Aren't we drifting into the realms of fantasy here? How in the name of Pan are we expected to get a dialogue going with the likes of Man?'

'It is not beyond the bounds of possibility,' Drew replied. 'Do not be hasty in rejecting this proposal. With a little effort and discussion I am sure you could come up with an idea for an appropriate form of communication; it just needs a little thought. Now if you will pardon my back, I will take my afternoon siesta.' Drew executed a ninety degree turn on his perch and slotted his head under a wing. 'Give my regards to your brother Cory,' came a muffled parting shot.

As the three friends left the barn, Sheard's last view was of another owl pellet hitting the floor with a splat. He grinned: 'The final and ultimate dismissal,' he said to himself.

They skirted the farmyard warily in anticipation of another attack from the cat, but it seemed to have gone to ground to lick its wounds and they found themselves back on their homeward path without further incident. Scally took his leave of them, saying he would fly back to Cory and Fag, to give them an update on their meeting with Drew.

'Well keep a tight reign on what you say in front of that Fag,' Sheard warned. 'We don't know anything about that dude; he could be a foul-weather friend for all we know.' Scally nodded and was gone.

Scumble and Sheard reached the edge of the common in the late afternoon sunshine; there was nothing to be seen except for the grazing cows standing in a bunch near the gate, peacefully chewing the cud and waiting for their full udders to be emptied. The two friends took advantage of the warmth and quietness to settle down for a short rest undercover of the hedgerow, keeping a watchful eye out for predators through the stalks of the long grass and cow parsley. The sun was about to set when they eventually entered Park Woods to make their report to Sunnifa. They found her with Patience, who had recently given birth to what she emphatically described as her very last litter.

'Only one little hoglet this time but just look at her: my beautiful Bliss, my little earth angel.' Patience leaned over the baby with a mixture of adoration and pride. 'My smallest litter by far,' she murmured, 'but she will always be special because she will be my last – I'm getting too long in the tooth for this sort of thing. I don't care how many handsome wandering hogs dally at my door; I shall turn a blind eye and a deaf ear in future!'

Scumble moved closer and regarded his sister. She lay, fast asleep in the nest of leaves and grass; pale pink with her baby white spines looking like pimples just beneath the skin. 'Bliss,' he said joyfully. 'She certainly is a little earth angel, I hope Cory and Spike get here soon to see her.'

'Where is Cory?' asked Sunnifa, 'Is he alright?'

They moved away under some trees so as not to disturb the mother and baby and Scumble, with Sheard interrupting enthusiastically, told Sunnifa of their adventures since they had left her.

'Cory will be fine,' said the kindly Scumble, when he saw the look of consternation on Sunnifa's face. 'Scally has probably found him already and they'll come back together.'

'I don't know what he will make of Drew's advice,' pondered Sunnifa, 'I hope he doesn't think it was all a wasted journey.'

Sheard nodded in agreement but Scumble cried, 'No, I don't believe so. Cory will see Drew's idea's as something to be considered carefully; there are things he said that none of us would ever have thought of on our own. And remember, Cory's journey has given him the chance to meet a rat from the Dark Wood. He must have got *some* information from him. When he returns we will know much more about Mad Maggie Minchin's place than before he went.'

'He will know what the rat chooses to tell him – no more, no less,' Sheard shrugged. 'But is the rat friend or foe I wonder – is he a spy?'

'Cory's no fool,' Scumble replied, 'and neither is Scally. We must trust to their good judgement.'

'And to Pan,' added Sunnifa; she glanced furtively around. 'We don't want any of his trickery!'

Just then there came a rustling in the undergrowth and a hot and dishevelled hedgehog burst upon them. He was panting in great gasps and a thin film of blood trickled from an open wound above one eye. One of his legs was also bloody and he dragged it painfully behind hind him as he approached the horrified trio.

'Why it's Bugle!' cried Scumble, 'Whatever has happened to you?' He rushed to support the wounded hog and led him to a soft grassy patch where he could lie down.

'Disaster!' wailed Bugle, 'Absolute disaster!'

'Calm down pal you're with friends now,' said Sheard. 'Tell us the worst, what's happened?'

Bugle looked fearfully around and then back to where he had emerged from the undergrowth. He took a shuddering breath and fixing his eyes on Scumble told of the fight with the Dark Wood rats and how Trefoil and Orva had been captured and taken off to Mad Maggie's place. 'We fought hard but they were too many for us; we were all wounded, Orva quite badly. I was lucky, I got knocked down and managed to curl into a ball and roll a bit under some brambles. Don't know if they saw me or not, but they didn't interfere with me, thank Pan; my prickles must've put 'em off. Anyway I waited for what seemed ages before uncurling; even then I thought they might have left a guard and that I'd be pounced on. It was all clear though so I put my snout to the ground and followed 'em.' Scumble, Sheard and Sunnifa stared at him in disbelief.

'You did what?' gasped Sunnifa.

'Followed the beggars,' said Bugle and he licked his snout where some of the blood was now clotting. 'Don't know what I thought I could do, but I had to find out where they had been taken.'

'And you saw them taken to Mad Maggie's?' asked Scumble.

'Didn't actually see 'em,' mumbled Bugle, still busy with his nose, 'but when I got to the old house I saw a number of the rats who had fought us, standing about outside. They seemed to be guards. Big, powerful beggars they were. I hid for a while but there didn't seem anything more I could do. I could hear loud noises inside; could've been what you might call music. Nothin' I've ever heard in my life before – made my head ache. Some smaller rats came outside; they were rollin' around and shovin' one another and gigglin' and laughin' fit to bust. The whole place was weird. I didn't want to be caught so I hurried away and got back here as fast as I could.' He looked at them all pleadingly. 'Trevoil and Orva need help and quickly. What's to be done?'

Sunnifa looked at the three earnest faces in front of her and shook her head sadly, 'I don't think there is anything we can do for them at the moment. The crows that Cory sent to scout out the land reported back to me yesterday. They confirm what Bugle says about there being guard rats all around the place; big savage looking ones at that. There are also a lot of rats building a dam across the stream. You would not be able to get near the place without being seen and captured – or killed. The crows saw a rat running fast into Whylder Wood with three of the guard rats chasing it. It was caught and taken back inside Mad Maggie's house. It was screaming and struggling but no other rat tried to help it. What could we do against that, we are not fighters.'

'But we can learn to be fighters,' cried Bugle. 'Trefoil and I learned to fight with Orva.'

'Yes but to no avail,' Sunnifa answered matter of factly. 'If we are to make up a rescue party, we should need more volunteers and it will take time to get them.' She sighed and looked back towards the common; 'Hurry up Cory, we need you to make a decision.'

141

'I am inclined to agree with Sunnifa,' said Scumble. 'I'm sorry Bugle, but when we go we will need to go with strength. And you need time for your leg to heal, you can't march on that.'

Sheard twitched his tail angrily in frustration. 'We can't just do nothing, my friends!'

'No,' agreed Scumble, 'so why don't you and I go and find Braxton. He may need our help and if he doesn't then we certainly need his. What d'you think?' He turned to Bugle, 'Was there any sign of the badger?'

'No sign,' said Bugle. 'Orva took us almost to his door before we were attacked by the rats. We made one hell of a noise but he never put in an appearance. Either too sick or he's scarpered.' He winced as Sunnifa began to examine his leg.

'Then Scumble and I will investigate fo shure,' said Sheard getting up and dusting himself down. 'Come amigo, we have no time to waste.'

'Yes,' Scumble answered, 'Sunnifa, say our goodbyes to my mother and look after her and little Bliss. Tell Cory where we are going and say that we won't do anything foolhardy. Tell him that after we have been to Braxton's we will make our way back via the course of the stream; that way we may run into Spike and Aldin and his friends.' He looked at Bugle, 'Don't give up hope for Trefoil; he's a resourceful hog and there's a chance that Aldin, Heaton and Clowes might be in a position to help him. They look as if they could hold their own in a fight.' Bugle nodded resignedly and quietly accepted Sunnifa's ministrations to his leg.

***

So once more Scumble and Sheard set off into the woods, keeping to the path that Bugle had described to them. Scumble felt very weary but was determined not to complain, so he gritted his teeth and concentrated on putting one leg in front of the other. It was quite dark now and, as they made their way into Whylder Woods under the canopy of the trees, the light of the moon became more obscure. Scumble found that he had to keep his eyes on the ground in order not to wander off the path, which was covered in leaf litter and hard to distinguish from the surrounding undergrowth. Altogether it was a lonely and slightly forbidding place and he was glad of Sheard's company. The squirrel swung from tree to tree wherever possible calling directions to the little hedgehog. At one point they came upon a fallen tree that lay across the path and Scumble spent much time trying to negotiate a suitable place where he could squeeze underneath. The dense undergrowth either side was impenetrable in the dark, making it impossible to skirt around; so in the end he had to climb over the top. He eventually arrived on the other side, breathless and aching but triumphant.

By the time they reached the centre of Whylder Wood, the moonlight was totally obscured and they had to use their ears as well as their eyes in order to progress into the darkness. Sometimes they heard strange scufflings and rustlings and occasionally glimpsed a flash of yellow or green eyes that stared for a few seconds then blinked and went out. At one point Scumble felt they were being tracked and once he stopped abruptly, with heart pounding and spines erect, but nothing materialised and they went on their way unmolested. Eventually they arrived at what Sheard thought must be very near to Braxton's set. Scumble sniffed around and quickly picked up the scent which led them to a deep hole in the side of a large bank covered in thick brambles.

'This is it,' Scumble said. 'Heavy scent so if he's gone it wasn't long ago; doesn't smell too healthy though!' He wrinkled his snout at Sheard. Sheard stuck his head in the hole and called softly to Braxton. They were afraid to make too much noise in case they brought the guard rats running. 'Best go in,' whispered Scumble. They entered the set together but soon had to go in single file as the passage became narrower.

'What d'you know 'bout badger sets?' asked Sheard, turning his head to check they weren't being followed.

'Not much,' Scumble replied, 'but I do know they can be quite big and have lots of adjoining tunnels.

As they went further in the smell became more pronounced and Sheard muttered 'Gross,' but continued to follow the intrepid little hedgehog who was now picking up speed as he scented his way along one tunnel and then another. 'Hope we're not walking into a trap,' Sheard hissed. Scumble did not reply but all of a sudden he stopped and Sheard heard him catch his breath.

'We've found him,' he said.

Braxton lay in a shallow dip he had scraped in the ground at a place where three tunnels converged. There was more room here and the badger lay with his back tight against one of the walls which offered a form of protection to his blind side. At first glance he appeared to be dead but as Scumble quietly approached he saw the faint rise and fall of his chest and heard the rasp of laboured breathing.

'Keep a look out for unexpected visitors,' Scumble whispered to Sheard, whilst he gently ran his paw over the sick animal's body. 'Can't find any wounds,' he said eventually, 'but the poor fellow's obviously very sick.' Braxton opened his eyes and the hedgehog said quickly, 'Don't be alarmed; can you tell me what the matter is?'

'Poisoned,' rasped Braxton. 'Drank some tainted water and ate a dead shrew; didn't taste quite right but I was hungry and too lazy to be bothered…serves me right.' He closed his eyes and was silent.

'How do you feel – what hurts?' asked Scumble in a soothing voice.

'Pains in me stomach and chest; head's pounding. Been vomiting and me droppings aren't right.'

'Man, you can say that again!' muttered Sheard in the background.

Scumble threw him an angry look. 'Sheard, I will need a few things and it will be quicker for you to find them.' He stroked Braxton's cheek, 'Where do these tunnels lead apart from the Dark Wood?'

Braxton let out an involuntary moan and his face grimaced in pain. After a moment he said through gritted teeth, 'The tunnel behind me comes out on the edge of the wood, right beside a quiet lane. All other tunnels lead straight into the wood.'

'OK, Sheard,' said Scumble, trying to think as fast as he could, 'take the tunnel to the lane and find me some road-weed. Don't come back and tell me you can't find any; there are masses about. Make the leaves wet if you can, there should be some pools of rain water amongst the tree roots. Oh and if you see a birch tree get some of its bark.' As the squirrel turned to go, Scumble called softly, 'Be quick Sheard – be quick.'

When Sheard had gone, Scumble peered around into the darkness trying to weigh up the severity of the situation. Usually a badger's set was clean and dry but Braxton must have been ill for some time because many of the passages were fouled up and the air was fetid. There was no way that they would be able to move the badger, so the mess must be cleaned up instead. In the meantime Scumble sat close by the poorly creature, speaking gently and reassuringly to him. On Sheard's return with the requested items, Scumble chewed the wet road-weed leaves, masticating them into a pulp that was easier for Braxton to swallow. He sent Sheard away again to collect more rainwater as best he could and the ingenious little fellow returned with what he called an "old tin can". He then made a number of journeys transporting the water in an empty nut shell until the can was filled to the brim. Scumble fed Braxton some water and encouraged him to chew on the birch bark. The little hedgehog was feeling quite emotional and needed to clear his throat before speaking to the squirrel.

'Look Sheard, I've been thinking and it seems to me that you would be better off going to try and find Aldin and my brother Spike. Braxton will need help for quite a while yet; I'm happy to stay and look after him, but squirrels aren't meant to be underground, you'll be far better occupied outside. You will be quicker and safer in the trees when you haven't got me to worry about; maybe you will think of a plan to rescue Trefoil and Orva.'

'Well, I hear what you say my little dude and it makes sense. Can't say I feel comfortable down here; on the other paw, I'm not happy about leaving you.'

'I'll be absolutely fine,' Scumble relied. 'No arguments! When I've done all I can for Braxton – either way; I'll make my own way home, the way we came. I'll steer clear of Mad Maggie's and we will meet up later.'

So reluctantly Sheard said goodbye and left by the tunnel that led out to the lane, as he didn't trust himself to be able to find his way back through the tunnels they had come in by. It was true that he did not want to leave the small hedgehog by himself so near to danger, but he reflected on what Drew had said about using their different strengths. It was right that Scumble should stay with Braxton. Sheard was not needed there but he might be able to help Aldin, Heaton, Clowes and Spike more effectively. As he made his way through the tree tops he remembered Vincent the little caterpillar and he grinned to himself. That was a spunky little creature; he would be pleased to see him again.

CHAPTER 16

FABLES, MYTHS AND LEGENDS

After leaving the meeting in Bluebell Grove, the three rats, the caterpillar and Spike made their way over the top of the rise of the earth bank towards Park Woods stream. Aldin being a natural leader was in front, with Spike taking up the rear. Clowes had volunteered to carry Vincent and by trial and error they had found the perfect way to do this. The little caterpillar was now safely installed invisibly in the warmth of the hollow under the rat's front leg, where he clung tightly to the course chest fur.

Aldin was by and large a town rat; he had lived most of his life in a variety of homes dug painstakingly within the buildings of Man. He was a rat of ingenuity, quick thinking and courageous; he was a survivor. Competition for town rats was high; although food was plentiful, the numbers of rats competing for the best quality titbits made them all rivals and adversaries from the moment they left the nest. They learned to fight for everything they valued: food, homes, mates and pups. Aldin had earned respect from his opponents and had reached the stage where mostly he was left in peace. But there was a restlessness about him that sat uncomfortably with a safe and peaceful life. He found it all rather boring. Sometimes he had ventured out into the countryside to explore the wider world and on the last occasion had met up with Heaton and Clowes; two brothers who had lived all their lives on the banks of the River Rushlep. They bonded well and after one night of carousing on dregs of wine left behind on the riverbank, they agreed that they would set out to seek new climes, action packed adventure and with any luck their fortunes! *So here we are*, thought Aldin, *our first engagement;* which he hoped would not prove to be their last. He had not counted on being hampered by an overtalkative caterpillar and a sour faced, sluggish hedgehog.

They soon found the stream and on Cory's instructions proceeded to follow its meandering course through the woods. Heaton and Clowes appeared to be in their element on the damp boggy ground and unconsciously quickened their pace. Aldin also found the smell of the peaty earth pleasant and the sound of the trickling water tinkling over stones was refreshing and gave him a new spring to his step. Only Spike found the wet earth difficult to walk on; constantly slipping and sliding until he was worn out. Aldin was brought to a halt by a tap on the shoulder from Heaton and the message that they had lost Spike. Not wishing to raise their voices and attract unwanted attention, the party retraced their steps until they came upon Spike crouched on some damp moss under the protection of a briery bush.

'Having difficulties mate?' Aldin asked as Spike gave him a sullen look.

'Hedgehogs aren't made for this muddy ground,' said Spike, 'I can't get a grip with my paws.' Privately he was seething that Cory should have suggested this particular route, without a thought for how his brother might cope with the conditions.

'Well now, you know you don't have to come,' replied the rat, who had little patience for whingers. 'All credit to you for trying but if it's too difficult there's no shame in turning back. I'm sure Sunnifa would appreciate some help.'

Spike bit back a sarcastic retort and rose wearily to his feet. 'Look, I volunteered to come with you and Cory has authorised it. I want to come, I want to help, but do we have to go at such a fast pace: we're not in a race are we? Whatever we find we can report back to Sunnifa as and when; if we take longer, then what's to stop Cory from following us and we can report to him direct.' Spike waited with bated breath for Aldin's response. He had decided that if the rats left him, he would not return ignominiously to Bluebell Grove, but would continue to investigate on his own.

He was relieved therefore when Aldin replied, 'OK, continue with us for the present and we'll slow it down a bit; but I don't want to hear anymore complaints.' With that Aldin turned on his heel and immediately set off again with all of them in tow.

To be fair the pace was slower and by dint of concentration and determination, Spike was just about able to keep up with the others. He found that he had no time to think negative thoughts concerning Cory and on the whole, thought only of putting one paw in front of the other and keeping in Clowes tracks. Dusk had now fallen and with it brought renewed energy to the hedgehog, so he was surprised when Aldin came to a sudden stop and signalled for silence. The rat was peering cautiously at a spot a little way ahead of them, just to the right of the path. He advanced tentatively before beckoning the others on and indicating that they should remain quiet. A female rat lay on her side amongst the ferns and nettles; she was alive but only just and it was clear that she was dying. She was covered in deep bites and scratches, some of which had bled profusely before congealing into great clots and by the look of her dirty, mud encrusted, emaciated body, she must have been there for days. Aldin bent over her and drew in a quick breath when he saw the extent of her injuries. There was a gaping wound in her stomach which was alive with blow fly maggots; as he examined her she opened her eyes.

'We are friends,' Aldin whispered, 'what in the name of all that is good has happened to you?'

The rat's words came hesitantly and her voice was so low that Aldin had to bend closely to hear her. 'Tried to leave the colony,' she gasped. 'Not allowed; we were followed and they tried to take us back. Borage, my mate, was killed in the fight. I was left to die. No more use to them if I can't have pups.'

Aldin reached into a rain puddle amongst the roots of a nearby willow and gently wetted the rat's mouth. She weakly licked his paw and he caressed her cheek. Her eyes closed and her breathing became so shallow it seemed that she scarcely breathed at all. 'You are no longer alone,' he said softly, 'you are with friends and we will stay by your side.' Quietly the others settled down around her whilst Aldin continued to stroke her gently, uttering soft words: 'Deep peace and comfort of the quiet earth to you, my dear; deep peace of sun-lit meadows and shady woodlands; deep peace of pleasant pastures and welcoming hedgerows; deep peace of bright running waters.'

The little rat's torn body shivered slightly and was still. Aldin allowed his paw to rest protectively upon her for a while, before slowly getting to his feet, when Clowes restrained him with a paw on his shoulder. Then to Aldin's surprise his friend, with bowed head murmured a supplication to the God of the Pasture.

'Breathe on her almighty Pan, warm her with your breath. Take her to you and protect her evermore in new green pastures.'

'Let it be,' responded the others in chorus; whilst Aldin gave Clowes a puzzled look and received a wistful smile and a little shrug in response.

They found the body of Borage further up stream in the wet mud on the bank and Heaton carried it back to its mate, where they were buried together in a scrape Aldin dug amongst the tall green ferns. This whole incident had left them all emotionally drained and it was therefore decided to find a place of safety where they could spend the rest of the night. A short way on they found a gnarled old willow tree whose twisted roots spread across the path into the undergrowth on the other side. Pushing into the dense vegetation and snouting around for an acceptable supper, they finally settled down with the protection of the tree roots at their backs and felt secure enough to be able to relax at last.

As much as he disliked Aldin, Spike could not but help having a sneaking regard for him. He admired how the rat had taken charge and how no creature in the group had questioned his authority, because how he had behaved had somehow seemed so right. Nevertheless, Spike was not yet prepared to fully trust the rats and he resolved to stay awake and keep his ears open for any sign of treachery. He closed his eyes and listened intently to what was being said. The rats had been discussing how they might best approach Mad Maggie Minchin's now that it was confirmed how aggressive and depraved some of the rat colony had become. Vincent the caterpillar was adamant that they should allow him time to consult with the ants before they made any further move and it was agreed that he should attempt to contact the ants at dawn's early light. Once this was settled the talk became more fragmented and desultory. Aldin stretched himself out and remarked that it was a shame they could not make the night more comfortable by having a fire.

'Leave fires to Man is what I say,' said Heaton, 'much too dangerous! Remember the lightning that set fire to the old oak in Park Woods; been standing hundreds of years up 'til then I shouldn't warrant. And what about that truck we saw ablaze as we were travelling up the Rushlep. Burnt completely out they say and who's to know how many lives lost. Nah, we're better off without it.'

'I'm talking about fire that's under control,' said Aldin. 'Where I come from Man keeps it boxed up in one place and they get all the benefits with none of the disadvantages. Warmth,' he mused, 'heat that penetrates your very bones and takes away the aches and pains. And food! You wouldn't believe the tasty, succulent food you get when it has been cooked on a fire.' He patted his belly appreciatively at the memory.

'You and your town living, Aldin,' said Clowes, 'it's a wonder you wanted to leave the place at all, if it was that good.'

'Ah yes,' Heaton sat up and addressed the group. 'Now you must have heard the story of the town rat and the country rat?' He saw a number of perplexed faces and so continued, 'A town rat went to visit his country cousin. Now this cousin was rough and ready and lived a very simple life, but he loved the town rat and made him very welcome. They dined off wheat stocks, berries and roots pulled up from the hedgerows, but the town rat was not impressed. "You live the lifestyle of the most meagre of ants," he said disparagingly, "whilst in my house food is plentiful. Come back with me and you shall have an ample share of it." Well the country rat could not resist this invitation and so he returned with his cousin to the town house. When they arrived, the town rat took his cousin into a huge dining room where a table was laid with all sorts of splendid foods: bread, honey, cheeses, cakes and cooked meats. The country rat was delighted at the sight of such good cheer. "You were right in what you said,' he remarked, 'and I do indeed lament my own hard fate."

'You and your town living, Aldin, it's a wonder you wanted to leave the place at all, if it was that good.'

'Now scarcely had they begun to eat when the door opened and a man entered. Both rats scurried to hide and remained hidden for some time, hearts pumping with fear, behind a coal scuttle in the fireplace. But no sooner had they ventured back onto the table and the country rat was reaching for a succulent piece of roast beef, when the door flew open again and in bounded two hound dogs; baying ferociously and slobbering all over the carpet. With a shriek the country rat leapt from the table and disappeared under the wainscoting to safety, closely followed by his town cousin. When he had got his breath the country rat turned to his cousin and said, "You may well have many tasty foods to choose from here, but the price you pay is too great for me. I prefer my humble home with simple food, where I can live in peace and safety".'

Aldin laughed. 'Touché my friend,' he said. 'But I think you have not heard the other story about those two cousins.' He looked around for confirmation and continued. 'The town rat did indeed visit his country cousin and was unimpressed by the food he was offered. And at his invitation the cousin agreed to visit the town rat's house. On arrival, as before, he saw the table brimming over with all good things to eat and his mouth watered in anticipation. Just then the door opened and a huge ginger tom cat entered, its twitching tail held high in the air. The country rat was much bemused for he had never seen such a creature in all his life and he asked his cousin what manner of creature it was. "Ah," said the town rat, "let me introduce you to our illustrious leader

who dwells in this house. Go and make his acquaintance."
So the foolish country rat jumped down from the table
and gaily approached the cat who smacked him with its
paw, lifted him up and ate him.' Aldin grinned and looked
about him.

'For shame,' cried Clowes. 'You made that up to suit
your own view of life. What is it suppose to prove?'

'It proves the importance of exploration; of having
an inquiring mind and learning the lessons of survival
before life eats you up. There is no virtue in remaining in
one place all your life just because you think it's safe. You
will always remain naïve and easily duped.'

'Well it seems to me that if we were all rolling stones
there'd be no stability,' Clowes said. 'If no creature was
prepared to stay in one place then there'd be no place for
the rest of us to go back to.'

'Hmm,' Aldin raised his head and winked at Vincent.
'Then we must just agree to disagree, my friend; I'm too
tired to argue anymore.'

Clowes smiled but did not pursue the subject. 'Not much
moonlight tonight,' he remarked, squinting up at the sky.

'She's only in her first quarter,' said Heaton, 'she is
ruled by Ganesh.'

'Who's Ganesh, I've never heard of him?' said Vincent,
who wasn't at all sleepy and was thoroughly enjoying the
stories.

'Ganesh,' explained Heaton, 'is a god – he is the God
of Rats and smiles favourably on us. He has the face of an
elephant, with a long trunk and two tusks, one of which is
broken; he broke it one night when he was out riding on

his favourite rat and overbalanced. Ganesh loves his food – probably because most of it is cooked on a fire!' Heaton glanced slyly in Aldin's direction, but Aldin ignored him. 'Ganesh is rather self indulgent and too much eating has made him fat. When he fell off his rat the moon saw him and laughed. This angered Ganesh so he threw the broken piece of tusk at her and cursed her. And the moon disappeared. Every night after that was dark and dreary. There was no moonlight, not even any twilight. Well, as you can imagine, the other gods were very displeased about this; they found the darkness unbearable so they threatened Ganesh to amend his curse. Ganesh did not want to lose all his comforts so he did as he was told. And from that time onwards the moon is sentenced to wax and wane. She alternates between a shining fortnight and a dark fortnight, each period ending either with a full moon or a new moon.'

'As fascinating as your country stories are, I think we would be wise to get some rest before the sun rise,' said Aldin. 'We do not know what dangers tomorrow will bring. We need to be ready to face them. If you are all agreed I propose that we take turns in keeping watch, we don't want to be jumped on in the dark. I'll take first watch.'

They all said their goodnights and settled down as best they could, their heads filled with a mixture of troubled, fearful and excited thoughts, depending on the nature of each.

CHAPTER 17

ON THE BRINK

Spike woke the next morning having dreamed deeply and most vividly of the god Ganesh and the moon. Ganesh rode on a huge ginger cat, closely followed by two baying, slobbering hounds and together they pursued the moon relentlessly across the starlit sky. As he journeyed the plump god threw back his elephant-like head and trumpeted wreaths of white powder from his trunk. The powder hung like a doom laden embryonic sac in the sky and formed impenetrable clouds that soon obliterated the light of the stars. Eventually only the pale, cold beauty of the moon remained, surrounded by a halo of fire which burned clear and bright for a short while longer before it too was dimmed and finally blotted out, leaving the world in darkness and despair.

As Spike became aware of his surroundings he realised that the three rats were already up and about, foraging in the undergrowth for breakfast no doubt. It occurred to Spike that no one had woken him to take his turn of keeping watch and he immediately felt aggrieved. He got up seething with anger and busied himself with uncovering any bugs and grubs that would sate his hunger. When Aldin appeared Spike glared at him accusingly.

'Aren't I good enough to keep watch?' he said, 'Or is it that you don't trust me? What have you got against me?'

Aldin was polishing off what looked like a collection of rather tough stitchwort stems and finished chewing before he spoke. 'Don't take it personally kid; you're a youngster here compared to the rest of us. Clowes, Heaton and I are used to keeping watch at night. It was no hardship and it gave you and the caterpillar a well earned rest.' It was some relief to Spike to hear that Vincent had also been excluded from the night watch duties, but then of course the caterpillar was far too small to keep watch effectively. Within seconds Spike felt that once again he had been belittled, passed over and he allowed his dislike for Aldin to fester and grow. The morning light had a slight haze to it that promised a fine spring day and the group were just about to continue on their way when they heard a flurry of activity in the branches of a tree overhead. The three rats immediately flew together and stood back to back, claws out at the ready against any imminent threat.

'Whoa there!' called a well known voice and Sheard's face appeared amongst the foliage. 'Did I give you dudes a scare?' He chuckled and dropped to the ground in front of them. 'Chill out it's only yours truly.'

'OK. Nice to see you but keep your voice down,' Aldin said. 'Where have you come from and what are you doing here?' Sheard replied that he had a great deal of news to impart and that it would be best if they settled back down for a while to listen. Vincent was somewhat impatient at this as he was itching to get on and find his ants; however Aldin judged that they would be better equipped when they were better informed and gave instructions to gather around the squirrel and listen to what he had to say. 'Only don't take all day talking,' he warned Sheard. 'We don't want to be found hanging around here in the daylight.' And he told Sheard about the rats they had buried the previous evening. Sheard immediately responded by recounting what Bugle had reported concerning the capture of Trefoil and Orva.

'As soon as we heard, Scumble and I came to the Dark Wood to search for Braxton. Man, we found a pretty sick dude and Scumble stayed with him to help. I thought I'd be of more use to you. Found you quite easily y'know. If those guard rats are anywhere near as fierce and unfriendly as they sound we need to stay way down wind of 'em.'

'What news on Cory?' Aldin asked quickly, not wanting any of them to get more jumpy than they already were. Sheard laughed and told about the aborted plan to visit Clacks Farm. He told of the sighting of the burnt out truck which had seemed to precipitate Scumble into one of his weird trances; the pantomime of crossing the road culminating in Cory's fall into the drainage pipes and the decision to leave Cory to make his own way out.

'That was unfortunate,' said Aldin. 'So I suppose you still don't know where Cory is?'

'Oh yeah man, no worries; Scally is keeping an eye on him. When Cory was in the drain pipe he made the acquaintance of a rat from Mad Maggie's – called himself Fag. Seem to have pal'd up. Scally said they found an exit into the Rushlep and are making their way back together.

Well,' Sheard scratched his head, 'apparently not straight away. Fag wanted to show Cory a place he called "heaven".' Sheard looked sheepishly at the others. 'Can't make sense of it meself but knowing Cory he'll be back as soon as he can.'

Aldin nodded. 'This Fag is an interesting addition; let's hope he's a genuine ally and not a spy. I didn't have Cory down as naïve.'

'I'm hip to that,' said the squirrel. 'But even if he is a foul-weather friend it's wise of Cory to keep him close. Keep your friends close and your enemies closer, I always say.'

'Yes,' mused Aldin, 'and he may well learn much from the rat that we would not hope to gain in any other way.'

'Excuse me!' Vincent was getting tired of being ignored. 'Perhaps if we could just get a move on and I can talk to the ants, you might be very surprised at what we *could* learn!'

'You're right Vincent, and we will make a move immediately. Remember, this must be a silent march,' Aldin said.

As the others moved back through the undergrowth towards the path by the stream, Aldin held Sheard back and asked him what he had learned from Drew at Clacks Farm. Sheard briefly shared what advice the owl had given them and was surprised to see how much importance the rat seemed to attach to it. They followed the others back onto the path and it wasn't long before their nostrils were assailed by a foul smell. Heaton, who was in the lead, raised his paw for them all to stop.

'Must be fairly near now,' he whispered.

The place was silent and Clowes realised he could no longer hear the tinkling of the stream. He turned to look and noticed only a faint trickle of water. 'Streams dried up,' he said softly

Sheard tapped Aldin on the shoulder. 'If I get back into the trees I figure I could scout out the lie of the land without being seen. Are you cool to that?'

A smile hovered on Aldin's face for a fleeting second before he said, 'I'm cool, but go quietly and stay hidden. Don't do anything rash.'

Sheard was gone in a trice whilst the others waited out of sight, hidden by the underbrush. They did not have to wait long before the squirrel arrived back breathless and excited. 'Three guard rats visible,' he said. 'Seem to be guarding the pit where the smell is coming from. It looks as if they've unloaded some of the pit's contents – bags and boxes and things stacked up on the edge. They've also built a dam across the stream, made a good job of it too, if you ask me.'

'Well done Sheard,' said Aldin. He looked at Vincent who had crawled out from under Clowes' leg and was now perched on his shoulder. 'What do you want us to do to find your ants?' he asked the little fellow. Vincent was balanced on his tail, his body stretched upwards as high as he could reach. He quested with his feelers in each direction.

'Back into the wood,' he said. 'We need to find a dead tree or tree stump.'

They retraced their steps through the undergrowth into the gloom of the closely growing trees and very soon came across a small tree trunk lying on its side. It was dead and rotted but still giving life support to a number of lichens, fungi and insects.

Clowes placed Vincent on the bare wood and they all stood back a fraction to watch what, if anything, would happen. At first it appeared as if the caterpillar had gone to sleep and Spike raised his spines in irritation. Gradually however, they could see that the grub's little body had begun to vibrate and secrete a clear liquid that slipped slowly and subtly into the cracks and crevices of the tree bark. For a while nothing else happened until Heaton noticed an ant crawling towards Vincent along the length of the trunk and pointed it out to the others. As soon as this little visitor was noted more put in an appearance, following the leader along the trunk or emerging from the cracks in the bark. Dozens upon dozens of ants converged upon the caterpillar until he disappeared from view and all the onlookers could see was a writhing mass of dark brown bodies that bubbled and boiled like an erupting lava flow.

Some minutes elapsed before Clowes, with a worried frown, stepped forward to rescue Vincent from what they all now feared was a lethal attack. Before he could do anything however, the ants on the periphery of the mass began to pull away and disappear back into the tree. Others quickly followed and before long Vincent's body became visible as the last remnants of ants retreated back into obscurity. Clowes bent over the caterpillar and gently blew warm breath on him. The little grub stirred and sat up to a sigh of relief from the onlookers. Vincent turned and surveyed them all.

'Well?' said Aldin.

'Well!' the caterpillar replied. 'I must begin with the awful news that Orva the stoat has been brutally killed.' There was a general gasp of dismay.

'And what of Trefoil?' cried Spike.

'He remains a prisoner,' said Vincent; 'I will come to him in a bit. In general it is as we suspected, the white powders have tempted too many rats and it is turning them brainless. Their behaviour is erratic – aggressive and emotional. They have also taken to fermenting berries and leaves to make a potent drink which renders them even more brainless. A group of rats have taken control of the others and the colony has become like a prison, with punishments and death to those who try to flout the rules. Many of those who are free of the drugs and the drink want to leave but are prevented by the guard rats. All gestating females and those of pup-bearing age are confined together. When the pups are weaned they are taken from the mothers and kept in a room elsewhere. Some of the pups are deformed and the worst of these are kept separately in a room on their own. All pups, healthy or deformed, are looked after by the priests.'

'The priests?' Aldin looked puzzled.

'There is a bird with a broken wing that the rats keep in a nest in a room. She is called Iya Nla and she has set up a group of rats called priests. The priests are supposed to look after the colony but the ants think that it is they who are destroying it. Orva and Trefoil were captured during an Initiation Ceremony of the priests and Orva was offered as a sacrifice to the gods that they worship.'

'But Pan wants no sacrifices made to him,' said Heaton.

'No man! He prefers to take his own!' Sheard cut in.

'They are not worshipping Pan,' explained Vincent. 'The gods have names that the ants have never heard of before. But they are powerful gods and the priests are in awe of them. When the rats were erecting a stone idol to the gods it toppled over and crushed some of them. Their bodies were skinned and the priests now wear the skins as cloaks. It makes them look bigger and more powerful and they strike fear into the colony.'

'How many are these priests?' Aldin asked.

Vincent shrugged. 'The ants are not so good at counting I'm afraid, but they are at least one less than they were. One of them was pushed into the bottom of the pit and his body lies there still.'

'Never mind that, what about Trefoil?' cried Spike impatiently.

'The bird is trying to save him,' Vincent answered unexpectedly. 'She is growing weaker and is in much pain but she has a good brain and has spun the rats a story that all hedgehogs are protected by the Moon Goddess Ishtar. The bird has let it be known that Ishtar has given the gift of prophecy to the hedgehog and at the moment the rats believe that they would call down the wrath of the goddess if they hurt Trefoil. But some of the Priests suspect the story and it has been decreed that Trefoil must prove he has the gift of second sight. If he fails the test he will be sacrificed like Orva.' Vincent surveyed his now silent audience, 'What's to be done?' he said with a tremor in his voice.

'We must force an entry and rescue Trefoil,' cried Spike. 'Come on, there's not a moment to lose!'

'Now hold hard,' said Aldin. 'Your sentiments are to be admired Spike, but foolhardiness is not the answer. We must think through a strategy first. We will be no help to Trefoil if we all land up as prisoners.' He turned back to the caterpillar, 'Well Vincent, I think we all owe you an apology for doubting your powers. That was pretty impressive what you did just then and it seems clear to me that you are indeed able to communicate with the ants. Can we rely on their continued help do you think?'

'I don't think we can bet on it; they are feeling the effects of remaining so long in the polluted ground. Their plans are to move on as soon as they can.'

'It's understandable, they have done well already, and we cannot expect them to do more. Come, let's get nearer to the place, but keep quiet and keep under cover.' As quickly and quietly as they could, they retraced their steps back to the stream and cautiously approached the place where the poisonous smell was coming from. The three guard rats were in view, talking by the side of the pit. One was sitting on a battered box that had obviously been excavated from the hole along with the other bags and containers. 'I would very much like to investigate that pit,' Aldin said.

'Nuff said,' Sheard replied. 'I can deal with those three doofers with my eyes shut. Give me five minutes and I'll have cleared the way for you.' Without waiting for a reply the squirrel disappeared through the tree tops and reappeared perched on a branch only feet away from the guards. He proceeded to throw verbal abuse at the guard rats; all the time running along the branch and hopping up and down, screaming and chattering in excitement. The guards were visibly annoyed and much bad language was exchanged between them and Sheard, but despite this they remained where they were and made no attempt to chase him. Eventually they turned their backs on the squirrel and ignored him. Sheard, ever the quick thinker, dropped to the ground and, gathering a pile of small rocks and stones from the crumbling walls of the house, proceeded to lob the missiles at the guard rats. A particularly well aimed stone caught one of them on the back of his head and with a howl of anger he turned and charged at the squirrel threatening to 'Wring his bleeding, scrawny little neck.'

Sheard made off at a sprint with all three rats on his tail. They disappeared into the undergrowth and could be heard crashing about. As the sounds grew fainter, Aldin, Heaton and Clowes hurried over to the pit and Aldin climbed down into the hole whilst the other two stood watch.

Spike watched all of this through a thicket of tall ferns, his eyes unblinking as he fought to stem his rising feelings of hate and frustration. Why was he always the one to be left on the sidelines? Why was he never given the chance to prove himself? Why did no creature like him? Full of self-pity, he had even forgotten the dangerous predicament of Trefoil. He saw Aldin's head appear over the lip of the hole and witnessed a huddled conversation between the three rats. Heaton then disappeared into the hole with Aldin, and Clowes was left alone at the top. There was still no sight or sound of Sheard or the guard rats, so on impulse Spike pushed through the ferns and made his way swiftly towards the other side of the boxes and bags where he was hidden from Clowes. He noticed that a bag had been gnawed through at one corner and there was some spillage of white powder on the ground. He sniffed at it gingerly and then snouted and snuffled around the bag. All of a sudden there was a shout and the three guard rats burst through the thicket and accosted Clowes. Spike curled into a ball and froze.

'Who the 'ell are you, what you doin' 'ere?' Spike heard the surly guard's question and Clowes' calm reply.

'Good morning cousins. I was just wondering where everyone was. I have come with news for the leader of the colony. Would you be so good as to take me to him?'

'What news? Who d'ya think yer are, the friggin post-rat?' The rat scowled at Clowes.

'The news is for your leader's ears only, it is important he learns of it; it will be the worse for you no doubt, if he does *not* hear it.' Clowes moved forward, 'I imagine it's this way; don't fret yourselves I will find him myself.' He continued walking purposefully towards a gap in the wall of the house.

"Ere not so fast,' a second guard rat called after him, 'you can't go in there on yer own, yer need ter be escorted.' The three guard rats exchanged glances bordering on panic and rushed after Clowes. All of them disappeared through the gap in the wall.

Spike uncurled and made sure the coast was clear before reaching a paw into the hole in the bag and extracting a package of silver paper. He sniffed it quickly before placing it in his mouth and held it in his cheek pouch. No sooner had he done this when Aldin and Heaton climbed out of the pit, dragging with them the lifeless body of a rat. After ascertaining that all was clear they dragged the body back into the undergrowth and looked for Spike.

'Where...? Oh there you are,' said Heaton as Spike appeared. Just then Sheard dropped from a tree in front of them making them all start.

'Nerves getting the best of us,' muttered Aldin. 'Now look you two; Heaton and I will stay here in case we can be of help to Clowes and Trefoil. Sheard, I suggest you make your way back and report to Cory as soon as possible. Tell him we need reinforcements and not to be too long about it.'

'No worries innit,' said the squirrel. He gave a puzzled glance at the dead rat who seemed to be wearing a second skin and head mask. 'Who's the dude?'

'Probably one of the priests,' Heaton answered. 'Why are you still here?'

'I'm gone,' said Sheard. And he was.

Aldin turned his attention to Spike who seemed to be in some state of agitation.

'You have a choice Spike; follow Sheard back at your own pace or, if you're up to it, find your way to Braxton's and give your brother Scumble some help.'

'Right,' mumbled Spike. 'Where's Vincent?'

'With Clowes,' Aldin said curtly. 'Let me worry about him.'

Spike left the two rats and continued through the undergrowth for a time, his thoughts in turmoil. He had been dismissed, sent on his way whilst that parasitic turd of a caterpillar was carried about and feted like some sort of hero. Why should he endanger himself by trying to find Scumble? It was the same old story, always expected to look after his brother. Well he wouldn't, not this time. He resolved to stay hidden for a while and see what they were all up to before returning to Park Woods; secrets, always secrets that excluded him. He grinned suddenly as he remembered his prize. Well *he* had a secret now and as he watched and waited he could taste a little more of the precious white powder whilst enjoying the privacy of his own company.

CHAPTER 18

HEAVEN AND THE EARTH ANGEL

Cory, Scally and Fag spent the best part of what was left of the night resting in a sheltered spot on the bank of the Rushlep. By mid morning, following a fairly sumptuous breakfast, Scally left them to join Sheard and Scumble; after being given instructions by Fag as to where he might find them on his return.

'Come on sir, follow me,' Fag climbed to the top of the embankment and looked back down at Cory's worried expression. 'I assure you it won't take long; we can join your friends before the day is out.'

Cory was not totally convinced that he should be deviating from his original plan, but he liked the little rat and after all he owed him his life. The hedgehog was not a ditherer so he resolved to accompany Fag for a while at least. He felt that it couldn't be a complete waste of time, any chance of furthering their friendship might prove very helpful in the future. His limbs ached from the previous day's exertions but the best cure for that was more exercise he thought stoically and so, head down he dug in his claws and climbed the embankment.

'It really isn't far sir,' said Fag excitedly. 'Just along the hedgerow and here...' he stopped and pointed to what could have been an old rabbit burrow. 'Here sir, we go through here and then you will see.' Fag scrabbled into the hole and within seconds had disappeared from view. Cory took a deep breath and followed. It was a bit of a squeeze and he had to lay his spines flat along his back in order to get through. The passage led under the hedgerow and then continued under a Man-made wall. By the time Cory emerged, Fag was already standing a few feet away with his back to him, gazing with rapture at a huge expanse of short, springy grass the like of which Cory had never seen before, not even on the common. The texture was smooth and velvety, like the skin of a mole and it was a lush green with no yellow patches or unkempt weeds; the edges were trim and straight and tidy. Spring flowers of all types and colours grew together abundantly in clumps, making patterns and designs most pleasing to the eye. Trees of different shapes and sizes stood proud and naked in the sunshine, free of the entanglement of brambles and nettles; some were adorned with heavily scented blossoms and everywhere looked clean and fresh with no sign of blight, rot or decay. Further in the distance was an expanse of shimmering water with some brightly coloured birds. In the centre was an island with a pretty little ornamental pagoda. Fag raised his front paws high above his head.

'Lookee, lookee, lookee,' he squealed with joy. 'What did I tell you sir? Oh my, oh my; knock, knock, knocking on heaven's door.' He spun round to face Cory. 'When I die this is where I want to come,' he sighed, 'but it's too good for the likes of me.'

'I doubt that,' said Cory, 'but it's certainly beautiful, what's the place called?'

'Otterly House sir; but these are only part of the gardens, they go on for miles and the house can't even be seen from here. One day when there is time I would like to explore the whole place. In fact,' he said wistfully, 'I have a dream to live here, but I don't think they would want rats.'

'No,' Cory rested a paw on Fag's shoulder, 'I don't think you would get a friendly welcome.' He noticed Fag's dejected expression and patted him on the back.

'No reason why you can't visit as often as you like though; as long as you keep a low profile eh?'

'Do you really think so sir?' said Fag, cheering up a little. 'I think that I must not return to the colony because they will never let me leave again.' He pointed into the distance ahead, 'Shall we go down to the lake and see the ducks? They are most marvellous creatures – they come from a place called China.'

'Then we shall go and see them, but afterwards we must start back for home, I'm worried that some of my friends are in trouble.' With a nod of assent, Fag led the way and before long they arrived at the lake which housed a number of water birds: a large flock of geese and various species of ducks. Cory was immediately drawn to some ducks with wonderfully coloured, ornate plumage. On seeing the visitors one of them swam over in stately fashion. His orange face feathers glistened in the reflection of the clear bright water and his orange back feathers were held regally in full sail. Altogether he was an imposing bird and Cory was not surprised when Fag whispered that this was a duck from China and quite rare.

'Hello, it's Fig isn't it, if I recall correctly?'

'Fag, your highness.' Fag all but fell into the lake he bowed so low. 'May I introduce my friend, Cory? Cory this is Chan Shen, he is a spiritual thinker.' Fag was obviously in awe of the proud and beautiful bird.

'How do you do,' Cory amended his bow to a nod of the head. 'Er, what a fine place you have here, it is to be envied I'm sure.'

'Do not be envious; it is the art of counting another's blessings instead of your own,' intoned Chan Shen, fluffing out his chest feathers. 'It is a lack of appreciation of your own uniqueness and self-worth young hog. Each of us has something to give that no other creature has.' The duck archly lifted a rainbow coloured wing and preened himself. 'You know,' he added, 'that envy eats nothing but its own heart!'

'Oh, er quite!' Cory replied rather lost for words; it would seem that the duck from China was a rather literal duck

'Of course some might say that fortune in life is dealt out disproportionately.' Chen Shen preened under his other wing and admired his reflection in the water. 'Unfairly some may argue but it is all in the grand scheme of Tai-Yueh-Ta-Ti, our great benefactor. We should all be content with our lot. It is disrespectful to be anything else wouldn't you say?' His little black beady eyes appraised Cory with a hint of arrogant indifference.

'Well, erm, I think that we should certainly make the best of what is given to us,' Cory struggled to find the right words, 'but I don't think there is any harm in striving to better ourselves. Er working hard towards it I mean, not just taking it for granted or being complacent or lazy or…' Under the steady scrutiny of the duck, Cory faltered to a halt.

'So Fig,' Chen Shen dismissed Cory and turned his full attention on the deferential Fag. 'How is life treating you since we last met? I notice there is even less of you than I remember.' He gave a rasping laugh. 'Be very careful young rat, if you turned sideways you would disappear!'

Fag felt extremely uncomfortable at this remark and nervously launched into a lengthy explanation of why he was so slight of figure; the scarcity of good wholesome food where his colony lived and the hard daily grind that was his lot in life. 'I'm referred to as "Fag the drudge", your worship, there is no time, nor enough provisions to put on weight.'

'Oh dear,' replied Chen Shen dipping his head to snap up a plump little water beetle. 'That is most unfortunate. But look at it this way, Fig: it is an ideal opportunity to show your mettle. Do not fall into the trap of constantly complaining, nobody likes a whinger.'

Cory felt he would burst with indignation. 'Fag is no whinger! He has proved himself to be the best friend any creature could want!'

'Indeed,' said the duck. 'Then may I offer some advice to you Fig – keep no friends that are not equal to yourself. It shows a smallness of character to seek in others what a superior creature seeks in himself. Now I really must take my leave of you, please feel free to come again, Fig.' Ignoring Cory, Chen Shen turned imperiously and began paddling away.

'Well really!' cried the exasperated hedgehog. 'Who does he think he is; the jumped-up, pompous, self-opinionated popinjay!'

'Oh sir, do you not think him wise?' The little rat said in a small voice.

'Fag, I think him a self serving, pretentious twit. You are twice the creature he is, never forget it. Now come on we really must be getting back.'

On the way back, Cory asked Fag what he had meant by saying the colony would not allow him out again if he returned. Fag said that he was unsure except that those who had tried to make a break for it had been caught and punished; some killed and made examples of.

'The priests make a big deal out of breeding,' the rat said. 'We are told how important it is to replace those we have lost. The death rate is high in that poisonous atmosphere. Young females are kept apart from the rest of the colony in the breeding rooms. All male rats are promised visits to the females, but I have never been chosen and I don't know of any other male rat except the guard rats. They make no secret of it and swagger about and make fun of the rest of us.'

'What about the priests?' Cory asked.

Fag shrugged. 'Who knows; at first we were told that all priests would be celibate but since Iya Nla has become sick, there is no creature to monitor this and I suspect that some of them at least are doing just what they please.'

They had chosen to walk back along the banks of the Rushlep to make it easier for Scally to find them and sure enough the crow put in an appearance about mid afternoon. 'Hail and well met,' he squawked, landing on a low tree branch in front of them. 'Glad to see you safe and sound and none the worse for your adventure – Cory, Lord of the Drains!' He opened his sharp black beak, threw back his head and laughed uproariously.

'Hmm,' Cory muttered, 'Don't push your luck bird brain. What news from Clacks Farm?' They sat under the hedgerow while Scally told of the meeting with Drew and how the owl had suggested they brought the state of affairs at Mad Maggie's to the attention of Man.

'Course he didn't offer any suggestions as to how we might do that. All talk and no do, if you ask me. A working bird in the paw is better than two sages in the bush any day say I!' He related the incident of the farm cat and how he, Sheard and Scumble had fought it off. 'Quite impressed Drew I think; leastways he was more inclined to listen to us afterwards.'

'Scumble and Sheard must have got back to Park Woods by now,' said Cory. 'Let's make tracks; Sunnifa may have news of the others.' He tried to keep the anxiety he was feeling out of his voice.

As Fag moved away along the embankment, Scally said quietly to Corry, 'So how was heaven?'

'Beautiful to look at,' Cory answered, 'and the residents were beautiful too.'

'And?' said Scally with a glint in his eye.

'The place seemed a bit soulless, a bit contrived… Man-made you know; not for the likes of us woodland creatures. My mother always says "all that glitters is not gold". Never really knew what she meant 'til now. The duck we spoke to was full of its own importance; led a privileged lifestyle; safe and secure – appeared to have little idea how the rest of us live. I think Fag liked it though, but perhaps that's not surprising considering where he comes from.'

'Yes,' said Scally, 'I've been there on occasions and it struck me the same way. I would be more inclined to believe in its heavenly qualities if the creatures that remain there did so from choice.'

'What do you mean?' said Cory, puzzled.

'Didn't you notice?' Scally explained, 'All the ducks' wings are clipped, they can't fly away. I'll see you back at Sunnifa's,' he called as he launched himself into the air.

Cory and Fag made good time back to Park Woods, with only a brief exchange of words as Cory explained where he lived and the names of some of his friends and relations. He was not sure what plans the little rat had, but for the time being he seemed content to remain with Cory. The first thing they saw as they approached home was Sunnifa and Cory's heart leapt with joy, even more so when she ran into his arms and kissed him enthusiastically.

'Cory so good to see you, I had begun to worry until Scally arrived and said you were on your way. And you must be Fag,' she said, turning to the rat and giving him a warm smile. 'I believe you saved Cory's life.' Without hesitation she leaned forward and deposited a kiss on his cheek. 'Come,' she said, 'there is much news to tell you.' They followed her through the trees, Cory with mixed feelings of happiness and anxiety, whilst Fag, who had never been kissed in his life before, was in a state of euphoria.

'I don't think you know that you have a sister,' Sunnifa said to Cory as they approached his home. Patience was waiting, a look of pride on her face, although she had acquired some extra worry lines. Bliss was happily occupied fascinated, by a group of worker ants, but when she saw the visitors she tottered on her baby legs back to the nest, where she hid behind her mother, peeping out shyly at them.

'There, there my dear,' soothed Patience, 'this is your big brother, Cory and…?'

'Fag madam, I am happy to make your acquaintance.'

'Go with Sunnifa, my love, and let me talk to Cory.' Patience ushered the tiny hedgehog towards Sunnifa, who took her paw and led her away.

'Such a pretty baby, Mother,' said Cory, 'Well done.'

Patience frowned. 'You must see that there is something wrong with her. Her spines came through a while back but they have not changed colour. She remains white all over and her eyes are pink. I thought there was trouble enough with the twins; I did not think to have another unusual child. I fear it will make her life very difficult.'

'I think not Mother, she is so pretty and if her nature remains as sweet as it is now then no creature could fail to love her. Don't see difficulties where there are none. She will be well loved and protected by all of us, I promise'

'Excuse me for being forward, madam,' Fag said, 'but I have seen that condition before, it does not only affect hedgehogs but all species. Some say it is a blessing from Pan and that these pups are special and I agree. She must remember to keep out of the hot sun and she will need to take more care when hiding from danger. You have a beautiful daughter, be happy and very proud.'

'Yes, thank you, Fag,' Patience smiled, 'I *am* proud of her, my little Bliss; my earth angel.'

Cory and Fag made their way to Bluebell Grove where they were soon joined by Sunnifa, Bugle and Scally. The story of Orva and Trefoil confirmed Cory's anxious feelings and when he heard how Scumble and Sheard had set off on their own into the Dark Wood he cursed his decision to visit Fag's heaven. He had wasted valuable time and who knew what else had gone wrong in the meantime. He fought to keep an optimistic approach in front of the others but he wondered how long he could keep a positive front up. He was relieved therefore when the pressure was taken off him in the shape of Sheard, who came bounding and chattering into the grove.

'Greetings fellow creatures, hail and well met,' the squirrel cried.

'Sheard, good timing!' said Cory, with heartfelt sincerity. 'What news, where is Scumble?' Cory peered around wanting so much to see the little hedgehog with his blackened prickles.

'Left him with Braxton, he's safe enough,' Sheard said seeing Cory's anxious look. 'Using his healing skills to good purpose man, the badger's in the best of paws.' He turned his attention to Fag. 'Greetings young rat, we have heard of your swimming exploits concerning our leader and we thank you.' He looked at the rat long and hard. 'It would seem you have changed camps, I hope we are not harbouring a viper in our nest.'

'That's enough Sheard!' Cory said sharply. 'Now tell us what you've been doing.'

Sheard needed no further encouragement and launched into relaying his meeting with Aldin and company. Cory kept him more or less on the straight and narrow, bringing him back to the point whenever he tried to deviate into the realms of exaggeration and fantasy, so that it was not long before they were all aware of the current situation.

'Aldin requests that you bring reinforcements as soon as possible to rescue Trefoil and Clowes… oh and Vincent too of course.' Sheard finished his narrative breathlessly.

'I'll call another meeting immediately,' said Cory. 'The rest of you go and speak to as many creatures as time will allow. Tell them I'm holding a meeting here first thing tomorrow.' He paused for a moment then added, 'Don't tell them precisely what the meeting is about and let their curiosity bring them here.' They all dispersed quickly and silently, leaving Cory and Fag alone.

'Nothing I can do here at present sir,' Fag said slowly, looking down at the ground. 'I'm sorry about your friends; I'm ashamed of what my colony has become.' He lifted his head and perused Cory's worried face. 'When the time is right and if it will be beneficial sir, I will return to Mad Maggie's so that you will have a friend on the inside.' With a lump in his throat, Cory put a paw on the little rat's shoulder.

'Come,' he said, ' let's go try some recruiting in Whylder Wood.'

***

From her vantage point hidden amongst the tall grass, Neldar watched Cory and Fag make their way up the earth-bank and over the top into Whylder Wood. Neldar was bored; she was bored, bored, bored and pinched with jealousy; bored of her life, restricted to domesticity and playing nursemaid to Bliss; jealous of Sunnifa, her popularity, her never failing good spirits and the mutual love between her and Cory. How Neldar's heart had beat with excitement when she first saw the returning Cory this afternoon, how she had wanted to run and greet him and hold him in her arms. But Sunnifa had got there first and Cory had not even been aware of Neldar's presence. Now she remained hidden, feeling an outcast from the group, excluded from their company and their plans. She refused to return to Patience, it would only mean being lumbered with Bliss again. Neldar did not much like her own company and on a whim decided to track Cory and Fag; it would provide an afternoon's entertainment. She followed their route into Whylder Wood but they had completely disappeared. The wood seemed dim and suffocating compared to her Park Woods' home and she was just debating whether to continue or go back when, who should appear through the undergrowth but Spike.

'Well hello Neldar,' Spike chortled in a rather off-putting way. 'Fancy seeing you here, it must be my lucky day: lucky, lucky, lucky.' He leered at her with eyes that weren't quite focussed and gave her a wink.

'Spike,' she said, feeling confused, repelled and attracted all at the same time. 'Are you alone, where are the three rats and the caterpillar?'

'Oh don't worry about them, sweetie,' slurred Spike. 'They're old and ugly enough to take care of themselves. Now come here to me and see what I've got.'

Neldar giggled but continued to regard him cautiously. Spike took something from his mouth that glinted briefly in the muted sunlight. 'Come on,' he said enticingly, 'I want to show you a little piece of heaven.'

CHAPTER 19

IN AT THE DEEP END

Clowes, followed by the three guard rats entered the cellar through the gap in the wall and took stock of his surroundings. He noted the marble altar with its artefacts of worship on display, in particular the dried head of the unfortunate stoat. He also noted the large stone statue of a shaggy beast wearing a wreath of deadly nightshade on its head. The smell from the pit was less noisome inside but nevertheless it was still prevalent and took on a sickly quality when mixed with other smells of sweat, stale wine and dried blood. In one corner, a priest in ceremonial robes was busy with a group of musicians practising a composition of rhythmic sounds on instruments roughly fashioned from cans, jars and bottles salvaged from rubbish dumps or possibly from the pit itself. The music was primitive but not without a certain charm and under other circumstances, Clowes thought he might well be tempted into dancing to it. The priest stopped conducting when he noticed the guards and the music came to a discordant halt.

'Why do you disturb me?' he said sharply. 'You have no right to come...' His voice trailed off when he saw Clowes.

'Excuse us, Ware,' said the first guard rat, 'this visitor demands to see our leader. He says 'e has important news to impart.'

'Well take him to Baldlice,' snapped Ware. 'You should have gone the other way, don't bring strangers into the cellar again or it will be the worse for you.'

Clowes stepped forward quickly and bowed to Ware. 'My news is for the bird er… Your Grace, the knowledge of her wisdom has spread far; it is *she* whom I have been sent to see.'

Ware wrinkled an already wrinkled face. 'Who has sent you?'

'I have come from a deputation of creatures who live, for the most part, in Park Woods. There is growing concern over the pollution of the stream and the poisoning of the surrounding vegetation.'

'Hummph!' grunted Ware. 'Can't see it's any business of theirs. We are perfectly capable of handling the problem ourselves.'

'Even so,' Clowes stressed, 'the problem is spreading and areas other than your colony are becoming infected. If I do not return with an acceptable answer you will shortly be receiving many more visitors.'

Ware waved his paw theatrically towards the cellar steps. 'The bird is sick; take him to Baldlice,' he ordered the guard rats. 'And do not disturb me again.'

As they reached the top of the steps a female rat appeared and bobbed her head to the lead guard rat. 'Iya Nla is awake and wishes to question the visitor,' she said.

The guard rat seemed undecided. 'My orders are ter take 'im ter Baldlice,' he said through gritted teeth.

'Baldlice cannot be found; I was sent to find him only a few minutes ago but to no avail.' The female rat answered with bowed head. 'Iya Nla will see him instead.' The guard rat looked as if he was about to argue the case when one of his companions reminded him that they had left their post outside and should return promptly; so somewhat grudgingly the largest of the guards escorted Clowes into the swift's room and took up a position by the door alongside the regular duty guard. The other two guards returned to their post outside after ordering the female rat to continue looking for Baldlice.

'And if you still can't find 'im, report to another priest. I'm blowed if I'm goin' ter take the rap fer allowin' a stranger on the premises!'

As soon as he was left alone Clowes wasted no time in approaching the swift. He saw that she was indeed very sick but although her eyes were dim they radiated intelligence and compassion. She saw before her an honest rat, strong in both mind and body and she clutched at what remained of hope that her prayers had been answered. It was with a great sense of relief that she found Clowes' mind receptive and his thoughts easy to interpret. Information was exchanged between them relatively quickly. Trefoil sat resignedly at the back of the room within an eight pointed star that had been roughly drawn out on the floor. He was tethered to the ground by his leg. He regarded the animated communication with mounting excitement until he was distracted by something tickling his chin and recognised Vincent the caterpillar who had come to rest on the hedgehog's snout.

'Well hallelujah!' whispered Trefoil, with an eye on the guards at the door, 'the bleedin' cavalry's arrived!'

'Shsh, shut up and listen,' snapped the little bug. Trefoil listened as though his life depended upon it, which of course it did.

It wasn't long before a commotion outside the door heralded two more guards, but these were certainly of a higher rank and looked much meaner. They entered the room and demanded that Clowes accompany them to be questioned by the priests. The swift nodded her head briefly in assent and he followed his escort out of the room.

The guards kept tight lipped as they walked along the corridor and refused to be drawn into any conversation by Clowes so he used the time by looking about him; noting a large crumbling staircase and a number of rooms, some with doors in various disrepair and others open to the elements. The house smelled of damp in addition to the all pervading pit fumes; but all in all it was the kind of building much favoured by rats. He was led into a large room containing two internal doors both shut, where a giant of a guard rat – a hulk of muscle and sinew, was standing with his back against one of them; seated in the centre of the room around a large flat stone that served as a table, were four priests recognisable as such by their cloaks of dried rat skins.

'Ah,' said one, 'our visitor. Allow me to welcome you to our humble abode. May I inquire what exactly we can do for you?'

Clowes surveyed them all in turn, refusing to be intimidated. 'As I explained to one of your colleagues in the cellar, I represent the inhabitants of Park Woods and parts of Whylder Wood. We are concerned about the poisons coming from the pit close by. The poisons are spreading and causing pollution in the stream which, as you must know, eventually runs into the River Rushlep and beyond.'

'We are addressing the problem,' one of the priests said. 'The stream has been dammed and we are looking into the possibility of diverting the waters further up; bypassing the pit area and channelling them back into the dry stream bed nearer to Park Woods.'

'That sounds like a major construction project,' Clowes replied. 'Who considers this feasible; are any of you engineers?' He was met by stony stares, so decided to plough on. 'Let me fetch assistance from other woodland creatures; many heads could prove better than just a few when it comes to sharing knowledge.' He smiled encouragingly around the table. One of the priests stood up and pushed its head piece back from its forehead so that its face could be seen. She was a female.

'You are our cousin and in that respect – and in that respect only – we have allowed you into the colony. It is ludicrous to suppose that we would willingly allow our privacy to be violated by creatures that are not even of the rat family. We are responsible for the welfare of the old and infirm; the sick and the dying and for the pups which are the lifeline and future of the colony. Do you think that we would invite the rank and file of predators into our midst? If so you are more foolish than I first imagined.'

'Forgive me,' said Clowes. 'Perhaps we could come to some agreement as to another meeting place: a mutually acceptable one.'

'Enough!' cried another priest, 'We waste time bandying words with this newcomer...'

'Come, come,' said a third in silky tones. It turned to face Clowes. 'We must not panic unnecessarily; perhaps after all it is Pan himself who has provided the gift of this pit for our use. Indeed some of its contents have healing powers, it is not all bad. I have an abundant faith in Nature herself: given time she will learn to counter the poisonous elements. Those of us who are strong enough to remain here and survive will breed immunity in our pups. The new race will be stronger, perhaps invincible. Go back to your friends and reassure them that we have everything in hand here. It is understandable that they have been concerned but tell them there is no need to worry further. We have a capable engineer to divert the stream,' he indicated a priest at the other end of the table, 'and our breeding programme comes on apace. We will soon have ample workers for the manual labour.'

'Perhaps before you return you would like to see our nursery?' the female priest turned to the other priests for their agreement.

'If it will put your mind at rest we would be proud to show you what we have achieved recently against all odds,' said the silky toned voice again. 'Scabious,' he called the head guard rat, 'take this rat...er...' he looked at Clowes, 'I fear we are unaware of your name good sir.'

'It's Clowes... er... Reverend and I would be honoured to be shown around.'

'Scur, open the door,' said the priest.

The huge guard rat pushed heavily on the door which opened wide enough to allow Clowes, Scabious and the priest to pass through. Inside were a great number of rat pups at different stages of development; from those just weaned to others on the verge of puberty. The sound was deafening but as soon as the visitors entered, silence fell abruptly. The room was big with a high vaulted ceiling, but there were no windows and only a little light came in through a gap in the roof. Fallen masonry lined the walls but nothing else could be seen, save for dozens of dark furred bodies. The floor was carpeted with them and many sat atop the rubble of bricks around the walls. The light filtering through the roof revealed rotted, exposed beams thick with young rats; their long tails hanging pendulously down into the room. It stank and Clowes fought hard against putting his paw over his nose.

'It's incredible,' he managed to say, 'however have you done it?'

'We have worked hard – yes,' replied the priest. 'The females have been most co-operative and are willing to produce more litters than is usually expected. But there... unusual problems beget unusual resolutions. Perhaps now you will think better of us, Clowes. We have been innovative in maintaining the size and strength of the colony. We are confident we will overcome the problem of the polluted stream.' He smiled imperiously.

'I notice that some of the pups are deformed,' said Clowes, 'presumably that is because of the poisonous atmosphere and the foodstuffs that have become tainted?'

'Indeed,' answered the priest, 'but as you can see, deformed rats are in much lower numbers than healthy ones and the deformities are slight – not a problem.'

'I am amazed that you are able to collect enough food for all of them. They seem well fed, how do you manage it?'

'Ah,' the priest replied, 'that *was* a difficulty at first but we put our minds to solving it successfully. Ingenuity you know; ingenuity and hard work, that's the answer.' He laid a paw on Clowes' shoulder, 'Now I think it is time to be going. Your friends will be wondering about you.'

They retraced their steps back into the other room and the priest gave orders to Scabious and another guard rat, Scarlic, to escort Clowes off the premises.

'I wonder... Reverend... if the young hedgehog I saw in Iya Nla's room, might accompany me back. I know his family and they would greatly appreciate his return. Please accept my apologies on their behalf if he has been a nuisance to you, but you know what the young and foolhardy are like; always getting in the way and poking their noses where they are not wanted,' Clowes said with a chuckle.

The priest smiled politely and ushered Clowes out of the room. 'I only wish that I could comply with your request,' he said, 'but I am afraid it is out of my paws. It is for the head priest to make that decision and I am afraid that Baldlice is not available at present. The hedgehog in question transgressed the rules of the colony and as a consequence was due to be put to death. Iya Nla – the Great Mother – however, believes he is a prophet from a Moon Goddess called Ishtar... I know nothing of these matters you understand... but it has been decreed that he will make reparation by showing us his powers at a ceremony tomorrow night.'

'But surely this is too harsh?' Clowes argued. 'He is a youngster, how could he transgress the rules so badly that he faces possible death? What rules can these be?'

The priest's smile faded: 'The rules that keep the colony running smoothly; strict rules that govern a large number of rats. Without that structure we would risk anarchy.' He paused and called to the guards, 'I will say my farewell to you, please allow Scabious and Scarlic to see you off the premises.'

With that, the priest turned on his heel and left. Clowes had no choice but to march along the corridor between the two guards. As before they refused to reply to any remark he made and so he spent the time going over in his mind what he had just seen and heard. He was so deep in his thoughts that when Scabious stopped abruptly he knocked into him and had just opened his mouth to ask where they were when something crashed into the back of his head and he blacked out.

***

Back in the nursery, Atol pushed his head piece back and surveyed the other priests. 'Let me confirm that we are all agreed this rat should not be released for the present. Has anyone changed their mind?'

'We are agreed, Atol,' said Gram. 'But it's likely if we keep him too long we will be besieged by his friends.'

'It seems to me that he is a subtle rat,' said Wimund, 'I am not convinced that we can believe all that he says. I cannot envisage a collection of different species banding together to fight a common cause. He has exaggerated the numbers for his own purpose. In truth I think that his friends are few and do not include creatures other than his own kin.'

'Hmm,' Atol considered, 'and yet he did seem genuinely interested in the hedgehog's welfare. But there are ways and means of getting round this... we will cross that bridge when we come to it. And talking of bridges,' Atol looked at Holt, 'where are we in *those* plans engineer?' Muted laughter greeted this and everyone visibly relaxed.

Much later when the other priests had gone, Atol sat alone reflecting on the day's events. A noise at the door made him look up as a female rat entered breathlessly. Atol stood up and held out his arms: 'Luthian my dear, what a pleasant surprise. Come, I have something for you.'

Luthian crossed the floor with downcast eyes. 'My Lord,' she whispered.

CHAPTER 20

CLOWES KEEPS HIS HEAD ABOVE WATER

Clowes awoke with a thumping headache and a feeling of disorientation. He was lying on the ground in a cell-like room: floors and walls of concrete and no window. There was a door in front of him but on investigation it proved to be locked or at least wedged shut. He groaned, of all the idiotic things he had done in his life this probably capped the lot. In truth, he had been taken unawares; he had become complacent and let his guard down. Now what? Was he in line to be the next sacrifice? Were he and Trefoil to be used as bait to trap the friends who would inevitably come to attempt rescue? He felt that they were dealing with lies and treachery everywhere. That one priest in particular was not to be trusted, he felt sure. How did the saying go, "one may smile and smile and be a villain"? Yes he had been made vulnerable and he must think clearly and try to improve his position or he would be no help to any creature. The swift, Trefoil and Vincent had their brief and so had Aldin and Heaton. He must not jeopardise their stories; somehow he must align himself with the priests. He heard voices outside, the door scraped slowly and noisily ajar: he had a visitor.

A rat entered and stared impassively at him. 'Well Clowes, I must apologise for my overly enthusiastic guards. It appears they suspected you of initiating a rescue attempt on the hedgehog and as a result took rash and inappropriate action. I can only reiterate my apologies and assure you that the guards in question have been severely reprimanded.'

Clowes immediately entered into the spirit of the falsehood. 'I have spent an uncomfortable night under your roof...er... Reverend, through no fault of my own; but I will accept your apology. Erm... I assume you are the priest I spoke to last night? It is difficult to judge without your ceremonial robe.'

'My name is Atol and I am a priest yes – but I am not the head priest. Baldlice seems to have gone to ground somewhere at the moment. I think, on reflection, that it would be wiser to prolong your stay with us, until there is an opportunity to discuss you and your friend's concerns with him on his return. I hope this will not prove too inconvenient to you? As recompense I would like to extend an invitation to you for tonight's ceremony. I am sure you are most interested in how and what the hedgehog will prophesy.'

'Indeed,' Clowes replied. 'I have heard a little of the Moon Goddess Ishtar and her prowess. It will be very interesting to hear her speak through the mouth of a hedgehog. Perhaps she will have some advice on how to counteract the poisons of the pit.'

'My feeling is that the pit is a gift from Pan,' said Atol. 'I cannot see that Ishtar would deliberately set herself against the Great God.'

'Perhaps not,' mused Clowes, 'after all she is not so great herself: she was bested by Ganesh.'

'Ganesh? Who or what is Ganesh? You speak in riddles!'

'Why Ganesh is our very own god,' said Clowes. 'He is God of the Rats; I am surprised you are not aware of him.'

'Never heard of him,' snapped Atol. 'Perhaps he is a figment of your imagination.'

'I assure you Atol, where I come from the stories of Ganesh are well known. If I could have a little refreshment I would be happy to tell you about him.' Clowes made himself more comfortable on the floor and gazed up at the rat. Atol gazed back for a few seconds before calling out to the guard to bring food and water. He was inclined to dismiss Clowes' story telling as just that, a ruse to waste time and ingratiate himself with the priests. However, the idea of having a God of Rats was an intriguing one and if believable could be used to good purpose in future. Atol decided to encourage Clowes, at least for the present.

When the refreshment had been brought and Clowes had had his fill, he proceeded to recount the tale of Ganesh, with his elephant-like head and his quarrel with Ishtar the Moon Goddess. At the end of the story, Atol frowned and stroked the end of his snout.

'So what you are saying,' he said, 'is that Ganesh is more powerful than Ishtar?'

'It would seem so,' Clowes answered. 'The curse he put on her to wax and wane remains still. She has not broken it and has not returned to her former glory of shining her full light every night. But of course we do not know for certain; it may be that she *chooses* to wax and wane. She may prefer it.' Clowes chuckled, 'It certainly gives her a well earned break. I suspect it is because of her predilection to wax and wane that she is known as the Goddess of Reincarnation – that she appears to die but can then come back to life. Whatever the reason she is certainly no creature's fool.'

'And Ganesh is?' said Atol sharply.

'Not at all; in fact he is known to have great wisdom.' Atol nodded to him to go on. 'Well,' continued Clowes, 'the story goes that Ganesh had a brother, Kartikeya. Their parents showed them both a marvellous fruit. Hidden inside was the nectar of supreme knowledge and of immortality. To get the fruit the brothers had to compete. The winner would be the one who could run three times round the world and come back first. Kartikeya left immediately, flying on his peacock. Ganesh was overweight and knew that he and his rat could not beat Kartikeya; so instead he waited upon his parents, showing great respect and devotion. When they asked him why he did not start his journey round the word, he replied: "My parents are the whole universe, in them is located the world – I do not need to go further than where they are". And so,' finished Clowes, 'his parents were so impressed that Ganesh won the contest and the fruit; proving at the same time the importance of cleverness and quick wits against speed and physical strength.'

Atol smiled a crooked smile. 'A lesson that *you* have truly learned my friend, I think. But I will give you the benefit of the doubt. It is a good tale and one I would want to believe. It illustrates clever trickery that Pan himself would be proud of. It would seem then that whilst Ishtar may have the power of reincarnation, her adversary has the power of supreme knowledge and immortality. I think therefore that Pan *would* favour Ganesh over Ishtar in any competition.' He called for the guard to open the door. 'Make yourself comfortable, Clowes. A guard will come tonight to escort you to the ceremony and I will have you placed at my side.' He paused, 'You have gone some way in persuading me of your good intentions. Do not disillusion me.' With that he turned tail and departed.

***

Baldlice shifted his aching limbs on the makeshift bed of dried grass and leaves and wearily opened his one good eye. He had lost track of time and realised he was not aware of whether it was day or night. How long he had been in this half comatose state he did not know. He realised that the bird must be anxiously awaiting his return but he lacked the energy or indeed the desire to attempt getting up. A number of empty silver paper wrappers surrounded his bed and he wondered how they had got there. He had no recollection of having made any recent journeys into the pit and yet his pain was only a dull ache, suggesting he had taken medication within the last few hours. In fact the wooziness he felt indicated he had taken more of the powders than was necessary. *Was he losing his memory? Was he losing his mind?* A slight noise behind him and a shadow on the wall told him he was not alone. He tried to speak but his throat was so dry he failed to utter a sound and the effort to continue trying was too much. He heard the rustle of paper and a paw appeared briefly on his sighted side. It placed another parcel of medication within his reach and withdrew. Baldlice held his breath and waited but nothing else happened and after a few minutes he had to conclude that he was alone once more.

CHAPTER 21

SPIKE FINDS LOVE

S pike and Neldar lay in the late afternoon sunshine that filtered softly through the dense canopy of leaves in Whylder Wood. Every so often Neldar giggled and gave Spike a playful kick, but they were both too tired to resume any further lovemaking. Although their bodies were pleasantly fatigued however, their heads were busy and thoughts whirled around inexorably. Neldar loved the effect that the white powder had given her; never had she ever felt so excited, relaxed or abandoned in the whole of her short life. It had taken away all her self doubts and anxieties and left her, for a while, without a care in the world; she had experienced the euphoric feeling that nothing ever really mattered. Her earlier longings for Cory were currently obliterated and her lovemaking with Spike had given her new energy and a sense of well being. She believed that she had found the answer to life and was amazed that it all could be so easy. She rolled over and tickled Spike on the belly.

'Gerrof,' he mumbled. Spike's thoughts were a confusing mixture of shades both light and dark. He felt elation, which was to be expected; but surprisingly he also felt regret, although he could not quite imagine why. He was also feeling the effects of withdrawal symptoms from the powder. In his bid to make Neldar receptive to him he had rashly given her all of what had been left of the powder. It had certainly done the trick but it meant that his current craving had to go unfed and as a result he was becoming irritable. He was beginning to find Neldar's company tiresome.

'No need to be so disagreeable,' Neldar retorted. 'So it's true what they say then.'

'What's true?' Spike rolled over with his back to her.

'You've got your own way and now you're not interested in me any more,' Neldar feigned a little hiccup and a tearful voice.

Spike sat up abruptly and heaved a sigh. 'Look, don't start picking on me. I've been on a long journey and faced danger to get that powder. I'm tired… that's all.' He lay back down and closed his eyes.

'Well, it's funny you weren't tired earlier on,' argued Neldar. 'You weren't tired at all!' she muttered resentfully. After a long silence she said, 'I don't suppose you know you've got a new sister now, do you?' Spike didn't answer; in truth his latest adventures and the aftermath of the powder had left him exhausted. The news of a new sibling did not fill him with joy, just resignation that his place in the pecking order would inevitably be that much further down. He heard Neldar get up and sensed her shadow as she stood over him. 'I'm going,' she said, 'it's boring here.'

He felt that he should say something so managed to mumble, 'See you later,' before falling into a fitful sleep.

When he woke it had grown chill and Neldar was nowhere to be seen. He was stiff, his head ached and his eyes smarted; he felt that the best thing to do was to return home and rest up as best he could. He made his way over the earth mound down into Park Woods and home to a much relieved Patience, where he was given a warm welcome. Bliss lay fast asleep in a comfortable nest and Spike found himself intrigued by the little white hog. His eyes were constantly drawn to her throughout his conversation with Patience and Sunnifa, who had come to give him the news of Cory's meeting. Under the soothing influence of Sunnifa and of his home, Spike found his earlier irritation slipping away. He decided to attempt to sleep off his hangover and then offer his services to Cory in the morning.

He awoke early and felt somewhat better, although his eyes were very watery and his head still a little muzzy. He lifted his snout and sniffed the morning air; it promised to be another fine spring day. As he gazed about he was surprised to notice Bliss curled up alongside him, sleeping soundly like the proverbial baby that she was. Spike sincerely hoped that her attachment to him was not going to prove burdensome. He had experienced enough of that sort of responsibility looking after Scumble. Nevertheless, the heat of her body next to his and her innocent belief that she was safe in his shadow gave him a warm glow, which he could not deny made him feel good. He assumed that Cory's meeting would be held in Bluebell Grove as before and decided to start straightaway before he changed his mind; he could breakfast when he got there. He uncurled as quietly as he could and with rather stiff legs made his way towards the trees.

'Wait fo' me, wait fo' me Thpike,' and there was Bliss; first running by his side then darting in front almost tripping him up.

Spike stopped. 'Now look, Bliss,' he said gruffly, 'you can't come with me, I'm going on a long journey with Cory and you are too little to come.' He peered down at her and tried to smile kindly. She smiled back with such a trusting, sunny disposition, that Spike felt a genuine affection flood through him. Why, he was amazed — he loved his little sister.

'Come and have some breakfast with me first then,' he said. 'But we mustn't be long or Mother will be worried.' Bliss smiled even more and the tear that had lodged in the corner of one eye trickled down her cheek and was quickly wiped away.

'Yeth pleath Thpike,' she said.

So they went through the trees together and found a warm hollow covered in flowering wood sorrel where Bliss sat down, whilst Spike collected a number of tit bits for their meal. It was pleasant eating together and sharing the choicest pieces. They played the game of "one for you, two for me", which had Bliss rolling around in glee and laughing a high tinkling little laugh that made Spike laugh out loud too. Afterwards they lay relaxed, content in each other's company. It was still early and the woodland basked in a quiet, still peacefulness. In the silence Spike sensed an all pervading watchfulness; but it was a benign watchfulness, that gave him no cause for concern. He felt that he and Bliss were wrapped in a protective bubble of time and for a brief moment all was well with the world.

'Tell me a thtory Thpike,' the little voice broke in on his thoughts. Now Spike was no story teller but he wanted to please Bliss, so he cast his mind back to when Patience had sometimes found the time and inclination to send her sons off to sleep by telling a story in quiet, soporific voice.

'Did you know that the fox is very clever and knows many things?' he asked the little hedgehog.

Bliss gazed expectantly at her brother. 'No Thpike, go on.'

'Well he does,' Spike continued, 'and the hedgehog knows only one thing – but that is enough.' He smiled at Bliss and they both settled down comfortably against a tree root. 'Now the fox was a wily old creature and he was for ever tricking the farmer, getting into the poultry yard and stealing the chickens. He was always boasting to other creatures how clever he was, cleverer than all the rest of them put together. One day the hedgehog asked if he might go with the fox to the farm and watch how he managed to get into the poultry yard. Now usually the fox would not want any other creature to learn from his tricks, but he thought the hedgehog so stupid that he did not consider him to be a threat, so he said that he could accompany him. But the fox was not aware that the farmer had grown so angry about losing many of his favourite chickens that he had dug a deep pit all around the poultry yard and covered it with small branches and leaves. As the fox and the hedgehog cautiously approached the chicken house they heard a creaking and a cracking under their paws and before you could say "Pan in a predicament", the branches of the trap gave way and they fell into the bottom of the pit.'

'Ooooh!' said Bliss softly and she placed her little paw on top of Spike's.

Spike continued, ' "Well this is a sorry state we are in," said the hedgehog, "the sides of the pit are too steep to climb, but I am sure that you have a brilliant plan to get us out." But the fox only looked bewildered and when the hedgehog continued to press him for his escape plan, he turned sulky and refused to speak. After a while the hedgehog said that he felt sick; in fact he felt so sick that at any moment he would have to vomit into the pit and he apologised in advance for any inconvenience caused. The fox in his disgust picked up the hog by his snout and hurled him out of the pit. The hedgehog curled into a ball, and on landing, remained unhurt as he was protected by his spines. The hedgehog called down his thanks to the fox and pretended to make his way home, chuckling as he went. The poor fox called out to him asking for help, pleading for advice; so the hedgehog told him to lie still and pretend to be dead. After a while the farmer came to see what he had caught in his trap and he was very pleased to see that he had caught the chicken thief. The fox held his breath and did not move and so the farmer thought that he had broken his neck in the fall. He grasped him by the leg and threw him into the bushes. When the farmer had gone the fox got up and ran home. He was very grateful to the hedgehog and ever since the fox and the hedgehog have been friends.'

Bliss smiled up at her brother and placed a little heart shaped wood sorrel leaf on the back of his paw.

'So there you are!' Spike and Bliss looked up to see Neldar standing there. 'I've been looking for you everywhere.'

'Well we're here as you can see,' said Spike, feeling his happiness slip away. 'Thought I'd spend some time with my sister,' he gave Bliss' paw a squeeze.

'You'll be late for the meeting,' Nelda remarked, looking behind her towards Bluebell Grove. She stood blocking out the early morning sun and the two on the ground were suddenly bathed in shadow.

Spike got up. He felt anxious and uncertain. 'Must go,' he muttered. 'Grateful if you would take Bliss back to Patience.'

'Now look here!' Neldar frowned, 'What if I want to come to the meeting as well?'

'Do you?' asked Spike with sinking heart.

Neldar regarded him haughtily. 'Shan't go where I'm not wanted,' she eventually replied. She waited for Spike to invite her, but when he didn't she continued, 'Well off you go then, don't let me spoil your fun!'

Spike glanced in the direction of Bluebell Grove; it seemed imperative that he went as soon as possible. 'It won't be fun, Neldar,' he said as kindly as he could. 'Cory is getting an army together; they will be expected to fight if needs be. Please look after Bliss for me.'

Neldar looked down and studied her toes. 'Fine,' she said and without another word to Spike she called to Bliss and started walking away.

Spike bent and kissed Bliss tenderly on the cheek.

'So there you are... I've been looking for you everywhere!'

'Now be a good girl and do what Neldar says. I will come to see you as soon as I get back.' He watched the little figure run after Neldar then turned and hurried towards Bluebell Grove, hoping that he would not be too late.

Neldar was furious, she would make Spike pay for his disinterest. How dare he use her and then throw her aside like some half digested, unappetising bug. She felt sick; not just because of his coldness towards her but because she missed how the white powder had made her feel. She wanted to feel like that again. She knew that if she could only feel the confidence and elation she had felt the day before then she could win Spike back. She stopped abruptly with the exciting thought that, even better, it might be possible to make Cory feel like that about her. Now that *would* be something to aim for. She smiled to herself and then became aware of Bliss sitting at her side looking up at her.

'Where we goin' Neldy?' she asked.

'The name's Neldar,' Neldar snapped. '*I'm* going to Whylder Wood to follow Cory and Spike,' she heard herself say.

'Thpike said to take me home. Mother doesn't know where I am. Let's go home Neldy.'

'Look!' shrieked Neldar, 'We'll go home later, see! I'm going up stream and...' Neldar paused and gazed hard at the little white hoglet, 'Spike said you are to do what I say – didn't he?'

'Yeth,' said Bliss softly.

'So come on then, we're going this way.' Neldar led the

way towards the earth bank that would lead them down to the stream. She figured that if they followed its course upwards they would come to the pit where Spike had found the white powder. With her head full of whirling thoughts, Neldar picked her way carefully between the roots and brambles whilst Bliss did her best to follow.

***

When Spike arrived in Bluebell Grove a number of creatures were already there and Cory was in full flow explaining the current situation at Mad Maggie's. Sheard saw Spike and beckoned him over. He went and stood by Sunnifa and Bugle and looked around at the crowd. There were a dozen hedgehogs; about the same number of squirrels; eight stoats and four weasels. Bede was looking pleased with himself: he had managed to bring one other male rabbit, introduced as Dering, a big muscular buck who looked as if he would be useful in a fight. He had also co-opted a number of female rabbits, as does were deemed to be the best diggers. A scrawny rat stood at Cory's side and the branches of the nearest trees were occupied by a good number of birds; most of them crows who looked upon Scally as their leader. No Braxton and no Freeman. All in all Spike thought it a poor turnout and it could hardly be called an army. He remembered the size and aggression of the guard rats at the pit and felt this paltry gathering was a lost cause.

'How strong are the opposition?' a weasel called out. 'How many of the beggars are we likely ter have to fight?'

'I have to be honest with you and say that at this stage we have no idea of numbers,' Cory replied and was met with a hubbub of noise. He raised his voice and cut in quickly, 'Whatever the numbers it is very likely that most of them will be sick and weak by now. I do not envisage any fighting – we go to negotiate; to parley and seek an agreed resolution to our shared problems. Our numbers will show solidarity. They will see that many different species in Park Woods and Whylder Wood all feel the same way.'

'Bugger talking, we want revenge for Orva!' shouted one of the stoats and the others cried, 'Aye – we'll take the beggers down for Orva!'

'You will fight only if you have to,' Cory said in a quiet but firm voice that carried across the grove. 'You will fight when I say so and not before. If we cannot agree on this you can leave now. Orva was a brave, courageous stoat and we honour her.' He paused and surveyed them all. 'The rat colony has three more of our comrades: Trefoil the hedgehog, Clowes the riverbank rat and Vincent the caterpillar. It must be our priority to recover these three creatures unharmed. I think the best way is through negotiation first; backed up by a show of physical strength. At this moment we do not know how the leaders will receive us, let us not be the first to attempt violence.'

'Orva's death was violent,' cried another stoat. 'How can we have peaceful negotiations with rats who cold bloodily slit another creature's throat?'

Fag stepped forward and spoke in a small but earnest voice. 'It's true that some rats have become vicious and cruel, but we are not all like that. Some of us have escaped and there have been others who have lost their lives trying to escape. We truly regret the manner of Orva's death.'

Cory held up a paw as noise erupted again. 'Fag is right; we do not know how many rats were involved in the killing. It may have only been one or two. At this moment we cannot penalise the whole colony for the actions of a few. Let us try to get more information before we charge in recklessly.'

'And how d'we know we don't 'ave a spy in our midst?' a weasel shouted, pointing at Fag.

'Because I say so,' replied Cory firmly. 'As I explained to you earlier, Fag has proved his loyalty and I will vouch for him.'

Bugle raised his paw. 'I vote we do as Cory says, but I also vote that we go without any further delay. Perhaps Trefoil is facing his ordeal of prophecy at this very moment and we stand here arguing.'

Cory turned to face the agitated hedgehog. 'I'm pretty sure that Trefoil will not be tested until there is enough moonlight to ensure the right atmosphere. If Trefoil is to speak for the goddess, then Ishtar must be seen to be present in some form.' He paused, 'And let us not forget the bird, it would seem that she is on our side and if that is true then all is not lost.'

'Let's go!' cried Sheard.

'Let's go!' squawked Scally.

'Let's go,' said Cory.

Spike looked at the little heart shaped leaf he had been clutching in his paw; he raised it to his snout and gently breathed in the scents of a beautiful memory. With a sigh of resignation he followed the raggle-taggle army out of the grove.

***

Along the stream bed further into Whylder Wood the ground was damp and boggy. The dense vegetation screened out the sunlight and the place where Neldar had chosen to hide was dark and gloomy. There was no bird sound, no sound at all; even the stream had run dry leaving the wood eerily silent. A dank, musty smell pervaded the still air and altogether Neldar was beginning to think she had been rash in starting this journey. She felt she was being watched by something unfriendly, but whenever she turned suddenly to catch it out, all she saw was the same desolate view of dark crowded trees and heavy tangles of ferns and brambles wet with the cold morning dew. She shivered. If she hadn't wanted another taste of the powder so badly she would have turned in her tracks and made for home, but the magical powder now loomed so large in her thoughts that she had little room for anything else. She pressed herself against the trunk of the willow tree and waited, hardly daring to breathe. Every few minutes she could hear Bliss calling, but as time passed the sound grew fainter, the little hog was travelling out of ear shot.

'Neldy…Neldy…where are you? I'm lost Neldy… where are you?' The cry became a wail that gradually disappeared into the distance. 'N..e..l..d..y…!'

Neldar sunk to the ground with her back to the tree and covered her face with her paws. What was she doing? How could she justify her behaviour? What would Spike think of her? What would Cory? The atmosphere of the Dark Wood became oppressive and the presence she felt intensified to something malevolent. She peered out apprehensively between her paws. But the lure of the white powder was becoming too much to bear. She would resume her initial plan: collect some more powder and then, when she felt more confident she would search the wood for Bliss and take her home. It wouldn't be too difficult, how far could a baby hog get? No doubt she would find her curled up asleep eventually, no worse for her adventure. Neldar got up and set her snout northwards; she would continue following the stream bed until she reached Mad Maggie Minchin's.

CHAPTER 22

REFLECTIONS OF THE NOT SO GREAT & GOOD

The priest stood and stared at himself in the Spirit of Self-Perception. The mirror reflected back a tall, straight-backed, well-built rat, an imposing rat he thought; one to be reckoned with. He smiled and pulled back the headpiece. Atol had always been a handsome rat but he considered that the ceremonial cloak and the status that Head Priest of the nursery had conferred upon him had both added to his good looks. He loved the power it gave him: the power to influence, the power to manipulate. He would not relinquish that – never – there was nothing he wouldn't do to get what he wanted. Everything was going his way, he felt invincible. The bird was on her last legs and it wouldn't be long before they could hold a burial service for her. He would ensure it was a sumptuous affair; a memorable occasion for the rank and file to appreciate and it would serve to elevate his position even more. He turned his head and looked up at the balcony where part of the nest was just visible. The bird no longer had the strength to raise herself and look down into the cellar without help. Atol turned back to the mirror with a sly grin. He had seen to it that her helpers had been depleted. Baldlice was now a gibbering wreck thanks to Atol's intervention into the old rat's medication. For days now he had been fed a high strength mixture of powders which had rendered him useless. And the lovely Luthian, he had her well and truly in his pocket. There wasn't much she wouldn't do now for the promise of more powder. He made a mental note to examine Luthian; she should be ready to pup soon and he would need to make contingencies for the birth of the litter. It must be a private affair where he could keep his progeny safe and secure from potential enemies. He planned to establish a dynasty where his name and his deeds would be remembered for generations to come.

He gazed at himself in the mirror again and smirked; yes he was a force to be reckoned with. He felt only contempt for the other priests, they were all weak. Ware had become obsessed with his music and disregarded everything else going on around him. Wimund had acquired religious mania. It was incredible to him that for all her intellectual abilities she showed complete naivety and gullibility in her belief in the powers of the Sacred Stone; it impaired her judgement and she had become a pain to work with. Gram might be physically strong but he had no brain and was easily manipulated. He and Earle had opposed Atol on many occasions but since Earle had been disposed of, Gram had meekly come on side. Atol gave a fond glance to the empty spot on the altar where the Spirit of the Impaler usually lay and a frisson of lustful excitement flowed through his body. It was an aphrodisiac – to determine who should live and who should die: that was the ultimate power.

His nursery project was progressing well with the help of Scabious. Scarlic and Scur needed watching, they were prone to act instinctively; without orders at times, but their loyalty to him was in no doubt. With due consideration Atol believed there was no other creature intelligent or perceptive enough to recognise his true nature. The bird suspected him, he was aware of that, but she was in no position to do anything about it now. Just the one helper left: the female rat Myrtle, who was less than nothing! Of course there was always Holt. Atol had come to no final conclusion about Holt. He was affable enough and clever too; perhaps clever enough not to attempt to stand in Atol's way. Holt may well prefer to keep his head down and go along the path of least resistance. Atol frowned, it angered him that he was unsure about Holt; he did not fully trust him and yet there was no evidence to indicate why. Perhaps it was because he felt envious of Holt's obvious popularity within the colony. Atol shrugged and dismissed this thought with the contempt it deserved. What was popularity compared with power – nothing! No, he could deal with Holt if and when the time came.

He was left with the one major dilemma that he had and that was how he viewed the intruder, Clowes. Now there was a rat that showed both intelligence and quick wits. A rat that might be of good use to Atol to bring about all that he planned. Or he might prove his downfall. Yes he had mixed feelings about this rat and he was prepared to reserve judgement on him for the time being. One thing he was certain of was that he coveted the rat's coat. Clowes was half a head taller than Atol and his pelt was thick with an enviable sheen to it. It would be far grander than his current one. It had been his idea to use ceremonial cloaks in the first place and a stroke of genius to use the pelts of dead rats. Dead rats were plentiful and even if they weren't they could always be acquired easily enough. How simple it had been to hoodwink the other priests. He delighted in the knowledge that he could manipulate their thinking so easily to the point where some could not recall who had first come up with the idea and some, in their misplaced arrogance, believed themselves to be the initiator. Atol preened and almost purred with pleasure; how Clowes' pelt would distinguish him above the other priests; what status it would confer. It would ease his way into being accepted as High Priest once they were rid of Baldlice. He looked into the mirror again and imagined the shining pelt over his shoulders with the long tail hanging heavily behind; the distinctive headpiece fitting closely over his skull: regal, majestic. He was tempted but he would bide his time; he would give the captured rat the benefit of the doubt for now.

Atol had recently taken to wearing a wrist decoration. It had been brought to him after a foraging raid and he had wanted it as soon as he set eyes on it. It shimmered and sparkled as it caught the light and it seemed most precious to him. Luthian had devised a way for it to be worn on his wrist and it fitted him well. He held it up to the mirror and saw once again how it suited him. With

Clowes' pelt he would make an inspiring figure at future ceremonies. That was something to look forward to. In the meantime there was tonight's ceremony to prepare for – the testing of Trefoil. Atol did not know whether he wanted the hog to prove himself or to fail. He was ambivalent about it; a cruel smile played around his mouth, either way would be exciting. He gave one last affectionate look at the things on the altar and, as he made his way out of the cellar, he gave an irreverent pat on the leonine snout of the Spirit of the Sacred Stone.

CHAPTER 23

TREFOIL & THE MOON GODDESS

The party was well underway when Clowes was led into the cellar, sandwiched between Scabious and Scarlic. He was placed next to Atol at the altar, who acknowledged him with a curt nod. Ware was on his podium conducting the band. The band now consisted of ten prodigious musicians; playing an assortment of timpani and percussion – empty vessels which had been refined into acceptable musical instruments by adding the contents of water, earth and stones. There was also some innovative, if roughly made, wooden frames with dried rat pelts stretched tightly over them and the cellar now throbbed with the beat of African drums. Ware was in his element; he was the maestro; lord of the dance; a musician extraordinaire. Forget religious altars, craven images or gods and goddesses; forget the presence of other priests, Iya Nla or the hedgehog; they were all secondary diversions. The Muskrat Ramblers took centre stage and Ware gloried in the fact that he could turn his back both legitimately and disdainfully on all other things.

Clowes noted that the red velvet cloth had been taken down from the wall and now covered the altar. In its place a large five pointed star and a circle had been drawn onto the crumbling brickwork. In front of this was a raised dais. Clowes lifted his head to the balcony above and saw the bird looking down at him. Her nest had been pulled further forward and built up higher to give her a better view of the proceedings. A female rat stood in attendance. There was no sign of Trefoil, nor Vincent come to that, and Clowes wondered how the caterpillar was faring. Many rats were already dancing and pounding the floor with exuberance; soon to be joined by others once they had partaken of the alcohol and drugs on offer. Wine was ladled out copiously from large containers set up by the exit gap in the outside wall. White powders were bartered and paid for stealthily in the murky corners and dark recesses under the balcony. Clowes counted five priests in all; including Atol and Ware. He thought he recognised the female priest who stood behind the altar on the other side of Atol. A short but sturdy priest had positioned himself close to Clowes, but his face was covered and he was unrecognisable.

The tempo of the music quickened and some of the dancers began to move around the floor. An attractive female rat gyrated past; lost to the pulsating throb of the drums; her face blank, expressionless. There was no doubt that the beat was intoxicating; some rats had begun chanting rhythmically, repetitively, but their voices were thin compared to the noise of the music and could not dilute the power of the drums. Clowes felt an irresistible urge to join the dancers on the floor; the sound was becoming an all encompassing, pounding rhythm in his blood and his body felt driven to respond. He started to sway and his feet involuntarily began to move. He felt a restraining paw on his shoulder.

'Be careful, don't get carried away,' a soft voice whispered in his ear.

He turned and looked into the eyes of the priest who stood close to him. The priest stared silently and impassively back. Clowes felt a tingle of excitement; did he have an ally, here at the centre of power? He turned back to the dancers hardly daring to hope that help might be at hand. More and more of the rats were now whirling around the floor; caught up in a frantic world of their own, oblivious to all else. Clowes saw one rat grab the tail of another and clamp the root of it between his teeth, leaving his front paws free to continue the improvised and frenzied movements of the dance. Soon others had followed suit until there were a dozen or so rats irrevocably fastened together in a circle, each fixed firmly to the one in front by their tails trapped in immovable locked jaws. The circle of rats gathered speed as they spun faster and faster, until they became a dizzying blur that pulsated in time to the throbbing beat. The rotating wheel dominated the dance floor and as other rats became aware of it they faltered and moved back to stand against the walls and watch, mesmerised by the hypnotic gyrations. Just when it seemed that the whirling rats would have no choice but to take off and fly around the room, Atol brought the situation to Ware's attention and the music came to an abrupt finish.

In the ensuing silence, Atol raised his paws and cried, 'All praise to the Spirit of the Sacred Stone. Hail and all praise to thee!' There were a few faltering attempts to respond to his cry, but those rats who were not left breathless by their exertions on the dance floor, were transfixed in a state of shock. As the music ceased, the circle of rats had fallen to the floor and lay there motionless, with no attempt to get up or extricate themselves from each other. That they were still alive was true as could be witnessed by their heaving sides and rasping gasps, but their eyes remained tightly shut and there was no other movement. Thick bubbles of mucus oozed from their nostrils and blood seeped from their mouths where lips, curled back, revealed teeth still grotesquely clamped down upon each tail.

'All hail to the Spirit of the Sacred Stone,' cried Atol once more. 'All praise to thee. Accept our offering of love and dedication as we devote our lives to thee, oh powerful one.' He turned and indicated the stone beast, which now proudly displayed the dead stoat's pelt draped about its shoulders.

Clowes saw the female priest throw back her head and join in. 'Oh praise to thee Spirit of the Sacred Stone. Oh praise to thee. All praise to thee.'

Gradually the rats standing on the dance floor began to respond and before long they had found a rhythm to the chant that they repeated over and over again. With a covert nod Atol indicated to Scabious and Scarlic to have the circle of rats removed and it eventually took two dozen guard rats to man-handle the inert bodies through the outside exit. Atol allowed the chanting to continue a while longer until it had mounted to a crescendo; then he jumped on top of the altar and raised his paws for silence. A dim glow from the rising moon was just becoming apparent and the rays filtering through the broken roof caught the decoration on his wrist, sending sparkles of shimmering light across the darkened cellar.

'You have done well, my friends,' he cried. 'The spirits are pleased.'

'What's 'appened ter me brother?' An inebriated rat swayed towards the altar. 'Where've you taken me brother?'

Atol gazed down at the rat imperiously. 'If your brother was part of the ring of dance he will be outside along with his fellow dancers.' He held his paws aloft once again to quieten a growing restlessness. 'Those who chose to join the ring of dance were encouraged to do so by the Spirit of the Stone,' Atol intoned loudly. 'The ring of dance is a test to the loyalty of those who partake. Those who are loyal, true and without guilt in their love for the Spirit of the Stone will survive; no harm will come to them. Those who do not survive the ring of dance shall be proclaimed guilty of harbouring doubts in the powers of the deity; their death is a just and rightful punishment.'

"Ere me brother was alright 'e was. 'E weren't guilty of…of… what you said.' The rat turned and appealed to the crowd behind him.

'If he was without guilt then he will survive,' Atol repeated. He beckoned Scarlic over. 'Perhaps you wish to go and see your brother. Scarlic will accompany you.' The rat, still protesting was hurried out of the cellar by Scarlic and two other guard rats.

'Now,' continued Atol dismissively, 'we come to the purpose of the evening: the testing of the hedgehog.' All eyes turned to the cellar steps where Trefoil appeared, led by two guard rats and followed closely by the enormous Scur. They made their way through a now silent throng, to the pentacle on the wall where Trefoil was placed rather unceremoniously onto the dais. Atol pointed dramatically towards the balcony and cried loudly. 'You have all witnessed the occasion at our last ceremony when Iya Nla declared that the hog had special powers...'

'Let Iya Nla speak for herself,' the priest next to Clowes cut in quickly.

'By all means,' replied Atol silkily. He gestured towards the balcony, 'I was trying to save your strength Iya Nla, but please let us hear your version of it.' He turned back to the crowd, 'Quiet for Iya Nla,' he shouted. A hush ran round the cellar as all eyes turned to the frail bird, whose head could just be seen above the parapet.

She waited a few moments longer to be sure of their full attention then said in a firm voice, belying her frail appearance, 'At the Initiation Ceremony, following the death of the stoat, I interceded for the life of this hedgehog. It is important that you all understand why he should not be sacrificed thoughtlessly.' She paused to regain her strength. 'I have travelled far and crossed many lands, far larger than any that you have seen, living here in this small woodland. I have learned many things; many stories and many truths. The Moon Goddess Ishtar has always been the protector of hedgehogs; she has an affinity with them. She is the Goddess of Truth and Justice and the Goddess of Reincarnation. To harm any hedgehog deliberately risks bringing down her wrath; she is known to have no mercy when she brings retribution.' There was a low undercurrent of noise as Iya Nla paused for a few seconds again. Clowes could see that she had made an impression on the rats; they still saw her as the figure of authority. 'This hedgehog's name is Trefoil,' the bird continued, 'and through him tonight we shall see the power and hear the voice of Ishtar. I ask only that you join together in our prayers to call down the Moon Goddess.' She looked towards the altar. 'I ask that the priests lead us in the prayer.'

Clowes heard Atol give a quiet chuckle but then he cleared his throat, bowed his head and began to intone. 'Oh hear us Ishtar – Moon Goddess. Hear us call to thee. Come to us through this, your vessel – this humble hedgehog. Ishtar, Goddess of Truth and Justice – make yourself known to us, your servants. Ishtar, Goddess of Reincarnation – that gives life after death; show us your power, dazzle us with thy wondrous might.' Atol raised his head and flung out his paws, 'Ishtar!' he cried, 'Ishtar!'

The crowd took up the cry and following his stance, threw back their heads, 'Ishtar! Ishtar!' they cried in unison.

Incredibly, as if by some divine power, the half moon suddenly appeared from behind a passing cloud and the rays of light filtering through the broken roof became brighter. A ghostly white face pressed itself against a gap in the roof and a button black eye surveyed them all silently. A number of rats screamed while others shouted more loudly, 'Ishtar! Ishtar!' Clowes saw Atol recoil and look with consternation at the female priest, who seemed mesmerised by what was happening. It looked as if pandemonium would ensue when, as suddenly as it had appeared, the face was gone.

Before any rat had a chance to deliberate with its neighbour on this mystifying phenomenon, Trefoil began to speak. His head fell forward and his eyes were closed, but his voice rang out clearly and with authority. 'Ishtar sees all!' he cried. 'Ishtar has come and she sees all!' A hush fell on the crowd and they waited with bated breath to hear what the hedgehog had to say. 'Ishtar, the all seeing eye of heaven sees…' Trefoil lifted his head and raised his closed eyes to the roof: 'Secrets – Deception – Lies!' he proclaimed. 'Ishtar sees murder; murder most foul; witness the blood; oh witness the bloody knife!' There was a buzz of agitated restlessness and the priest next to Clowes stepped forward.

'What murder?' he asked, 'Who has been murdered?'

Trefoil remained motionless with eyes closed. 'Ishtar knows all things and Ishtar answers,' he spoke again. 'The priest lies in his own blood at the bottom of the pit.' He raised his voice, 'Black blood under the moonlight! Ishtar denounces this sacrilegious murder and Ishtar accuses.'

'Who?' asked the priest, 'Who does Ishtar accuse?'

'This is ridiculous!' interrupted Atol and pushed the priest to one side. 'Brothers, Sisters, I beseech you all to stay calm. We will investigate this claim to see if there is any truth in it. Let us determine if the hedgehog speaks true or falsely.' He jumped down from the altar and strode quickly over to the gap in the wall, where he turned and faced the crowd again with paws high in the air. 'A selection of you will come to bear witness to what we find. Come!' he indicated half a dozen of the nearest rats. 'Scabious!' he shouted, 'Bring half a dozen guards as well. The rest of you stay here! Scur, Scarlic, guard the exit.' The chosen party exited through the gap leaving a cellar full of shocked and bewildered rats.

The priest near to Clowes called to a couple of guards. 'Take the hedgehog back up to Iya Nla,' Clowes heard him say.

'But if he escapes?' one of them asked.

'Tether him if you have to but take him out of here quickly.' He glared at the guards, 'You heard what was said about the goddess, if anything befalls this creature we will have to contend with her anger. Take him back to safety at once!'

'You do not have the authority to make that decision, Holt,' the female priest frowned, 'Atol will be displeased.'

Holt nodded to the guards and they ushered Trefoil up the cellar steps and out of sight. 'He will have other things on his mind when he returns,' the priest, whose name Clowes now knew as Holt replied. 'I believe that what he has prophesied will prove to be true. Do you doubt it, Wimund?' Holt spoke directly to the female, but Clowes felt again a sense of closeness with the priest, as if he was deliberately including him in the conversation.

Wimund sighed. 'Well it is out of my paws now. But I refuse to stand here not knowing what is going on out there.' She pushed her way through the crowd towards the exit.

'Come,' said Holt to Clowes and they both followed her.

It took some minutes of remonstrating with Scur and Scarlic before they eventually pushed their way outside and joined the group of rats standing in the moonlight. Atol was in front looking towards the pit, his mouth hung open and he appeared transfixed by what he saw. Some crates and boxes had been excavated from the pit and stood randomly at one side. Their edges were dark and sharply defined, silhouetted against the moonlight, except for one box which was half covered by something black and indistinct. It looked like the figure of a large rat sitting hunched over; its head in its paws. As they watched it began to moan and wail. The watching rats shuddered and all took a step backwards except for one: Atol stepped forward peering into the half light intent on unravelling this mystery. Was the figure real or just a ghostly phantom? He crept nearer. Suddenly the figure rose up with a blood curdling screech. It was a tall rat dressed in a priestly ceremonial cloak.

It pointed a claw at Atol and cried: 'Murderers! Killers! Betrayers! I seek justice – Ishtar seeks justice! The Moon Goddess resurrects me to seek justice. I will have no rest until justice is seen to be done!'

'It's Earle,' whispered Wimund. 'It's got to be Earle. Oh Sacred Spirit of the Stone save us, protect us from this... this thing!'

Atol stood his ground on shaking legs but when the apparition stepped down from the box and started slowly towards him, its claw still pointing accusingly, his courage finally gave way and he turned and fled. Without hesitation the other rats followed suit and within seconds all had disappeared back inside the cellar. Only Holt and Clowes remained outside, facing the now static figure. Clowes raised his paw and the figure did likewise; then it turned and walked away into the darkness.

'You know more of this than you let on, I think,' said Holt. 'But have no fear; your secret is safe with me. We can perhaps be mutually beneficial to one another?' He looked directly at Clowes with an honest open gaze.

'I think that yes, we must learn to trust each other, my friend,' Clowes replied sincerely.

Holt touched Clowes lightly on the shoulder for a moment. 'Come,' he said, 'it will be interesting to see how Atol handles this.'

Inside, the cellar was buzzing with noise and confusion. Atol could be seen in close conversation with Scabious; they stood at the bottom of the cellar steps, their heads bent closely together. Wimund was gesticulating wildly to Ware and another priest, whose face was a mask of fury. Scarlic was directing the guards; positioning them amongst the rats on the dance floor with orders to calm things down and keep control. Scur wandered around with a vacuous, expressionless face, shoving rats roughly out of his way and looking – for what, Clowes was unsure. The huge guard rat eventually made his way over to the exit and blocked the path of any rat who might be considering an escape. Clowes looked up at the balcony but Iya Nla was not to be seen. Just as he thought he might take advantage of the general confusion and attempt to find Trefoil and rescue him, he heard Scur roaring. Clowes turned and saw that the rat was half in and half out of the exit and seemed very excited. Holt immediately hurried over and Clowes followed closely. He could hear Atol's heavy breathing just behind him.

'What! What now?' Atol screamed, elbowing Clowes out of the way. Scur said nothing but stood back to allow the priest to pass through. Holt and Clowes quickly followed. Outside, in contrast to the pandemonium inside, all was quiet and calm under the moonlight. The boxes could still be seen next to the pit, but the figure had gone. Atol breathed a sigh of relief. 'Pull yourself together Scur, what's all the fuss about?' Scur pointed at a dark bundle lying on the ground further away near to the trees. It looked big enough to be the body of a rat but it did not move. 'Right,' said Atol, 'we go together.' He looked at Holt, Clowes and Scur in turn and they all cautiously approached the bundle. At a withering look from Atol, Scur slowly lent forward and prodded it. Nothing happened. Somewhat emboldened, Scur gave it a good kick. The bundle flopped over revealing the dead face of Earle, half concealed by his ceremonial cloak. Atol bent over it reassuring himself that it was just dead flesh and bone, not a ghostly creation of Beelzebub. He flipped it over again and the back of the cloak was seen to be covered in dried blood. Holt stepped forward quickly and lifted the cloak to reveal a deep knife wound in Earle's back.

'So,' Holt muttered, 'Ishtar was right.'

'Ishtar, smishtar!' sneered Atol. 'The hog was right but is that the same thing I wonder?' He regarded Clowes with a certain suspicion. 'Perhaps the hog got his information elsewhere.' Clowes looked surprised and shrugged. Atol wrinkled his snout, 'The hog will be interrogated later in private. In the meantime let's get this body back to the cellar.'

Earle was a large rat and his inert body was literally a dead weight but Scur picked him up as if he were a pup and slung him over his shoulder. Inside, the dead body was laid at the feet of the stone beast and Holt appealed for silence.

'The prophecy from Ishtar has proved true,' he said in a quiet but firm voice. 'The hedgehog has proved to be the mouthpiece of the Moon Goddess. The priest that you see here was Earle and he has been mortally wounded – stabbed in the back.'

'And here is the knife that did it!' Scabious came down the cellar steps holding the knife aloft. There were gasps all round. Atol strode over to Scabious and took the knife; he examined it minutely and then measured its blade against the wound in Earle's back.

He turned dramatically to face the crowd and held the knife high. 'This is indeed the weapon,' he cried. 'The blade has been wiped, but there are still traces of blood. Who has dared to use the Spirit of the Impaler – this sanctified knife – for such a sacrilegious act? Who is guilty of this heinous crime?' Atol glared around and met stony silence. Some brave rats met his gaze but were soon cowed into casting their eyes down. There was much shuffling of feet and furtive glances amongst them. 'Where did you find the knife?' Atol asked Scabious.

Scabious narrowed his eyes and looked into the crowd, scrutinising faces. 'The knife was found with Baldlice,' he proclaimed loudly. 'He was apprehended attempting to hide it.'

Baldlice appeared at the top of the steps, escorted by two guards who marched him down into the cellar and up to the altar facing Atol.

Clowes heard Holt catch his breath. 'My father!' he whispered. Baldlice was a sorry sight. He was frail and bent and visibly shaking. His eyes were watery and he had a runny nose.

'So, old rat,' Atol said softly, 'your time has come I think.' He regarded Baldlice almost benevolently. 'Tell me; was it that you feared losing your position as head of the colony? Did you see this respected and well-loved priest who now lies at our feet as a threat?' Baldlice appeared not to understand what was happening to him. He looked about him vacantly but for a moment seemed to recognise Holt who stepped forward to support the feeble figure.

'Can you not see my father is confused? He is ill,' said Holt. 'He should be questioned privately.'

'Ishtar wishes justice to be seen to be done tonight,' Wimund cut in. 'The rest of the colony should witness his trial.'

'This is no fair trial, it's a witch hunt!' said Holt. 'My father is ill; he is unable to speak for himself.'

Atol bent down and spoke directly to the prisoner. 'Baldlice, did you or did you not take the life of this rat lying here? Answer me now, do not prevaricate!'

'Baldlice was a sorry sight. He was frail and bent and visibly shaking.'

Baldlice hung his head and mucus from his nose dripped onto the floor. Wimund shuddered with distaste. 'I…I… do not understand…' Baldlice mumbled. He looked at Holt pleadingly.

Holt held his father's arm and rubbed his paw affectionately. 'Father, Earle has been killed. He was stabbed in the back. This guard rat,' he indicated Scabious who stood with folded paws and a smirk on his face, 'says he found the knife – the murder weapon in your room.'

'No!' cried Baldlice. 'I have no knife… I have no knife.'

Atol raised his voice so that it rang clearly around the cellar. 'You are accused of stealing the Spirit of the Impaler from the altar. You are accused of following the priest known as Earle and of stabbing him in the back and pushing his body into the pit. You are accused of taking the bloody knife back to your room and of trying to conceal the evidence when the guards came to search a few minutes ago. How do you answer the charges?'

'Father?' said Holt gently.

Baldlice wiped his watery eyes with the back of his paw. 'I… I do not know. I do not… remember.' His body sagged between Holt and the guard rat and they strove to hold him upright. Clowes looked up at the balcony hoping for some intervention from the bird but she was not to be seen. The priest, who Clowes had seen earlier talking to Wimund, pushed his way angrily up to the altar and remonstrated with Atol.

'Enough of this equivocation,' he shouted. 'This murderer has effectively been caught red-handed. He wears his guilt like the old shabby coward that he is. Ishtar demands that justice is done. She herself has led us to the culprit's door and we would do well to heed her. I for one do not want to incur her anger.'

'You speak sense, Gram,' said Atol. He raised his paws for the crowd's attention and addressed them loudly. 'The Priest Gram is right. Ishtar the Moon Goddess sees all and it is by her that we have been led to this guilty rat. See him as he cowers before you. Baldlice, our once bold and effective leader, now stands indicted of this shameful deed. What possessed him to do such a thing? To violently take the life of a good and venerable, well respected rat like Earle?' Atol paused theatrically. 'It is the sickness of old age my friends; the greed to hold on to the privileges of leadership at whatever cost; the fear of being dispossessed of the power enjoyed by him alone for so many years. Yes – selfishness and greed walk hand in hand with jealousy... dishonesty... disloyalty and the ultimate sin... murder!' He held out his paws beseechingly to the crowd, 'What should be done with him?'

'Take his life! Take his life like he took the life of Earle,' screamed Gram.

'Aye, aye!' some of the crowd took up the cry, while others looked fearful and uncertain. Noise broke out around the room.

Holt gave a quick glance towards Clowes then jumped up onto the altar. 'Brothers, sisters; hear me, hear me!' The noise abated fairly quickly when it was seen who addressed them; Holt had earned himself a good reputation for his work in building the dam. 'Let us not be hasty in our judgement. It is true that Baldlice, my father, is sick, but that is all the more reason to give him the benefit of the doubt...'

'Doubt! There is no doubt as far as Baldlice is concerned!' interrupted Gram. 'Let us put an end to this now. Let us make a sacrifice of the murderer to Ishtar in recompense for ever having doubted her hedgehog.'

Atol suddenly noticed that Trefoil was no longer in the cellar. 'Where's the hog?' he whispered fiercely to Wimund.

'Holt gave orders to have him taken back to Iya Nla,' she replied. 'I told him you would be displeased.' Atol glanced quickly above but there was nothing to be seen. He strove to keep his anger under control; he suspected trickery, but was powerless to point the paw at any individual. He mouthed orders to Scarlic amid the mounting hubbub, to check on the hedgehog's whereabouts. Then he jumped upon the altar next to Holt and waved his paws to calm the crowd down.

'It would seem that we are not all agreed on what should be done.' He held his paw high to stem any further outbreak of argument. 'That is nothing to be ashamed of. In fact we should be proud that we are a thinking race of rats – we are not barbarians. We respect the gift of life that the great Pan has given us. Therefore good friends, let me suggest another way. Let Baldlice be put to the test; let the gods decide whether he is innocent or guilty. I propose that he is given trial by water. If he is innocent then he will live. If guilty, he will drown. It is a fair test and the responsibility is taken out of our paws.

'Agreed!' shouted Gram.

'Agreed' said Wimund.

Atol looked at Holt, who quietly answered, 'Agreed.'

'Agreed!' cried Scabious, coming back down the steps.

He nodded his head as Atol looked inquiringly at him. 'The hog is in Iya Nla's room with two guards. Iya Nla is in a deep sleep or else she is unconscious,' he whispered. 'Either way she will not contest our plans tonight.'

Atol smiled and felt relief: control was still in his paws. 'Brothers and sisters we have made the right decision, but it has been a long night and we are all tired. Let us retire to sleep now. We will begin to prepare for the test of Baldlice tomorrow.' He smiled ingratiatingly at the crowd. 'Go now my friends, we will reconvene tomorrow.' He waved a paw towards the exit and as the rats began to move, Atol beckoned to Scarlic and Scur. 'Take Baldlice back to his room and place guards outside. When you have done that return and we will dispose of Earle's body; it is unseemly to let it remain here. Holt, we will discuss this further in the morning.' He turned his back on Holt and looked at Clowes with a smile. 'Well cousin, it has been an eventful night has it not? There is much for you to report back to your friends, but not now I think. Scabious escort Clowes back to his room. Er – for the time being you understand Clowes, until we resolve this wretched problem of Baldlice. Scabious, the knife stays with you for safekeeping.'

Left alone, Atol passed a weary paw across his tired eyes. Tonight had been an emotional journey; a roller coaster of a ride and it was still not over. But he had handled it well: he had emerged top rat. It did not surprise him; although there had been a few brief moments when he had doubted himself, in his heart he believed himself to be superior, unbeatable. He allowed himself a little chuckle and leaned back against the altar... and froze.

Peering down at him was the ghostly white face, visible in part through the holes in the roof. As before only one coal black eye could be seen but its unblinking stare bore down upon him, penetrating his very soul. Great Pan what was it? Atol felt the hairs on the back of his neck stand up in fright and as he opened his mouth to scream he heard a thump behind him. Spinning round he glimpsed the beast, Sacred Spirit of the Stone and the face seemed to be alive with malevolence. The moonlight playing about its snarling mouth revealed pale, razor sharp fangs and the deep eyes full of dread, stared implacably back at him. Transfixed in horror, Atol became aware of a commotion up in Iya Nla's room. He smelt the stink of an alien creature, a smell of predator; he heard growls and then loud cries from the guards. Suddenly the cellar rang with piercing screams, followed almost immediately by a threatening silence. Atol was rooted to the spot with fear; mute with terror. The smell assailed his nostrils and he saw movement up on the balcony. A black head appeared above the parapet and a moon beam caught the light of baleful yellow eyes and a glint of sharp, white, canine teeth. Atol moaned in anticipation that the thing would launch itself off the balcony and come straight for his throat. Instead it drew back and Atol heard it sniffing and snuffling around the bird. He prayed that it would sate its hunger on her old bones. If it started in on her it might give him time to escape. He moaned again as the head came into view once more; this time it seemed even larger. The moonlight was too feeble to illuminate the creature properly but it was enough to throw its shadow across the wall of the cellar.

The shadow was grotesque. The creature appeared to have a long thin body with a huge, spiky mane of hair around the back of its head and on its shoulders. Whilst Atol was held in thrall, it gave a strange rasping cough, drew back its head and disappeared. Atol held his breath; what if it came down the cellar steps? He was a sitting duck; he didn't even have the knife to defend himself. As the minutes went by he began to relax, he couldn't hear anything and the smell had gone. He felt alone. He looked up at the roof but the white face with its probing black eye had gone also; he breathed a sigh of relief. He returned his gaze to the beast but the Sacred Spirit of the Stone appeared to be just that, a block of stone.

With pounding heart he crept up the cellar steps, listening intently for any further signs of the creature's whereabouts; but all was now silent. *Scarlic and Scur should be on their way back by now,* he thought and, taking courage, Atol called loudly for the two guard rats. He approached the bird's room cautiously and stopped in horror. The rats that had been guarding Trefoil were lying on the floor, their bloodied heads torn from their bodies. The hedgehog was gone.

CHAPTER 24

FORTUNE FAVOURS THE BOLD

The meeting between Aldin, Heaton and Cory with his raggle-taggle army, had been a joyous one; especially as Freeman the fox and Drew the owl had both joined them early enough to play additional and valuable roles in "the plan". All had silently witnessed the "resurrection" of Earle, hidden amongst the trees in the shadows. Heaton had played his part of the ghostly apparition to perfection and it was hoped that the priests had been unnerved enough to render them confused and incapable of effective retaliation. The plan, as hurriedly devised by Aldin, Heaton, Clowes and Vincent when they had first discovered the body of Earle in the pit, was deemed a rousing success. It had been the icing on the cake when Drew and Freeman had volunteered to be included. Drew had timed his two appearances on the roof brilliantly; whilst Freeman had shown courage and initiative in entering the colony alone, dispatching a number of guards and rescuing Trefoil triumphantly.

The young hedgehog now sat in state, surrounded by a respectful and attentive group who were hanging on his every word. On Aldin's instructions they had all removed further undercover, inside the gloom of the wood and away from the smell of the pit. Trefoil, after many interruptions and questions, both to the point and totally irrelevant, managed eventually to bring them all up to date on what was happening in the rat colony.

'Don't suppose I know everything,' he qualified, 'but once I got down into the cellar I could see fo' meself 'ow the land lay. 'Course the bird was able ter tell me a bit before 'and. Funny that… didn't seem ter talk much at all but sort of read me thoughts and let me see 'ers. Clever that. Anyway it seems that she suspects this priest called Atol as being the leader. Seems to think he's dangerous – a nasty piece of work; she an' Clowes 'ad a similar conversation before 'e was taken away by the guards.'

'How is Clowes?' asked Heaton. 'He waved to me after my performance, but we couldn't speak, there was a priest standing beside him. How are they treating him?'

'Don't know fo' sure, it looked like he was a prisoner, but that particular priest, name of Holt, seems friendly enough. 'E was the one who ordered the guards ter take me back to the bird – or Iya Nla as they call 'er. I was glad of that, made it easier for the cavalry ter rescue me.' Trefoil laughed out loud, 'Blimey yer could've bowled me over with a caterpillar's whisper when Freeman bounded inter the room; 'e made short work of them guards, serve 'em right the bleeders.' He rubbed the bruised leg that he had been tethered by. 'Joke was tho' that Freeman couldn't pick me up – altho' I'll give 'im 'is due, he tried.' Trefoil looked over at the fox with affection. 'Anyway, as you know now, I was carried away ridin' on the back of 'is neck. Felt like a bleedin' circus act!' He laughed uproariously and they all joined in. Bugle, who was sitting close by, could not take his eyes off him he was so relieved to see his old friend safe and sound.

'Do you know what has happened to Vincent?' Cory asked. 'Is he still there do you think. Would it be possible for him to make his way out without being seen?'

'I think 'e could get out if 'e wanted to, but I think 'e'll stay. Probably keep the bird company; she's very sick yer know. She might ask 'im to find Clowes an' stay with 'im,' Trefoil shrugged, 'but your guess is as good as mine. Plucky little feller without a doubt.'

Sheard had been quiet for longer than was normal, he sat up straight and looked around the collection of creatures. 'Well, pardon me for asking but what happens now? What's the plan?'

'I think the immediate plan must be to talk things over before taking action,' said Cory. 'Aldin, we would welcome your advice, what do you think?'

The rat sat squarely and calmly on a tree root, he was relaxed and when he spoke his voice had the quiet authority that commanded attention. 'I am mindful of the owl's advice,' he said looking at Drew with respect. 'We have complied with some of it already in that our group represents a variety of different species. We have learned to put our differences behind us and unite in a common cause against a shared enemy. I understand that Drew also stressed the importance of learning as much as possible about the enemy and that is something that I whole heartedly agree with. The more weaknesses we can uncover in the enemy the better placed we will be to deal with them. This priest – Atol, according to what Drew and Freeman witnessed, seemed totally in awe of Earle's resurrection and of Trefoil's abrupt departure. We can only hope that the fear he showed was because he now believes the Moon Goddess to be a force to reckon with. We have to assume that he failed to recognise Freeman as a fox and saw him instead as some magical, ghastly creature sent by Ishtar. My feeling is that we need to strike while the iron is hot. If Atol *is* unnerved and perhaps doubting his own strength, then he will not be thinking clearly; in which case we need to push our advantage home. I think we should send a deputation to confront him.'

'Yes I agree,' said Cory. 'The loss of Trefoil will have surprised and confused him. I fear for the life of Clowes under these circumstances and we should do all that we can to rescue him as well. But which of us should go to confront Atol and what should be our angle?' He looked questioningly at Drew.

The owl blinked slowly several times and after a little thought replied, 'We assume that Atol is the leader but at this stage are not absolutely certain. We think we may be dealing with a creature that, for want of a better word, is deranged and therefore irrational. We do not know what support he has; who is loyal or who will *remain* loyal to him. But what we *do* know for a fact is that not all rats agree with him. There are those that question his policies and his actions and it is those rats who we must first try to get on side.' Drew paused for a moment then continued, 'In contrast to Atol therefore, we must show ourselves to be reasonable creatures. It is my feeling that the deputation should remain firm and rational in their arguments. Stand your ground but do not be overtly confrontational. Offer help to divert the stream and be forceful in your argument that this must be done immediately. It would be helpful to ask that the bird is included in your discussions and also Clowes, so that you can gauge whether he is happy to remain there or not. I will leave it to you to decide who will be part of the deputation but the group must be seen to be backed up by creatures prepared to fight if all else fails.'

Aldin nodded, 'I agree; let's rest up for the remainder of the day and ask for a meeting with Atol tonight. The presence of the moon may help us.' So it was agreed; look-outs were set around their camp whilst the other creatures made themselves comfortable for sleep. Sheard saw Aldin, Cory, Drew, Spike and Fag in deep discussion and went to find Scally.

'Feels like we're wasting time here man,' he said. 'I'm going to have another shot at recruiting some more help.'

'I'll come with you,' the crow replied, 'You'll probably get us all into trouble left to your own devices.'

'Bozo!' cried Sheard. 'Come on then.' The squirrel slipped quietly away through the trees and Scally followed.

***

Atol had spent a restless night and morning trying to come to terms with what had taken place the evening before. It unnerved him to find that he could not sleep and that his mouth was still dry with fear. There seemed to be no explanation for the mysterious things that had happened, other than the incredible notion that Ishtar the Moon Goddess really did exist. This bizarre idea went against everything Atol believed in and he was never wrong! Part of him believed that he had been tricked, but he could not work out how and he ground his teeth in frustrated anger. The white face on the roof, appearing not once but twice had sent him into a paroxysm of fear where, against all rational judgement, his senses screamed out that it was Ishtar herself whose cold gaze held him in thrall. The reincarnation of Earle could not be easily explained away; many creatures believed wholeheartedly in ghosts, so who could prove that they did not exist, certainly not Atol. Finally that heart stopping moment when the awful apparition made its appearance on the balcony, coinciding with Atol's presentiment that the Sacred Spirit of the Stone – the beast – was imbued with life. At the time he had assumed that Trefoil had been rescued by Ishtar's sacred lion, some mystical, magical creature and a reincarnation perhaps of the stone beast itself. The horror of it had unnerved him so much that he had failed to send out search parties to track the hog. Now in the cold light of day he could see how lax he had been. Control had been snatched from his paws and he had been reduced to a quivering, muddled-thinking wreck. Atol was aware that he needed to speak to Holt about arrangements for the trial of Baldlice, but for the first time in his life he found he lacked the courage to proceed. He doubted his ability to stand up to Holt and parry the arguments the other priest would inevitably put forward to spare his father. His thoughts turned to Clowes and he felt an urge to talk to the rat again. Clowes had already inferred that he doubted the powers of the Moon Goddess and Atol felt the need to hear this reassurance again. On his way to the prison cell he made a detour into the cellar to check how work was going for the trial by water. Gram was the only other priest in sight but he appeared to be directing operations satisfactorily so Atol decided to leave him to it. He turned to make his way back up the steps when he noticed something else had been added to the altar collection. Going closer to inspect the object more thoroughly, he was startled to see that it was a creature carved from the same substance as the Spirit of the Impaler, the bone handled knife. He picked up the ornament and examined it. It was a four footed creature with large ears and an extremely long nose. Atol had never seen anything like it before but from stories he recalled from pup days he would hazard a guess that it was an elephant. Remembering what Clowes had said about the Rat God, Ganesh, Atol excitedly tucked the ornament under his arm and hurried off to find him.

Clowes had heard of Trefoil's escape; indeed no creature within Mad Maggie's could fail to have heard, the whole place was buzzing with the news. Clowes was pleased to note that the undercurrent of whispers were largely an indictment against Atol. It had shown that he was vulnerable; that he was fallible and as is so often the case when a tyrant is proved to be losing his grip, he became the butt of many a rat's jokes. Of course, for security reasons and indeed self-preservation, the guard rats were not overt in their censure, but there was certainly some covert dissension within the ranks. Scabious continued to rule with a rod of iron however and no rat questioned the loyalty of either Scarlic or Scur. Clowes was undecided as to whether the momentous outcome of last night's proceedings had put him in a stronger or weaker position. When he had been left for those few minutes outside with Holt and had watched Heaton dressed as Earle turn and walk away, he had almost made a bid for freedom. Almost, but not quite; a few seconds hesitation and he lost the chance. Fate had decreed that he return to the cellar. So here he was back in the cell and little enough in ideas as to how to improve his lot. He worried now that he had not made his escape priority, armed with the information on Atol's prolific breeding project. Now Aldin and the others would have no idea of the colony's strength. Well what was done could not be undone and he would have to make the best of it. He heard voices and the door began to creak open. Atol entered and Clowes noted how distracted and flustered he appeared to be in comparison with the composed and steely figure he usually presented.

'Er good morning Clowes; I trust you had a good night?' Atol shifted his eyes around the cell and then down to the object he was cradling in his paws.

Clowes coughed politely to gain his attention. 'Can't say sleeping on this hard floor allows for a comfortable night Atol – let's hope I won't have to spend another night here eh?'

Atol ignored the question, he placed the ornament in front of Clowes and stepped back to admire it. 'Now what do you make of this?' he asked.

Clowes studied the figure for a few minutes, noting Atol's growing impatience. 'Well,' he finally said, 'it's a figure of an elephant; a white elephant none the less. White elephants are very rare you know.' He looked up at the priest who could barely contain his excitement.

'I knew it,' he squealed. 'And what did you tell me about Ganesh, God of the Rats?'

'Aha I see where you are coming from,' said Clowes. 'Yes indeed Ganesh is said to have the head of an elephant. Where did you get this?'

'It was on the altar this morning,' cried Atol. 'It had been placed on the exact spot where the Spirit of the Impaler is usually kept. At the moment Scabious has the knife in safekeeping until Baldlice undergoes his trial. But look Clowes look,' Atol caressed the elephant, 'it is made from the same substance as the knife, is that not a coincidence. What do you suppose it means?'

Clowes fought to stay calm and think clearly, this was his moment to become an ally in Atol's eyes, a friend and mentor possibly. He made to touch the ornament and then looked up at Atol. 'May I?' he asked. Atol gestured his permission. Clowes examined it closely then laid it gently down again. 'This is finely made by Man and must be highly prized by them. I assume one of your foraging parties found it but I cannot think why it was thrown away in the first place, unless it was because of the damage.' He indicated one of the tusks that had been broken in two. 'Now that *is* a coincidence.' He regarded Atol seriously, 'Remember that Ganesh only has one tusk.'

'I think it is more than a coincidence,' Atol cried excitedly. 'It is a sign from the Rat God himself – a sign to show us that he is with us – to protect us – do you not think so Clowes?'

'It looks pretty much that way, Atol.' Clowes frowned, 'Can't say I've ever really believed these stories of gods and goddesses, always thought they were just interesting myths. But we can't easily dismiss what happened last night; there was definitely something strange and unreal going on. If the Moon Goddess exists then, by the same token, so must the Rat God. I think you are right Atol: this elephant is a sign from Ganesh himself and there is nothing more amusing to the rat god than to thwart Ishtar's wishes.'

'And are you still of the opinion that Ganesh is the stronger of the two, that he is the more powerful?' Atol searched Clowe's face eagerly.

'Oh that is without doubt,' Clowes replied. 'All the stories I have ever heard, tell of how Ganesh has bested Ishtar. In fact we only have to look at the sky on a cloudy night to see that any old cloud can easily hide the light of the moon, no matter how hard she tries to shine. The elephant has always been linked with clouds because of its shape and colour. All elephants are said to have strength and power and wisdom, but a white elephant like this one is extremely rare and is the most powerful of all.' Clowes picked the ornament up again and handed it to the priest. 'Keep it safe Atol. It is the symbol of the rat god and he has sent it to you.'

'I expect you have heard of the hog's escape late last night,' said Atol. 'Some may say it was a spectacular rescue involving a grotesque, unidentified creature. I saw it myself; a vague outline you understand, but nevertheless it was lion shaped and could very well have been Ishtar's sacred familiar. Whatever it was however is neither here nor there, the outcome is the same: I have been made to look a fool in the eyes of the colony.'

'Oh I cannot think that,' Clowes cut in quickly, 'perhaps a few ignorant silly rats – a minority. From what I hear, you continue to stand in good stead with the rest of the colony.'

'I must reclaim my authority,' said Atol, ignoring Clowes. 'We will go ahead with the trial of Baldlice tonight. I must be seen to be in control again or we risk anarchy. The colony must witness the punishment of the transgressor... if transgressor he be.'

'Yes,' said Clowes. 'Is there any way that I can have a role in the proceedings? I would very much like to be part of it.' The priest regarded him gravely and Clowes met his gaze.

'Why not,' Atol laughed. 'It will be harder for Holt to influence *you*, a stranger, in his bid to save his father.' He paused, 'Yes, I think it an admiral idea. I am going to see Holt now and you shall come with me.

***

Bliss had wandered far into the depths of Whylder Wood, where the trees and vegetation were thickest and hid the light and the warmth of the afternoon sun. She had given up calling for Neldar and the eerie silence, save for the occasional rustling of the undergrowth as she pushed her way through it, deterred her from calling out again; to be completely on her own like this was a new experience for the little hoglet and she felt uneasy. Surprisingly however, Bliss did not feel particularly fearful, despite the gloomy dampness and strangeness of her situation. She felt proud that she had managed to find food to sate her hunger and she had quenched her thirst from a rain puddle caught in the snarl of tree roots. *This could be an exciting adventure, she told herself, and I must be brave and not panic.* She knew that Freeman the fox sometimes came this way and if she met him then she wouldn't be afraid because Spike had said that the fox was a friend of hedgehogs. She thought of Spike and her eyes misted over, what if she never saw him again? It had been such a happy time when they had been together; she had felt safe and contented, but it had been all too brief. A sound of snapping branches, crackling undergrowth and coarse voices broke her thoughts. Instinctively Bliss rolled into a tight ball and lay still under cover of some dock leaves, hardly daring to breath. Four rats pushed their way out of some brambles and looked around.

'Wrong again Titus!' one of them said, 'Don't know why I always listen ter yer. You've got no bleedin' sense of direction; looks like we're bang in the middle of nowhere.'

'Not fer the first time neither,' a second rat grumbled. 'There'll be 'ell ter pay if we get back late. The trial is ternight.' The four of them stood huddled together, uneasily, looking over their shoulders furtively. An unnatural stillness had fallen over the woodland; the air had become thick and suffocating. The rats sensed a watching presence, menacing, threatening, although there was nothing overtly to be seen or heard.

'Gettin' out of 'ere, somethin' not right,' muttered the rat called Titus. Without another word he bolted back the way they had come.

'Bleedin' coward,' said another and then quickly followed. The two rats left, gave a final glance around. One of them looked directly at the little white hoglet but his eyes passed over her, blindly.

'Go, go,' he whispered with a shudder and within seconds all the rats had gone.

As quickly as it had come the menacing quality lifted from the place where Bliss lay; the sounds of the woodland seeped back into the silence and a ray of sunlight found its way through the canopy of leaves to play about the little spines of the hoglet, infusing their whiteness with a warm golden glow. Bliss stirred and cautiously uncurled. For a few seconds she thought she caught the faint sound of tinkling pipe music, but then it was gone. She sniffed the air but could detect no hint of danger, so with out further ado Bliss continued on her journey. She had no preconceived plan as to where she was heading but she allowed her instincts to take her naturally and unchecked along a variety of pathways. She felt safe somehow, as if some powerful presence guided and protected her, so that when she smelled an unknown scent she felt no fear, only curiosity. The scent emanated from a deep hole dug into a bank of earth covered in thick brambles and as she approached nearer she distinguished the comforting scent of hedgehog mixed with the alien scent of an unknown creature. Whilst she hesitated at the entrance pondering on her next move, there was a sound of hurried paw-steps inside accompanied by a soft, if rather tuneless, humming. A snout was pushed out through the hole followed by two bright beady eyes, framed by a halo of prickles.

'Hello,' it said emerging to reveal itself to be a small hedgehog, with burnt black spines on its backside.

'Hello,' Bliss answered, her little heart thumping with joy. 'You mutht be my bwother Thcumble.'

CHAPTER 25

ECHO'S STORY PART 2

It is often the case when we torment ourselves worrying over some perceived impending problem that, once confronted, it never presents itself to be the demon we had anticipated. So it was that when Echo eventually plucked up the courage to cross the road, she did so surprisingly smoothly with no incident. Encouraged by this small success she negotiated the obstacles of trees and bushes easily enough, at the same time keeping a watchful eye out for breakfast. Her vigilance was rewarded when she glimpsed movement amongst some litter of leaves and with a swift, if somewhat clumsy descent, she secured herself an appetising vole. With both mind and body fortified therefore, she continued her journey in better spirits than the day before. Her instructions had been to fly in a north easterly direction where she would eventually come upon The Grange, so this was what she intended to do. Echo had no idea how far she would have to fly and so she tried to conserve her strength by taking frequent rests and in this way gradually become more proficient at stopping and starting. The woodland on the other side of the road was less dense than Whylder Wood and after a while the trees began to thin out even more.

Echo found herself flying over hedgerows and across fields, some of which contained sheep with new born lambs. The innocent joy of these little gambolling creatures caused her spirits to lift and she flew on with growing hope in her heart.

She reached what she assumed must be The Grange by mid afternoon: a large, grey stoned house surrounded by gardens; some outbuildings and beyond those about three acres of arable land. Alighting on a fence behind the house near to a thatched dovecot, she took stock of her surroundings. The dovecot appeared to be uninhabited, but there were a number of twittering swallows lined up along the roof of a barn generating an air of excited noise and activity. Echo watched in fascination a couple of birds pull straw from the rapidly balding dovecot roof and carry it up to the eaves of the house, where they disappeared. A few moments later they reappeared to repeat the seemingly tireless procedure over again. Overhead swallows circled gracefully, the white markings on the long forked tails flashing brightly in the sunshine. For the first time since the terrible accident Echo felt at peace, she closed her eyes and bathed in the warmth of the afternoon.

She was rudely awakened by something thudding into her and a sharp pain on the back of her neck. Immediately she felt another thump which almost knocked her off her perch.

'On your way!' screamed a swallow, swooping about her head. 'Clear off!' This was obviously no welcoming committee: Echo saw that she was surrounded by a mob of angry swallows that seemed hell bent on dislodging her from the perch and driving her away. Two of the birds dive bombed her simultaneously, whilst the rest set up a continuous screeching of disapproval; presumably outraged at the audacity of her presence. It was almost more than she could bear, coming so unexpectedly at the end of such a long and hard journey. Echo had no more fight left in her and with drooping head and tail, shuffled her feet abjectly and prepared to leave. She was halted just before take off by the arrival of two pretty pale brown and grey doves with pinkish breast feathers and black neck collars. It soon became apparent to Echo that they were trying to help her as they buzzed the smaller birds, scattering them in all directions.

'Leave her alone,' one cried, 'she's doing no harm.' The dove elegantly circled Echo then flew straight at a swallow who had stubbornly ventured too near once again.

'Bullies!' yelled the second dove. 'Who do you think you are? What gives you the right to drive others away? You don't own this place!' Both doves came to perch one each side of Echo. 'And another thing, you can stop stealing the straw off our dove cot for your mangy nests.'

The first dove drew herself up and puffed out her chest. 'Yes, nothing but bullies and thieves; absolutely beneath contempt!' The swallows were so taken aback that they could think of no appropriate retaliation and so retreated, somewhat huffily to the barn roof.

'Sorry about that,' said the first dove, turning to Echo and appraising with obvious admiration, the attractive blue-grey head with the bright yellow ring framing the dark eyes. 'That's the trouble with some birds, they get mob happy.'

'They're not all bad,' said the second dove; 'but they tend to get uppity and need to be pulled down a peg or two from time to time.'

'Well, I'm very grateful to you,' replied Echo. 'I couldn't have fought them all on my own and I am too tired to argue. Thank you for your help. If there is anything I can do in return just say the word – er as long as it doesn't involve flying more than ten feet off the ground!'

'Sounds interesting,' remarked the first dove. 'Can you elaborate?' Echo was just about to give them both a boiled down version of her adventures when they were overwhelmed by a cacophony of noise from the swallows. Looking in that direction Echo caught a glimpse of two boys sneaking furtively through the barn door. The swallows on the roof appeared to be in a state of panic and more desperate cries could be heard coming from the inside of the barn.

'What's going on?' she asked the doves.

'Boys after the eggs I shouldn't wonder,' answered the second dove. 'They've been here before, curse them.'

'Greedy thieves!' screamed the other dove hopping about in anger, 'Get away, be off with you!'

Echo did not have time to think about what she was about to do; she was driven by anger and a sense of injustice. Instinctively she flew hard and low towards the barn and swooped in through the doorway. She could see the two boys at the far end of the building. One was helping the other to get a grip on a rafter so that he could climb higher. A number of nests containing glossy white eggs with reddish speckles were lodged between the topmost rafters, where they joined the eaves of the roof and some adult swallows were unsuccessfully attempting to prevent the boys reaching them. Uttering a raucous cry, Echo flew fast and furiously straight at the boys who both tumbled to the ground in surprise. She came up against the barn wall and wheeled around majestically, talons held out ready to pounce.

'Leg it!' cried the bigger of the two, dabbing at a gashed knee. 'It's a bloody kestrel.' He made for the barn door like a bat out of hell, with his companion in crime hard on his heels. Echo followed at a slower pace only to make sure that they did not have second thoughts about returning and saw them disappear around the side of the house and hurtle up the drive towards the main gate. She remained keeping a watchful eye on them until they were safely off the premises and then flew wearily in search of a place to rest.

She perched for a while on a high gate post at the entrance to a pretty walled garden, where she had a good view of the house and its surrounding court yard. Reluctantly she began gathering her breath in preparation for departure, but soon she was joined by a small party of twittering swallows, who settled noisily on top of the wall beside her.

'We all thank you for what you just did, it was generous of you after the way we behaved; please accept our apologies,' said the spokesman.

'We were only doing what every responsible parent would do to protect our fledglings,' said another swallow, 'after all, under other circumstances it might have been *you* stealing the eggs.'

'But she didn't!' snapped a third, 'And I for one am very grateful. I think we should extend a welcome to her to rest here if she chooses to.' He looked at Echo with head cocked waiting for her reply.

Echo smiled and sighed with relief. 'I should be very glad to accept your invitation. I will stay tonight and go first thing in the morning.'

So it was agreed and Echo was left in peace to settle down. She was in some dilemma as to where to lay her head as there was no way she could remain on the post throughout the night. She fluttered down into the walled garden hoping that it would afford some sort of protection and tried to lose herself amidst the tangle of rhododendron roots. It wasn't ideal but the best she could do to avoid alarming the swallows again by encroaching on their territory. Overhead she heard the cooing sound of doves and looking up saw them both sitting on the wall regarding her with surprise.

'Not the best of places to try and sleep,' remarked one. 'Three cats and two dogs live here and they all roam around freely at night.'

'Well I shall have to take my chances,' said Echo feeling foolish and a little irritated, 'unless you've got a better idea?' The two doves had a huddled, muted conversation together which Echo could not hear, and she had just decided to ignore them and try to get some shut eye when one of them spoke to her again.

'There's an empty nest under the eaves of the scullery out house. It's old but serviceable; doesn't look as if Freya will be using it this year and if you don't like heights then it probably fits the bill.'

'Yes and it's much safer than where you are now,' said the other dove. 'Come on and we'll show you.'

Echo was too tired to argue; so without a word she followed where they led and found that the nest suited her purpose very well. It was a bit of a squeeze but all in all quite comfortable and not high enough to make her feel dizzy. 'Very grateful,' she murmured, 'thank you.' She closed her eyes and immediately fell into a deep sleep.

***

She awoke the next morning having dreamed of flying free and with abandon; high in the sky. She felt exhilarated, full of anticipation, something she had not felt for a long time. There was something about the nest that brought back her first fledgling memories; a sweet scent of grasses and flower petals that had once been cosseted by friendly breezes and danced in the warmth of the sun. But this nest, though similar, was not the same as the one at home. This nest contained all manner of interesting things: winged seeds, the inevitable straw from the dovecot, feathers, even scraps of paper; all held together by a sticky saliva that shaped it and gave it substance and security: a sense of continuity. Echo knew that the nest had seen many years and known many chicks and she felt safe in its sturdy, timeless embrace. Raising her head she saw a marbled mackerel sky above her and wondered if it heralded a warm spring day. She felt hopeful that it would. Already the early morning sun had tinged the edges of the clouds with gold and a forget-me-not blue sky peeped shyly between. It was time to go. Echo said her goodbyes to the doves who, helpful to the end, gave her directions to Great Bowden Water and assured her that she would be welcome back whenever she chose to come. A quartet of swallows wished her good luck and accompanied her out of The Grange and across two fields, before respectfully saying their farewells and returning to keep a watchful vigilance over their eggs.

Echo spent the next few hours in much the same way as she had done the day before: flying low in short bursts and resting frequently. However, she hardly dared admit to herself that there *was* a difference. Her visit to The Grange had bolstered her confidence and given her new found hope that with determination, she might successfully overcome her disability. Flying over open land she felt a rush of joy that surpassed even the feeling of elation experienced when she had first left her fledgling nest. Instead of the heart stopping anxiety each time she approached a particularly challenging high hedge she began to feel the excitement of self-belief; the feeling that that she could outface her fears and doubts. Taking courage in both talons, Echo literally rose to the challenge and soared over hedges and across patchwork fields effortlessly. Looking down she could see the beauty of the world beneath her; the different shades of fertile greens, browns and yellows as the sunlight began to shine more strongly through the rapidly diminishing clouds.

By the time the sun was high in the sky, directly above the grasslands and bare furrows of newly ploughed earth waiting to give birth, the colours had become brilliant and incredibly varied. Spiked dark green leaves of unripe wheat, the ears just emerging shyly from the stems stood illuminated; in direct contrast to the neighbouring pastures with their mixture of pale yellow and olive green prairie, cocksfoot and fescue grasses. A small herd of cows swayed languidly under a beech tree at the end of one field, grazing contentedly and occasionally strolling out of the shade to supplement their diet with the pretty creeping white clover that grew in close companionship with buttery yellow meadow flowers.

Echo flew low over a field where the young spring barley plants were pushing their delicate pale green leaves through the orange-brown earth. She watched a fox trot up the pathway of a bare tramline through the crop to the top of the field, where it disappeared into the hedgerow. For a while she rested on the lowest branch of a small field maple tree and caught sight of the fox again as it squatted amongst tall shady grasses under a hedge; its watchful eyes concentrating on a field of stubble, burnt umber in the sunshine. The stubble was alive with all kinds of mouth watering creatures: vole, shrew and field mice; also a banquet of insects – black ground beetles, little seed weevils, spotted red and black ladybirds, a variety of tasty ants and scurrying arachnids. The whole scene was accompanied by the soporific drone of the bumble bee and buzzing flies. Echo left the tree and made a dive for a tiny shrew scampering through the tangle of cut roots and broad leaf weeds, but she misjudged the distance and missed the little creature by inches. Landing heavily and ungracefully amongst the vegetation she immediately peered around hoping that the embarrassing incident had not been witnessed. Her eyes met those of the fox; a vixen who had positioned herself a few feet away and who was staring impassively at the kestrel.

'Yes well…' said Echo ruffling her feathers, 'changed my mind at the last second; mustn't be too greedy, I have my figure to consider.'

The vixen grinned. 'Of course,' she said; 'lucky ol' shrew eh?'

Echo extricated herself from the stubble and with a haughty expression attempted to salvage some dignity. However the vixen's grin was infectious and before she could stop herself Echo began to giggle. The giggle turned into a laugh and before she knew it Echo was cackling hysterically with tears streaming down her face. The vixen joined in and it was some minutes before they both regained enough composure to calm down and study each other seriously. The vixen's remark about the fortunate shrew had reminded Echo of something her brother Marlin had said about the less fortunate early morning earthworm, and she suddenly felt an overwhelming sadness that quickly dispelled the mirth.

'My name is Tait,' said the vixen. 'Anything I can do to help?'

Echo was about to dismiss this offer as having no practical value to herself when she remembered Scumble and all that was happening back home. 'My name is Echo,' she replied. 'There is nothing you can do for me, but you could be a lot of help to some of my friends.' She told Tait of the evil things going on in Whylder Wood and how some of the woodland creatures were trying to put a stop to it. She mentioned Freeman's story and his dead mate Wilda and finally she spoke a little of her own history and why it was that she felt powerless to help until she had regained her confidence to fly properly. 'First, before anything else, I have to get to Great Bowden Water to search for my brother and my father.'

The vixen looked sympathetic. 'I know of Freeman and Wilda, I'm sorry to hear what happened. She paused and scented the air; glancing over her shoulder across the field to where some over wintered wheat stood pale golden yellow in the sunlight. 'This is my home,' she said quietly, 'I don't usually wander into the woodland areas, but...' She saw the sadness in the kestrel's face, 'I will go to the woods and see if I can be of any help, I'm not afraid of rats.'

And so it was that they parted; Echo continuing in a north easterly direction and Tait promising to pay Whylder Wood a visit as soon as she could. As Echo flew on, the low undulating landscape became flatter. She crossed grassland, bare fields of red-brown earth lying fallow and a glorious field of bright yellow rape seed. As her spirits lifted once again so did her flight path, until she was able to look down onto a grassy field and notice a little trail of rodent urine glistening in the sun. Instinctively she glided and wheeled back to hover tentatively over the spot before diving down with talons out to capture a field mouse that had just emerged from its hole. The death of the little fellow was quick, unannounced and what is to be hoped, painless. Perhaps the loss of one small mouse was not so much to pay for the joy and growing self confidence that it gave to the kestrel and who knows how, but that it might prove significant in the overall grand scheme of Pan.

As the afternoon sun fell lower in the sky, throwing purple-blue shadows across the ground, Echo sighted what could only be Great Bowden Water. The reservoir stretched as far as she could see; rippling and shimmering breathtakingly towards the distant flat horizon. A number of water birds and fowl had made it their home and there was much activity going on. Echo settled herself comfortably in the branches of an alder tree and surveyed the scene before her. A black and white moorhen with a splash of red across its face picked a way through the reed bed on bright yellow legs, delicately pecking at the shallow lapping water. She watched it make its way into a mat of flowering bog-bean; the little white blossoms tinged with pink, coyly revealing their lining of tiny hairs. Further along the water's edge, two tufted ducks were building a nest amongst the reed-mace and clumps of tall purple loosestrife. They could be heard quietly bickering about what made the best nesting materials, but Echo considered it to be an affectionate bickering. Across the open water many different types of geese bobbed in garrulous unison, excitingly exchanging news and gossip as if there was no tomorrow. Echo sighed contentedly, she felt at home here and understood why her parent's had always chosen to visit. She scanned the skies frequently but, disappointingly, there had been no sign of her father or her brother.

There were a scattering of trees nearby and also some tall structures of what appeared to be artificial, Man-made trees. These towered above the rest and made Echo feel dizzy just to look up at them. They were all topped by a large flat platform and on one of these a great nest of small branches and twigs had been built. As she looked, a large bird lifted off and with a slow, heavy flight traversed the reservoir back and forth, searching the water's surface. Echo tracked his progress with great interest, marvelling at his strength and grace and the awesome wingspan. As he approached her he stopped, wheeled around and hung almost motionless in one spot whilst scanning the waters below. Suddenly without warning he dived steeply, wings swept back, talons outspread and plunged into the water disappearing beneath the surface. Echo gasped and anxiously held her breath; he reappeared clutching a fish and after mounting a few yards into the air proceeded to shake his plumage furiously, scattering droplets of water far and wide. Then

273

with consummate ease he returned to the nest where he deposited the fish in front of the female bird who was patiently taking her turn in the incubation of their prospective family. Echo watched for a while longer but gradually the warmth and the friendly reassuring sounds around her sent her drifting into a light, dreamless sleep.

A loud splash woke her just in time to see the great bird retrieve another fish in exactly the same fashion, but this time he landed on a thick bare branch of a tree close by. He was a handsome looking bird; dark brown feathers above and white below with short, thick grey-green legs covered in sharp thorny spines that enabled him to grip onto the slippery fish. His head was white, with a broad dark brown stripe running up from his back across the face to his eye. Echo watched, fascinated as he skilfully used his sharp hooked beak to shred and devour the meal. She was so lost in amazement at this wonderful bird that it was some minutes before she became aware that he was regarding her with an air of puzzled concern.

'Oh do forgive me,' Echo called out to him, 'I didn't mean to stare. It... it's just that I've never met a bird like you before. I'm... I'm wondering if perhaps you may know my father, he comes here a lot.' Her voice faltered and she lapsed into silence under his scrutiny. Part of her wondered if she might end up being the dessert to his fishy main course and she hunched her shoulders and drew in her head defensively. She felt a rush of air and heard a flutter of feathers followed by the creak of a branch. The bird had flown nearer and was now perched only a few feet away.

'Kestrels often come here,' he said in a low and conversational tone, 'but I don't know any of them personally. There have been three or four around recently but they have all gone now. I heard that one had lost his mate and was thinking of returning to Spain where he had once come from.'

'Did you hear how he had lost his mate?' whispered Echo fearfully.

'In a thunderstorm I believe, but I know nothing more,' answered the bird. 'You seem to be in trouble,' he continued kindly. 'You look a little underfed to me, perhaps I can be of help; there are plenty of fish in Bowden Water.'

Echo shook a tear from the tip of her beak and took a deep breath, 'I've never eaten fish.'

'Well it looks as if you've never eaten much of anything else either. Fish won't harm you.' He put his head on one side and gazed at her cajolingly. 'I'm an osprey,' he said gently, 'I am not your enemy. My name is Raedan.'

Echo felt that he was telling the truth and even if he wasn't she felt that she didn't really care. If her father had gone back to Spain then it was likely she would never see him again and she was rapidly losing hope that Marlin was still alive. Plucking up courage she flew across to the osprey and perched next to him. He smiled benignly and offered her a piece of fish which she scoffed greedily. After some minutes of silent eating Echo felt pleasantly replete and thanked Raedan sincerely for his hospitality.

'Perhaps you would like to tell me what is troubling you?' he said. 'I have time enough to listen before the sun goes down when I shall return to my mate on the nest.

Our chicks are due to hatch soon you know. It's our first brood,' he said proudly.

So Echo recounted all that happened to her since first leaving the fledgling nest. It was tempting to gloss over the worst parts, especially her own stupid, thoughtless behaviour, but she was a truthful soul and kept the account as honest as she could. 'Well,' said Raedan when she had finally come to the end of everything she could remember, 'you've certainly been through it, my dear. Not the best start in life I must admit but you're still here – alive and flying!'

'Hardly flying,' Echo retorted, 'limping more like. And anyway that's not the point; the point is that because of me my mother is dead and probably my brother too. My father has gone away broken hearted and… and… and I killed a man,' she finished mournfully.

'And you of course are the centre of the world I suppose!' Raedan said emphatically. 'Come on Echo, stop beating yourself up. None of what you did was deliberate with malicious intent was it? The events were accidental as I see it; a culmination of an inexperienced young bird, a storm and a man driving recklessly. Of course you feel sorrow, you have lost loved ones but you can't go through the rest of your life feeling such consuming guilt. No wonder you can't fly properly.'

Echo was startled. 'You think I can't fly because of my guilty feelings? I thought it was an injury I got when the truck hit me.' She looked in surprise at the osprey.

'Are you still in pain then?' Raedan asked. Echo thought about this for a moment before acknowledging that she had not been in pain for some time and that there appeared to be no physical reason why she experienced dizziness and nausea when flying high. Raedan chuckled. 'You seem to be a courageous little bird, I'm sure that if you put your mind to it you would overcome this supposed disability. If you like, I will help you.'

'But what if I fail?' Echo muttered half to herself. 'I can't take anymore bad news.'

'Well you got here didn't you, why should you fail? Positive thinking, that's what's needed. Surely true courage is daring to go from one failure to another without losing the will to keep trying. Come on Echo, your story proves that you *can* be determined so let's give it a go. Have some rest now and we'll begin lessons first thing in the morning.' With a sympathetic smile the osprey said his goodbyes and flew away up to his mate high in the nest.

Echo watched him go with thudding heart and a crawling feeling in her belly. She knew that what he said made sense but she hoped that he would not expect her to reach the frightening heights of that precarious looking nest. The evening was warm and the alder tree provided the protection she needed, so Echo decided to spend the night where she was. She moved along the branch so that she could rest against the trunk of the tree and by and by managed to sleep, if somewhat fitfully, until she heard the first sounds of the dawn chorus. A melodious blackbird led the choir and his joyful full-throated song filled the kestrel with hopeful anticipation of what the day might bring. Comfortingly in the background the wood pigeons provided the accompaniment of their timeless chant: 'U-

NI-ted, U-NI-ted, U-NI-ted.' Looking down from her vantage point she spotted a little ringed plover with its yellow eye ring and black neckband pecking up its breakfast at the water's edge. With great dexterity it then picked up a small pebble and ran along the reed bed where she assumed it was building a nest. So many birds busily engaged in preparation of new life. Life went on regardless, no matter what catastrophes happened and Echo determined then and there to face the day with confidence.

She thought she had better make a start at getting her own breakfast; it wouldn't do to expect further handouts from Raedan and so she took off across the grassland keeping a beady eye out for any signs of food. Her concentration was rewarded when she homed in on the rapid movements of something small hidden amongst the long grass. As she had done the day before she wheeled around and made a dive in the direction of the movement, however this time she was not so lucky and her outstretched talons missed the tiny creature, whatever it was and it went scurrying away with a tale to tell to its nearest and dearest. Her immediate reaction was to give in to her feelings of frustration and despair, but just in case Raedan might be watching she shrugged her disappointment off and took flight again. Her perseverance paid off and at the third attempt she managed to secure breakfast: a vole and some grubs. Feeling fortified she returned to the alder tree where Raedan was already waiting.

So passed what proved to be a very pleasant morning. Raedan was a good, patient teacher; he did not belittle or tease and gradually Echo found increasing confidence in swerving, wheeling, diving and stooping. It was hovering that was still the most difficult to perform and without the skill to remain motionless above a piece of ground so that she could pinpoint precisely where her prey was, her dives mostly ended unsuccessfully. The crux of the matter was that she needed to find the warmer air currents that would help to support her motionless flight and this could only happen when she was prepared to go higher. The first time she lifted more than ten feet nausea overwhelmed her and she dived for the ground. With Raedan's encouragement however she found that she could fight the feeling at least so that she remained airborne and in time the nausea became less frequent. By midday things had improved so much that she was seriously thinking of journeying onwards. She had attained the ability to rise high enough to be introduced to Raedan's mate and to overhear the long suffering osprey ask in no uncertain terms when the prospective father would be taking his turn on the nest.

After a particularly successful stoop, where Echo, closely following her mentor, dipped her talons in Great Bowden Water then rose up almost vertically towards the welcoming blue sky; it was agreed between them that she was ready to go solo. The question was where? On first hearing the news that her father had likely returned to Spain, Echo had harboured thoughts of going in pursuit; but it would be a difficult journey fraught with unknown dangers and if she successfully navigated all that, how was she to find what part of Spain her father had made for? The more she mulled over the odds of ever finding him, the more she had to accept the probable impossibility of it all. Since Scumble and she had parted, Echo had been haunted by the sight of his little blackened rump disappearing away through the undergrowth and the loss she had felt – still felt – at his absence. Her mind was made up: she would return to Whylder Wood and Mad Maggie Minchin's if necessary, in search of her friend. Once this decision had been made, Echo felt at peace; her whole being told her it was the right thing to do and as a consequence was impatient to begin her journey. She planned to fly high and fast to reach The Grange as darkness fell; spend the night in Freya's nest once more and be ready to offer her help to Scumble and his friends the next day. Raedan seemed delighted at her decision. He told her never to forget that she was some bird well worth knowing and he would be happy to welcome her back anytime she visited Great Bowden Water again. As Echo took off and turned in the direction of The Grange, his parting words rang in her ears:

'Remember Echo, bravery is being the only one who knows you are afraid.'

CHAPTER 26

A HELLISH PLACE

The trial by water was to take place soon after dusk and Gram had been overseeing the preparations most of the day. A barricade of branches was erected across the top of Holt's dam where the priests and other important rats would stand to witness the test. On instructions from Atol, Scabious had overseen the construction of another, temporary dam a few yards further down stream; it was nowhere near as stable as the other one but would serve its purpose for the time being. The brackish, polluted water contained between the two dams was deep and gave off a sulphurous stink; the poisonous vapours could be seen rising insidiously above the surface. Baldlice would be expected to swim across these waters and climb out up the steep bank on the other side unaided. A failure to do this would inevitably end in death by drowning and be irrefutable proof of his guilt. The surrounding ground along the nearside banks of the stream had been cleared to accommodate as many rank and file rats as possible, although there would not be room for every rat. Ware had been given the job of devising a lottery that would determine who would be present and who would not. The idea had caused dissension and ill feeling in the colony and Ware only added fuel to the flames by his dismissive attitude to the perceived unfairness of the whole proceedings. Rats who were interested in attending, and most were, had been ordered to line up and Scabious had gone down the line painting the arm of every fifth rat with a yellowish strong smelling ointment retrieved from the pit. Initially the recipients were looked upon as being the lucky chosen ones; although this opinion was reversed later when the ointment was found to cause a painful skin rash. A number of well connected rats were able to buy their waterside places and certainly neither Ware nor Gram were averse to being flattered or bribed.

Atol was in a state of heightened excitement and anxiety. In spite of his private rejoicing in what he believed would be an ignominious end to Baldlice, his mind stubbornly remained preoccupied with thoughts of Ganesh and Ishtar. Whether the god was with him or the goddess against him put him in a constant flux of uncertainty, and the dilemma was inhibiting him from making any decisive plans. Nevertheless, he derived a sense of power and solace from the feel of the Spirit of the Impaler, which he had retrieved from Scabious and now wore tucked into his wrist band against the inside of his arm. The knife was a comfort to him and he frequently caressed it under the protection of his ceremonial cloak. He stood now before the altar, the quietness of the cellar in stark contrast to the noise outside, and gathered his thoughts. Once Baldlice was despatched in disgrace, the way would be open to seize the mantle of High Priest and there could be no effective opposition. Holt would automatically be tarnished by his father's disgrace and with any luck would leave the colony. Once alone outside it would be an easy matter to have him quietly killed.

Atol passed his tongue over dry lips; soon Luthian would pup and his dynasty would begin in earnest, unchallenged – the supreme power. These uplifting thoughts were interrupted by Scarlic arriving to inform him that a deputation of woodland creatures had requested an audience with him and were waiting outside. When he learned that there were only half a dozen or so, Atol's first inclination was to send word that he was too busy to see them; he privately determined to have them all put down if they continued to remain and argue. On second thoughts however, he resolved to speak with them and satisfy himself that they were no real threat. At that moment Wimund entered the cellar and Atol called to her to follow him outside with Scarlic, where he beckoned to Gram and Scur to accompany them also.

A little way down from the activity at the dam, a group of animals stood not far from where Atol had first seen the ghost of Earle. The recollection unnerved him, especially as just at that moment a passing cloud revealed the face of the rising moon. In the sudden silver light Atol saw that the group included two hedgehogs, a large rat, a weasel and a muscular looking rabbit. As he approached he also noticed a small, scrawny rat that he recognised and fought hard to suppress a surge of anger. The two groups stood regarding each other impassively and Atol felt an unexpected sense of relief as he regarded each individual before him. In a one to one fight he considered that only the large rat, the weasel, the fierce looking rabbit and possibly the larger of the two hedgehogs would be anything like a threat. Atol pictured the nursery room filled now to capacity with his army of mutant rats and knew that these pathetic creatures in front of him would never get the chance of a one to one fight, they would be hopelessly outnumbered. He smiled and addressed the large rat.

'I must apologise in advance for what must be a very hurried meeting. As you can see we have almost completed our preparations for an important ceremony that must take place soon. What is it that you want?' He gazed with a supercilious stare at Aldin whom he considered must be the leader and was completely taken aback when the larger of the hedgehogs spoke.

'We represent the inhabitants of Park Woods and Whylder Wood,' Cory said softly but firmly. 'There is growing concern over the poisoning of the stream which is used daily by all living creatures in the area and further beyond where it feeds into the River Rushlep. We note your concern also and are impressed by your engineering skills in building the dam. This has effectively stopped any further contaminated water from flowing down through the woods and for this we are grateful.' Atol opened his mouth to reply but Cory doggedly continued before the rat could make a sound. 'We have come to offer our services to help redirect the stream further up the source so that the woods can have clean water again.'

'There is no need,' Atol snapped. 'We have rats a plenty that will do the job in half the time, our schedule is to begin tomorrow.'

'Perfect,' said Aldin, 'we will work through the night and you will be ready to take over in the morning. By the way, I believe my friend Clowes is staying with you at present, perhaps we could utilise his help also?' Aldin directed his question to Wimund.

'Erm… I…' Wimund looked uncomfortable and Atol interrupted.

'Clowes has kindly offered his help to me in tonight's ceremony; he is getting ready as we speak. Now…'

Cory broke in effortlessly, 'In that case before we make a start on the work we would very much appreciate a short meeting with the bird you have in residence. Her fame has spread far and wide and many would like to hear more about her circumstances.'

'The bird is dying,' Atol replied harshly. 'She is unable to see any visitors.'

Wimund gave Atol a searching look then said apologetically: 'Iya Nla broke her wing when falling into the colony. We have done all that we could to relieve her pain and keep her comfortable, but she grows weaker by the day and I am afraid there is nothing more that can be done for her.'

'Enough of this shilly shallying,' Gram cried impatiently. 'We are wasting precious time listening to these nonentities.' He turned to Cory, 'Go back to your homes and tell those you represent that the colony will deal with the situation. We will do what has to be done in the morning.'

'Yes,' Atol found new power in his voice. 'Even if you worked all night what progress could you hope to make?

Why, only the rabbit and the weasel can be said to be anything like expert diggers. Go home and don't waste your time. Scur, Scarlic please see them off the premises, call more guards if you have to.' As Atol turned to go he suddenly remembered the scrawny black rat and spun back to give him a steely stare: 'I do not know what *you* are doing here but I will see you inside. Scarlic see that you ...'

Aldin's voice cut in. 'Surely you did not think that we came here alone? Of course we have brought others. It will take a small army to divert the course of the stream; we are under no illusion of how much work it will take. Our friends are camped out in the woods nearby.' He spoke to Wimund, 'We did not wish to alarm you by bringing too many strangers close to your door.'

'Utter tosh!' Gram snorted, whilst Atol peered into the surrounding vegetation with furrowed brow.

'Be quiet!' he snapped at Gram. 'Look around.'

The rats stood silently searching the area intently and gradually, under the moonlight many eyes became visible, some low on the ground, some midway amongst tall nettles and others high up in the trees. It was difficult to gauge how many animals were there because the vegetation that hid them appeared to be constantly moving and when one pair of eyes blinked shut another pair opened somewhere else. As Atol moved forward to see more clearly, a cloud covered the moon and plunged everything into shadow. Immediately the confused rat was consumed by his doubts regarding Ganesh and Ishtar. He seethed with anger, what did this mean? Who of the two was most powerful and to what ends were they wielding their powers?

The hedgehog spoke again. 'We will take our workers around the other side of the building so that we do not hold up your ceremony. We will work through the night and expect to have much completed by the time you send a party to relieve us tomorrow. Come.' Cory indicated to his group to follow him along the path that would take them around the front of the house. As they made their way a paw fell on Fag's shoulder.

'I believe the Master wishes to see you inside,' said Scarlic. Cory turned to remonstrate but Fag shook his head.

'I'll go inside sir,' he said with a wry smile. Scarlic kept a restraining paw on the little rat and they walked together back towards the cellar opening.

Cory watched them until they disappeared with sorrow in his heart. 'I am not sure that we will ever see that little feller again,' he muttered. 'I fear we may have rushed into this unprepared; we lack inside information on the strength of this colony.'

'Come,' said Aldin, 'our plan is the best we can make it in the given circumstances. We have no time to lose and a good plan now is better than a perfect plan next week!'

Cory sighed. 'I do not like the shiftiness of that spokes-rat, I sense trickery – I smell a rat, an evil rat.' He looked around at the rancid, dying vegetation and wrinkled his snout at the acrid vaporous air. 'This is a hellish place.'

Well,' Aldin replied pragmatically, 'you know what they say my friend: if you're going through hell then keep on going.' He laid a reassuring paw on Cory's shoulder, 'We need to go before we attract any more unwanted attention.'

So the group moved off towards the front of the ruined house, where they would take the longer route around to the waters further upstream. The rustling in the surrounding undergrowth increased and shadows followed them.

***

Fag was led into the cellar and told to wait. The two guard rats in the doorway glanced swiftly at the abject little bag of bones with scant curiosity, before turning their backs emphatically upon him in preference to the more interesting activities outside. He took advantage of his isolation to familiarise himself with the layout and contents of the room and he immediately noticed the balcony above housing a large bird's nest: home of the dying Iya Nla no doubt. His eyes fell on the head of the stoat sitting on the altar, dried purple blood staining its neck, alongside the other artefacts that had also been given pride of place. Finally he stared in horror at the stone statue placed in front and to one side of the altar. The beast itself was frightening enough with its sharp canine teeth, lips curled back in a ferocious snarl; it looked for all the world as if it was about to spring off its plinth and tear him limb from limb. But the most horrific thing of all was the substance of the necklace that had been placed over its head. About a dozen mummified rats hung suspended from the creature's shoulders; each rat held in place within the macabre circlet by the attachment to its neighbour's tail. Fag moved cautiously nearer and saw how the teeth were cruelly clamped down on the root of the tail, gripping it mercilessly and the place where each were joined was covered with crusted blood and faeces.

'Ah I see you are admiring our latest sacrifice to the Spirit of the Stone. A most unusual and impressive adornment do you not think?' Atol came down the cellar steps tight lipped and smiling. 'So young Fag, I believe that is your name?' Fag nodded as Scarlic and another guard rat placed themselves beside him. 'Absent without leave,' Atol mused. 'But worse than that I think; fraternising with the enemy. What do you have to say for yourself?'

Fag made a concerted effort to look the priest in the eye: 'Your Reverence, I do assure you that it was not my plan to abscond, but rather circumstances beyond my control dictated my fortune; for good or otherwise. I lost my way in the Park Woods drainage system and was never able to catch up with my attachment scouting party. I am small and weak as you can see Reverend Father, and during a heavy rain storm I was washed down the pipes into the fast running Rushlep. The hedgehog you have just spoken with pulled me to the bank and saved my life.'

Atol snorted derisively. 'And why should a hog attempt to save the life of a rat may I ask? It goes against everything that is natural.'

'Indeed Your Reverence, and I was as mystified as you. But he truly seems to be a hedgehog with radical new ideas. He believes in co-operation between the species; especially in the business of resolving shared problems. It is amazing how many different species he has co-opted to help with the stream diversion.'

'And do you not see the weakness in his arguments,' barked Atol, 'colluding with stoats and weasels and who knows what other predatory creatures he thinks he has in tow. He has no jurisdiction or control over natural enemies; he only makes himself and those that follow him vulnerable. Where do your loyalties lie, Fag? How much have you told him about the strength and size of this colony?'

Fag hung his head. 'This is my home, Reverend Father and I would never put it in danger. I believed that the colony would welcome help.' Atol regarded the bowed, contrite figure before him and then glanced quickly up at the balcony where he saw Myrtle looking down.

'Here girl, how is the Iya Nla?' he called.

'Not well,' Myrtle replied softly. 'I fear she has not much longer to live.'

Atol turned to Scarlic. 'Take this silly, naïve youngster outside. He will be the little aperitif before the main course. We will test him for his loyalty in the trial by water before Baldlice is tested.' He looked long and hard at Fag with narrowed eyes, 'Swim strongly with courage little rat and your life may be saved.' Atol turned again and bounded up the cellar steps. 'Scarlic,' he called back over his shoulder, 'let it be known that the trial takes place in fifteen minutes, I have something of importance to do before then.'

Atol entered the swift's room and approached the nest. Myrtle barred his way.

'Iya Nla cannot be disturbed at the moment Master, she is sleeping deeply.' Atol clasped the knife against his arm inside his cloak and gazed about the room.

'Who has been helping you look after the bird since Baldlice became sick?'

'No rat Master, 'Luthian has not been here for days; I cannot find her.'

'Luthian has been given another role to play,' said Atol, fingering the knife. 'You will be relieved of your duties here very soon. Remember where your loyalties lie. You have done a good job so far and I will not forget it.' His gaze lingered for a moment on Myrtle's face then he was gone, running up the corridor towards the nursery.

Myrtle shuddered and bent close to the nest. 'It's alright he's gone,' she whispered, 'but I'm sure he'll be back soon. We need help urgently. Think Vincent – think!'

Atol passed the nursery and continued down the corridor alongside the infirmary, which stank of death and sickness, and down a flight of steps that led to the birthing rooms. Here lived the majority of adolescent and gestating females; the rooms were patrolled by elder females and heavily guarded. As he entered, Atol was besieged by the piercing noise of mewling pups and as far as he could see across the room were lines of females waiting to give birth; in the process of giving birth; or suckling their young. Pups big enough to have left the nest to explore the world further, would soon be collected up and moved to one of the segregated nursery rooms. A female guard rat approached and ushered him through a gap in the wall into a quiet, empty corridor.

'You pre-empt me,' she said, 'I was about to send for you. Luthian has been delivered of four pups, ten minutes ago.' She saw him frown and continued, 'It happened too quickly to reach you, I think you must have been somewhere outside.'

'No matter, I'm here now,' Atol said, biting his lower lip. 'Show me…'

'Wait!' the guard cried and she put a restraining paw on his arm. 'I'm afraid it has not gone as planned: the pups are mutant.'

'I am not averse to mutant rats,' Atol said through gritted teeth, 'how mutant? HOW MUTANT?' he shouted as the female seemed undecided what to say.

'It's bad, Master,' she replied softly, 'I think that they are too weak to live.'

Atol followed her along the corridor to a small room at the end and pushed roughly past her through the doorway. Luthian lay on bedding made of moss and leaves; she looked ill. She had been trying to suckle one of the pups which now lay comatose across her breast. Three other sickly pups mewled on the floor nearby. One was attempting to make its way closer to the bedding but with no progress as it was devoid of legs. All the pups were grossly malformed and it was clear that none of them would ever lead a normal life.

'Get out,' Atol said quietly to the guard. Luthian looked up in alarm at his voice and cried out.

'Master please… Master…!'

'GET OUT!' Atol screamed and the guard disappeared. Luthian was scrabbling to retrieve the pups from the floor but she was too weak and could not reach them. She held the one on her breast tightly to her.

'Please Master, let me keep them, let me keep them… we can try again… I'll keep well away from the pit and I won't take anymore of the white powders. Please!' she screamed as the priest came nearer.

Atol looked down at her in ice cold rage. 'All my work wasted,' he said softly caressing the knife as he spoke, 'weakness, weakness; how I despise weakness. I judged badly in you my dear, you have let me down.' Luthian saw him withdraw the knife and with a cry turned away from him to protect her pup. 'I AM A RAT MORE SINNED AGAINST THAN SINNING!' screamed Atol as he plunged the knife into the three pups. Reaching across the bed he ripped the fourth pup from her arms and dashed out its life on the bloodied floor. He gazed down at Luthian's hunched figure before pulling back her head and exposing her throat…

Atol could not move for some minutes and waited for the rage in him to subside. Slowly and deliberately he wiped the knife's blade clean on the bedding then slipped it back into its hiding place under his cloak. Without a backward glance he left the room; summoned the guard to clear up the mess and made his way back to officiate at the trial by water.

CHAPTER 27

TRIALS & TRIBULATIONS

A hush fell on the crowd as Gram, Ware, Wimund and Atol took their places behind the barrier on the bridge of the dam. They were flanked by Guards of the Elite, a newly appointed cohort of guard rats; young, strong and fiercely loyal to Atol, their one Master. Guards of the Elite were made up of rats that had proved themselves to be fearless in combat and skilled in survival at the military training school run by the priests. All had originally come from the nursery and many bore the marks of some sort of abnormality. Guards of the Elite were led by Scabious and were distinguished by yellow bands tied around their wrists. The bands had been chewed and stripped from bags in the pit and many a rat had been burnt in doing so, but took pride in surviving this baptism of fire. The Guards of the Elite and the VIPs on the bridge had been issued with masks; rags scavenged from dumping grounds, as some protection from the noxious vapours rising from the stream. Many of the rank and file rats had also attempted to cover their snouts with a variety of vegetation against the fumes; others were high on white powders and alcohol and had become inured to the poisoned air they were breathing in.

Atol stepped forward and addressed the assembled rats along the bank of the stream. 'Brethren, we are here to witness the testing of our Brother Baldlice.' This was greeted by a few muted cheers and an undercurrent of mutterings. 'Trial by water,' Atol continued raising his voice, 'is a test devised by the gods and is a fair and just way to prove a rat's honesty and integrity. If Baldlice can swim across this water and climb out unaided then he speaks truly and we will accept that he is innocent of the murder of Earle. But...' he paused and surveyed the upturned faces of the crowd, 'if he sinks and drowns then he proclaims his guilt to all.' A further buzz from the crowd was quelled as Atol raised a paw high in the air: 'Brethren, before Baldlice is tested, it has been decreed that we test one other rat.' Atol beckoned to Scarlic and Scur, who advanced to the edge of the bank holding Fag between them. Atol pointed dramatically at the little rat: 'This recreant absconded whilst on an official scouting party. For reasons known only to himself he has now returned. We welcome him back into the fold, but his loyalty must be proved beyond doubt. We ask the gods the question, is this rat loyal to the colony or has he been planted as a SPY?'

A buzz of conversation broke out and Fag took advantage of the interruption to assess his situation. He gazed across the stream, noting its width and checked the steepness of the bank on the other side. Holt had had the dam constructed across the widest point to spread the pressure of the rising water evenly, but even so in comparison to the Rushlep, the stream was quite narrow.

Fag had swum the river many times and was used to its strong current; the water of the stream posed no such problem, but he was well aware that its poisons could prove fatal. When he was thrown in he must use all his skill not to submerge completely and once in the water he must strike out immediately and keep in a straight line, he could not afford to linger. The far bank was steep and covered in a mass of overhanging bushes, with tangles of nettles and creeper. This might help him climb out more easily but he must be careful not to get himself snarled up. He felt himself being gripped a fraction more tightly and saw Atol raise his paw, all noise ceased; for a few seconds it was as if the priest had stopped time, nothing moved, then with a swift jerk his paw descended and Fag felt himself flying through the air. He landed with a splash and in accordance with his plan struck out for the far bank keeping his head above the water, his eyes shut and his lips pressed firmly together. Whilst he swam he could hear and see nothing; only his sense of smell and feeling remained. The water stank and he was aware how cold it was; how it lapped his chin and sought insidiously to penetrate his mouth. He remembered his last swimming adventure with Cory and fancied he could almost hear his friend splashing and panting behind him. It comforted him and gave him something to focus on, so it came as an unexpected surprise to find himself at the far bank much quicker than he had anticipated. With relief he clutched at the overhanging tendrils of a bush covered in bindweed and hauled himself, slipping and sliding out of the water to an uproar of cheers and clapping. Fag lay on top of the bank shivering and gasping for air, his thin body looking even more skeletal now that it was soaking wet.

'The gods proclaim him innocent!' cried Wimund. 'His loyalty is vouchsafed.' Her words were greeted by more cheers.

'Fag! Fag! Fag!' chanted the crowd.

Atol glared at Wimund. 'You are quick to pronounce judgement,' he sneered. 'Perhaps you would like to oversee the rat's recovery. Arrange for him to be taken inside and go with him.' Turning his back on her, he addressed the crowd. 'Fag has proved his worth; he has also proved that the trial is just: it *can* be achieved.' He indicated the far bank where two guard rats and Wimund were helping Fag to his feet. 'We honour the rat,' he proclaimed loudly, encouraging the crowd to continue their cheering enthusiastically. Some had picked up sticks and were thumping them against the trunks of trees.

Undercover of the commotion, Atol spun round and strode across the bridge to where Holt and Clowes had appeared supporting a limp and sagging Baldlice. As he approached them a cloud obscured the moon's face leaving everything in shadow.

'You see,' Atol whispered quietly to Holt, 'the trial is achievable; if your father is innocent he will survive.'

Holt glowered. 'My father is ill, can you not see that it is impossible for him to swim the stream?'

'Come, come my old friend,' said Atol gently to Baldlice, 'you are old yes, but nevertheless an experienced and courageous campaigner – are you not? Prove to me that I can still trust you and that you are innocent of the murder of Earle.' Atol stepped forward and, putting his arms under the old rat's ceremonial cloak, warmly embraced him. Holt and Clowes strengthened their hold as Baldlice sagged even more and with drooping head he was half carried to the water's edge.

Atol hurried back to his place on the bridge and without further delay, held a paw up for silence once again. As he swept his paw downwards Baldlice was dropped into the water. For a few seconds his cloak billowed out around him and appeared to be keeping him afloat, before his body sank beneath the surface, dragging the cloak down after him. A few rats called out, shouting encouragement and all eyes watched the growing ripples spreading out across the stream, waiting for the old rat's head to reappear. But there was no sign of him. No last minute reprieve as his tired and aching body dropped heavily to its final resting place, succumbing to the weight of the waters above it.

'The gods speak yet again,' intoned Atol. 'Oh Bretheren, my heart is heavy; that one so once respected, so favoured and privileged should choose to end his days in so despicable a manner: murder, the unforgivable sin; born out of envy and greed. A lust for power brothers and sisters, and for that the gods have rightly brought him down.' He paused for effect until he had gained every rats' attention. 'Baldlice has been found guilty and has justly paid the price.' He threw back his head and raised a triumphant clenched fist to the moon as it showed its face once again from behind the cloud. 'Gram, I will leave you to organise dispersal of the crowd. Tell the other priests we will meet privately tonight and discuss what should be done about the diversion of the stream.'

'Yes High Priest...Your Excellency,' a jubilant Gram replied.

***

Atol made his way into the cellar and went to look for Holt, but he was not in his room. Holt's ceremonial cloak lay in one corner; he had chosen not to wear it this evening. Atol glanced around, the room was empty and there were no signs of life in the corridor outside. He quickly knelt beside the cloak and wiped the bloodied knife blade clean, then rearranged the cloak so that the stain did not show. Then with measured step he left the room and started in the direction of the nursery. He was elated; how simple it had all been; how easily the knife had slid under the old rat's ribcage and then up towards his heart. Even Ganesh had helped by blocking the moon's light at just the right moment to hide the bloody deed. Yes it would seem that Ishtar was indeed less powerful than the Rat God and under the protection of Ganesh he would prove invincible. A surge of power ran through him like a bolt of lightning and he could not refrain from laughing out loud. Even the stupid Gram had anticipated his next orders that he now be referred to as the High Priest. He could not envisage that any other priest would contest this... except perhaps Holt. He shouted to a guard to send Holt to him and then remembered the female rat that was looking after the bird; Myrtle he thought her name was. He turned in his tracks and retraced the corridor making for Iya Nla's nest, he licked his lips: he had plans for Myrtle. As he passed the top of the cellar steps he was distracted by a commotion down below and went to investigate. Two of the Guards Elite had pushed their way into the cellar from outside, closely followed by Scur who was holding something gingerly in his paw.

'We have an intruder Your Excellency,' said one of the guards, as Scur came forward and showed his prize. The huge rat raised his paw high and dangled a little creature by its snout in front of Atol. For a moment the priest was taken aback, thinking it was Trefoil returned to haunt him and his eyes flicked upwards half expecting to see the white face with its probing black eye looking down on him. But it was a female hedgehog that dangled before him and a terrified one at that. Atol surveyed her slowly allowing her terror to grow and then showed her the knife.

'When Scur releases you, you will remain uncurled... if you roll into a ball I will kill you,' he said quietly. 'Do you understand?' The hedgehog could not speak because of Scur's grip on her snout, but she blinked rapidly and Atol accepted this as affirmation. He nodded to Scur who bent down and dropped the hog on the floor. 'What is your name and what are you doing here?' Atol continued in a quiet but menacing tone.

'Neldar,' she whispered; the hog was visible trembling.

'Neldar?' repeated Atol. 'Well Neldar you had better make an effort to speak up or I shall think you are being deliberately obstructive. DON'T WASTE MY TIME HOG, I ASKED YOU WHAT YOU ARE DOING

HERE!' Neldar burst into tears and between snuffles managed to say that she had come to try some more of the white powder from Pan's Pit, but that there didn't seem to be anymore left and she was feeling quite ill so could she please be allowed to go home.

'Some *more* of the white powder,' said Atol with a steely glint in his eye, 'and how may I ask did you obtain white powder in the first place?'

'S… s… some hog gave it to me, he found it spilled from a packet at the edge of the pit. Please sir my head aches, my stomach hurts and I can't stop shivering. Please let me go sir, I… want… to… go… home.' Neldar lifted up her head and wailed, tears coursing down her cheeks.

Atol regarded her for some minutes, allowing her fear and desperation to build up.

'So,' he hissed finally, 'we have before us nothing but a cheating thief… and a thief with the audacity to make demands. What a sorry spectacle you are my dear.' He looked at Scur: 'Have her killed in whatever way amuses you best. She will do well as part of tonight's celebratory menu.'

'I have heard that hog is a delicacy, High Priest,' said Scabious coming down the cellar steps. 'It is best baked slowly underground until the spines can be ripped cleanly away. The meat is then tender and succulent.'

Atol laughed, 'That I must try: Scur, keep her in a secure place tonight. We will have her baked in the warm earth tomorrow.'

'Nooooooo!' screamed Neldar, 'Noooooo! Please sir, I could be useful to you. I… I have information… things

'Please let me go sir, I… want… to… go… home!'

you would wish to know. Spare my life and I will tell you.'
Atol and Scabious exchanged glances.

'Go and guard the exit, don't let any rat in,' Scabious
ordered the Guards Elite.

'So?' Atol folded his arms and towered over Neldar.
'Begin!'

Neldar began falteringly, then more confidently when
she realised she had the three rats' undivided attention.
She explained how she had been introduced to the white
powder by another hog in Park Woods, who had found it
by the side of Pan's Pit. How she had delighted in the
effects of sniffing and eating the powder and resolved to
find the pit and gather more for herself. 'Please believe me
sir, but I did not realise it belonged to you. It is said by the
woodland folk that it is Pan's present to all of us.' She
gazed up at Atol in doe eyed innocence. 'We are all Pan's
creatures are we not sir?'

'Go on,' said Atol ignoring her question.

Neldar continued by saying that when she arrived at the
pit she had to remain hidden because there were a number
of other creatures led by a hog and a rat all camping in the
underbrush nearby. Also there were fierce looking guard
rats marching about. Neldar paused, but urged on by Atol's
inscrutable, steely eyed expression, she continued sheepishly
that she had finally managed to gather what was left of the
spilled white powder and was able to enjoy its effects secretly
in her hiding place. 'But it's all gone now sir,' she whimpered,
and it has left me feeling... not right. I... I'm ill sir – please
help me.' Atol closed his eyes for a moment, but said
nothing and waited for her to continue.

'We will learn nothing of importance from this pathetic creature,' said Scabious. 'She wastes our time. Scur, take her away!'

'I do know something,' cried Neldar. 'I do, I do.' She waited for a response but when none was forthcoming she continued: 'They found a dead body of a rat in the bottom of the pit and they hid it under the trees.' She gazed wide eyed at Atol who was now staring fixedly at her, his expression like stone. 'The guard rats had gone inside and did not see, sir. A rat... I think he was called Heaton, disguised himself with the dead rat's cloak and sat on a box by the side of the pit. All the others hid in the underbrush. I was curious sir, so I stayed to watch. A while later a white owl flew down onto the roof of the building and peered through the broken slates, it was a large owl sir and I was becoming very frightened. I could hear music and shouting coming from inside then all went quiet. Some rats came outside... I think that you might have been some of them?' Neldar looked from Atol to Scabious to Scur for reassurance but received none. 'Well,' she continued, 'Heaton... if that was his name... stood up and pointed his claw at the other rats. He said something sir... something about a Moon Goddess and retribution but I didn't understand what it meant. He started walking towards the rats and they all ran back inside. All except two sir. One of them waved to him and he waved back then they went inside and Heaton took off the cloak and together with the other rat and a couple of hogs they moved the dead body out from under the trees and laid the cloak over it, then they disappeared... I didn't see them again. I went and hid myself away from the pit and I was so tired that I went to sleep, sir. I think I've been asleep for a long time; when I woke up I was shivering and felt sick. I came back to the pit to find more white powder because I think it will make me feel better. There's none left sir, but I didn't take it all... it wasn't me, others have been there as well.'

Atol drew in breath loudly and clenched his jaw, grinding his teeth in suppressed anger. He had been tricked; yes he had suspected *something*, but not this. It was clever and had been well executed. He would not have credited mere woodland creatures with the cunning and audaciousness to succeed with such a plot. It must be kept quiet; if it got out he would be a laughing stock. He fought to get himself under control.

'Who were the ringleaders in this?'

'I... I told you sir,' Neldar replied, 'I saw two rats and a large hedgehog and later another hedgehog appeared. Oh and there was a squirrel I think.'

'And how many creatures were in the underbrush?' Scabious asked. 'Speak up girl or it will be the worst for you. How strong was the party?'

Neldar looked beseechingly at Atol. 'I don't know, they were hidden; but I could see eyes, I think there were not many though sir.'

'Take her away,' hissed Atol. 'Keep her under guard, I may wish to question her some more.' He turned his back ignoring Neldar's cries for help. 'GET HER OUT OF MY SIGHT!' he shouted at Scur. 'Scabious if this story gets out I will hold you personally responsible: do you understand? Get up a search party immediately for Holt and that traitor Clowes. And Scabious – I want them ALIVE!'

***

Atol lent on the altar, breathing heavily as waves of anger pulsated through him. Was the bird in it too? She had been the one to start the story of Ishtar. Was it co-incidence that Clowes had embellished it or, as was more likely, had his orders come from the bird? If the Moon Goddess was a fabricated fairy tale then what of Ganesh; did the Rat God exist or was he also just a figment of Clowes' imagination? Atol stroked the image of Ganesh on the altar; where had the carving come from if it was not a sign from the Rat God himself? Atol lifted his head and gazed directly into the Spirit of Self-Perception. The cloak with its macabre rat hood lent a commanding authority to his physical appearance. He still looked every inch a High Priest, despite the doubts and insecurities whirling round inside his head. The awesome reflection helped him to calm down and get his thoughts under control. He had been tricked and in effect had lost Trefoil his hostage – but a worthless hostage, so what? The rescue of the hedgehog had still not been explained but that must also have been part of the trick and he would worm it out of some rat or some hog soon enough. He glanced at the leonine statue of the Spirit of the Stone with its gory mummified necklace and smiled grimly. He *must* have been rattled to think that crumbling relic had ever been imbued with life. He regarded his image in the mirror again; perhaps this wasn't such a catastrophe, perhaps he had gained more than he'd lost. He had got rid of Baldlice and now he had good reason to get rid of Holt as well. Colluding with the enemy and what a treacherous silver tongued enemy Clowes had turned out to be. Atol would savour the moment when he regained power over that rat. He would have him skinned alive and wear the coveted pelt with pride. He gazed up at the roof, remembering the white face and black eye that had rendered him frozen with fear for a while. Oh yes, some creatures would pay dearly for that. Slowly he turned and looked up at the balcony with a scowl; the bird would be the first to pay. He shot up the cellar steps and came to an abrupt halt at the edge of the nest. The bird had gone!

At first Atol could not comprehend what had happened; his eyes were playing tricks on him. In desperation he bent down and explored the nest with his paws in some expectation that he might touch the bird even if he could not see her. The nest was warm; she could not have been gone long, but gone she most definitely was. He swung round searching for Myrtle but there was no sign of her. How in the laws of Pan could the bird be missing? It was impossible for her to have escaped by herself and it would have taken a dozen rats to transport her any distance. Were there so many rats that would dare be disloyal to him? Was he in danger of being usurped before he had even officially been proclaimed the leader of the colony; before he could found his dynasty? Where was Myrtle?

Atol raced along the corridor to the nurseries, barking orders to the patrolling guards to fetch Myrtle and bring her to him. He pushed his way through the entrance to the first nursery and found Scarlic wielding the Spirit of the Impaler, in charge of apportioning out the evening food rations. The place stunk like an abattoir and the floor was stained with blood and excrement. Monstrously formed young rats had been herded into a fenced-off pen at the end of the room, whilst slaughtered carcases hung suspended from the ceiling waiting to be cut and sliced by the knife. Guards of the Elite were busy transporting the meat and offal to the nursery next door where Atol's army of young rats were fed.

'Scarlic,' snapped Atol, 'I need you; bring the knife.' He retraced his steps to the reception room and was met by Scur and a group of Guards Elite.

'No sign of Holt or that prisoner rat, Yer Excellency,' said Scur, 'the 'ole colony's bin searched, top ter bottom.'

Atol's rage knew no bounds; it was as if a wall of red fire obscured his vision and if he had held the knife at that particular moment he would have plunged it into Scur's belly, which was much on a par with Atol's eye line.

'GET SCABIOUS!' he screamed, 'GET HIM HERE IMMEDIATELY!' Scur backed out of the door, lost for words and Atol entered the second nursery followed by Scarlic and the Guards Elite. The army of mutant rats had grown in size and stature since Clowes had first been introduced to them and they were now fully adult. As Atol entered the room a reverential hush fell.

'We are surrounded by treachery and deceit,' muttered Atol to Scarlic, taking the knife from him and slipping it into his wrist band. 'We must assert our authority before it is wrested from us; when Scur returns take him and these fighting rats to the stream where those cunning, conniving creatures are working. I want them all annihilated; spare none, except for the traitors Holt and Clowes... bring those two renegades to me.'

'I hear and I obey, Your Excellency,' Scarlic replied joyously.

CHAPTER 28

TYING UP THREADS

H olt and Clowes, heads bowed, watched the ripples spreading out across the stream and the edge of the ceremonial cloak disappearing beneath the water. Oblivious to the noise from the spectators on the bank and to the mocking oratory from Atol, the two friends turned away in sorrow and returned to the cellar. Once inside they sped up the steps to Iya Nla's room where they found Myrtle in attendance. Peering down into the nest Holt gently greeted the bird and gazed at her intently. As she returned his gaze her heart quickened with excitement; relief flooded over her and she started with the pleasurable news the priest imparted.

'Why has it taken you so long to make your secrets known to me?' she queried. 'Why did you prevent me from reading your thoughts?'

'Oh Great Mother, my mind is my own and not to be taken lightly by others. But I am free to give it when I choose,' Holt replied.

'And I am grateful,' said the swift. 'It is good news that you bring. It gives me hope that there are more like you who are willing to fight this evil that I, in my ignorance, have unleashed.' She looked up at Myrtle with clouded eyes, 'Take Myrtle with you and protect her; I sense she is in danger here and there is no time to be lost.'

Myrtle crouched by the nest, 'I will not leave you, Iya Nla, to die here alone and friendless.'

'There is nothing more you can do for me, my dear,' the swift sighed, 'and I would have you safe. Besides, Holt and Clowes have better need of you. Don't be afraid for me Myrtle, my time has come and I am ready to go wherever that journey takes me.'

'Yes Myrtle, Iya Nla is right, you must come with us,' said Clowes. 'But where is Vincent, is he alright?'

Mrytle stood up and shook her head sadly. 'He went for help a while ago but we have heard nothing. I imagine he was trying to find you Clowes, he is so tiny, I am afraid for him.'

'Don't be, he is a resourceful little bug and his size can only help to keep him hidden.'

'Come,' said Holt, 'we must go quickly; there is much to be done. Farewell Iya Nla and do not blame yourself for causing this evil, as you put it. What you and my father did was with the best intentions I know that; you have nothing to reproach yourself with.' Holt knelt before her and touched her face softly, 'May the love and protection of Pan watch over you.'

So Holt, Clowes and Myrtle said their farewells and left the room. Holt ordered the guards to keep a careful watch on the dying bird and to see that she received anything she asked for. 'She is Iya Nla: the Great Mother and has earned our devotion and respect,' he said. Then the three rats made their escape along the corridor.

Fag lay on a bed in the infirmary. Before leaving, Wimund had given the guard in attendance instructions to have him dried off and given food and water. The little rat's mind was in turmoil; it had been no surprise to him that he had swum the stream successfully but he was worried about the effects the polluted water might have on him. Already he could feel a tingling – a crawling sensation on his skin; not particularly unpleasant but a reminder that he may not have got off scot free. Fag was no stranger to the infirmary; he had been a sickly pup and had spent much of his infant years here. Later one of his many jobs had been as an orderly, where he had tended the sick and disposed of the dead. He felt quite at home here and knew Eric the current orderly on duty well enough not to feel threatened. Fag did not trust Atol to keep his word about accepting him back into the colony and he certainly did not believe that the trial by water had convinced the High Priest of Fag's innocence. Atol would do what suited his own self-serving plans best, regardless of other facts or others' opinions. Fag wanted to find Clowes and Vincent to let them know they had an ally. He also wanted to visit the sick bird and offer any help that he could give. But before that he knew that his first priority was to get back to the stream and wash himself clean; and to do this he would need to go further up towards its source where the water was uncontaminated.

He looked around the room. The infirmary was crowded with sickly rats; some of old age but most with ailments arising from the pit and its poisons, and Fag could see that Eric was run off his feet trying to attend to their needs. Most of the beds were crowded together but down at the far end in a corner was a bed with an occupant all on its own. If Fag was to get to the stream he would need to exit from that end of the room and so he waited until an errand had taken the orderly away, before leaving his bed and making his way quickly in that direction. He hoped that the lone rat had not been segregated for quarantine purposes; he didn't want to run the risk of catching anything contagious on top of everything else. He approached the bed gingerly and froze. The rat was withered and shrunken and obviously very ill; his eyes and nostrils were gummed with mucus, but he was still recognisable by the distinctive scar running across his face – it was Baldlice. As Fag stood rooted to the spot, uncertain what to do next, he heard the sound of paw steps and turning he saw Eric coming towards him followed by Holt and a large rat who he assumed must be Clowes. Accompanying them was a female rat who Fag had seen only once before but who's name he knew to be Myrtle.

'Fag,' squeaked Eric, 'as you can see we… er… this is important… er… you must understand…'

'Relax Eric,' Holt spoke quietly. 'I am sure that we can all trust Fag in this matter.'

'I am glad to see you sir,' Fag said to Holt, 'and I am more than glad to see that Baldlice still lives, although he is very sick sir, if you don't mind my saying.'

'Yes, and it's imperative that we get him out of here and as far away from this poisonous atmosphere as soon as possible. Clowes and Myrtle here are willing helpers but we are all ignorant of the best route to take.' Holt looked expectantly at the little scrawny rat. Fag nodded animatedly. He was overjoyed to know that he might be of some help to this priest who commanded so much respect and to Clowes who was a friend of Cory and to Myrtle who was... his heart missed a beat.

During his early, sickly days, the infant Fag had discovered a secret room that backed onto the infirmary and a passage that subsequently led to the old Minchin stable block and coach house. The room was once part of the servants' quarters but had been boarded up and the windows bricked over later, at a time when money was running out. He was not sure who else knew about the room, he had certainly not told any rat, keeping its existence safely hidden for whatever purposes it might prove useful to him in later life; but he was certain at least that the secret room was not public knowledge.

'Perhaps if you good rats would support Baldlice, I will show you a way,' he said proudly.

Holt and Clowes lifted Baldlice lightly from his bed as if he was made only of hollow bones and gristle, and with Myrtle and Eric in tow followed Fag to where a rotted and splintered piece of furniture stood against the crumbling brick wall. With a furtive glance around him to ensure that they were unobserved, Fag scurried into the darkness under the pedestal. Halfway along he found the broken wainscoting and levered a section free, beckoning the others to follow. The aperture was small but posed no great difficulty and soon they had all managed to squeeze through and Fag pulled the piece of wainscoting back into place behind him. It fitted perfectly and would be hard to detect under any normal search conditions. He straightened up and appraised the room, anxious to reassure himself that it was just as he remembered it would be. There was no change: the room was empty and austere but felt secure and safe. Fag bent down by the far wall and loosened a couple of bricks.

'There is a passage here that leads to the old stables,' he explained, 'and thereafter to wherever your hearts' desire, dear friends.'

'You are nothing short of genius!' cried Clowes. 'There is more to you than meets the eye, my brave little cousin; I am honoured to know you.'

Holt placed a paw on Eric's shoulder. 'My father is not strong enough to journey any further tonight. Would it be possible to bring some bedding in here to make him more comfortable for the present?'

'I will do that, Your Reverence, leave it to me,' the orderly replied.

'I will help you,' said Myrtle, 'and we will bring back medication as well, Reverend.'

'My name is Holt,' said the priest, 'I want no other name, thank you both. We will rest here for the night and discuss our plans for the morning.' He squatted down with his back against the wall and closed his eyes wearily.

Clowes and Fag made Baldlice as comfortable as they could, then settled down nearby to rest. It was not long before Eric and Myrtle returned with dried leaves and grasses to cushion the old rat's bones. Myrtle had also brought clean water to bathe his eyes and face and some pungent white flowering valarian which Eric believed would relieve his pain. They brought the news that a storm was brewing so it was lucky they had found this dry hideout.

'Before we bed down for the night sir, may I ask what rat it was that so courageously stood in for you father in the trial by water?' Fag asked.

Holt sighed. 'He was a rat from the infirmary, Fag. He had died a natural death earlier in the day and Eric here was good enough to inform Clowes and myself. It was with much regret that we decided to use him for the purpose of the trial. I regret the lack of respect; but needs must when the devil rides and I was desperate to save my father.' Holt gazed with concern at the sickly rat on the bed. 'I understand he was taking the white powders for some time to relieve his aching bones. I was not aware of it until he became addicted to the drugs and lost control over when and how much to take.'

'Iya Nla was worried about Baldlice when he stopped coming to see her. She suspected that there was treachery at work,' said Myrtle. 'She suspected it was some evil work of Atol's, but we didn't know for sure. Of course Iya Nla suffered dreadfully with pain when Baldlice stopped bringing her the white powder; but the good thing about it was that, without the powder she began to regain her power to read minds.'

'Yes,' replied Holt, 'and I think that we have you to thank, Myrtle for keeping her alive so long and if we could have devised a way to transport her here with us we would certainly have done so. No creature deserves to die alone.'

The company all nodded in agreement and for a short while fell into silence until Eric said that he had better return to the infirmary before the next duty officer discovered his absence.

'Before you go, Eric,' said Myrtle quickly, 'have you any news of Luthian, she was a good friend of mine and I miss her dreadfully.' Eric faltered and looked to Holt for guidance, but the priest seemed not to know what was expected from him. Eric gazed at the floor for inspiration and finally made an effort to speak.

'I am afraid to have to tell you that Luthian is dead,' he muttered. 'It was reported to some of us by a female guard from the birthing chambers. It... she... the pups she bore were too deformed to live.' He looked at Myrtle. 'They were Atol's pups you know. The guard said he was incensed with rage; out of control. He killed the pups and killed Luthian directly afterwards.'

'It can't be true,' Myrtle sobbed. 'Perhaps it's not true?' she looked beseechingly around at the others and back to Eric.

'It's true alright,' the orderly said softly, 'the guard witnessed it from the corridor... Atol left her to clear up the mess. I'm sorry to give you such bad news; please don't cry so, her death was quick and she knew little of it.'

'But no consolation to you I am sure Myrtle,' Clowes said, putting his arm around her. 'If we didn't know it already we can now be assured that we are dealing with a demented rat.'

'And a dangerous one at that,' said Holt. 'There will be more atrocities I am certain; there is no knowing what his deranged mind is capable of.'

After Eric had left them, the rest of the night was spent in whispered conversation; exchanging histories and experiences until eventually a deep, but troubled sleep overtook them all. Except for Fag who remained awake, keeping watch over the others; especially Baldlice, gently attending to the sick rat's needs.

***

When Vincent left Iya Nla's nest, urged on by Myrtle to get help, he had only a vague idea of where to go. Ideally he wanted to find Clowes, but he had no knowledge of the layout of the house and even if he had was ignorant of where he might find the rat. To cap it all, Vincent was not feeling well; in fact he had to admit to himself that he felt extremely poorly. He decided to climb upwards and get out onto the roof, in the hope that some air might make him feel better. There had been a lot of activity going on outside all day, with much comings and goings prior to the trial by water and Vincent could still hear a lot of banging and shouting. He hoped that the high vantage point might give him sight of any creature or creatures that might be able to help Iya Nla; if only he could attract their attention. It was a long climb to the top but eventually he pulled himself painfully out onto the remaining slates of the roof and lay gasping for breath. He felt sluggish and lacked mobility, but he knew what it was, it had happened before. He was shedding his skin and growing a new one, and he expected to be fully re-clothed and recovered before the end of the day. Nevertheless, this had come at a most inopportune time and he felt frustrated by his current uselessness. From his position he could see guard rats and worker rats busily constructing a safety barrier across the width of the dam where obviously some of the VIPs would be standing. A little way further down the stream a second dam had recently been completed although Vincent noted that it looked pretty unstable. The basin between the two dams now contained a deep pool of oily, brackish water, its surface covered by vaporous fumes. His heart went out to Baldlice, who had always been loyal and responsive to Iya Nla, until his addiction to the drugs had struck him down. It would take a miracle to save him from this deathly trial.

Vincent was finding it difficult to breathe the air was so polluted and he turned his reluctant thoughts back to the job in hand. He could see no rat that might conceivably be of help in rescuing the bird and to continue looking only made him feel faint. This journey had made him worse not better and the thought of having to crawl back inside and instigate a search for Clowes filled him with dread; he just wasn't up to it. Nevertheless there was no alternative, it had to be done and he quested with his feelers to find an opening for the return journey. As he moved forward a bolt of pain shot through his aching body and he lost consciousness.

He awoke sometime later; how much later he did not know but he could hear shouting below and Atol's voice rising above the noise in a mock salutation to the life and death of Baldlice. So there had been no miracle. Vincent gingerly shifted his body weight on the slate, but there was no more pain. The dull ache remained though and he felt very stiff and uncomfortable. He wasn't sure whether he was capable of climbing back down  to the nest. He sighed and pointed himself resolutely towards the cellar when there was a flurry of feathers and a welcome breeze overhead, and the soft plopping noise of something heavy landing on the roof beside him.

'Excuse me but don't I know you?' said a voice and looking up he saw a kestrel. It was the kestrel from the meeting in Bluebell Grove – how long ago did that seem now. His hopes lifted.

'I'm Vincent,' he said, 'and I think we do know each other, but I don't know your name.'

'Echo,' she answered, whilst peering down at the busy scene below. 'Whatever's going on? Have you seen Scumble?'

'It was a trial for one of the rats: trial by water. Most of the rats are gaga, off their faces on drugs and alcohol. I think Cory is out there somewhere but I don't think Scumble is with him. Look Echo,' Vincent turned to her excitedly, 'there's a bird inside the house; she's wounded… in… in fact she's dying, but she has been a friend to us and we want to help her escape. She can't fly but you look strong, Echo. I know you told Cory you couldn't help but you're here now, please re-consider.'

'Where exactly is she?'

Vincent peered down through a broken slate. 'Directly underneath,' he said, 'in a nest on the balcony above the cellar; but you won't be able to reach her from here. You're going to have to find an entrance big enough with room to fly into the cellar and out again. I don't know if it's possible' He looked up at her with stiffening neck, 'I think that you must hurry or everything will be too late.'

'I'll try,' she replied and with thumping heart Echo took off from the roof and circled the house looking for a convenient opening. At one side of the building, where part of the roof had caved in, she hovered twenty feet in the air assessing her chances of getting through the hole without damaging her wings. For a few seconds a feeling of nausea flooded over her, but she fought down her panic and concentrated on what Raedan had taught her; once she had calmed herself she could hear his sensible, steadying voice in her head. On a wing and a prayer she dropped straight into the gap and with a sharp twist and turn of her body found herself hurtling along a corridor until she emerged into a large vaulted room with the remains of a balcony hanging precariously to one side. Echo slowed her speed and circled the room a couple of times; this must be what Vincent had called the cellar. She shuddered: it was dark and dank and smelt of death. She caught sight of the nest on the balcony and landed skilfully beside it. The noise made the swift look up.

'Vincent sent me,' the kestrel said without any preamble, 'I have come to take you out of this awful place; my name is Echo.'

The swift spoke but Echo heard only a whisper. 'It...
it is hopeless my dear. I am too weak to help you; I will be
a burden.'

The kestrel bent her head nearer to catch the faint
reply and in doing so smelled again the familiar fragrance
of sweet grasses and flower petals with the imperceptive
hint of spices. 'What is your name?' she asked softly.

The swift closed her eyes and a tear trickled down her
cheek. 'I have almost forgotten, but a long time ago I was
called Freya.'

'Freya, there is always hope.'

The kestrel rose above the bird and gently clutched the
frail body, cradling it in her talons, she rose higher judging
the weight and adjusting her balance. There were shouts
from the guards in the corridor but as she flew past them
they made no attempt to stop her and stood with bowed
heads in respectful silence. Echo traversed the corridor
once more and with a twist and a thrust emerged through
the gap in the roof and flew away through the trees. A
storm was threatening with distant rumblings and dark
grey, elephant-like clouds were beginning to fill the sky.
But Freya was unaware of them; she only knew that she
was flying once again – gliding – buoyed high on warm air
currents, soaring effortlessly. She banked and dived;
swooping deliciously downwards and the rush of cold,
clean air as she drove through was exhilarating; liberating.
Her little heart beat joyously; at last she was going home...

Once clear of Whylder Wood, Echo beat her wings
more strongly and together they rose higher and higher
until what could be seen of the land beneath them was

lost in obscure purple shadow. The waxing moon came out from behind a cloud and lit Echo's path, until the grey stoned Grange could be seen at last as a silver silhouette against the darkening sky. The kestrel lowered Freya gently into the sweetly scented nest under the eaves of the outhouse and settled down quietly beside her. The swift's eyes were closed and as she breathed in the familiar scents of her home and heard the faint comforting twittering of her friends the swallows, peace stole over her erasing her doubts and fears. Freya felt the warmth of her mate again at her side and the excited chirruping of their young. She opened her eyes to see the kestrel nearby and sighed contentedly. 'Thank you Echo,' she whispered, 'there *is* always hope and I was foolish to lose sight of that.' She closed her eyes once more and fell into a deep sleep, whilst Echo continued to keep watch.

For some time now, dark clouds had continued to bank high in the sky and the distant thunder was becoming more pronounced. Freya stirred and sighed so quietly that Echo had to bend low into the nest to hear her. The bird's eyes fluttered briefly but she did not speak. Her chest rose and fell for the last time and her little heart ceased to beat. Freya had embarked on her final journey, a great flight into the unknown, perhaps at last to stand before her maker. Echo murmured her farewell, touching the sleeping bird tenderly on her cheek then took flight, wheeling around the barn before flying fast and furiously back to Whylder Wood and into the eye of the storm.

***

As soon as the kestrel had left him, Vincent resolved to go back inside under cover. The fumes outside on the roof were stronger than they had been in the cellar and he thought that if he could just return to Iya Nla's nest, Clowes might be able to find him. With a great effort he pushed his way back through the hole in the slate and clung on for dear life to the underside of the roof. Vincent was frightened: his sluggish body was not responding to his instructions. Afraid of falling, he spun some sticky threads to attach himself more securely to the cellar ceiling. He was at a loss to know what was wrong with him; he had finally shed his old skin but the new one was hard and unyielding. For a moment his heart leapt into his mouth as he completely lost grip and fell with a sickening lurch. The sticky threads held and anchored him, but the momentum left him swinging in dizzying circles for a few seconds, before he found himself hanging vertically and impotently some fifteen feet above the floor. The shock knocked the breath out of him but when he tried to gasp in more air, he found that his throat was constricted by the ever hardening skin that now bound and swaddled him tightly. Terrified and unable to breathe, the little caterpillar fought to release himself, but inexorably his new suit of clothes continued to grow and to bind him. His muffled cries for help went unheard and as the membrane of the carapace began to cover his eyes, the last thing Vincent saw was the snarling grin of the alien Spirit of the Stone with its gruesome bloody necklace – before his world ended.

CHAPTER 29

LET BATTLE COMMENCE

Hope springs eternal so it is said and that is a comforting thought. But what is so gratifying about hope is that when trouble finds us, alone and desperate, help often comes when we least expect it and from an unlooked for source. So it was that Braxton found himself in the ironic position of having his life saved by no other than a humble hedgehog; a species always considered to be the badger's sole enemy, apart from Man himself of course. Not only was this particular hedgehog apparently a weak and insubstantial specimen but it had been joined later by a tiny junior hoglet who, at first sight appeared even more peculiar. Under normal circumstances Braxton would have ordered them off his territory and aggressively defended his solitude. As it was he had to admit that he welcomed their presence and was much appreciative of their attentions. At first the tiny hoglet had proved to be a bit of a nuisance, always getting in his way and interrupting his periods of contemplation. But she was a sensitive little thing and soon learned to temper her exuberance and cleverly match the old badger's moods like for like. He was growing very fond of her.

'Thought I was a gonner,' Braxton said, for what seemed to Scumble the hundredth time, 'thought I was a gonner.'

Scumble had achieved miracles with the badger's set, working hard to clear away the foul debris. It had taken days to sweep everything clean and he had trekked long distances through Whylder Wood to find sweet smelling herbs and grasses to line the tunnel floors. Bliss had done her part too and enthusiastically helped collect fresh leaves from the healing plants that Scumble pointed out to her. Braxton had made a brilliant recovery and although he was fairly long in the tooth had taken on a new vigour under the hogs' attentive care. Their rescue mission had been a success and Scumble began to consider what his next move should be. He wanted to make his way to Maggie Minchin's just to see if his help was needed there and he hoped to persuade Braxton to go as well, as a deterrent to any violent ideas the rats might have. He knew however that the pit and its poisons was no place to take Bliss and regretfully accepted that before anything else he would have to take her back to Patience.

It was early June and the day had started well with blue skies and meltingly warm sunshine. They had spent much of the time lazing outside under the protection of tangled hawthorn and hornbeam, saying little; each with their own thoughts. As the afternoon wore on however, dark clouds came rolling in and the pleasant warmth became muggy and oppressive.

'Shouldn't wonder if we 'ad a storm soon enough,' Braxton said, looking up at the sky and sniffing the air, 'bit ominous I'd say.' Scumble agreed wholeheartedly and felt an unexplained wave of panic for a split second before shaking it off.

'Perhaps it's time to go inside,' he said in what he hoped was a cheerful voice.' Just as he said this there was a rustle in the tree behind him and the distinct noise of a cracking branch.

'Bloody tree rat!' said Braxton, looking in the direction of the noise and getting to his feet quickly with a frown.

'Ooooooo... bloody twee wat!' exclaimed Bliss, jumping up and down. Scumble turned in trepidation, prepared to face he did not know what, when he heard the welcome sound of Sheard.

'Yo! Greetings one and all,' cried the squirrel, swinging down from the tree and landing in the middle of them. He beamed delightedly, 'Sheard at your service and overjoyed to see you all fit and well; especially you good sir.' He directed his remarks to Braxton, 'Er... not exactly over fond of the "tree rat" moniker if you don't mind my saying; so grateful if you'd bin it.' He bent and peered at Bliss, 'Don't want the little'un picking up bad habits do we?' He gave her a wink and she giggled happily.

'Great to see you, Sheard,' said Scumble. In the company of the high spirited squirrel, his earlier disquieting feelings had all but disappeared. 'We were just debating what would be our best course of action now.' He looked enquiringly at the squirrel. 'What's the news?'

Sheard settled down with his back to a tree. 'You'd better make yourselves comfortable; there's a lot to tell.'

So Scumble, Braxton and Bliss were brought up to date on the happenings at Mad Maggie's. They cheered at the news of Trefoil's rescue by Freeman; Bliss said that Spike had told her that foxes were their friends and when she met Freeman she would give him a kiss. Braxton looked askance and told her not to be so foolhardy. They listened in amazement to the clever trickery that Cory and Aldin had planned and carried out, with Heaton pretending to be the dead priest, Earle. Sheard explained how the bird and Clowes had deliberately made Atol anxious and confused about Ishtar the Moon Goddess and how Drew's appearance on the roof had thrown the rat into a paroxysm of fear. Atol appeared to have become completely deranged; but he couldn't just be dismissed as simply mad, for his actions were overlaid by cunning and evil as well. He had slit Orva the stoat's throat on the altar and it was likely he had had a hand in many other killings. Sheard said that he and Scally had left the rescue group to try and recruit more helpers. They had left Cory and Aldin planning a deputation to meet Atol and the other priests to discuss diverting the clean waters of the stream down into Park Woods. At the time of their leaving; Clowes, Vincent the caterpillar and the sick bird remained inside Mad Maggie's and it wasn't clear whether they were prisoners or remained there of their own free will. What Cory and Aldin and the rest of the group hoped was that there might be some rats that were disenchanted with Atol's leadership and would be prepared to help them. Cory had already made an ally in a little rat called Fag, who had given them information about what was going on inside the colony.

By now the earlier threat of bad weather had turned into a promise and the black clouds dictated that they should either retire inside or move on. Sheard was adamant that he at least should return to Mad Maggie's. He had spread the word that help was needed there and he was impatient to oversee any late volunteers. He did not want to pressure Braxton into coming with him if he was not yet strong enough so he was overjoyed when the badger volunteered of his own accord.

'Seems I owe these little hogs a big favour,' he said, looking fondly at Scumble and Bliss. 'At any rate, I've a score to settle with those thoughtless rats.'

So, accompanied by a distant rumbling of thunder, Sheard and Braxton said their goodbyes and disappeared in the direction of Maggie Minchin's house.

Scumble watched them out of sight with mixed feelings and then ushered Bliss back inside the badger's set. The inclement weather had postponed his plans to return his little sister to Park Woods so there was nothing else to do but play the waiting game. He and Bliss spent the next hour talking about their likes and dislikes, their hopes and dreams. Scumble learned how much Bliss loved Spike and the generous young hog was delighted that his brother had at last found himself such a loveable little admirer. He was well aware that Spike was now very likely to be in a dangerous position and Scumble felt a longing to be with him. It was frustrating to be out of the action with no part to play in what had developed into a risky but exciting adventure. The sound of thunder was getting more frequent and a flickering light in the sky indicated that the storm was travelling closer. Telling Bliss to stay where she was, Scumble went to the entrance of the set to sniff the air for rain. Just as he put his head outside he came face to face with a fox. It was difficult to know who was the most startled but Scumble being the hospitable hog that he was immediately exited the set and approached the vixen with a welcoming smile.

'Why you must be Scumble,' she cried, looking at his blackened hindquarters. 'What an amazing coincidence. I must surely be getting near to Mad Maggie Minchin's, which is a comforting thought as I seem to have walked for miles.'

'I wouldn't choose the word comforting when speaking of Mad Maggie's,' Scumble replied, 'it's a nasty, dangerous place you know.' They both jumped in alarm at a flash of blue lightning shortly followed by a loud clap of thunder. Scumble wrinkled his brow. 'We're going to get wet in a minute,' he said and then added, 'how do you know my name?'

So Tait recounted her meeting with Echo and the promise that the kestrel had extracted from her to come and offer her help in Whylder Wood. 'I knew Freeman and his mate Wilda; I hear that she died a very painful death. I will do my best to do whatever needs to be done.'

The first drops of rain began to fall and on an impulse Scumble said that he would show Tait the way and then return to Bliss. 'I'm not sure what use I can be against aggressive rats,' he said, 'but I feel so useless staying here. If we hurry we can pick up the trail left by Sheard and Braxton.'

He scurried back into the set and instructed Bliss to remain where she was until he returned. 'I won't be long, have a little sleep and I'll be back before you know it.' Bliss however had other ideas and insisted that she must meet the fox first as Spike had told her that foxes were their friends. Scumble was sceptical and privately thought that his brother had been a little over generous with this view of the cunning predator; nevertheless he did not want to frighten Bliss unnecessarily so he led her outside and introduced her to Tait.

'Now go back inside and take a nap, there's a dear and I will be back before you know it.' Bliss nodded trustingly and Scumble re-joined Tait, feeling a bit guilty but nevertheless determined to see some action for a change.

They set off in the direction taken by the squirrel and the badger and found the trail easily enough by keeping their snouts close to the ground. It wasn't long before they reached what had once been, the original owner, Alderman Minchin's front garden, now a forest of overgrown weeds and nettles. There was no sign of Sheard or Braxton but they could hear what sounded like angry shouting in the distance behind some outbuildings that might at one time have been a stable block. It was difficult to tell because the storm was now directly overhead and the noise of the thunder was deafening.

'Go back Scumble,' shouted Tait, 'go back to Bliss. I can find my own way from here.'

Resignedly Scumble said goodbye to the fox and pushed his way through the soggy undergrowth with the intention of retracing his steps back towards the path. He hadn't taken more than a few steps however when he felt an inexplicable and overwhelming urge to deviate from his route. Spurred on by a curiosity that would not be denied, he abandoned his earlier plan and abruptly veered to the right in order to inspect the crumbling ruins of the building more closely. He could smell the sulphurous fumes and had a desire to see for himself what manner of Man-made objects could give off such a stench. But as he skirted a side wall of the house Scumble became uneasy – he sensed a malevolent watchful presence. He shivered and without warning his back spines stood erect. The evil emanating from the building grew stronger the further he went until it threatened to engulf him. The little hog felt the beat of his heart quicken and the pounding of his blood obliterated all sound, leaving him lost in a cocoon of silence. On the brink of panic Scumble collapsed and began to fit – eyes glazed and body arching in jerks he entered a dark, nightmare world where he was forced to face his demons alone. His terrified cries attracted the attention of a rat that emerged from a gap in the brickwork and studied the distressed hog implacably for some minutes before calling three of the Guards Elite. Scumble was held down and bound tightly with strips of cloth. He was then dragged inside the house, along a corridor and bumped unceremoniously down the steps into the cellar.

'Put him on the altar,' ordered Scabious, 'and wait for me outside. I'll deal with this myself.'

Once left alone Scabious examined the prisoner closely; Scumble had ceased to call out and was quiet – deathly quiet. His eyes were shut and his breathing shallow; the rise and fall of his chest almost imperceptible. Scabious reviewed his options. He was aware that there was some sort of fracas going on outside upstream and that this had probably been instigated by Atol. He had not been privy to Atol's plans lately and missed their nightly plotting together. He missed Atol's authoritative manner and his quick, perceptive mind. The rat was losing his reason for certain and Scabious had lost faith in the deranged creature's right to leadership; the priest's judgement had become questionable; his orders that Holt and Clowes be found and brought back alive were ludicrous. So much easier to have them killed somewhere away from prying eyes; to bring them back risked rebellion. Holt had always been popular and had the leadership qualities that would attract many of the disenchanted and doubting rats; the son of Baldlice would provide a rallying point. Scabious was aware of how Luthian and her pups died; indeed the gory tale had travelled round the colony quicker than a flying fart from a flatulent fire-fly and it was being whispered everywhere that Atol had lost the plot. Taking stock of the current situation, Scabious saw a distinct possibility that his own star was in rising ascendency; he was convinced that he was now stronger than Atol. The time was ripe to jump Atol's sinking ship and set himself up in opposition. He regarded Scumble steadily: how might he use the hog to the best advantage, to discredit Atol and further his own ends at the same time? He had noticed Atol's increasingly unhealthy preoccupation with the moon and his apparent fear and distrust of all hedgehogs. In his opinion Atol had lost the ability to rationalise and to recognise truth from myth. Scabious decided to play on Atol's fears and unhinge him even more. He left the cellar and went to find him.

***

When Tait left Scumble she made her way towards the stable block and then around to the other side of it. Immediately in front of her was a small crowd of animals, mostly stoats and weasels, but also a few large rabbits, who were sitting rather uneasily alongside a family of ferrets only recently arrived in Whylder Woods. The eloquent and persuasive Sheard had done well to coerce so many additional volunteers. Tait pushed her way through to where Sheard and Braxton the badger were discussing tactics and introduced herself. Further up stream they could see some of Cory's "army", for want of a better word. They were strung out along the far bank, intent on repelling dozens of rats who were attempting to swim across what had become very deep and dangerous waters. The storm was now directly overhead and lent its terrifying authority to the turbulence of the scene below. The scudding iron grey clouds covered and revealed the face of the moon intermittently, whilst the general darkness was lit spectacularly every few minutes by flashes of blue-white lightning bolts.

In poor imitation of Holt's brilliant engineering, Cory, Aldin and Heaton had attempted to construct two dams higher up the stream. Most of the rabbits, all does as they were the best diggers, had been set the task of digging a trench. It began a few feet away from the far bank, stretching out towards the woodland on the far side, with a view to creating a new stream bed that curved around in a large semi circle, skirting the poisoned pit, and finally joining the old stream bed further down in Park Woods. Once the digging had been completed the final stage would be to open up the remaining few feet of the bank and let the water through. The two temporary dams were an attempt to control the fast running water and were supposed to work more like the sluice gates of locks found on the river; but no creature there had the skill or experience to make a proper job of it. The second of the two sluice gates was holding up relatively well but the other was constantly being washed away by the build up of the powerful current. Only the strongest swimmers remained in the water, striving to shore up the ever increasing gaps with anything suitable they could find to hand. Cory and Dering the rabbit strained to keep their backs braced against the first sluice gate, willing the whole unstable pile to stand firm.

Freeman the fox – jaws snapping, and Heaton – wielding a club-like stick – were balanced precariously on the second sluice gate, posing a threat to any rat who ventured to attempt a foothold. Aldin had climbed a tree to view the surrounding area and ascertain the opposition's strength and numbers. His voice could be heard above the storm shouting instructions whenever he saw a weak and vulnerable spot that needed to be plugged. There were skirmishes in the stream where invading rats came up against those trying to shore up the dam, but the torrential rain and general turbulence of the water rendered any serious fighting ineffective. Sheard, Braxton and Tait could see that some rats had managed to crawl up the far bank and were now engaged in combat with the stoats, weasels, squirrels and hogs that Cory had deployed there; but many were becoming exhausted and had turned back towards the nearside bank.

'Now's our chance!' cried Braxton. 'Let's get 'em when they try to get out this side.' He made a dash out into the open along the bank towards the fight.

'Yo!' Sheard yelled, turning to face his co-opted volunteers. 'Follow me lads and let's give 'em what for!' With the foolhardiness of inexperience and enthusiasm, the newly recruited fighting battalion chased in disorderly fashion after Braxton and Sheard, oblivious to Tait's cries of objection and Aldin's frantic waving and calling from

across the stream. All but Tait arrived in time to repel most of the returning rats from climbing out of the water and those that had managed to crawl up the bank were being caught, tossed into the air and dispatched unmercifully by the badger. 'Go to it lads,' yelled Sheard. 'We've got the buggers on the run!'

But Tait was uneasy and with her eyes on Aldin, she shrunk back covertly into the undergrowth just as another cohort of rats emerged from their hideout in a surprise rear attack against Sheard and his gallant heroes. As the squirrel turned and cried a warning, the rats in the water took advantage of the confusion and began climbing up the bank. Braxton and Sheard were now caught between two frontal attacks and would soon be surrounded: they had been out-flanked and out-manoeuvred.

***

Bliss waited for what she considered to be an absolute age and still Scumble had not returned. It was all very well him telling her to go to sleep; as if any self respecting hog could sleep when friends and family were in danger, let alone the fact that the noise of the storm made it impossible. She poked her head out of the set and surveyed the sky. She found that she was excited rather than afraid; it was her first experience of thunder and lightning and the noise and flashing lights thrilled her. The rain promised to be refreshing after the oppressive clammy evening and without further ado she decided to take a little walk and meet Scumble on his way back. The walk however proved to be longer and more arduous than she had anticipated and she arrived at what could only be the ruined Mad Maggie Minchin's house feeling exhausted and a little worried that there was still no sign of her brother. By now Bliss was soaked through and very uncomfortable so she thought her best bet was to find enough shelter to keep her out of the wet. She made her way along a side wall and eventually came upon a large gap where the brickwork had collapsed. Looking around to see if she was being observed, she cautiously entered the house and found herself in a long corridor. The floor and walls were wet with rain so she journeyed onwards to find somewhere dry. There did not appear to be any creature about; she could not hear or see any signs of rats, but there was a nasty smell which made her wrinkle her little snout. She arrived at a flight of steps and was about to go down when she noticed a room to one side with what looked to be a bird's nest on the edge of the crumbling floor. Curiously she went to investigate and found the nest to be empty. It looked warm and inviting however and smelt of familiar dried grasses and leaves that made her feel homesick. Bliss decided that she would have a little sleep here before returning to the badger's set. So she climbed in, curled up and within minutes was snoring gently.

CHAPTER 30

KING OF THE ROAD

Fag was restless and could not sleep. He could hear the sounds of quiet breathing all around him and was glad that the others had found rest and peace if only for a while; but the little rat was in pain. His skin had become inflamed and the burning sensation was getting worse. He decided that he could wait no longer and that he must make an attempt to wash himself in the clean waters of the stream. Silently he left his makeshift bed and cautiously removed the bricks that led to the passage leading to the stable block, and with a quick look over his shoulder, disappeared into the opening. Once inside the passage he could hear the noise of heavy rain beating down onto the roof and by the time he reached the stable block he was aware that a storm was raging outside. Outside, Fag stood with arms outstretched and face turned upwards welcoming the cooling water washing over him. As he stood wondering whether this wetting would be enough to cleanse the poisons from his body or whether it would be more prudent to immerse himself properly further up in the stream, he became aware of fighting going on along the bank to the right of the stable block. There was also fighting on the far bank and a commotion of rats and other creatures in the agitated waters of the stream itself. Fag saw Heaton and Freeman defending what looked to be a pretty unstable dam and he caught sight of Aldin shouting orders and instructions on the other side. He looked in vain for Cory but could not see him. Of the group of fighters nearest to him, Fag recognised Sheard and realised that the squirrel and his team were getting the worst of it. The stoats, weasels and ferrets were fighting valiantly and the badger was right in the thick of it, tossing up bodies of rats before catching them again and shaking them to pieces. Even the normally docile rabbits had grouped around the badgers hindquarters bravely defending his rear. But they were outnumbered and as quickly as the rats were despatched, so more came poring out of the undergrowth or climbing out of the water and up the bank relentlessly. Fag heard Aldin shout to Freeman, who took a flying leap from the dam to lend his weight and sharp teeth to the battle; whilst at the same moment another fox dashed from behind the stable block, passed Fag at lightning speed and crash landed in the middle of the melee sending a number of rats racing for cover.

Taking advantage of the temporary change in circumstances that this element of surprise had generated, Fag beat a hasty retreat back the way he had come with the intention of rousing Holt and Clowes to come and help. But the two had anticipated him and just then rounded the corner of the stable block to meet him head on.

'Wondered where you'd got to,' muttered Holt, looking about him quickly and swiftly assessing the situation. 'Two types of rats,' he said. 'See the ones with yellow wrist bands; they're the ones to go for. They're loyal to Atol and know no other life; they'll fight to the bitter end. The others are getting tired already, their hearts aren't in it. I'm going to try and win them over to me, it's just possible they will come; it's worth a try anyway. Clowes go and help Sheard… Fag… you my friend are not cut out for fighting, but I have a special assignment for you.'

The little rat stood to attention and listened intently. 'Yes sir, you can count on me,' he said and with that turned tail and disappeared back into the stable block.

Holt watched Clowes run to join Sheard and then took stock of what was happening across the stream. Aldin had joined Heaton on top of the makeshift sluice gate and together they continued to repel any rats from gaining a footing. There were a few desultory skirmishes along the far bank but on the whole the numbers of rats attempting to swim the stream had dropped considerably; for the moment at least. The worst of the fighting continued to be on this nearside bank where a section of rats fought ferociously and fearlessly, with a conviction that was proving to be unstoppable. Holt made his way towards them and swung himself up into a nearby tree where he ran nimbly along a branch until he was positioned right overhead. His movements coincided with a flash of lightning, followed almost immediately by a crack of thunder, which attracted attention from those below. But before he could speak, a large rat that Holt recognised as Scarlic shouted and pointed up at him.

'See… see the traitor Priest… son of a murderer… our Master wants him alive!' Some of the Guards Elite began to climb the tree in pursuit of him but Holt was pleased to see that many other rats hesitated and appeared to show relief at his presence.

'Friends!' he cried, 'Fellow rats, for what reason are you fighting? Why all this killing? Hasn't there been enough death in the colony without adding to it – and for what? It's insanity! The stream needs to be diverted and we should all be working towards that aim.' Holt moved back along the branch and deliberately stood heavily and painfully on the paw of the first Guard Elite who was reaching up to him. 'You all know me,' Holt continued. 'You know I want what's best for everyone, not just a privileged few. Join with me now, give me your aide and together we will build a new and healthy colony.'

The rat who's paw he stood on tried frantically to swing himself free but only succeeded in losing his grip entirely and plunged to the muddy ground where he lay inert; the breath having been knocked out of him. Scarlic screamed abuse at Holt and then turned on the rats that were obviously in awe of Holt and listening to his words intently. As Scarlic spun round to gauge who might be contemplating shifting loyalties, he caught sight of Clowes standing relaxed and composed next to a squirrel. Scarlic supposed this to be the very same squirrel that had been reported by guards for causing trouble a few days earlier.

'Look, look!' Scarlic shouted, 'Our cousin the spy… the renegade! He came with silver tongue and wormed his way into the Master's trust. And now he fights against us! The Master wants him alive! Take him alive! Take them both alive!'

'Quick,' said Sheard. 'Run!'

'I'm going nowhere,' hissed Clowes. 'I'm –'

'Run!' screamed Sheard in his ear. 'Run like you've never run before... and trust me.' Without another word Sheard turned tail and sped along the bank before veering off into the undergrowth. Clowes hesitated for a second before following the squirrel and they both disappeared from view. Instinctively Scarlic followed; roughly pushing rats out of his way and adding to the confusion by shouting at the Guards Elite to follow him and apprehend Holt all at the same time.

Sheard set a fast pace and Clowes followed, although he was perplexed at what the squirrel thought he could achieve by running away. Surely it would have shown more sense to stay and help Holt win the rats over to their side. But he had committed himself to running now so he focussed all his energy on not being caught. He could hear the crashing of pursuit behind him and concentrated on not allowing it to get any closer. Clowes was a strong rat who normally kept himself fit and agile but the last few days of incarceration had left him feeling stiff and clumsy and he hoped that Sheard was not planning to run far. He hurdled a fallen log and took a moment to glance behind him; there were more than a dozen rats in pursuit, Scarlic in the lead, all distinguished by their yellow wrist bands. Clowes put his head down and increased his effort.

As he ran, Sheard's mind was racing; going over and over the plan he had been constructing ever since his visit to Drew the owl. He had seen the opportunity when he was at Braxton's but had only realised back on the bank

345

that this might be their one and only chance to put it into action. He had had no time to explain to Clowes and he hoped that the rat trusted him enough to keep running. They had been approaching their destination along an unfamiliar route but Sheard was confident he was leading in the right direction and there, sure enough, he recognised the large earth mound where he and Scumble had first encountered Braxton. He prayed to Pan that neither Scumble nor Bliss were around to pop their heads out at just the wrong moment. Looking straight ahead he raced past the set and came out onto the lane. He immediately turned left and continued at a pace along the middle of the narrow track.

'Where? Where?' gasped Clowes running a few paw steps behind.

'Follow me!' was all Sheard managed to say. They could hear shrill shouts a little way back and it seemed as if Scarlic and his rats were gaining on them. 'Road ahead,' puffed Sheard, 'turn left and keep close to the edge. When we come to where the embankment runs downhill, turn off and make yourself scarce: pronto my friend.'

'But what…' Clowes was confused.

'In the lap of Pan old pal; we're in the lap of Pan.'

Neck and neck they reached the end of the lane and turned onto the main highway. Clowes kept well over into the side of the road, listening intently for any engine noise, but surprisingly there was none and all he could hear was rasping breath and the claws of the pursuers clicking on the wet tarmac behind them. His heart was pumping and cold rain water choked him as he desperately tried to gulp in more air. 'Can't go on much further,' he gasped.

'Lights changing soon; not long now,' Sheard answered. 'When I tell you to go pal, you go... pronto.'

They were approaching the grass verge where the embankment dropped steeply away; at this point the road climbed upwards over a hump back bridge that hid the view on the other side. Above the noise of the storm Clowes could just detect the noise of engines and almost immediately the bonnet of a VW Camper Van appeared over the brow of the bridge.

'Go-go-go!' cried Sheard and Clowes veered off to the left, careering down the steep embankment head over tail and landing unceremoniously in a ditch full of muddy water at the bottom. Sheard slowed down perceptively and moved out to the centre of the road where he continued to run in a distracted ziz-zag fashion. Scarlic and the Guards Elite were almost on him when Scarlic realised that Clowes was missing. As he stopped to look about him Sheard darted across the road in front of the van, closely followed by a number of guard rats. The squirrel made it by the skin of his teeth but heard the satisfactory squeals of those who had not. The van came to a shuddering halt, causing a red Peugeot behind it to swerve sharply across the road where it ploughed into more guard rats that were standing bemused and befuddled at this unfamiliar turn of events. A little Nissan Micra – unaware of the two stationary vehicles now blocking the road – appeared over the bridge, engine racing and with a screech of brakes buried its nose in the back of the van.

Scarlic, beside himself with rage at the decimation of his troops, gave a harsh cry of triumph when he realised all vehicles were now at a standstill and, mustering the last of the active guard rats bounded across the road towards Sheard with murder in his heart. But Sheard had anticipated him and was already making fast progress back down the road the way he had come.

The squirrel was enjoying himself; he found the danger exhilarating and was euphoric that his plan had worked so well – so far. But he would not be satisfied until he had taken out all the rats. As he had expected the lights had changed again and he and the pursuing rats were now directly in line with the oncoming traffic. The rain, in its efforts to either help or hinder – Sheard was uncertain which, had become a torrential sheet of water obscuring the vision of every creature, Man or beast, on the road. The cascade beat down upon the tarmac sending high sprays of water bouncing back up and the noise of its drumming supplied a rhythmic accompaniment to the ear splitting claps of thunder overhead. Squinting through the avalanche of water, Sheard could just make out the hunched shape of an approaching Ford Transit. He held his nerve and waited until the last second before spinning round and leaping high over Scarlic who, with claws outstretched was just about to grab him. Scarlic's momentum carried him irrevocably forward into the path of the vehicle and straight under its front offside wheel.

'Geronimo!' screamed Sheard attempting to hurdle the following guard rats in the same way. But he missed his footing on the slippery road and in a tangle of arms, legs and tails they all disappeared from sight under the Transit's front grill. With a dexterity born from years of experience on the road, the driver brought the Transit to a graceful halt alongside the stationary Peugeot. The hazard lights began to flash.

***

A number of drivers had by now left their vehicles and were standing in desultory fashion, undecided as to what was the best thing to do; the exception being the Ford Transit's driver who was rapidly calling the appropriate authorities on his mobile phone.

'May Allah protect us!' cried the VW Camper's driver bending down to examine four dead rats partially hidden under his vehicle. 'These rodents are sadly misshapen; I've never seen anything like it before in my life. Why d'you suppose they were running all over the road like that?'

The lady from the red Peugeot gave a scream. 'Good Lord! Look at this lot here. Oh I can't bear it. To think we've killed them all!'

'Well at least *we're* alright,' said the girl from the Micra Nissan coming to join the others, 'that's the main thing. Oh my God! Look at my car!' She attempted half-heartedly to disentangle the car from under the Camper's rear axle.

The lady from the red Peugeot sniffed disparagingly. 'Shouldn't have been driving so fast should you!'

'Now look here –' But the girl was interrupted by the Ford Transit's driver who was staring at the little pile of bodies dispatched by his van.

'More rats,' he called out, 'and they all seem to be wearing plastic wrist bands. D'you think they've escaped from some laboratory?'

'Well if they have we'd best not touch 'em,' said another motorist, who was also on his mobile, 'could be contagious. I make it about sixteen don't you?'

'There's another one here,' shouted the Ford Transit's driver, as he discovered Scarlic squashed on the tarmac. 'Well bugger me we've also got ourselves a squirrel.' He bent closer and whistled softly through his teeth. 'Jesus Christ, never seen anything like this before, it's bizarre,' he muttered. As he seemed rooted to the spot the others walked back to join him and gazed with wonder at a little squirrel lying in the road. The force of the impact with the Transit had flattened Sheard's lower body, but his upper body remained unharmed; his head was erect and one arm was held aloft with the little clenched paw raised as if in triumph towards the sky.

From his vantage point on the grass verge amidst a cluster of drooping red poppies, their heads bowed by the rain as if in sorrow, Clowes surveyed the scene of devastation before him. It was clear that he could do nothing for his friend and with a heavy heart he hurried down the embankment to carry back the awful news. As the rat disappeared into the undergrowth he heard a distant wail of sirens.

CHAPTER 31

SPIKE TO THE RESCUE

Scarlic's last garbled words on the bank of the stream had so confused the Guards Elite that most had instinctively followed him as he chased after Clowes and Sheard. Their rapid departure had left only three guards, one of whom still lay on the ground in a daze after falling from the tree. It was a simple matter, therefore, for Holt to press home the advantage of accepting his leadership and with relief found himself heavily supported by the other rats. The two mobile Guards Elite quickly made their escape along the bank to join the contingency of other Guards Elite who were intent upon accessing the sluice gate; stoically defended by Aldin and Heaton. At a nod from Holt; Braxton, Freeman and Tait followed in quick succession to add their weight to the skirmish. Holt decided to swim his troops across the stream to give support to those who were fighting to hold the second crumbling sluice gate and to lend more paws to the digging of the new stream bed. But as he rallied his rats around him in an attempt to encourage them to face the turbulent waters once again, he heard a shout from Aldin and became aware of a large black cloud heading swiftly towards them from downstream. In trepidation he faltered on the bank, unsure of what foe was now come against them and he cried to his troops to stand firm.

***

Cory was rapidly reaching exhaustion in his endeavours to prop up the sluice gate. The water had been rising steadily as the incessant rain continued to feed the stream and it now lapped dangerously around his snout. 'Can't stay here much longer,' he gasped to Dering, 'we're going to have to let the whole thing go.' The rabbit was taller than Cory and as yet was only battling the water up to his chest; he cried out to the hog to go for reinforcements whilst he attempted to hold the barrier together for a little longer.

Cory paddled his legs frantically in an effort to raise his head above the bank, where he saw Sunnifa and Bede directing dozens of female rabbits in the digging of the trench. He could see that they had made good progress despite the foul weather and he took heart from the fact that this achievement stemmed largely from the valiant and so far successful exertions of those who continued to repel the attacking rats. As he turned to look further along the bank in order to call for more help, he heard Dering shout a warning and almost immediately was engulfed in a huge wave of water that swept him inexorably downstream. Dering also was taken; along with the debris of branches and vegetation from the now totally demolished sluice gate. For a few moments respite the two half-drowned creatures came to a halt against the struts of the second sluice gate before it too gave way to the power of the water and sent them tumbling and spinning onwards. Aldin leapt to safety on the opposite bank but Heaton lost his footing and disappeared under a mass of spreading detritus. The cascading, turbulent water now took control and sought to re-establish its freedom after being so constrained. It poured over the bank and into the trench; filling it to capacity within seconds. At the sound of desperate cries and gurgles, Bede dived in to assist some of the younger, smaller rabbits who had been thrown into a panic by the unexpected disaster; whilst Sunnifa ran along the bank shouting for help. As she did so everything went dark, and looking fearfully upwards, she saw a black cloud approaching fast up the stream.

'It's Scally!' cried Spike, who had arrived breathlessly at the sound of Sunnifa's cry for help. And indeed it *was* Scally heading up a large contingent of crows – a murder of crows the wily bird would have called them – ready to do battle against any and all that were considered to be the enemy. Following close behind in the slip stream was the amazing sight of a kestrel and a white barn owl. Speechless, Spike waved them over to the trench and a number of the larger birds immediately began a rescue mission: retrieving the half drowned rabbits from the water and laying them gently under the trees to recover. Scally led the rest of the birds back downstream where a scowling Scur, ears flattened and water cascading off the top of his large domed head, was directing more Guards Elite across Holt's dam. The crows worked in unison; dive bombing the rats until all but a few had been knocked into the polluted waters of the basin or into the waters of the stream.

Scur had never in his life before known such spirited opposition; his unusual size and bullying nature within the colony had always opened up easy routes to privilege and influence, allowing him to carve out a powerful niche for himself that had, on no occasion until now, ever been disputed. He was at a loss to know how to regain the advantage; he had not seen Scarlic since the start of the fighting and Scabious and Atol seemed but a distant memory to the dull witted creature. Whilst Scur wavered on the brink of the stream, Scally wheeled about and flew with raucous cries right at him and would have pecked out his eyes if he had not jumped full tilt into the water. As the waters closed over his head he felt the sharp teeth of some creature take hold of his hind foot and as he prepared to shake it off more sharp teeth closed around his other leg. Scur fought to release himself but to no avail; he was being pulled slowly and relentlessly downwards. Instinctively the heavy, water-laden rat reached out for something to cling onto and found the struts at the bedrock of the dam. He hugged the struts closely, bubbles escaping from his snout as he strove to withstand the weight on his legs. Almost at his last gasp, a bolt of pain shot through him and his foot became free; he kicked out aggressively with it, colliding with something sharp and painful before his other leg was free. The momentum carried him upwards and his head broke the surface where he gulped air into his screaming lungs. Scur slowly and painfully hauled himself out of the water and up the bank where he lay panting and gasping, momentarily blinded and deafened by the water. Both hind legs were bleeding profusely: one foot was bruised and swollen whilst a toe and a claw were missing from the other, which was also cruelly pierced by a number of hog spines.

***

For some time now Spike had been feeling restless and anxious. This discomfort had initially given him energy and spurred him on to repel the swimming rats attempting to gain a hold on the bank. He fought bravely and selflessly alongside Trevoil and Bulgar, who had eagerly coached him in the arts of attack and defence as learnt from Orva the stoat. Spike had felt elated at their easy acceptance of him and for the first time in his life had felt included in what he dared to hope might be the beginning of a lasting friendship with the other hogs. It was only when he heard Sunnifa call for help that he left them. His spirits were raised at the arrival of Scally and the party of birds and looking across the stream he could see that Holt had taken control of many of the rats there. The Guards Elite were getting the worst of the fight with Aldin, Braxton, Freeman and another fox he did not recognise; whilst further down he could see Scally and his feathered followers, making mince meat of another troop of Guards Elite. In truth it would seem that the rats had been well and truly routed and it should not be long before the fighting would fizzle out and they could all withdraw to lick their wounds and count their losses.

But, for some reason the anxiety would not leave him and Spike searched his mind to seek the answer – but a fog was in his head. He felt cold and trapped, unable to move and his breathing had become laboured. Some voice called to him; he lifted his head and gazed with misty eyes downstream and then across to the ruined house. It was Scumble... Scumble in trouble... Scumble in the dark and calling to him; Scumble inside his head and needing him – something about his little sister – something about Bliss. Spike raced along the sodden bank towards the dam opposite Mad Maggie's; blind and deaf to all else other than that his brother needed him. Holt's dam was free of Elite Guards, most of whom had drowned or escaped to who knew where; but there on the other side of the stream was a huge rat lurching towards an opening in the wall of the house. Spike paused for a moment to quell the fear that threatened to engulf him. He noticed that the rat was badly wounded in both back legs and this gave him the impetus to move forward once more. With a feeling of impeding doom, Spike traversed the hazardous dam as quickly and as carefully as he could.

CHAPTER 32

BEAUTY AND THE BEASTS

A calm and implacable Scabious led a furious Atol down the steps into the cellar.

'Here, My Lord, the hog lies here on the altar,' he indicated Scumble; a still, silent form lying stretched out on the marble slab. Atol, desperately trying to contain his rage, examined him, noting his smallness and the blackened prickles of his back spines.

'Hmm not a very prepossessing specimen is he?' He stood back and regarded Scabious intently through narrowed eyes. 'And is this... this puny creature the reason you have sought to disturb me and bring me here to waste my time? The thing is dead – do you suppose I am interested in a dead hog, eh? Answer me!'

Scabious inclined his head. 'Before he died the hog prophesised retribution from the Moon Goddess: I believe the storm heralds the wrath of Ishtar.'

'The wrath of Ishtar!' screamed Atol, 'I spit on the wrath of Ishtar! WHERE HAVE YOU BEEN? I sent you to find Holt and Clowes – have you found them? It would seem not! Are you helping Scarlic and Scur to deploy our forces upstream? Obviously not! Instead you choose to parley with hedgehogs and attempt to undermine *me,* your Master. There is nothing to fear from Ishtar, her power is over. Look... look at the black clouds sent by Ganesh, they all but cover the moon's light. Wrath of Ishtar my hind paw, the storm is the wrath of Ganesh! The storm is with us not against us. The rain will flood the banks; it will destroy any digging those ridiculous creatures from Park Woods have managed to achieve.' Atol thrust his face into the face of Scabious and said menacingly, 'Do not set yourself against me Scabious, or you will face *my* wrath and that is enough to fear. The loss of my protection will finish you... you have made enough enemies in your time, anyone of them could turn, or be turned against you. Do not underestimate me; I have not come this far to fall at the last hurdle. Now show your loyalty to me: go and aide Scarlic and Scur. And Scabious, do not return until you can report that the battle is won and all miscreant Park Woods creatures are dead or fled!'

Atol watched Scabious disappear through the outside exit with rage in his heart. None of his plans were coming to fruition; he was thwarted on all sides and now when he looked at Scabious he smelled treachery; was he to be usurped before he had even been anointed? Recently Atol had been plagued by a number of headaches and today's events had set off another particularly nasty one. It was debilitating and he felt weary. A flash of lightning lit up the cellar and a crack of thunder startled him out of his self preoccupation; Atol felt the hairs on the back of his neck stand up and a shiver of fear ran down his spine. He squinted at the snarling shape of the beast – Spirit of the Stone, fearful of detecting signs of life in the monster. But all seemed as normal and he let his breath out in a hiss of relief. He turned his attention to the hog on the altar and bent to examine it more closely. It was lifeless. He flipped it onto its back and the white and vulnerable belly presented itself to him. The pathetic creature had not even had time to curl into a ball before it went to meet its maker. He stroked the knife lovingly and then reverently touched the elephant icon of Ganesh. So what if the hog *was* already dead, he would offer it anyway to the Rat God; his very own god, the God of Supreme Knowledge and Immortality. Atol pulled the red altar cloth from under the body and threw it to one side. He raised the knife in a gesture of defiance to Ishtar just as another crack of thunder split the heavens.

'Wha' yoo doin' t'my Thcumble?'

The voice came high and clear above the noise of the storm and the rat spun round with a scream of terror, just as the cellar was again illuminated by a bolt of blue-white light. High above him, silhouetted against the cellar wall, was the shape of a small hedgehog, but it was no ordinary hog. Atol's knees gave way and he cowered trembling before it. The erect spines were moonlight silver with a luminescence that was awe inspiring and the light that shone between was pure gold, radiating a halo of incandescent angelic fire. The light blinded Atol and he could not see the face but he heard the voice again only louder now.

'I *thed* wha' yoo doin' t' my Thcumble!'

The hog, if hog it was, spoke no language that Atol was familiar with and he had to deduce that the creature was something supernatural... something akin to the moon! Atol began to whimper uncontrollably; he groped frantically behind him for support and clutched the cold marble slab of the altar. With a shrill keening sound he embraced the elephant icon of Ganesh and prayed for deliverance to the god. And his prayers were answered in the shape of Scur. The huge rat lurched into the cellar bringing with him a trail of blood and half the contents of the swollen stream, together with the stormy elements of both the weather and his rage.

With indescribable relief Atol pointed up towards the shimmering hog. 'Kill it, kill the horror; kill it NOW!' He slumped against the altar still clutching the elephant icon and shaded his eyes from the light shining down on him.

Scur was grateful for the orders that precluded him from having to think for himself any longer and with the cowardliness of the inherent bully he noted the comforting diminutive stature of his adversary. With a ferocious roar of intent he propelled himself forward and launched his wet and damaged body at the balcony. He hung suspended for a moment, dripping blood, before beginning to haul himself slowly upwards. Bliss screamed and as she did so Spike appeared in the doorway.

The first thing that Spike saw was the snarling Spirit of the Stone with its gruesome necklace, lit by a glowing light from above. His eyes flew upwards and he failed to see the gibbering Atol cowering down in the shadows. Instead he perceived what at first he thought to be some celestial heavenly body until he distinctly heard it call his name: 'Thpike...Thpike!' and realised it was his little sister, Bliss. It was Bliss; how in the name of Pan had she got here? All fear left him as he watched Scur resolutely swing his gross body, paw over paw, higher and higher to where Bliss stood. With a cry of anger, Spike charged the length of the cellar and leapt upwards to clutch desperately at one of Scur's bleeding legs, where he swung momentarily like a weighted pendulum. The rat roared in pain and tried to shake him off, but Spike hung on grimly. With concentrated effort, using teeth and claws, he began to climb with dogged determination up the damaged appendage, encouraged by the rallying cries from Bliss.

'Hang on Thpike, hang on Thpike!' she cried excitedly, jumping up and down. But they were to be the last words that Spike heard as an enormous clap of thunder drowned out all else and a final deadly bolt of electrical current zig-zagged across the sky. The lightning made spectacular contact with one of the last remaining trees in what had once been Alderman Minchin's prized arboretum. In slow and stately fashion it bent gracefully, then broke irrevocably to the will of the elements and came crashing down onto the side of the house. All light was erased from the cellar; in the darkness Scur and Spike plunged to the ground and were buried under a deluge of falling bricks and masonry.

Brick dust obscured the vision of the supernatural being from Atol, but from the corner of his eye he saw a dark leonine shadow block what little light was left filtering through the door and smelled again the predatory alien smell. With a terrified scream he made a bid for freedom up the cellar steps and disappeared from view.

CHAPTER 33

TAKEN AT THE FLOOD

Cory lay battered and bruised; lungs full of water, his glazed eyes open but seeing nothing. The hedgehog had fought long and hard to ride the wave of terror that had swept many creatures downstream, where they had been washed over the banks or smashed cruelly against the solid struts of the last remaining dam – Holt's dam. Now the turbulence had dissipated and Cory's body bobbed gently in the lapping water against the sides of the dam on the bed of the stream. Something told him that he had to move upwards toward the light but he was tired and comfortable where he was. He had vague memories of trying to help Heaton attack a huge rat... was it Heaton? He wasn't sure now. He remembered sinking his teeth into the huge rat's leg and tasting its blood. He remembered hanging on for grim death whilst being shaken and jerked around in the water. He remembered something like a battering ram crashing into him and knocking him unconscious. Was he still unconscious and dreaming? He felt warm and snug, the dark was comforting; the velvety water rocked him like a baby and he succumbed to its hypnotic rhythm.

Something bumped against him and he felt himself propelled upwards a few inches; another nudge and he rose again. Cory kicked out with irritation; he wanted to be left alone. Against his will his eyes began to focus and he noticed the water had taken on an opaque greenish glow in the light filtering down from above. Beneath him was a dark shape that rose to meet him and another nudge sent him upwards once more. He was reminded of the little rat Fag, who had saved him when they crossed the River Rushlep; years ago it seemed now and involuntarily his legs began paddling and he pointed his nose towards the surface. At this instance what had been a dull ache in his chest exploded into indescribable pain that became increasingly excruciating. His snout broke the surface of the stream with a cry and his unknown saviour continued to propel him forwards to the water's edge, where he was pushed unceremoniously halfway up the bank. Coughing and spluttering, Cory lay in a daze of pain. He felt paws gently opening his snout and clearing his mouth of the vile tasting, slimy weed. He vomited up a gush of dirty water and with an exhausted groan sank back onto the ground. His gaze fell on Dering who was regarding him with a concerned expression.

'Are you alright Cory?' the rabbit asked. 'Are you alive?'

Cory breathed a heavy sigh and with all the strength he could muster gave a grin.

'Well unless angels have long ears and whiskers I guess I must still be of this world,' he said. 'I owe you my life Dering, which isn't much of a catch I'm afraid as I already owe it to some creature else.'

Dering looked puzzled but decided not to pursue the conversation as Cory was looking decidedly weak. 'Got washed over the bank,' the rabbit said, 'but I could see there was some sort of a fight going on under the water which involved Scur. Heaton surfaced for a few seconds; he had hold of Scur's foot and was being attacked by three Guards Elite who dragged him back under. Then Scur was dragged under and I dived in to help drown the bugger. Got attacked myself then and eventually had to make for the bank again. I think I was the lucky one... I haven't seen Heaton since. I came back to search and was I relieved to find you. Thought you were dead at first, but it just goes to show you can't keep a good hog down.' Cory noticed that Dering was covered in bites and scratches and one of his ears was shredded. The rabbit saw his look of horror and shrugged. 'Not as bad as it looks,' he said. 'Anyway you should have seen those rats after Heaton and I had finished with them.'

Cory sat up; his breathing had become easier and he examined himself for injuries. He could see none that were immediately apparent but Dering said that he had lost a few spines from the top of his head. Cory put his paw to his head and gingerly felt a sore bald scalp; as he did so he heard a cry of concern and looked up to see Sunnifa racing along the bank towards them.

'Cory, oh Cory, thank Pan you're alright,' she bent to examine his sore head and he grinned ruefully up at her.

'Battle scarred for life, I shouldn't wonder,' he said. 'Hope it doesn't put you off me.'

Ignoring this self-pitying plea for reassurance Sunnifa proceeded to report all that had been happening up stream.

'We lost three does,' she said sadly, turning to Dering. 'They were drowned in the trench but Bede and Drew and Echo and... and some of the bigger crows managed to save all the others; they are recovering in the long grass under the trees. I gave orders that they are not to be moved until they have got over the shock. Some of the stoats, weasels and squirrels are guarding them. I left Trefoil and Bulgar in charge. I... I hope I did right? The does are vulnerable to the rats but I'm afraid they may also be a temptation to the stoats and weasels.'

She looked at Cory questioningly and he nodded encouragingly. 'We can only put our faith in Pan and trust to their better judgement, Sunnifa. They fight alongside us, not against us; we can't weaken our defences by allowing doubts to grow. But it's good news about the return of Drew and Echo, especially Echo, I had lost all hope about her.' Cory stood up and looked up and down the stream. There were a few half-hearted, desultory skirmishes going on but in general the battle appeared to be over and the storm had passed into the distance. 'Any other news?' he asked.

Sunnifa pointed across the stream to where Holt, surrounded by a number of rats, was engaged in close conversation with Aldin and what looked to be a very subdued Clowes. 'I think that Holt has got a good following of rats now, leastways they're not attempting to swim across and attack us anymore.'

As she spoke Aldin left the group and ran downstream to Holt's dam and crossed over. He hurried up to Cory with a grave face. 'Sad news my friend,' and with a deep sigh Aldin related all that Clowes had reported concerning Sheard.

It was a devastating blow to the listeners and Cory had to blink rapidly to keep back the tears. 'It was obviously planned,' he said. 'How long had he been thinking about it I wonder?'

'Who knows,' Aldin shrugged. 'He was always a mouthy little devil and yet he kept that one close to his chest. Apparently there are almost twenty rats lying dead on the road; many of them with deformities and a number of men taking an interest in them. I thought we might up the tally by taking more bodies up there.'

'Good idea,' Cory replied, 'and as it was Drew's original suggestion he can be in charge. Echo will be of help and Braxton and Freeman of course. They can all carry the dead quite easily. Tell them to leave a trail of bodies for the men to follow from the road back through the wood to the pit.'

'Will do,' said Aldin. He turned somewhat distractedly away and scanned the banks where the water of the stream now lapped gently against them. 'Haven't seen Heaton for a while,' he said softly. 'I don't suppose...?'

'We were together in the water fighting with some of the Guards Elite,' said Cory. 'One was a big bugger... name of Scur I think.'

'We haven't seen Spike for a while either,' said Sunnifa. She saw the worried expressions on Aldin and Cory's faces and continued, 'Look, I'll go and take your message to Holt and Clowes whilst you start searching for Heaton and Spike. She hurried quickly across the dam and made her way towards the rats upstream.

Cory, Aldin and Dering traversed the dam slowly, calling as they did so, but there was no reply and with resignation they knew they would have to search in the water. Without delay, Aldin dived straight and determinedly off the top of the dam. Cory and Dering no less determinedly scrambled down its sides, entered the water once again and struck out for the stream's murky depths. It took a while for his eyes to become accustomed to the gloom and Cory had to fight down the waves of panic washing over him in remembrance of what had only just recently been a matter of life and death for him. He gritted his teeth and plunged deeper; he had no intention of letting any of his friends down. The earlier fighting had churned up the bed of the stream and the water was still dark and cloudy with mud and weeds. Cory could just make out a moving shape in front of him and by its size he guessed it was Dering. The rabbit had a strong hind leg kick action and was making good progress. Cory saw him dive lower and he followed more slowly trying to get his body to acclimatise gradually to the added pressure. A dead rat surrounded in bubbles of blood floated passed his face and almost immediately he saw another one caught up in a tangle of weeds. Two more lay cold and still on the bed of the stream. Then he saw Aldin and Dering pulling at something half hidden amongst the struts of the dam. He moved forward quickly to help and they were soon able to free two rats entwined tightly together in their death throes; neither one seemingly prepared to let the other go. Aldin and Cory rose to the surface pulling the rats behind them with Dering pushing from below. Safe on the bank they prised the two dead protagonists apart and in sorrow contemplated the awful spectacle. One was a large Guard Elite, his deformity of eight malformed legs making him resemble something akin to a drowned giant spider. The other rat was Heaton and in his jaw, with vice like grip, he clenched the bloody toe and claw of Scur.

**

Holt was directing evacuation operations. The sick bay and birthing rooms had been cleared and rats were being moved slowly away from the building on the backs of other rats, or on make shift stretchers, or whenever possible by their own volition. Holt had entrusted the old guard force with getting them all as far away from the pit as possible. They had been directed to follow the stream until it flowed under the hump back bridge and then use a nearby culvert which would take them safely under the road to the other side. They were then tasked to continue onwards, keeping the stream to the left and using the protection of the trees and tall grass to hide from prying eyes. Somewhere along that path they would reach a safe haven where they would find Fag, Myrtle and Eric the sick bay orderly. The grossly deformed occupants in the nursery posed a more difficult problem and after much discussion it was decided to release them into Whylder Wood and trust to Pan and their own self preservation instincts to determine their future.

Clowes was taking a leading role in directing the removal of dead bodies to the road side verges and making sure that an appropriate trail was left so that Mad Maggie Minchin's and the pit could be easily discovered. The road had been sealed off by a police cordon but as it was now quite dark Drew, Echo, Braxton and Freeman had no difficulty in placing the bodies without being detected. Scally was beside himself with grief and had flown over the body of Sheard a number of times, squawking mournfully; but there was nothing more to be done for the courageous little squirrel and with heavy heart he witnessed his friend being put into a sack along with Scarlic and the Guards Elite. The crow perched high in a tree where he was able to see the long line of departing rats making their escape towards the culvert under the road. They looked a sorry lot and for once Scally had doubts about whether it had all been worth it. Despite their constant bickering he would miss Sheard immensely and there had been other losses too; all manner of creatures who had given their lives for the cause. Would it make a difference? Would things get better? He decided to go and find Cory and then seek out Scumble, who he had not seen or heard of for a while.

Scally found Cory by Holt's dam, together with Aldin and Dering and the body of Heaton. It had been decided to carry Heaton as far away from the pit as possible and find a suitable burial place further upstream. Aldin asked that Clowes be informed and without further ado Scally went to impart the sad news. Before leaving, he reassured Cory that he would then spend time looking for Scumble and Spike and would begin his search at Braxton's.

Cory watched Aldin and Dering carry Heaton along the bank of the stream and disappear into the cover of the trees. He felt sick to his stomach and crossed over the dam almost blinded by tears. He called Spike's name and immediately heard an answering cry; but it was a strange, unknown voice and he hurried towards the sound with beating heart. As he approached the house a creature emerged from a gap in the wall and turned to face him. It was a fox, a vixen and she carried a bundle wrapped in a red cloth. On seeing him she laid the bundle at her feet.

'I think you might be Cory,' she said; 'am I right?' Cory could only nod and looked at her enquiringly for an explanation. 'I'm Tait and I think you know who this is.' She picked up a corner of the cloth and revealed a little ball of white spines.

'Bliss?' cried Cory. 'It's Bliss! Whatever is she doing here? Is she alright... is she alive?' he started forward to examine her.

'She's alright, but it's probably better if we let her sleep now, she's had a bit of a shock.' Tait related how she had seen Spike follow Scur into the cellar of the house and she had run to join them just as a bolt of lightning struck a tree which had then fallen across the roof of the building. When she entered the cellar Spike and Scur were nowhere to be seen, but she could see Bliss lying unconscious on top of a pile of rubble. 'I was sent to help you by a kestrel named Echo,' Tait explained. 'I met your brother Scumble at the badger's home in the woods. Scumble

371

showed me the way here and then he turned back to be with Bliss. I haven't seen him since and I don't know how Bliss got here.'

At this moment Holt appeared and suggested that they lose no time in vacating the area as it was likely that Man would be arriving on the scene very shortly. 'We need to be well on our way out of here before they come,' he said. 'I am just rounding up all the stragglers before leaving myself.'

Cory nodded and asked Tait if she would kindly take Bliss away to safety. 'I will catch up with you as soon as I can,' he said and turned to the rat. 'I'll come as soon as I can Holt, but in the meantime I'll take my chances. I must keep searching for Spike.' So Holt and Tait said their farewells and Cory watched them hurry away along the bank.

He heaved a big sigh and fixed his eye on the gap in the house wall. As quietly as he could he approached the threshold and peeped in. The fallen tree threw everything into darkness and the only light was what filtered through the entrance. Brick and cement dust lay heavy in the air and it was difficult to breathe. Cory noticed the steps across the far side of the cellar; they were littered with debris but still appeared to be usable. He listened intently for any sound of voices or movement but detected nothing. All was silent. Cory wrinkled his snout, the place reeked; there were the sulphurous fumes from the pit but there was also an underlying noisome smell of stale wine and blood. He saw the Spirit of the Stone with its pitiful necklace of death and shuddered.

'Spike,' he whispered and then a little louder, 'Spike.' There was no reply. He nosed around the pile of rubble on the floor and started to scrape some of it away. He began slowly and cautiously, but then his efforts became stronger and more frantic. He knew what he would find. All his senses cried out to him; so that when he eventually uncovered part of the remains of Spike and Scur it was a calamitous confirmation of all his anxious forebodings. Scur lay on his back, his big dome head partially buried by a jagged block of stone. Spike was attached to the huge rat's hind leg, his sharp teeth deeply penetrating the flesh and sinew and it looked as if it would be impossible to separate them. Spike's eyes were closed as if in peaceful slumber and a wave of emptiness and loss swept over Cory. Here lay the most exasperating of hogs he had ever encountered; mean, moody and secretive but in the end, brave and steadfast, Spike had died a hero. With tears running down his face Cory softly nuzzled his young brother and whispered his gentle goodbyes.

He took one last hasty look around before hurrying outside and along the path taken by the others. As he passed through the exit he sent a little draught of air upwards where it played with, what looked to be, a tiny shrivelled brown leaf suspended by threads from the cellar ceiling. The leaf spun and jiggled for a moment in the draught, then hung inert once again.

CHAPTER 34

NEMESIS

Time passed and in the cellar the dust settled. Three bodies lay cold and still whilst a fourth hung suspended, awaiting its rebirth. A tiny opening appeared at the bottom of the leaf-like chrysalis and as the minutes ticked by the opening widened as something from inside sought to free itself from the confines of its bondage.

***

Atol reached the top of the cellar steps with thumping heart, and without a backward glance made for the nurseries. *Great Pan! He had smelled again that fetid alien smell of the creature that had rescued the hog Trefoil. Ishtar's leonine familiar? How could this be? Where was his protector Ganesh?* He burst into the first of the three nursery chambers and found Wimund, Gram and Ware sitting at the table.

'Where have you been?' asked Wimund sharply.

'Where have *I* been?' Atol cried incredulously. 'Where have *I* been? Where have YOU been is more to the point! Have you seen what has happened out there? WE HAVE BEEN ROUTED! MOST OF THE GUARDS ELITE

HAVE BEEN KILLED!… MASSACRED!' The rat groaned and clutched at the table for support. He drew in a deep breath and let it out slowly through clenched teeth. 'You sit here complacently, as if waiting for supper to be served, whilst out there my kingdom has been usurped.'

Wimund folded her arms on the table top and examined her claws. 'It seems to me, Atol, that you have brought this on yourself. Why order an attack on those Park Wood creatures? They were only doing what we would have had to do eventually. The facts cannot be ignored: the pit has polluted the waters of the stream and a fresh tributary must be made.'

Ware shuffled his feet uncomfortably. 'Wimund is right,' he muttered. 'Why deplete our own resources when the Park Wood creatures offer us a labour force for free?'

'I'll tell you why you fools,' Atol glared at each one in turn. 'Has it never occurred to you that without a new tributary we have sole water rights? All other creatures

would have had to pay whatever we asked to gain access to clean water. The colony would have grown rich… we could have been rich beyond our wildest dreams.' Atol scowled at Wimund, 'And not only rich but powerful; the power to command… the power to decide how things are run.' He thrust his face into Wimund's. 'Power not just within the colony but over the whole territory; I'm talking supreme power here Wimund, and don't tell me *you* wouldn't have wanted that.'

Gram licked his lips. 'Are we truly defeated? Can nothing be salvaged?'

A Guard Elite entered the room and Atol went swiftly to meet him. Wimund and Ware exchanged glances whilst Gram kept himself apart in a bid to remain circumspect. The three priests could not hear Atol's hurried whispered conversation with the guard so it was a shock when he returned to them to report that men had arrived outside and were examining the pit.

'It's over then,' said Gram rising from the table, 'I'm off.'

'And I,' echoed Ware, moving hesitantly towards the door.

'Cowards to the last,' Atol sneered. 'You never deserved to be priests in the first place; Baldlice was already losing his powers of judgement when he proposed you. Why run now? Do you think you can outrun men? They will seize you before you get twenty paw steps from the house. Stay! Stay and keep hidden. How many hiding holes have we already discovered here? Dozens – we can lie low until the men go, they cannot stay forever.'

'Why should we want to stay?' Wimund asked. 'There is nothing left for us, the colony has gone.'

Atol threw back his head and raised his paws towards the heavens: 'Oh ye gods! Have these imbeciles no vision!' He glared around at them, 'We will establish a new colony. A stronger, better colony; founded upon our own progeny, it will rise like a phoenix from the dust and the ashes.'

'But that is the point, don't you think,' queried Wimund, she spread her paws wide. 'This is *all* that is left to us...

dust and ashes. We will grow sick and die and our progeny will sicken and die also. There is no future for us here.'

'Oh ye of little faith; do you not observe the Guards Elite? Have they not proved that Nature has already begun to adapt our species to suit the circumstances in which we find ourselves? In a few more generations who knows what strengths the colony may have acquired, what unique talents some rats will have been born with.' Atol looked at Gram and Ware who were reluctantly hovering by the door. 'Come, I ask only that you stay for a while at least. Help me resurrect the phoenix?'

Gram laughed, 'Now *you* are being the imbecile, Atol. Are we to found this new dynasty with only one female?' He glanced slyly at Wimund, 'And an old one to boot!'

Wimund jumped to her feet with a snarl and Ware said quickly, 'Our priestly vows at Initiation bind us to celibacy.'

Atol sensed his headache, which for a time had lodged itself in a small corner of his brain, pushing out insidious tentacles until his pulsating head felt it was about to burst. 'Your priestly vows Ware, are no longer relevant. They were of the world that is now gone.' Atol smiled grimly through his pain. 'Besides they were only ever made as a sop to Iya Nla; if you chose to uphold them then more fool you.' He turned to Gram. 'As to your observation Gram, that just goes to prove how blinkered you are in more ways than one. Have you never noticed that some of the Guards Elite are female?'

Gram looked surprised and stopped edging towards the door. 'Well then,' he mused, 'I will go along with what you say at the moment.' He looked at Ware and Wimund for agreement, 'It can't do any harm to lie low for a while until the men have gone at least.'

'I'll take my chances outside,' Ware faltered. 'I have no wish to remain here.'

'And I will go with you,' Wimund said, moving swiftly towards the door.

'I think not,' said Atol. 'You have wasted enough time already with your pathetic arguments.' Four Guards Elite entered the room. 'It would be folly to leave now, you would not escape capture and you could well lead the men into discovering those of us who will be hiding in the house.' He nodded to the guards and both Ware and Wimund were seized roughly. 'Throw him in one of the dungeon cells, until he comes to his senses,' said Atol, indicating Ware. He looked at Gram with narrowed eyes, 'I'll leave you to find your own hiding place,' he said. 'We will talk later.'

Atol strode across the room and pushed a brick away from a pile of rubble in the corner revealing a small hole in the wall. He stood back and held out a paw towards Wimund, 'Come my dear, whatever Gram chooses to think, I believe that you are not too old. In a perverse sort of way I find you quite attractive, at least our offspring will have a modicum of intelligence do you not agree?'

'I feel nothing but revulsion for you Atol,' Wimund cried struggling with the guards who held her tightly.

Atol grinned. 'Do not object too strenuously my dear, I am afraid it only excites me even more.' He climbed through the hole and Wimund was propelled across the floor and pushed unceremoniously through the gap to join him. Gram made a quick exit through the door before any of the guards decided it might be wiser to apprehend him.

***

The metamorphosis of the little caterpillar into adulthood was nearing completion. It hung head downwards, proboscis and antennae quivering. The butterfly had as yet only vague memories of a previous existence but instinctively knew that it was dangerous to remain where it was. It concentrated on pumping the blood around its body to inflate its wings. Until they were fully inflated and had dried out, Vincent knew he would be unable to fly.

***

Dusk had fallen outside and the men had gone leaving the banks of the stream a mess of furrows and churned up, foul smelling slurry. The sound of car engines disappeared into the distance leaving everything silent. Atol crept quietly down the cellar steps. His headache had gone and he felt elated. He was wearing his priestly cloak and stood once more in front of the Spirit of Self-Perception. It was covered in brick dust and now bore a crack along its length but Atol wiped it clean and saw that his image was just as imposing as ever. His recent power over Wimund had been like a much awaited aphrodisiac; it had given him renewed confidence; he was energised and he had thought of an amazing idea. It was staggering in its audacity and earlier in the day he would not have dared to try and pull it off. But now he knew it was what was meant to be; it was ordained. He busily cleared the altar around the dead hedgehog which still lay belly up. He touched it and felt its unyielding hardness. The blood would now have clotted and would not flow freely as a sacrificial offering. However, Atol drew the knife from his wrist band and studied the notched blade. It was discoloured with the stains of other life bloods and now he would add his own. He cut the bindings away from Scumble and tossed them onto the floor. Then, holding his arm over the hog, he cut into the flesh on the inside of his wrist letting the crimson blood that welled out drip onto the sacrifice. He felt no pain.

'Oh Ganesh,' he intoned, 'My Lord and Master. Hear me, your servant and your follower. Come to me oh my illustrious God. Look down upon me with favour and fill me with your strength to do your bidding.' Atol let more blood fall onto Scumble, where it trickled across his belly and dripped onto the marble top of the altar. 'Oh Ganesh,' Atol raised his paws high and the blood trickled down his arm and splashed onto the floor in front of the Spirit of the Stone. 'Oh Mighty One, help me to serve you; help me to raise a temple in your honour; help me my God of Supreme Knowledge and Immortality; give me the power to build a colony of rats worthy of your greatness.'

As Atol knelt before the altar he heard a noise above of heavy stentorian breathing and with wonderment he observed two elephantine legs descending the cellar steps. As they got nearer, the rest of the body came into view: a huge grey figure with elephant-like head and a long trunk. He had done it; Ganesh had materialised for *him*. He had called him and the God of Rats had come. Atol jumped to his feet in a frenzy of euphoria and waved his arms excitedly. 'Here, here. I'm here Ganesh. Your servant is here.'

Ganesh stooped and peered closely at the rat; he quested with his trunk around the tiny figure whilst Atol fell to his knees in adoration. Ganesh straightened up and the god towered over his tiny acolyte. Atol raised his eyes to witness the glorious being and for a few rapturous seconds they locked onto those of the Divine One – before he was enveloped in a thick cloud of suffocating white powder. The rat felt the particles of death enter his lungs, burning his throat as it went down. His now sightless eyes succumbed to the onslaught of scalding, corrosive poison and he screamed in terror and pain before his airways blocked and took away all sound. Gagging and choking, he feverishly tried to gulp in more air; but the air was deadly – devoid of life. Clutching impotently at his burning throat, Atol fell blindly to the floor. His last conscious thought was, *Why?*

***

The man in the protective suit scrutinised the dead rat then picked it up by the tail and regarded it more closely. At first sight he had taken it to be deformed, similar to those already found outside the building, but now it was apparent that the second skin was merely a loose covering worn by the rat as if it were a cloak. It was bizarre. The whole place was bizarre. He dropped the rat into a sack and peered around the cellar. A pile of rubble on the floor had been disturbed revealing the bodies of a huge rat and a small hedgehog locked together in what must have been a fight to the death. The man placed them into the sack. He examined the dried head of a stoat and placed it gently into the sack also. As he did so he caught sight of a stone statue, a rampant mythical, lion-like creature wearing what appeared to be some sort of fur necklace. Breathing nosily through his oxygen cylinders he moved to investigate and was struck dumb with horror. The necklace consisted of twelve mummified rats joined by bared teeth and bloody tails. Dear God! The place looked as if it had been used for some sort of satanic Black Mass ceremonies. With revulsion he dropped the circle of rats into the now bulging sack and secured the top. He swept his eye back over the artefacts on the block of marble stone. There was another dead hedgehog and this one seemed to have been burned at some point, the back spines were blackened. He dropped it into a second sack and with relief made his way up the steps to freedom as fast as he could.

CHAPTER 35

INTERLUDE

In the gathering gloom Echo watched the men piling up the sacks and loading them into a van. The men were dressed strangely; covered from head to toe in grey suits and all wore some sort of breathing apparatus. She guessed it was because of the pit fumes. She did not know why she was here, only that she was restless and unhappy. No creature had seen Scumble since Tait. Braxton's set had been searched thoroughly by both Scally and herself to no avail. Her heart was heavy with loss for the little hedgehog and she could not bear to think that he might be suffering somewhere without help or friendship or that he had died a lonely, solitary death. She planned to wait until the men left and then attempt to search Mad Maggie's house and surrounding area until she was satisfied that Scumble was not there. As she sat patiently she caught a tiny movement from the corner of her eye and a butterfly fluttered onto the branch beside her. It was brown in colour with ragged edges to its wings so that when it remained still it looked for all the world just like a leaf.

'Hello again,' it said in a tiny voice. 'Echo isn't it?'

The kestrel peered closely in surprise. 'That's good camouflage,' she replied, not knowing quite what else to say; she had never conversed with a butterfly before.

'Yes,' agreed the butterfly, 'better than looking like a bird dropping don't you think?'

'Vincent? Vincent!' cried Echo. 'Oh Vincent it's wonderful to see you; everything has been looking so dark lately with no good news at all.'

'No matter, I can change that.' And Vincent proceeded to tell her about the scene he had witnessed in the cellar. 'Look!' he cried, 'That's the man I saw – he's carrying two sacks; one of them contains a hedgehog and I think it must be Scumble.'

The Man picked his way carefully between fresh mounds of fallen masonry. As they watched he stopped and crouched down to inspect something hidden amongst the broken bricks and stone. He lifted the something up gently in his gloved hands and placed it in the sack with Scumble. One of his colleagues called to him and he waved a reply before setting off as quickly as the cumbersome suit would allow towards the van. As he arrived another van pulled in alongside and two men minus the strange clothing jumped out. They appeared very interested in the contents of all the sacks and it seemed that they wanted to take some of them away in their van. This generated a lengthy conversation with much gesticulating and loud voices. Finally, just when Echo felt she could stand it no longer and was preparing to fly down to look in the sacks herself, an agreement was reached. A few sacks, including the one containing Scumble, were separated from the large pile and loaded into the second van. The men got in and the engine started up.

'I shall follow that van,' said Echo. 'You go and find the others; just follow the stream north until you come to three elm trees – you can't miss it. They will be delighted to see you, Clowes especially.'

The second van's engine fired into life and the two vehicles moved slowly in single file out towards the road. Echo tracked them both for a while until they came to an intersection, where they turned in opposite directions. The one going right bore the logo of skull and crossbones and the name:

XPEDIENT PEST CONTROL.
VERMIN EXTERMINATOR.

LAND & FORESTRY ENVIRONMENTS.

Echo followed the one going left, on which was written:

WOODLAND WILDLIFE RESCUE CENTRE.

The van trundled along quite slowly and the kestrel had no difficulty in keeping up with it. They had not travelled more than about five miles when it turned off through a gateway and continued down a long drive, eventually stopping at the rear of a group of one story buildings. Echo perched in a nearby chestnut tree and remained hidden amongst the thick foliage. She watched the men unload the sacks and carry them inside one of the buildings.

The rescue centre and wildlife hospital was a charitable concern operating mostly on public donations and whatever monies it could raise itself. Dedicated to the rescue of sick, injured, orphaned and traumatised animals and birds; it was proud of its success rate, not just in saving lives but on providing the necessary after care and, whenever possible, eventual release back into the wild. All multiple arrivals were initially taken to a reception room and sorted in terms of priority for treatment.

'Only one vet on duty at the moment I'm afraid,' said a girl in a blue overall. 'Here let me take this one.' She carefully picked up a weasel that appeared to have lost an eye and was covered in bites and scratches. 'Sweet Jesus!' she muttered and hurried away with it. The two men proceeded to place the other animals in suitable cages to await attention.

'Two hedgehogs in this one,' said one of the men. He lifted them carefully out of the sack and placed them on a bench. 'One looks dead already, I'm afraid and the other isn't much better.'

The other man came to look. 'Unlikely they'll need a cage. Put them in this box and let the vet decide what to do with them.'

The box was placed back on the bench and the men departed, shutting the door quietly behind them. One or two of the injured made little groans or snuffling noises but overall a feeling of peace and calm pervaded the room and most of the little creatures remained as if in a state of suspended animation, stoically waiting for whatever fate had been decreed for them.

The female hedgehog lying next to Scumble was barely aware of her surroundings. She lived in a nightmare of waking and sleeping; her dreams overshadowed by memories of an unyielding, cold concrete floor, impenetrable brick walls, silence and fear. She was weak from lack of food and her mouth was dry and parched from lack of water. Somewhere deep within her, Neldar knew that she was dying. Instinctively she moved closer to the creature by her side; although distant and cold it offered a semblance of comfort and companionship. She cuddled in tighter. Perhaps they were both awaiting the same fate she thought, recalling what the rat had said; waiting to be buried in the earth and baked to death. Perhaps they had already been buried and would soon be dug up and their spines ripped off in preparation for consumption. She shuddered and opened her eyes. Why was she still alive? Surely she wouldn't be eaten alive?

'Oh Pan have mercy on me!' she murmured. The hedgehog next to her was the lucky one; he wouldn't feel a thing, whereas she would have to face the horror alone. With a stifled cry she pressed herself against her dead companion, her heart racing with fear; eyes shut tight, Neldar waited for the gods to decide her destiny. And to the thudding of her heart beat came an answering response; faint at first, weak and fluttering, but gradually gathering momentum; Scumble's heart awakened with the joy of rebirth and began to pump the life blood round his comatose body.

***

Later that evening when most of the sick and injured had been taken from the cages to be assessed for treatment, the girl in the blue overall entered the room accompanied by a lady in a white coat.

'Put the kettle on there's a luv Sonia, I'm gasping,' the lady in the white coat said, sitting on the bench. She removed a shoe and began to massage her foot. 'What a night! I've never known anything like it before. I can't begin to imagine what's caused all these injuries unless the toxic fumes sent them all mad.' She peered into the box by her side and regarded the two hedgehogs. 'Have we run out of cages? This box will need a lid if it's the only container we've got left.'

'Don't think so,' Sonia replied opening up a tin and arranging biscuits on a plate. 'They were both dead – or pretty close to it. It's more likely they were put there for disposal.'

The lady in the white coat pulled some rubber gloves from her pocket and gingerly examined Scumble. 'This one's alive; he appears to be coming out of premature hibernation. He'll need to be kept warm and given access to food and water.' She squinted at him more closely, ' He's spattered with blood stains but I can't see any recent injuries… looks like his spines here at the back were burned at some point. He isn't a priority case.' She lowered him gently back into the box and picked Neldar up. 'This one is in poor condition: malnourished and dehydrated. Leave the tea for the moment Sonia, we need to make this little lass a special concern; if I'm not mistaken she's pregnant and very near her time.'

CHAPTER 36

AFTERMATH

The secluded spot immediately east of the three elm trees was an inspirational find by Fag and had proved to be a much needed haven of peace and tranquillity; providing recuperation and reflection for all. The place had once commanded a modicum of respect from the locals because it was the location for a modest but workable train service. Smeeton Briar Junction had originally served as an exchange platform for the Smeeton branch line. Staff at this lonely posting were housed in what had now become an abandoned and derelict cottage. Not surprisingly the humble junction inevitably fell victim to the powerful Beeching administration and when the branch line was closed down, the old railway track became a cycle-way and footpath known as the Briar Trail. Over the years however the track, lacking any official recognition or attention, had become overgrown with prolific, verdant vegetation and the memory of its original purpose all but lost in the annals of time. It was rarely visited by the fickle public. The bare structure of the cottage, minus its roof, windows and floors, remained nevertheless, with its tumbled walls of roughly hewn stonework, as a fitting complement to the beauty of the surrounding trees and plants. The stones had a smooth tactile finish to them where they had been lovingly weathered through the decades and they welcomed the embrace of the sun, storing up its warmth to give comfort to any living creature that chose to snuggle up in their protection. As well as the elms there was a cluster of sycamore and ash trees, their tangled leafy branches forming an imposing cathedral-like shelter against the elements and the whole place was surrounded with swathes of purple-pink rosebay willow-herb and white cow parsley.

When Fag, Myrtle and Eric the orderly eventually arrived, transporting Baldlice on a makeshift stretcher of sticks overlaid with bindweed; they immediately knew they had reached sanctuary. Together they constructed a shelter for Baldlice in a corner of the cottage walls, where he lay gratefully in the warmth of the late morning sunshine. Eric foraged around for medicinal herbs and began to teach Myrtle what he knew about their healing properties. Fag meanwhile took the opportunity to finally submerge himself in the clean, cooling waters of the stream. It offered some relief to his pain, for the sores on his skin had now become blistered; some of which were deep and suppurating. He returned uncomplainingly to Myrtle and Eric and the three of them worked hard in the next few hours gathering a variety of plants, berries and insects.

By mid afternoon when Holt arrived with an army of rats; some fit, others not so fit and some downright poorly; the sanctuary already had the beginnings of a cache of medical supplies and the semblance of a small food store. Many of the Park Woods creatures had decided to return to their homes and Bede had proudly led Dering – his hero – together with an assortment of courageous rabbits, back to the common where he trusted he would never have to feel ashamed of any of them again. Braxton, Freeman and Drew however had accompanied Holt, providing protection for the rats on the journey; whilst Tait brought up the rear carrying her precious bundle in the red altar cloth. A number of hedgehogs, Trefoil and Bugle included, together with an assortment of squirrels, stoats and weasels, who were either too traumatised or too lacking leadership to return to their homes immediately, tagged along as well. Under Holt's instructions, those who were able helped those who were not and whilst all were in some part suffering from shock, it was agreed that the "Three Elms", as it came to be called, offered the cheering prospect of hope for the future.

It was with glad hearts therefore that Cory, Sunnifa, Aldin, Clowes and Scally were welcomed on their arrival sometime just before dusk. Those who could keep awake set up camp to catch up on the news, pay tribute to friends who had given their lives and to mourn their loss. Both Aldin and Clowes were in low spirits about Heaton, but tried to rally in front of the younger creatures that looked to them to set an example. Unfortunately Scally showed no such restraint over his grief for Sheard and Drew finally had to take the crow to one side and explain gently but in no uncertain terms that if he could not compose himself it might be better if he returned to Park Woods.

Perhaps the most affected of all was Cory who sat with heavy heart trying his best to comfort others;

especially Bliss who, with tear stained face, clung to him with a fervour that would not be assuaged by any soft words that he could conjure up. The loss of Spike and his growing despair about Scumble rendered him almost impotent to speak with any clarity. When he considered the dead and observed the sick and injured he was struck with a terrible guilt that he had been the one to cause it all and to what purpose, he wondered? Park Woods still did not have running clean water. The depressed hedgehog bravely kept his anxieties to himself however and it was not immediately apparent to any others apart from the perceptive Drew. After reprimanding Scally, the owl made a point of settling himself quietly beside Cory, silently offering him the opportunity to speak out his fears.

'What was all this for Drew?' Cory faltered. 'What was achieved? We have lost so much and gained nothing as far as I can see. I started it all – me and my big mouth. Who in the name of Pan did I think I was?'

'You have achieved much,' Drew said gently. 'It's just that your sadness has taken away the power to see clearly. But for your encouragement and leadership, many of the woodland creatures would have ignored the warning signs. Their respect for you persuaded them to face up to the impending danger. What have you achieved? Why the pit will be cleared away now and the waters of the stream will run clean all the way down to Park Woods and beyond, with access to every creature. Did you suppose that the rat Atol would have shared the uncontaminated water for free? He had become as all despots become, greedy for power. Woodlanders would have had to pay dearly for their water; he would have held us all to ransom.' Drew surveyed the scene around them. 'Your actions released these rats from a regime of oppression and with the help of Holt they will have the chance to build a new and healthy colony. Atol took away their choice; Holt will give it back to them as all good leaders do. These last few days have taught us the value of standing up for what is right, despite the ultimate price that some have made. Always remember that a flock of unquestioning sheep will inevitably become prey to wolves.'

Whilst Drew was talking Aldin and Clowes had come to sit by them and nodded in agreement at the owl's word. 'If we had not heard you speaking that day in Bluebell Grove, Cory, we would have walked on by,' Aldin said.

'But then you would still have Heaton with you,' Cory answered.

Clowes shrugged. 'We might, but you can never be sure about anything. Besides what sort of a home would we have returned to? And both Heaton and I were determined to return home eventually.'

Aldin stared into the distance and said quietly, 'Heaton believed in having the freedom to choose the way he wanted to live. He believed it was worth fighting for.' He turned to Cory with a wry smile, 'You know most creatures don't really want freedom, because true freedom involves responsibility and most creatures are afraid of that. That was the main reason that I offered my help to you Cory, because you took on the burden of responsibility for those who were intimidated by it.'

His friends' comments went a long way towards healing Cory's feelings of despair and so he was able to show genuine delight when a tired but talkative butterfly made his appearance not long after, with the spectacular announcement that he was indeed *the* Vincent. The butterfly's news of Atol's death and the manner in which he had died brought both celebration and consternation to those still awake enough to apprehend it properly. Vincent was called upon again and again to repeat the story with as much detail as possible and there was much speculation about Ganesh; how dangerous he might be and whether they might now expect him to materialise here at Three Elms. Cory held up a paw to quell what was rapidly becoming hysteria and to reassure the alarmists that the supposed Ganesh was obviously one of the men sent to clear up the pit and that there was nothing supernatural about him at all. Vincent quickly confirmed this and it was generally decided that there really had now been enough excitement for the day and the best thing to do was to hunker down and get some sleep.

Gradually the noise quietened until eventually nothing could be heard but the stealthy breathing and occasional snoring from those in slumber. Vincent took the opportunity to relate what he had seen regarding Scumble. 'It looked very much like he was dead Cory, laid out like that on a hard stone slab. I'm so sorry. The man put him in a sack and Echo and I watched it being loaded into a van. Echo followed it and I know she won't come back until she can give a good account of what has happened to your brother.'

Cory nodded silently and thanked the little creature for his news. With a leaden heart he curled up for sleep next to Bliss, who was already well away, and entered a troubled dream world where he faced the lonely prospect of having to solve every creatures' problems when there were none apparently who could begin to solve his.

The next morning dawned bright and clear, with the promise of a warm and sunny day, fittingly apt for the end of June. Baldlice had spent a restful night and Holt praised Fag, Myrtle and Eric for their devotion to his father. 'It is likely that he is too weak to survive his illness for much longer,' he said sadly, 'but if we can make his last days ones of contentment then we will have nothing to reproach ourselves with.' Later he took Myrtle to one side and asked if there was anything the matter with Fag. 'He seems overly quiet. Not the jubilant rat I would have expected when faced with the prospect of a better and brighter future. Is he worrying about something?'

So Myrtle, with loving words, eventually learned from Fag what the matter was and she was aghast to see the raw weeping wounds. The acids in the polluted stream had slowly but surely eaten greedily into his flesh and where the skin was blistered the hair was beginning to come out in tufts. Eric recommended the red hips of the briery bush as the best healer for burned skin and Myrtle searched high and low along the banks of the stream and where the ground was wet and boggy she eventually found the plant, but with sinking heart saw that it was too early for the fruit to have matured. Myrtle cried tears of frustration because she had grown to love the brave little rat and could not bear to think that he should have to suffer any more. Together she and Eric used the next best remedy, crushing the leaves of dandelions and bindweed to make a soothing poultice. This remedy went some way in bringing relief to Fag's discomfort, but the best healing process of all was his source of wonderment that Myrtle cared for him and from that time on they were rarely out of each other's sight.

A few days later, Echo at last made an appearance and the weight of despair finally lifted from Cory when he learned the news that Scumble was alive and well. Echo had shown great resourcefulness in gaining a shrewd observation of the Wildlife Rescue Centre through its many windows and conveniently open skylights; where she had been able to track both hedgehogs from room to room and overhear fragments of conversation. Her news about Neldar was a revelation as there had been no evidence that she had ever been at Mad Maggie's, it being generally assumed that after losing Bliss she had returned to the safety of Park Woods. Of course there was much excited speculation as to who the father of the pups might be; but when Echo explained that out of three sickly pups born, only one had survived, the excitement became subdued.

'She was in a bad way,' said Echo, 'and lucky not to have lost all of them. It's a miracle she was taken to the hospital or most likely she would have lost her own life as well.'

Scally, hoping to make up for his previous over emotive, behaviour whispered to Cory that he would fly back to Park Woods and give Patience the good news.

'Thanks Scally,' said Cory gratefully. 'Tell her we will return as soon as Scumble and Neldar have joined us and are fit to make the journey.' He squeezed Sunnifa's paw as she nestled beside him. 'Now all we can do is wait patiently.'

And that was what they did; except for Freeman who was anxious to get back to his cubs. Tait said that she would go with him and Freeman could not hide his delight. They said their farewells with a particularly affectionate goodbye to Bliss, who throughout her life would always harbour a special fondness for foxes, and departed on their journey amidst much grins, nudges and winks from those left behind.

At last, one hot day in July Echo arrived, leading three weary but happy hedgehogs; the smallest of the trio being not much bigger than Bliss had been when she was first born. But what he lacked in size he made up for in spirit. He proved to be a feisty little fellow and it was soon established who his father was without Neldar having to say a word. She had named him Bearn but, to coin a phrase, he was a "chip off the old block" and quickly came to be known as "Little Spike". He and Bliss hit it off immediately and the little earth angel's sunny nature was happily restored to the relief of all. Remaining somewhat true to her own self-serving nature – for nature's are not changed that easily – Neldar found it difficult to confess her betrayal of Bliss, but opted to atone instead by becoming a caring and attentive surrogate aunt.

They decided to remain a further few days at Three Elms before attempting the final journey back to Park Woods. Those who intended to return to Whylder Wood said they would delay departure so that all could leave together and Braxton promised to stay awhile with Scumble before seeking out new quarters far removed from the pit. In the meantime Holt and his band of rats, being more than satisfied with the surrounding habitat as a new home, had already begun to carve out a niche for themselves amongst the welcoming tree roots and the shady area beneath the protection of the old railway platform.

Scumble remained a source of wonder and speculation to all; dividing those who were of the opinion that his "death" had been no more than a self-induced premature hibernation, from those who held to the belief that his "resurrection" had been nothing short of a miracle orchestrated by Ishtar herself. This was undoubtedly confirmed in their eyes when the last evening before their planned departure heralded an awe inspiring moon that hung sublimely in the clear sky: full bodied, radiant and pregnant with power. It drew the respectful gaze of every creature, who took the opportunity to unite beneath its light and give heartfelt thanks for the outcome of what had initially been referred to as "The Battle at Holt's Crossing" but which in time became known simply as "The Battle of the Storm".

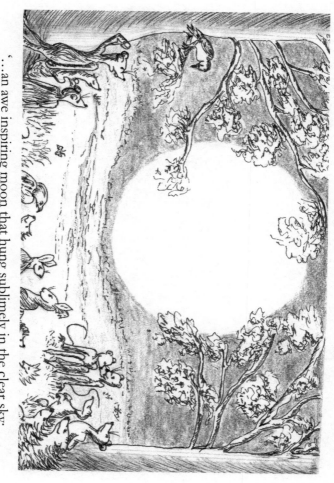

'...an awe inspiring moon that hung sublimely in the clear sky: full bodied, radiant and pregnant with power.'

EPILOGUE

Baldlice finally departed for his happy hunting ground one balmy evening in August with Holt at his bedside. What memories he had left in his addled brain cannot be certain but he died peacefully with a whisper of a smile on his old scarred face.

Cory made the trek back to Three Elms to visit Fag regularly and the little rat was always pleased to see him. He never fully recovered from his wounds, nor from the poisons that he had ingested; which generated bouts of sickness and fever every now and again. But when Cory offered to have him transported to "heaven" at Otterly House to spend his remaining days, Fag said happily that his earlier idea of heaven had been naïve and he had found his true heaven here with Myrtle at Three Elms. To prove his point he sired two healthy litters before closing his eyes for the last time some twelve months later.

Cory and Sunnifa had many happy years together and in the words of Atol founded a "dynasty" of hedgehogs between them. Although Cory was not always monogamous – what male hedgehog ever is – he was the first of his kind to remain with his females and set a precedent that a few brave followers tried, but often failed, to emulate. The "Battle of the Storm" was always a topic of conversation amongst any Park Woods creatures that came together for an evening of socialising; usually when the moon was full and youngsters were initiated into the courageous deeds of those who had taken part. For a time, much to his embarrassment, Cory was referred to as "Cory the Bold" and he was relieved and amused when it was later affectionately modified to "Cory the Bald".

Following the incident of the pit, both Park Woods and Whylder Wood became a National Nature Reserve; actively managed to foster more diversity and richness of species and habitats, but above all to offer protection from the likelihood of any similar dumping of toxic waste in the future. This was heralded by most woodland creatures as something positive to be welcomed, although the downside of generating public awareness was that the visits of men became more frequent. Aldin did not embrace this situation readily, considering it to be an over-interference with the natural scheme of things. 'For what is freedom,' he argued, 'if we are to be looked after all the time by some higher authority; especially if that higher authority directs everything for its own ends? How can we ever be sure that any of those god-like authorities are working to a well considered plan or merely just improvising as they go along?' Clowes, ever eager to debate any issue with his friend said that most creatures needed to believe in the presence of a higher power; some altruistic deity that could direct their lives to the good and provide a sense of security and worth. Aldin grudgingly accepted this, but remarked that it was a matter of opinion whether the deity in question could ever be truly altruistic when it was also perceived by many creatures as being the vengeful God of Retribution. It seemed to him that the validity of a higher being all boiled down to blind faith as opposed to reasoned judgement and he knew which one he plumped for.

'I think,' Clowes replied firmly, 'that you should not be too dismissive of the beliefs of other creatures or of faith itself. There is more to this world than we know.'

'Well so be it,' Aldin said, 'but like Heaton, I would always fight for the freedom to determine my own destiny and let all the gods and fate itself go hang!'

Cory listened carefully for he respected the opinions of both rats and so it was with diplomacy beyond his years that he ended the debate on a calming note by saying:

'Well there is truth in what both of you say; but all *I* know is that freedom is not worth having if it doesn't include freedom of choice, to believe what each of us wants to believe and the freedom to make our own mistakes without fear of reprisals.'

***

So all things must eventually conclude and the time has come to withdraw our benign – or as Aldin might see it – interfering presence from Park Woods. But what of Echo; does she ever find Marlin? And what happens to Scabious, Wimund, Gram and Ware? Well each of them will have their own stories to tell no doubt, but I shall leave *you* to determine what they are; for I have played god too long with the lives of these little creatures and will disturb them no longer. May peace and fulfilment be yours and in whatever name, shape or form it takes, may your god go with you.

ANGLO SAXON NAMES & MEANINGS

Aldin	Defender
Atol	Hateful
Baldlice	Bold
Bearn	Son
Bede	Historian
Bliss	Joy
Braxton	Brock's Town
Cory	Chosen
Clowes	Cleft in Hills
Drew	Wise
Earle	Chief
Fag	Drudge
Freeman	A Freeman
Freya	Queen of the Gods
Gram	Warring
Heaton	High Town/Hill

Holt	Wood
Lufian	Love
Mae	Kinswoman
Marlin	Falcon
Neldar	From the Alder Trees
Orva	Courageous Friend
Patience	Forest Dweller
Raedan	Advisor
Scarlic	Pain
Scur	Storm
Sheard	Of Splendid Valour
Sunniva	Gift of the Sun
Tait	Pleasant/Bright
Vincent	Invincible
Ware	Wary
Wilda	Forest Dweller
Wimund	Sacred Holy Peace